KU-417-749

The Saracen's Mark

Also by S. W. Perry

The Jackdaw Mysteries
The Angel's Mark
The Serpent's Mark

The Saracen's Mark

S. W. PERRY

CORVUS

Published in hardback in Great Britain in 2020 by Corvus, an
imprint of Atlantic Books Ltd.

Copyright © S. W. Perry, 2020

The moral right of S. W. Perry to be identified as the author
of this work has been asserted by him in accordance with the
Copyright, Designs and Patents Act of 1988.

All rights reserved. No part of this publication may be
reproduced, stored in a retrieval system, or transmitted in any
form or by any means, electronic, mechanical, photocopying,
recording, or otherwise, without the prior permission of both
the copyright owner and the above publisher of this book.

This novel is entirely a work of fiction. The names, characters
and incidents portrayed in it are the work of the author's
imagination. Any resemblance to actual persons, living or
dead, events or localities, is entirely coincidental.

10 9 8 7 6 5 4 3 2

A CIP catalogue record for this book is available
from the British Library.

Hardback ISBN: 978 1 78649 897 7
E-book ISBN: 978 1 78649 898 4

Printed and bound by CPI Group (UK) Ltd, Croydon, CR0 4YY

Corvus
An imprint of Atlantic Books Ltd
Ormond House
26–27 Boswell Street
London
WC1N 3JZ

www.corvus-books.co.uk

For Jane, as always

O, let the heavens give him defence against the elements,
for I have lost him on a dangerous sea…

WILLIAM SHAKESPEARE, *OTHELLO*

In 1589 the Sultan of Morocco sent an envoy to London. He received a rapturous welcome, even though at the time comprehension of the mysterious Islamic world was, at best, confused. Whatever the country of his birth, to the English a Muslim was a Moor, a Turk, or a Saracen...

PART 1

✠

The Kissing Knot

1

Marrakech, Morocco. March 1593

In the moment before they caught him, Adolfo Sykes was dreaming of oranges.

It was an hour after sunset, the third night of the time that some amongst the Moors called `Ushar, when the moon was almost full. In the gardens of the Koutoubia mosque the sellers of holy texts had packed away their books. The professional storytellers had departed, their audiences dispersed. From their high minarets the muezzins had called the city to the al-maghrib prayers, leaving the medina to the shadows and the scavenging dogs.

He loved the city at this time of night. He felt enfolded within its protective red walls. The cooling breeze from the Atlas Mountains filled the streets not with the scents of spices and human sweat, but with cleansing citrus.

Until he'd come to the land of the Moor, Adolfo Sykes had barely seen an orange, let alone tasted the succulent flesh. But now, after three prosperous years in Morocco, this agent of the Barbary Company of London – its founding stockholders the noble Earls of Warwick and Leicester – was ready to believe that paradise itself might smell like one vast orchard of orange trees.

He had almost reached his destination, the city hospital, the Bimaristan al-Mansur. Its high mud-brick walls were barely twenty paces ahead of him. And then this agreeable reverie was shattered in a single heartbeat.

Out of the night stepped two figures, their heads bound in voluminous *kufiyas* – a pair of monstrously fat-headed demons conjured up by some devilish *jinn*. In that instant Adolfo Sykes realized he had been a dead man from the moment he'd left his lodgings on the Street of the Weavers.

He had thought himself unobserved, no easy accomplishment for a small, somewhat bow-legged half-English, half-Portuguese merchant with a threadbare curtain of prematurely white hair that clung to the sides of his otherwise-unsown pate. An involuntary grunt of surprise escaped his lips. He stopped. Then he did what most are inclined to do when they have stumbled into what they suspect to be mortal danger: he came up with hasty reasons to believe he hadn't.

They are fellow Christian traders, he told himself confidently. Or Jewish moneymen from the el-Mellah quarter, those clever fellows without whom trade between Moor and European would seize up like an axle without grease. Whoever they were, they were not, under any circumstances, real or imagined, *assassins*.

The night suddenly seemed colder, despite the *djellaba* he was wearing, woven from the best English wool, and evidence – if any were needed – of the superiority of his merchandise. Fighting against a rising tide of panic, Sykes glanced quickly over his shoulder. A second pair of shrouded figures was standing barely two paces behind him, cutting off his retreat.

What happened next began with a moment of awkward comedy. First there was an odd little dance, as though five latecomers to a feast had all converged at the one remaining empty chair. Sykes, being a diminutive fellow and as wiry as a Barbary macaque, dodged sideways. He had a brief glimpse of himself as a free man, speeding through the darkened streets to safety – then to a ship that would carry him back to England where, as far as he knew, no one intended him violent bodily harm. Then a grasping hand caught a fold of his *djellaba* and a sideways kick swept his little bowed legs from under him. He went face-down onto the dirt, a plaintive grunt bursting from his lungs. He felt warm blood pool in his jaw, and the weight of a man's knee in the small of his back, almost breaking him. The darkness took on an even thicker patina as the man leaned over him, enveloping him in the folds of his robe like a falcon mantling over a stunned hare.

Even then, Adolfo Sykes was not yet fully ready to acknowledge the truth: that they had known he was coming, known where to lie in wait. That he'd been driven like game, the way the Berber tribesmen drove the desert gazelle towards their bows. In his tolerable Arabic he gasped, 'Purse... left side... my belt – take it. If God wills it, it's yours.'

The answer ripped away the last shreds of self-delusion.

'Do not insult us, Master Sykes; we are not common thieves,' said a voice very close to his left ear. 'It is not your purse we desire; it is the secret that you keep hidden from us in your infidel heart.'

English. Spoken with an Irish accent, by someone barely grown to manhood. The very last language he'd been expecting to hear.

Turning his head painfully towards the speaker, Sykes saw a cheek as pale as porcelain in the moonlight, a cheek flecked with a boyish attempt at a beard.

The voice then spoke some words in Arabic, presumably for his companions' benefit. It was not the unrefined language of the streets, Sykes noticed abstractly, but formal, classical Arabic, as if it had recently been learned by rote at the feet of a teacher. Sykes picked out the phrases 'It is him... it's the infidel who steals from the faithful.'

This offended Adolfo Sykes almost as much as the assault on his body. He had never stolen from anyone. Ask his customers. Ask the Christian merchants. Ask the Jews from the el-Mellah.

5

Ask the forty God-fearing English merchants who comprised the body of the Barbary Company – licensed by the queen's seal to hold the monopoly of trade between the princely states of Morocco and England – fine upstanding men, every last one of them. Men who counted themselves amongst the most forward-thinking in London, and who would expel him at the merest suggestion of stealing.

But what troubled him more than the slander was the voice: an executioner's voice, devoid of mercy.

Rough hands hauled Sykes to his feet. Making a poor attempt at bluff, he protested, 'I am the factor for the Barbary Company of London. As such, I am protected by the mercy of His Majesty Sultan al-Mansur. I have his written word upon it. I can show you.'

And it was true, after a fashion. The passport was in his lodgings, penned by one of the sultan's army of clerks, though as it was written in Arabic – which he could speak, but not read – it might, for all Sykes knew, be a shopping list.

The answer was brutally unapologetic. First there was a blow to the side of his head that made his knees buckle. Then they bound his hands and gagged him. He could tell at first bite that the gag was of a wholly inferior-quality cloth. Probably homespun by Berber tribesmen. It seemed to Sykes like the final, deliberate insult.

They manhandled him roughly through the same narrow doorway cut into the mud-brick wall of the Bimaristan from which they had emerged. He didn't struggle. They were young and much too strong for him. They had the law of the desert on their side: the weak always die first; and resisting only prolongs the agony.

Once inside, Sykes saw by the meagre light of an oil lamp an old watchman sitting in an alcove. His furrowed skin was as dark as *argan* bark, his beard white, like a crescent moon on a starless night. He left his seat, turned away and dropped to his knees, taking up the posture of a Moor at prayer. Sykes understood at once: this was not religious devotion, this was done so that he could later claim never to have witnessed the furtive, nocturnal arrival of a bound and gagged European.

For the place of execution they had chosen a room seemingly at the very heart of the Bimaristan, a chamber tiled from floor to ceiling with intricate mosaics, each tiny square of stone as polished as a mirror glass. He heard the one with the Irish accent engage in a brief but tense conversation in Arabic with his companions. He could understand only intermittent words, but he knew they were fortifying their own courage – boys on the verge of manhood, steeling themselves for a harsh rite of passage. He heard the prayer begin. '*All hu akbar...*'

In a way, he was glad it was to be here, in this little bejewelled chamber. Because cut into the flat ceiling was an opening in the shape of a six-pointed star, a window onto the limitless night, and once more he could catch the scent of oranges on the air. Paradise. Waiting for him. And all he had to do now was steel himself for the journey.

2

The south bank of the Thames river, London.
One month later

In the small hours of a deathly-still April morning two miles downriver from Westminster, three men climb silently from a private wherry. Caped against the bitter cold in heavy gabardines, they strike east from the Mutton Lane river stairs. They are heading for Long Southwark, guided through the empty lanes by the twisting flames of a single torch. Bankside is deserted. The unseasonably cold night is too raw even for thieves and house-divers. The timbers of the close-set houses rear out of the mist like the ribs of a fleet of galleys wrecked in the surf.

At the gatehouse on the southern end of London Bridge they come across the night-watch, warming their tired bones around a brazier that burns like a beacon warning of invasion. The three men pause, but only to confirm the address they have been given. There is a practised hardness in their faces that hints that they might be bearing steel beneath their cloaks. The watch lets them pass without question. They know government men when they see them. Arrests are always best made at times like this, when the subject is too sleep-befuddled to put up a fight.

Entering a lane close to the sign of the Tabard Inn, the three men count off the houses until they reach a modest two-storey property of lathe and plaster, close to a row of trees that marks the western boundary of St Thomas's hospital for the poor. With no show of pleasure at having reached their goal after such an uncomfortable journey their leader begins to hammer violently on the front door, as though its planks and hinges are personally responsible for the night's discomforts.

✠

Nicholas Shelby wakes with a start. He feels the rhythmic blows through the floorboards, through the frame of his bed, through the straw in the mattress, even in his bones. It is the sort of hammering that constables employ when arresting traitors – or calling physicians from their warm beds to tell them that the plague has finally crossed the river into Southwark.

He has been awaiting a call like this since the first cases of the new pestilence came to light last year. So far, the outbreak has stayed confined to the poorer lanes on the other side of London Bridge. But that hasn't stopped the Courts of Chancery, Wards, Liveries and Requests taking themselves off to Hertford to consider their business in healthier surroundings. So far, the liberty of Southwark has escaped. In the Bankside taverns, more than one wag has made the connection between the decrease in lawyers and the absence of plague south of the river where the bawdy-houses lie.

But Southwark has not escaped entirely. The Lord Mayor has ordered the closing of the playhouses and the bear-pits. As a consequence, an unwelcome lethargy has descended on the southern shore of the Thames. The purse-divers and coney-catchers have lost half of their trade at a stroke. In the stews, there are whores who have had only themselves for company since Candlemas, and the kindlier church wardens have stopped asking them their trade, when assessing the need for charity. Cynics say there are only two types of public places the authorities dare not shut, for fear of riot: churches and taverns. It all seems to Nicholas a grim

prelude for what would otherwise be a time of joy and festivity –
an impending wedding.

Fully awake now, he opens his eyes to the semi-darkness of
his rented room. On the clothes chest a single candle stands
close to guttering, as squat and fat as a lump of yellow clay
thrown on a potter's wheel. It fills the room with the smoky
smell of mutton grease. A film of moisture on the inside of the
window, and the absence of anything other than watery blackness beyond, tells him dawn must still be some hours off. It
is that hollowed-out time of the night when it is better not to
wake, when thoughts unchain themselves, when spirits walk
and old men die.

'The Devil take you and your godless knocking!'

The voice of his landlady, Mistress Muzzle, penetrates the
floorboards, caustic enough to strip limewash off a wall. Nicholas
hears a wheezing snort of indignation, followed by, 'I hope this is
not one of your patients, Dr Shelby! If it is, I'd be indebted if you
would ask them to fall sick at a godlier hour.'

Nicholas knows it will take his landlady a while to reach the
front door. She is a woman ill-designed for velocity. Struggling
into his hose and shirt, he wonders if he can beat her to it. As
he steps out onto the landing, he sees the flicker of an oil lamp
moving ponderously through the darkness and hears her voice
again, full of injured propriety: 'Anon! Anon! Do you expect me
to open the door in naught but my shift? What manner of place
do you think I keep – a bawdy-house?'

Even on Bankside, no one would confuse the upright Mistress
Muzzle's dwelling with a bawd's premises, thinks Nicholas as
he stumbles down the stairs. It is, however, the perfect place on
Bankside in which to start a medical practice: one room at street
level for seeing patients, accommodation above, and the land-
lady – the fearsome Mistress Muzzle – safely in her own domain

at the rear of the house. The only part they are forced to share is the front door.

In the light from the lamp, her pouchy face has the discomforted look of someone suffering a mild bout of colic. With an indignant explosion of breath and a theatrical jangling of her keys, she opens the door. Over her expansive shoulders, Nicholas can just make out three heads silhouetted against the misty night; a night turned a wet, muddy ochre by the light of a single flickering torch. A disembodied voice reaches him. No apology, just a bald statement: 'These are the lodgings of Dr Nicholas Shelby. Correct?'

'I am Dr Shelby,' Nicholas says, rubbing the sleep from his eyes.

'You are to come with us – at once.'

'By whose command?'

'By Sir Robert Cecil's command.'

So not the pestilence, then – but a close-enough second.

Mistress Muzzle turns back from the door. Nicholas sees her little eyes flicker over him, full of sudden mistrust. He knows what she's thinking: a member of the queen's Privy Council has sent for her tenant in the middle of the night. Therefore, at the very least, he must have poisoned someone. Has he been distributing papist pamphlets instead of medicine? Is he no doctor at all, but a charlatan prescriber of fake elixirs? And more importantly, by taking his rent, is she guilty by association?

For a moment Nicholas enjoys her confusion. But spacious, sanitary lodgings are not easy to find on Bankside.

'I'm not a wanted felon, Mistress Muzzle. Or a Jesuit – if that's what concerns you. And I *have* paid my rent until Trinity term.'

Unconvinced, she turns her head back towards the door and the men in the street. 'Is Dr Shelby under arrest?' she asks.

'Not at the moment,' says the one holding the burning torch. Wisps of smoke swirl upwards, disappearing into the cold, damp night and making Nicholas think of souls rising from a grave-yard. 'But if you want—'

The hammering has sounded so official that not a single occupant has dared open a window to see what is happening. No one wants to risk witnessing the apprehending of a traitor or the flushing out of a papist priest. Too many questions get asked, and there's always the chance of being mistaken for an accomplice. Much safer to wait for the public finale on Tower Hill or at Tyburn. And even though he knows himself to be an *almost*-innocent man, Nicholas can't help but acknowledge the little wormy knot of cold fear that writhes in his stomach.

'Do I have time to make myself a little more presentable?'

'Be quick. This is not an invitation to a revel, Dr Shelby. We have a wherry at the Mutton Lane stairs and the tide will soon begin to ebb. Bring what items a physician might normally have about him.'

'For what malady?'

'Sir Robert did not say.'

'Then how, in the name of Jesu, may I know what to bring?'

The irritation is clear in the man's terse reply. 'Whatever else is required, Sir Robert will provide it. Now *hurry*.'

'How long will you be away?' asks Mistress Muzzle.

'I don't know. Ask *them*,' Nicholas says, nodding at the men in the street. 'If anyone comes here needing medicine, tell them to seek out Mistress Merton. She'll be either at the Jackdaw tavern, or at her new apothecary shop on Dice Lane. Bianca will know what to do.'

For the first time that Nicholas has witnessed, since he moved out of the Jackdaw and into Mistress Muzzle's lodgings, his land-lady favours him with a smile. It is the warm, indulgent smile that some women are inclined to, whenever they think of impending nuptials. 'And if Mistress Merton herself should call here while you are away? What am I to say to her?'

'That's easy to answer, Mistress Muzzle. One way or another, I will be back in time for the wedding.'

✠

In the bedchamber of a modest property on Dice Lane, a short distance upriver from Mistress Muzzle's house, Bianca Merton wakes from a fragile, troubled sleep. She sits up against the bolster, the neckline of her shift damp against her skin. In the darkness she remembers two bodies falling through the night towards the cold, black surface of the Thames. She hears the slow, heavy slap as they enter deep water, the sound of ripples fading, like the tinkling of broken glass on a stone floor. She waits for them to disappear beneath the surface. But they don't. Their faces stay just below, watching her through the water with the cold, accusing stare of the dead. She squeezes her eyelids tightly shut. If I made a pact with God, she tells herself, when I look again, they will be gone. But if I made a pact with the Devil...

She counts to three and opens her eyes.

To her immense relief, there are no bodies tumbling, just shadows cast by the rushlight burning on the bedside table. A pact made with God, then. A righteous pact, not an evil one. Even so, she wonders if all murderers are troubled by such memories.

Her eyes linger on the crudely painted figures on the far wall, figures that must have triggered the illusion: two men, one prone, the other standing over him. The image is from the New Testament, the parable of the Good Samaritan. This house, she has learned, was previously owned by a Puritan who had wanted furnishings with a biblical theme, but couldn't afford expensive

13

Flemish tapestries. So instead he hired a man who painted tavern signs to decorate the walls.

They keep her company: Jonah and his whale, in the closet; Lazarus in the pantry; Daniel and the lion in the parlour where she takes breakfast. Daniel looks like a fat Bankside alderman. The lion, conjured from the painter's imagination, is an animal quite unknown anywhere else on earth. Bianca has learned to tolerate them all, including the Good Samaritan in the bedroom, except on those few occasions when he dances in the rushlight and reminds her of the night, almost two years ago now, when two men did indeed tumble through the darkness below the bridge.

When she had confessed her sin to Cardinal Fiorzi, before he sailed away back to Venice, he had told her that God would forgive her. The men she had led to their deaths were evil men. They had committed vile deeds in the service of Satan, and there was no sin in ridding the world of them. But to Bianca, in spite of all that, they were still men. And now they were dead. Absolution could not alter the hand she had played in their deaths.

She scolds herself. *I am not a murderer. I am a Good Samaritan. How many more innocents would have suffered if I had not done what I did? How many penniless Banksiders might have sickened – or, worse, died – if I'd stood by and allowed Nicholas Shelby to die?*

At the thought of him, she demurely adjusts her shift where it has slipped over one shoulder, and combs her hair with her fingers to bring at least a little obedience to those heavy, dark tresses that are always at their most ungovernable when she wakes. If he could see her at this moment – *Jesu*, what would her mother have said at the very idea? – he would think her skin still glowed with the warmth of the Italian sun. But that's because of the rushlight. She fears that five years of English rain have washed the real colour right out of her, along with almost every other trace of her Paduan upbringing. She touches her neck where it meets the shoulder – a neck that on Monday is swanlike, and on Tuesday as scrawny as the reeds that grow around the Mutton Lane river stairs. Yes, in candlelight a veritable Venus; but in the grey light of a morning in early April?

She consoles herself with the thought that Englishmen appear to like their women looking as pale as a cadaver. Caking your face with ceruse is all the fashion in smart circles. Even the queen paints her features with it, to make her skin as white as the best Flanders linen. Not that you'll see it on Bankside, save on the faces of the richer whores who favour it to cover up the ravages of the French Gout. She curses herself angrily, and recalls something her mother had often told her: *Bianca, my child, never trouble yourself with what a man may think of you. Thinking is not their natural disposition.*

Yet even as she stares down the bed to the wainscoting on the far wall, wainscoting that is painted a rich orange, she thinks it would be nice to have a little colour in her face for the wedding.

For once, no one tells Nicholas to sit patiently amidst the panelled elegance of Cecil House – one of the grandest beyond the city walls, set between the river and Covent Garden – until someone remembers his presence. No one instructs him to bide his time while the clerks and the men of law, the intriguers and the intelligencers hurry to and fro. No one mistakes him for a new gardener who has unforgivably stumbled through the wrong door. This time a weary-looking secretary in a black half-cape and gartered stockings shows him directly to Robert Cecil's study.

The Lord Treasurer's son has clearly been at work for some time, though dawn has yet to break. Hunched over his desk, his crookedness is smoothed by the night beyond the glass. His little beard cuts a dark wedge out of the neat white ruff that he wears over a doublet of moss-green velvet. To Nicholas, he could be an innocent-faced but malevolent little sprite reading spells from a parchment. Though he is about Nicholas's age, his eyes are those of a man who has seen all there is to see, good *and* bad. When he speaks, his voice is like the whisper of a blade drawn from its sheath.

'Dr Shelby, thank you for agreeing to come.'

It seems a strange thing to say, thinks Nicholas, when you've sent three men to drag someone from his bed – especially when you already pay him handsomely to be on call.

'I am always at your service, Sir Robert,' he says quietly, wishing it didn't sound so much like an admission of guilt.

Robert Cecil rises and steps forward from his desk. There is a tension in his little body that almost dares you to recognize its imperfection, to ask him to his face how it is that a small man with a crooked spine can make even the most powerful dance to his tune. Nicholas has heard the tavern-talk: that the queen calls him Elf, or Pigmy. Given that the Cecils know almost everything that occurs in this realm, he wonders how Sir Robert bears the insult. Perhaps his hard carapace is more a defence against life's slights than against the realm's enemies.

'Leave your gabardine there,' Cecil says, indicating a high-backed chair in the corner. 'I don't wish my wife to think I've summoned a Thames waterman instead of a physician.'

'Is Lady Cecil ill?' Nicholas asks as he unlaces his coat. 'Why didn't your man say?'

But Cecil merely regards him with a critical eye. 'Tell me, Dr Shelby, what *exactly* is it you spend my retainer on? That is the same white canvas doublet you were wearing when I sent you to spy upon Lord Lumley. When was that – two years past? Are you hoarding my stipend in case the Spanish come again? It won't save you, you know. They'll rob you of it and give it to the Pope to expiate their sins. So you might as well spend *some* of it on a good tailor.'

Nicholas tries not to sound sanctimonious. 'I spend a little on lodgings and food, the rest I use to subsidize my medical practice, so that Banksiders can afford something better than the usual charlatans who peddle false remedies. In return, I come when you call. It is what we agreed when I accepted your patronage.'

Cecil shoots him a look of mock despair. Then he opens the door and ushers Nicholas through into the panelled corridor. Candles burning in silver sconces throw their two shadows back against the oak wainscoting. In Nicholas's mind, one shadow is a man climbing the steps to a scaffold, the other a gargoyle watching from the crowd. Why is it, he asks himself, that whenever I'm in this man's presence, my thoughts turn inevitably towards a violent fate?

At the end of the corridor they stop before a set of doors, their panels carved with the Cecil crest. Sir Robert raps his energetic little fist on the timber and calls out, 'Madam, are you composed? Dr Shelby has arrived.'

The door opens onto a pleasant chamber hung with shimmering drapes and cushioned as Nicholas would imagine an Eastern harem to be. He remembers the craze for all things Moorish that swept London when the envoy of the Sultan of Morocco visited: *Tamburlaine* at the Rose theatre, shoemakers turning out oriental slippers, everyone gawping at the sight of dark-skinned men in exotic robes. Even Eleanor had insisted they turn their own chamber Turkish. But that was before...

He pushes the memory from his mind and follows Cecil into the room.

A slight, graceful woman of about thirty sits flanked by four ladies-in-waiting, an empty cradle at her feet. In her lap is a toddler, dressed in an embroidered smock that Nicholas reckons would set back a Southwark labourer the better part of a month's wages. He has met Lady Elizabeth Cecil, daughter of Lord Cobham and wife to the Lord Treasurer's son, before. And he knows she does not care much for him.

'Is there really no other physician in London to attend us, Husband?' she asks Cecil, putting her arms protectively around the child, who begins to grizzle loudly.

So it's the son I've been called to treat, thinks Nicholas. And his mother doesn't want me anywhere near him. This could prove a difficult diagnosis.

'Madam, you know my opinion of doctors,' says Cecil. 'I have suffered the best of them, certainly the most expensive. They did nothing for me. I remain as I was born – disjointed. To my mind, I count Dr Shelby among the few honest ones I've met. At the very least, he will not lie to us.'

It is the first time Nicholas has heard Robert Cecil speak openly of his condition. He takes it as a cue, looking directly into Cecil's wife's eyes.

'Lady Cecil, let us be open with one another. I assume you have heard what a few of the older Fellows of the College of Physicians say about me.'

His directness takes her by surprise. 'I have. They say that in some matters of physic you are a heretic.'

A sad smile – quickly mastered. 'And I do not deny it, Lady Cecil. When I discovered that what I had learned wasn't enough to save the woman I loved and the child she was carrying, there followed a period when I shunned all reason. I rejected everything I had been taught. I drank myself into insensibility, because it seemed the only medicine I could stomach. I lost my practice, my friends, my livelihood. I slept beneath hedges and I cursed God for letting me wake in the morning. When I recovered my senses – with the help of a woman I can only describe as a ministering angel – I swore I would only practise medicine that I could prove works. If I was to have faith in it, it must be physic whose outcome I could predict with some accuracy. That is an oath I do not intend to break. If it is not enough for you, I am content to return to Bankside and the bed from which your husband's men so roughly summoned me.'

Shocked by his honesty, Elizabeth Cecil drops her gaze to her son. She gentles him, but he keeps grizzling. 'I am not sure that recommends you, Dr Shelby, except as a man who loved his wife more than he loved his reputation.'

'As Sir Robert has just this moment said, madam, I will not lie to you.'

'Is it true you abjure casting a horoscope before you make a diagnosis?' she asks.

'Yes, it is.'

'Then how do you know what manner of cure is propitious?'

'I do not believe the stars influence the body nearly as much as is claimed, Lady Cecil.'

'But that flies in the face of all received wisdom, Dr Shelby.'

'Perhaps it does. But if you have a pain in your back in January, and after treatment it returns in August, how can the constellations guide me on what medicine I should prescribe? The stars are no longer aligned.'

He can see the confusion in her. Her delicate fingers fuss with the child's smock.

'And they say you do not believe in the humours of the body. Is that true?'

'Until someone can show me a humour, madam, yes, it is. Until I can touch it, examine it, replicate its influence in a reliable manner, I cannot in all faith insist it exists. Besides, it is taught that balancing the humours requires the drawing of blood from certain parts of the body. Would you have me bleed a child of William's age? He's barely two, am I right?'

'Of course not! William is *far* too young for bleeding,' she exclaims, more than a little horrified. She clutches the boy to her breast, as if she fears Nicholas will produce a lancet from beneath his doublet and advance upon the infant.

'But if bleeding works, Lady Cecil, why *not* bleed a child?'

'Because... well, because...'

'A child has blood flowing through its veins, just as the mother has. So if drawing blood is medically sound, why *not* bleed the child – other than to save it from the discomfort? That is where reason would lead us, is it not?'

He waits until he sees a flicker of self-doubt in her grey eyes.

'I'm not trying to trick you, madam. The answer is simple: because it *doesn't* work. I believe any effect is purely coincidental. I can tell you from my experiences in Holland, as a physician to the army of the House of Orange, that blood is best kept where it is – *inside*.'

Elizabeth Cecil seems intrigued now, almost enjoying a frisson of sedition. She turns to her husband. 'Robert, explain yourself: how is it that a man who spends his waking hours seeking out heretics invites one into his house – to administer to his son?'

'Madam, are you going to let Dr Shelby examine William or not?'

With a sudden obedience that surprises him, Lady Cecil sits the child on the nearest cushion, holding him gently by the arm. But there is nothing obedient in the look she gives Nicholas. 'Have a care with my son, Dr Shelby. He is not the child of some Southwark goodwife – he is a Cecil's heir. His grandfather is the queen's best-loved servant. Harm him' – a glance in her husband's direction – 'and not even her newest privy councillor will save you from *me*.'

'Look under his arms,' says Robert Cecil in reply, softly, as though he hopes no one else in the room will hear. 'Give me an honest report of what you see.'

Now Nicholas understands. Cecil fears his son might have contracted the pestilence.

Kneeling before the boy, Nicholas gives him what he hopes will be taken as a carefree smile. 'Tell me now, Master William, does your mother play Tickle with you?' He flutters his fingers. The boy grins. Nicholas looks up at Lady Cecil. 'Madam, will you assist me?'

Understanding him at once, she makes a fuss of the boy, pretending to pinch him on the side. He squirms away from his mother's fingers, laughing loudly and throwing up both arms in delight. Cecil looks on intently. If he objects to the frivolity, he keeps it to himself.

Nicholas gently holds the boy's arms aloft and studies the red patches that are clearly visible in the armpits. He knows at once what he's looking at.

He remembers that when he had his practice on Bread Street – before Eleanor's death; before the fall – his richer clients had taken a too-speedy diagnosis as a sign of sloppiness. They had wanted their money's worth. But he can sense Robert and Elizabeth Cecil's anxiety. There is no point in prolonging it. He stands up, finding himself stifling an unexpected yawn as the hour catches up with him.

'An irritation of the skin, Sir Robert, Lady Cecil. Nothing more. These are not buboes.'

'Thank our merciful Lord!' Robert Cecil's explosive release of breath is the first display of emotion Nicholas has witnessed since his arrival.

'But there is more,' says Elizabeth Cecil, restoring the child to her lap, where he starts toying with the edge of the cushion. 'His sleep has also been much disturbed of late. He spits out his milk-sop. He mewls a great deal. And my ladies tell me he has a fever.'

To Nicholas's ear, she sounds as if she's testing him. He lays a hand on the boy's forehead. It feels hot to the touch. He calls for a candle to be brought nearer, the better to see inside the child's mouth. 'You said he spits out his milk-sop. Does he swallow water with ease?'

Elizabeth Cecil looks at one of the ladies, who shakes her head.

'Inflammation of the columellae,' Nicholas says. 'If you look, madam, you'll see: there at the back of the throat.'

'What do you prescribe?' she asks.

'If you wish a strictly non-heretical regime,' he says, giving in to sarcasm and instantly regretting it, 'I'd suggest a purge to empty his bowels, and wet-cupping to draw blood from the skin. Possibly a small incision made under the tongue to take out the over-hot blood. That's what the textbooks would have me do.'

She smiles. 'Perhaps I was a little too hasty earlier, Dr Shelby. But a mother is entitled to be protective, is she not?'

'Of course, madam.'

'So?'

'For the soreness under his arms, a balm of milk-thistle and camomile. For the throat: a decoction of cypress leaves, rose petals, garlic and pomegranate buds, all in honey.'

Robert Cecil coughs, as if to remind them of his presence. 'I'll send a man to the apothecary on Spur Alley.'

'Husband, it is not even dawn—'

'What of it?'

'May I make a suggestion, Sir Robert?'

'Yes, of course, Dr Shelby.'

'Let me have Mistress Merton make up the physic for you. I'd trust her ingredients over anything a member of the Grocers' Guild puts in a pot. Half of it's likely to be dried grass and crushed hazelnuts.'

'Don't tell me you've run afoul of the grocers as well, Dr Shelby,' Robert Cecil says. 'After the College of Physicians, the Barber-Surgeons, and the Worshipful Company of Tailors, is there any guild in London you *haven't* upset?'

'The vintners speak highly of me,' says Nicholas in a flat voice devoid of frivolity.

'Perhaps I've been mistaken in my opinion of you, Dr Shelby,' says Elizabeth Cecil with a wry smile. 'I ought to know by now that a pearl is not to be judged by its shell.'

The clear reference to her husband catches Nicholas off-guard. He has always assumed Lord Cobham's daughter married the crook-backed Robert Cecil solely for the name. Until now, it had never dawned on him that love played any part in Cecil's life.

As they walk back to Sir Robert's study, Nicholas says, 'When your men hammered on the door of my lodgings, I feared it was the parish, come to tell me that plague had crossed the river.'

Robert Cecil glances up at him pensively. 'At present it seems confined mostly to the lanes around the Fleet bridge. One of Elizabeth's ladies has family there. So naturally I assumed the worst. Let us hope to God it can be kept in check.'

'The Lord Mayor has done the right thing, Sir Robert. As long as everyone keeps their dwelling clean and the street outside free of refuse—'

'And what would be your *heretical* view of the cause of this contagion, Dr Shelby?'

A weary smile. 'I know no better than any other physician, Sir Robert.'

'Men who don't think with the herd are often wiser than they know, Dr Shelby. Speculate.'

'I know that casting horoscopes and wrapping yourself in ribbons inscribed with prayers has no discernible – and, more importantly, *repeatable* – effect, if that's what you mean.'

'But its transmission: have you no views of your own?'

'It is held to move easily in tainted air, but how, and from where, I cannot say. Nor can I tell you why some who catch it die, while others live. That may have to do with age and constitution, but it is by no means certain. The disease is a mystery – an exceptionally malign mystery.'

'Well, the Privy Council has done what it can. The infected houses are to be shut up and a watch set over them. We've forbidden all fairs and gatherings within the city. The rest is up to God.'

'Then let us hope it dies of starvation, Sir Robert.'

'Amen to that. At present there's no talk of adjourning the Trinity term for Parliament. But if Her Majesty starts thinking of removing herself to Windsor or Greenwich, there will be a great leaving of this city, mark my words.'

Back in Cecil's study, Nicholas reaches for the gabardine he'd left hanging on a chair. Through the window, a faint grey line marks the boundary between the fields of Covent Garden and the still-black sky.

'Leave your coat a while longer,' Robert Cecil says, fixing him with an uncompromising look. 'I have something else to ask of you.'

Here it comes, Nicholas tells himself, his heart sinking. With Cecil, a summons is like the bark on a rotten tree: what is on the surface is not always what lies beneath. Peel away the layers and you're likely to find black beetles crawling about underneath.

'I want you to go on a journey for me.'

'A journey, Sir Robert? What manner of journey?'

'Quite a long one, as it happens. Are you familiar, by any chance, with the city of Marrakech?'

The courtier's little bejewelled index finger traces a line on the globe's lacquered surface, down the Narrow Sea towards Brittany, then across the Bay of Biscay, past Portugal, all the way to the African continent, almost to the point where knowledge ends. Here and there the fingertip ploughs through little flurries of waves, drawn simplistically as a child might draw the wings of a bird in flight. 'Saltpetre, Dr Shelby,' Cecil says as his finger runs southwards. 'It is all about saltpetre.'

Nicholas looks at him blankly.

'Let me explain. The Barbary Company was set up by Their Graces, Leicester and Warwick, to trade with the western nations of the Moor. We send Morocco fine English wool. In return, Sultan al-Mansur sends us spices and sugar.' As his fingertip reaches the Barbary shore, Cecil's eyes narrow. 'But that is not the sole extent of our commerce, and I must have your word that you will not speak of what I am about to tell you beyond this room – on pain of severe penalty.'

Nicholas wonders if this is the point where he should stick his fingers in his ears – but he knows full well that not actually hearing one of Robert Cecil's confidences is no protection at all. Reluctantly he nods his acceptance.

'Until some fifteen years ago,' Cecil continues, 'Philip of Spain – and his Portuguese puppet Sebastian – were masters of Morocco. Then the Moors rose up and expelled them. Now we send Sultan al-Mansur new matchlock muskets, to defend his realm against their return.'

'And in payment he sends us saltpetre,' Nicholas guesses.

'Which you, Dr Shelby, will know – from your service in the Low Countries – is a crucial component in the manufacture of gunpowder. Do you happen to know how many Spanish ships were sunk as a direct result of our gunfire, when Philip sent his Armada against us?'

'Not off the top of my head, no.'

'*None*,' Cecil says archly. 'Drake had to close with them at Gravelines before our cannon could do them proper harm. Moroccan saltpetre is amongst the finest there is. We need every ounce we can get, in order to ensure that if the Spanish snake comes against us again, we can out-charge his cannon.'

'But that still doesn't explain why you want *me* to go to the Barbary shore,' Nicholas says.

'I'm sure you will not be surprised to know that I maintain an agent in Marrakech, expressly to keep watch on our interests.'

It could scarcely surprise Nicholas less. The most isolated village in England knows the Cecils are the eyes and ears that ceaselessly protect England from her enemies. They have their people everywhere. Mothers warn their children that if they misbehave, the Cecils will see their faults almost as surely as God Himself.

'The man I employ as my spy in Marrakech is a half-English, half-Portuguese trader named Adolfo Sykes,' Cecil tells him. 'He is the Barbary Company's factor there. But in the past weeks three Barbary Company ships have returned to England without a single one of his customary dispatches. I fear some mischief has befallen him.'

'But why send me? Yes, I know a little about wool – my father is a yeoman farmer – but I couldn't tell saltpetre from pepper, if you put it on my mutton.'

Cecil gives him a condescending smile. 'Because to send just another merchant would be as pointless as sending my pastry cook. I need an educated man, Dr Shelby – someone who can assume an envoy's duties. If the Spanish have swayed the sultan against us, I want someone with the faculties to sway him back again.'

'But I'm a physician, not a diplomat.'

'Exactly. One of the sultan's close advisors – a Moor named Sumayl al-Seddik – is benefactor to a hospital in the city. My father had dealings with him when he came here with the entourage of the sultan's envoy some four years past. I'm sure you will recall the public tumult that accompanied the visit.'

'Eleanor and I were in the crowd,' Nicholas says, remembering. 'That was before...'

A moment's uncomfortable silence, until Cecil says, 'Yes, well... you can tell Minister al-Seddik that you've come as an envoy to foster ties of learning between our two realms. That should pass well enough as a believable reason.'

'An envoy who looks like a Thames waterman,' Nicholas says, throwing Cecil's earlier words back at him.

Sir Robert gives a diplomatic cough. 'If that's your only other objection, Dr Shelby, let me reassure you: I have more tailors than I do horses.'

Nicholas takes a steadying breath, so that his answer sounds appropriately resolute. Since the moment two years ago when he'd agreed to act as Cecil's physician, in return for a stipend that would allow him to set up a charitable practice on Bankside, he has known this time would come. Hasn't Bianca warned him enough times? *Nicholas, sweet, Robert Cecil offers nothing without a reason. There is always a price to be paid in return.*

He thinks of the last journey he undertook for the Lord Treasurer's crook-backed son. It had ended with two slack-eyed killers dragging him towards the centre of London Bridge and the river waiting below, the pain of the beatings coursing through his limbs and howling in his ears. If it hadn't been for Bianca's courage that night, he wouldn't be standing here now.

Yes, he thinks, a journey undertaken for Robert Cecil does not always end at the destination you are expecting.

3

In the shadow of the riverside church, St Saviour's market is in full cry. Competition for a sale is fierce. Drapers loudly proclaim the quality of their ribbons; farmers in from the Surrey countryside boast you'll find no better winter vegetables outside the queen's own gardens; cutlers swear on their mother's graves that their knives are newly forged and not pawned by destitute sailors laid off from the royal fleet. And weaving through the crowd, like pike in a shady pool, the cut-purses and coney-catchers hunt their prey.

Not that any of them would think for a moment of waylaying the comely young woman with the amber eyes who walks around the stalls with such an assured air, a wicker basket tucked under her arm, her waves of dark hair pinned beneath a simple linen coif. They've heard it said that if you try to slip your hand between bodice and kirtle to steal away *her* purse, you'll wake up next morning with a raven's claw instead of fingers. Bianca Merton is known to them. Bianca Merton is out of bounds.

And by association, so too is the curly-headed lad with dark eyes and skin the colour of orange-blossom honey who walks beside her.

Banksiders know Farzad Gul now, almost as well as they know his mistress. They greet him as if he were one of their own. After all, he is Bianca Merton's Moor, and thus something of a curiosity. His colourful slanders of the Pope and the King of Spain, learned from the English mariners who rescued him from shipwreck, have made him as popular as any Southwark street entertainer.

Today Farzad is making one of his regular visits in search of vegetables for the Jackdaw's pottage pot. Usually he would come alone, but with the wedding pending, Bianca has taken the opportunity to accompany him. She has the better eye for quality braids and ribbons with which to turn his battered jerkin into something a little more befitting a groomsman.

'An English wedding might not be the match of a Paduan one, or a Persian one for that matter,' she tells him sternly, when his interest in haberdashery fails at the second stall she drags him to, 'but I will not abide you looking like a vagabond, young gentleman.'

'No, Mistress,' he says, with downcast eyes.

'So then, you go and find us some of Master Brocklesbury's cabbages, and I will see to the ribbons. Meet me by Jacob Henry's oyster stall when you're done.'

'Yes, mistress,' Farzad says with a grin, knowing the choice of rendezvous means a cup of the best oysters to be found this side of the river.

As he heads deeper into the market, alone, Farzad Gul wonders where he might be now, were it not for Mistress Bianca. It is two years since he found himself cast up in this strange city. If his rescuers had not happened to stop at the Jackdaw tavern on their paying-off, perhaps he might have sold his cooking skills to a new ship, sailed away again to some other strange place far beyond the world he had once known.

Every day Farzad wonders where his mother and the other survivors of his family are. In his mind he can trace their soul-crushing progress across the scorching desert wilderness, from Suakin on the Red Sea to a slave market in Algiers or Tripoli, or Fez, or even Marrakech. But from there they fade away entirely; sold, undoubtedly – if they lived; turned from the boisterously argumentative characters of his childhood into living ghosts.

But living *where*? Sometimes he prays they never made landfall at all, but followed his father and his sister into heaven.

A jarring blow to his shoulder pulls Farzad back into the present. He hears a contemptuous 'Out of my way, heathen dog!'

Turning, he sees two lads of about his own age, dressed in the jerkins and caps of city apprentices. One has his hands in his belt and his elbows spread aggressively. 'And take your filthy Blackamoor eyes off me,' he snarls in an accent that, to Farzad, feels somehow familiar.

'I am no heathen, I am from Persia,' Farzad says pleasantly, refusing to rise to what is clearly a challenge. And to take the anger out of the air, he adds brightly, 'And the Pope has the breath of an old camel!'

To his surprise, his words fail to bring about the expected slapping of thighs and jocund howls of approval. The lad with the elbows rushes at him, hurling Farzad back into a cheese stall. Round yellow truckles tumble onto the cobbles.

Southwark street-fights can swiftly run out of hand. Knives get drawn. Sometimes even swords. Deaths are not unknown. So the stall-holders at St Saviour's are adept at putting them down before they get started. A burly weaver whom Farzad recognizes as a regular at the Jackdaw pins one of the apprentices in a vicious armlock.

'That's enough out of you, young master,' he says, giving the lad's arm a corrective wrench. 'If you've a mind for a brawl, you'd be better off back home in Ireland, taking your anger out on the Spanish, if they try a landing. We'll have none of your bog-trotting rowdiness here.' He releases his grip, thinking the apprentice has learned his lesson.

But he hasn't. He starts towards Farzad again, who is trying to put the cheeses back on the stall. 'One day soon I shall be a prince over the likes of you,' he snarls, his Irish accent thickened by his anger. He stares close into Farzad's face. 'We should permit none of your kind here. Our Captain Connell would know what to do with a Blackamoor like you.'

And lest there be any doubt about the sort of man this Captain Connell might be, he draws the blade of one hand across his own throat. Then he turns and walks away, beckoning his companion to follow.

Farzad watches them go, cold in his heart. Not at the insult – he's borne much worse – but at the mention of an all-too-familiar name: Captain Connell. It is a name Farzad Gul has long prayed he would never hear again. It is the name of the cruellest man in the whole world.

✠

'Tell me again, Nicholas: where?'

It is later that day, in Bianca Merton's apothecary's shop on Dice Lane. She has assumed what Nicholas calls her tavern-mistress's face – the one she adopts when a taproom brawl is about to kick off, someone exceeds his credit or a Puritan complains about the sinfulness of Bankside whilst asking directions to the Cardinal's Hat, all in the same breath. Nicholas marvels at how her features can change from exquisite to terrifying in an instant.

'Marrakech,' he repeats with a slight trace of discomfort, handing her the list of medicines he has promised Robert and Elizabeth Cecil.

She keeps her eyes fixed on the distillations, powders and medicaments: sweet clover boiled in wine for Walter Pemmel's sore eyes... saffron dissolved in the juice of honey-wort for Mistress Gilby's leg ulcers...

'It's in Morocco,' he says. 'Sir Robert showed me – he has a terrestrial globe, with all the lands and capitals—'

'I *know* where Marrakech is, Nicholas,' she says, brushing aside a pennon of ebony hair that has fallen over one eye. 'I was brought up in Padua and my father was a merchant, remember? I can name all the great cities of the known world, Christian *or* Moor.' She looks up again and begins to count them off on her lithe fingers, 'Venice, Aleppo, Lisbon, Constantinople, Jerusalem...'

'You can stop. I take your point: you know where Marrakech is.'

'Why does he want you to go *there*, of all places? If he wants spices, I know plenty of merchants on Galley Quay who import from Barbary.'

'It's about diplomacy,' he says evasively.

'Nicholas, you're a physician, not a diplomat.'

He gives her the answer Robert Cecil proposed as a masquerade. 'The Moors have a great tradition in medicine. Most of our medical texts were translated from Arabic versions of the Latin and Greek originals. He wants me to go there to discover what, if anything, we might learn from them.'

She fixes him with those unsettling amber eyes. 'You cannot go to Marrakech, Nicholas. The wedding – remember?'

'It doesn't matter.'

'What do you mean – *it doesn't matter?*'

'Because I'm not going. I told him No.'

The corners of Bianca's mouth lift into an incredulous half-smile. 'You *refused* Robert Cecil?'

'I'm not his slave, Bianca. I'm his physician.'

She taps one of the pots on the table, as if she's just checkmated him at chess. 'He didn't threaten to stop your stipend – force you to abandon your practice for the poor?'

'No.'

'Or threaten to have me hanged for a heretic?'

'No.'

'Because he's tried *that* line before, when he's wanted to coerce you.'

'No.'

'I suppose he swore on his mother's grave there was no one else he could trust to do the job but Nicholas Shelby?'

'Bianca, Robert Cecil has agents in more places than even you can name. I'm sure one of those will serve his needs more adequately than I. If he really must have a physician for the task, he can call on the College. Someone like Frowicke, or Beston. I'm sure they would be only too happy to spend three weeks at sea in a leaky ship full of rats and lice, so they can tell the descendants of the great Avicenna where they're going wrong.'

'Who?'

'Ibn Sina. He was a Persian physician. We know him as Avicenna.'

She comes out from behind the table, the hem of her gown swirling around her ankles like a willow in a summer squall. 'Well, I know that Robert Cecil is a snake. You *have* denied him – haven't you?'

'I told you, yes.'

She fixes him with a stern gaze and turns away before responding. 'Good, because for a moment I was sure you'd invented the whole story simply in order to disappear for a while – to avoid the wedding.'

✠

The Jackdaw has seldom looked so resplendent. Fresh paint gleams on the lintel. The ivy around the little latticed windows is neatly trimmed. The irregular timbers appear to be merely resting, rather than sagging under the three hundred years of travail they've endured, holding up the ancient brickwork. As Nicholas follows Bianca through the doorway, he catches the mingled tang of hops, wood-smoke and fresh rushes. From her place by the hearth, the Jackdaw's dog, Buffle, looks up at their arrival, wags her tail once and promptly goes back to sleep.

It has not been easy for Bianca to stay away, now that she's left the daily management of the tavern to Rose, her former maid, and to Ned Monkton. She suspects that if her apothecary shop was not doing such brisk business, she'd be poking her head over the threshold every other hour.

Almost immediately she spots Ned. He's standing in the centre of the taproom, casting an appraising eye at the scattering of breakfasters like a fiery-bearded Celtic chieftain after a good battle. Seeing her, he smooths his apron over his great frame and attempts a gallant bending of the knee.

'Mistress Bianca! 'Pon my troth, 'tis wondrous good to see you,' he says. 'Rose has the accounts ready, if you've come to see them. Just squiggles to me, but she assures me they're in order.'

'I'm sure they are, Ned,' Bianca says, with more confidence than she feels. Trusting Rose to keep anything in order – especially from a distance – has not come easily to her.

At the sound of Bianca's voice, Rose comes hurrying from the kitchen like a plump partridge flushed by a spaniel. Running a hand quickly through her black curls, she bobs in obeisance. 'Mistress, I wasn't expecting—'

Bianca smiles. 'Rose, dear, you don't have to courtesy. I've cancelled your indenture, remember? You're no longer my servant. You're not beholden to me in any way.' The faintest lift of a fine Paduan eyebrow. '*Unless*, of course, your accounting is deficient.'

An abbess accused of running a jumping-shop couldn't look half as horrified at the suggestion as Rose does. 'Mercy, Mistress! I've been diligent,' she protests, her cheeks blushing. 'Like you instructed: Walter Pemmel to have no credit beyond ninepence; Parson Moody to settle his slate promptly every Sunday, an' a penny on his ale each time he starts singing those songs of his – the one with the nuns in them...'

Nicholas listens with a sad smile of remembrance on his face, and wonders if it might be practical to rent just the downstairs room at Mistress Muzzle's.

'I'm sure you're doing everything to the letter, Rose,' Bianca says, giving her a belated kiss of greeting. 'To be honest, I'm more concerned about trade.'

'It *has* been quiet, Mistress,' admits Ned. 'But then all Bankside is quiet, given what's happening across the river. Strangers aren't exactly welcome these days. You don't know what they might be bringing with them.'

'Well, here is the man who can tells us first-hand,' Bianca says, fixing Nicholas with a challenging stare. 'You were chewing the cud with a member of the Privy Council this morning, Nicholas. What does your friend the Lord Treasurer's son say?'

'Apparently the pestilence is confined around the Fleet ditch and Holborn. But if the queen decides to postpone her new parliament and retire to Greenwich or Windsor, many in the city will take it as a signal to leave.'

'Those who have the luxury,' Bianca says fiercely.

'Yes. That's what I told Robert Cecil.'

She jams her fists into her waist and defiantly thrusts out her elbows. 'Well, we'll keep the place scrubbed clean, and burn rosemary and angelica in all the candle sconces. Fresh rushes every day, and if we have lodgers, then boil the bed sheets on Mondays and Thursdays. Use the pottage cauldron if you must, Rose, but for heaven's sake make sure it's clean before you do. I don't want the bed linen dyed brown and smelling of turnips.' She looks at Nicholas. 'Any other suggestions, Dr Shelby?'

'None that would be any more effective, Mistress Merton.'

'We could all run away to Marrakech, of course,' she says teasingly.

'Marry who?' Rose demands with a scowl.

'Marrakech. It's place, dear. A long way away. Nicholas knows where it is, don't you, Nicholas?'

For a moment Rose looks about to cry. 'But the marriage is to be here, on Bankside! It's all arranged. We've even hung up the kissing knots.' She points to the little woven balls of greenery hanging from the ceiling beams. 'There's a special one by the window, for you and Master Nicholas. Go on, we've all been waiting.'

'Rose!'

But Rose gives an impertinent toss of her head that has her black curls rippling across her brow. 'You can't be cross, Mistress – you said I wasn't indentured any more.'

Ned Monkton grins. 'You'll have to try it out, Mistress – see if it works. We all spent hours putting them up. Rose insisted.' He turns to the nearest booth, where an elderly man with a long threadbare white beard and a tight-fitting black cap on his head is taking his breakfast. 'Isn't that so, Master Mandel?'

Solomon Mandel, a Jew who lives in the lane beyond the public well, licks his fingers clean. 'Rose had me perched on a stool to put that thing up there,' he says crossly. 'Imagine it – me, at my age!'

'If I recall rightly, Master Solomon, you insisted on helping,' says Rose. 'And I vaguely recall you dancing a little measure while you were doing it.'

The image of the usually reserved Solomon Mandel dancing on a chair while he ties a kissing knot to the rafters is a startling one for Nicholas. Mandel is a reserved fellow who lives alone and goes about his trade – importing foreign spices – without fanfare. He has been a regular at the Jackdaw since shortly after Farzad's arrival became common knowledge on Bankside. He'd enquired, in a strange tongue, if the young Persian could cook a certain bread that neither Rose nor Bianca had ever heard of. When Farzad said yes, Mandel almost wept with joy. From that day on, he's arrived promptly at daybreak for his breakfast of *kubaneh*.

'You are a tyrant, Mistress Rose, a veritable tyrant, do you hear?' Mandel says, wagging a cautionary finger in her direction. 'Making an old man stand on a chair just so you can crow to all Southwark that you've witnessed Master Nicholas and Mistress Bianca exchanging a *kusch*.' He looks in their direction, his moist old eyes set far back in their caves. 'If it's going to happen, could you two please get on with it, so I can finish Farzad's excellent *kubaneh*?'

Seeing the trap that's been laid for them, Bianca begins to protest. '*Oh no, no, no...*'

'We have to go,' says Nicholas, coming to her aid. 'I'm bound to have patients to see—'

But the ambush has been too well set. The quarry is surrounded.

Farzad arrives from the kitchen, grinning all over his round face, while Timothy the taproom lad appears as if from nowhere and begins hopping from table to table, leading the customers in a rising tattoo of table-thumping. Ned and Rose all but march the couple to where the kissing knot hangs like a waiting noose.

There is no way out. Within minutes the event will be the talk of Bankside. *It's happened at last... Solomon Mandel saw it with his own eyes... Walter Askew, the waterman, was there having breakfast, and you know he's too stupid to lie... Mercy! – how long has that taken them?... I thought we were going to have to wait for the Second Coming before they saw sense...*

As kisses go, it's really rather unremarkable – hardly unbridled. It's not reticence that makes it so. Indeed, each has known this moment would come eventually. It's just that neither of them ever expected it to happen in the middle of the Jackdaw's taproom, to the enthusiastic approval of a dozen or more witnesses. Nevertheless, it's a kiss that falls a long way short of Puritan.

It is only when Rose's voice intrudes that Bianca and Nicholas notice everyone has stopped pounding the tables.

'Fie, Mistress,' she is saying, 'anyone would think it was you and Master Nicholas getting wed, and not me and Ned!'

Bianca puts her hands to her cheeks. They feel as hot as the sides of a bread oven. She runs her fingers through the dense waves of her hair, noticing the beads of sweat on her brow. A part of her wishes the ground would open up and swallow her. The other part wishes she hadn't invited Rose to use her chamber upstairs as her own.

And Nicholas? What is he thinking as he feels the extraordinary heat of her body through his fingertips?

In part, *absence*. Absence of guilt. Of grief. Of ghosts. Absence, at last, of Eleanor. And in its place, a growing understanding that it may indeed be possible for him to love two women and be faithless to neither. But most of all, he feels a desire that he thought was lost to him for ever.

All these thoughts – and more – tumble through their minds in the brief moment Nicholas and Bianca remain standing face-to-face, breathless, not quite able to believe they have finally crossed over from thought to deed. From past to future. It is a pause worth taking, because whatever public face they show now to Bankside, there is no going back.

'Fine, you've all had your fun,' Bianca says at last, raising her voice as a new outbreak of table-thumping closes the performance. 'If you want more entertainment, you'll have to wait for the Lord Mayor to reopen the Rose.' She points a commanding finger. 'Farzad – back to the kitchen. And those trenchers won't clean themselves, Timothy.'

Deciding that the only way to shut the door on what has just happened is by being strictly businesslike, she draws Nicholas, Ned and Rose aside. 'Before that happy little jape, Ned was telling us that trade is quiet. How quiet?'

'The regulars are still coming, Mistress,' says Ned. 'And we're still getting lodgers from the country who want to rest up before crossing the bridge. It's the trade coming in the opposite direction – down by half, at least. Anyone would think the Puritans have taken over the City Corporation.'

'Then we must bring in more custom,' Bianca says, adopting her practical tone. 'We need people with coin and the inclination to spend it.'

'Goodwife Shelby,' teases Solomon Mandel, curling his finger as he beckons to her from his nearby alcove. 'I might have the answer to your problem.'

Bianca crosses to his bench and kneels beside him. She feels her face glowing. She has the awful feeling it will never *stop* glowing. 'I am *not* Goodwife Shelby. It was a kiss, Master Mandel, not a marriage contract.'

Mandel sucks the crumbs off his thumb. '*Oh, the women in this realm! The queen won't marry. *You* won't marry. No wonder the gallants have nothing to fill their hours with but writing verse!'

Bianca leans forward and whispers sweetly, 'Perhaps you'd like to breakfast in the Good Husband. They won't cook your special bread, and if you choose the sprats, don't come seeking a cure for the flux from Master Nicholas.'

'*Ships*, Mistress,' says a chastened Mandel.

'What of them?'

'There are three Barbary Company argosies unloading at Lyon Quay,' Mandel says. 'The *Righteous*, the *Marion* and the *Luke of*

Bristol. They arrived from Morocco last week. Captain Connell is their commodore. He's an acquaintance of mine. We've traded spices together. Make him an offer.'

'Three ships – that must be sixty thirsty mariners at least,' Bianca muses. 'Tell your friend Captain Connell that he can drink here for free, and we'll stand his crew every fifth jug.' She looks at Ned and Rose. 'Do you concur?'

'Aye, Mistress,' says Rose. 'It's still your tavern.'

'And Master Mandel may have as much of Farzad's bread as he wishes, free until Easter. Does that please?'

'It pleases,' Mandel says with the sort wistful smile permitted to old men with good intentions. 'I'd ask for a kiss, too, but judging by the time it's taken for you and Dr Shelby to dance love's measure, I doubt I've got the years left in me to wait.'

She leans over and gives his beard a gentle tug. 'Then I'll have to dance a little faster, won't I?' And with that, she gives him a kiss on his mottled forehead.

As she walks away to re-join Nicholas, Ned and Rose, something makes her look back over her shoulder at the solitary Solomon Mandel. He is one of barely a handful of Jews still living in London, and the only one in Southwark. The few others of his kind live in the House of Converts on Chancery Lane. He is staring down at the crumbs on his trencher as though he's looking at the fragments of a life that was long ago lost to him. As if he's assessing the pieces, before making a final accounting of it. The sight fills her with a deep sadness.

Later, when she has cause to think of Solomon Mandel again, she will remember this moment. She will also remember something her mother once said to her: the gift of second sight is no use to anyone, if they don't comprehend what they're seeing.

4

There are men on Bankside who look as though they might kill you for stepping on their shadow. For the most part they take their ease in the darker taverns, the cock-fighting pits and the bear-baiting ring. Occasionally one or two might try their luck in the Jackdaw, requiring Bianca or Rose to point out the size of Ned Monkton's fists. But Cathal Connell, Bianca thinks, would put any one of them in fear of a cutting.

The captain of the Barbary trader *Righteous* is a parchment-skinned cadaver in a patched and padded russet doublet. He has the eyes of an old executioner who's forgotten what mercy is, though something tells her he's barely reached forty years. She can picture him staring at an empty horizon, wondering how long the rancid contents of the water casks will last, unsure of what he fears most: shipwreck or a safe landfall. Yet when he speaks, it is with the soft, dry voice of a poet.

'Well now, I see 'tis true,' he says, making an extravagant knee to her. 'The Jew did not lie. There is an Aphrodite hiding herself away in Southwark, amongst the thieves and the tricksters. A diamond lost in the midden – who'd have thought it?'

'Not an Aphrodite, Master Connell, more a Circe,' Bianca replies, trying not to stare at the salt-flayed skin of his face.

'Forgive the lack of education,' he says with a smile that would be self-deprecating if it didn't look more like an attack of the palsy, 'I'm a simple Irishman from Leinster.'

'Circe was a goddess who could turn men into crawling beasts by a single look. You'll probably have heard someone round here say that about me.'

A tight smile pulls the skin across the sides of his skull. 'I did hear something along those lines, when I made my enquiries.'

'You've made *enquiries*?'

'I don't care much for sailing into uncharted harbours, Mistress Merton. That's how lives are lost.'

'And what, pray, did you hear?'

'That you can heal. That you have the second sight. That you're the one witch nobody dares hang.'

She smiles as if he's paid her a great compliment. 'It's a pity they haven't found anything new to say about me.'

'I was told you once were taken up by Robert Cecil for being a Catholic. And instead of the scaffold, somehow you came back in the queen's own barge.'

'They're inventive, the people of Southwark.'

'So it's a lie?'

'Part of it.'

'Which part?'

'The barge. It belonged to the Cecils, not the queen.'

She watches the uncertainty playing in his eyes and tries not to laugh. But there's no doubt in her mind that he has the capacity for great violence. She supposes that if a man spends his life facing the worst that storm and ocean can hurl at him, then perhaps the violence one man may do to another is a small thing by comparison.

'I have to admit I was surprised by the offer,' he says. 'Me and my crew don't often get invited into taverns; we usually get invited to leave them.'

'If your coin is good, and your men's behaviour moderate, you're welcome, Captain Connell. And if not, Master Ned over there eats rowdy boys the way a whale eats little fishes: in vast numbers.'

Connell glances to where Ned is clearing away a trencher from a recently vacated booth. 'God's nails, he's a big bugger, ain't he? Is he yours?'

'Mine?'

'Your man. That's something else I heard about you: that you are betrothed.' He runs a hand over the tight stubble on his scalp. The rasping sound makes Bianca think of someone scrubbing a bloodstain out of a winding sheet.

'The only people betrothed here are Ned and Rose,' she says. 'That's her over there, with the dark ringlets, serving your men their ale.'

'When's the wedding? My fellows like to see a wedding – gives them a proper sense of home to hang on to.'

'The day after tomorrow. We're holding the feast here, so if you want to take advantage of my offer, I'd ask you not to act like mariners ashore are sometimes inclined to act. I don't want Rose to have to spend her wedding night bathing Ned's knuckles.'

Connell makes another exaggerated bow. 'I shall have my boys be on their best behaviour, Mistress Merton. The queen herself would not be discomforted by their manners.'

'Then you're welcome, Captain Connell.'

'And this man of yours – will he be there?'

'I told you, there isn't "a man".'

'That is not *quite* what you said. Enquiries, remember? He must be some manner of fellow, to have snared such a one as you.'

'I haven't been *snared*, Captain Connell; I'm not a hare.'

'Then a vixen, perhaps?' He gives her a look of hungry appraisal. She tries not to shudder.

'Best behaviour, please, Captain Connell. Or else Circe will have to consider employing her magic again. What shall it be? I think turning you into a boar might suit.'

Her jibe seems to please him. 'Aye, I could see myself as a boar, Mistress Bianca – tenacious and unpredictable.' He makes twin tusks out of his index fingers, thrusting them out from his chin.

'To be honest with you, I was thinking more of flayed, salted and hung up for eating, after all the quality beef has gone.'

✠

With a ban imposed on public entertainments, the lanes of Bankside are unusually quiet. The street tricksters have retired to the taverns, where they attempt to gull each other in the warm, partly to keep their sleight of hand sharp, partly to relieve the boredom. In the bear-baiting rings the bearward watches old Sackerson staring out through the bars of his cage and wonders if he's enjoying the respite, though in the spirit of Christian compassion, Sackerson – being in the twilight of his life – is only baited now on special occasions. And a wedding isn't one of them.

It is to be an Easter wedding. After a night of rain that has the earth yielding to the boot like damp mortar, Monday brings a bridal gift of clear skies.

Ned Monkton – and Nicholas, his appointed groomsman – arrive at the Jackdaw to the accompaniment of the musicians from the closed-up Rose theatre. With rowdy but joyous display, they search the tavern for the bride, to carry her away from her former estate. She and her maids – of whom Bianca is matron – resist just long enough to satisfy convention, filling the Jackdaw with joyous shrieks as they flee from one room to another.

The procession leaves promptly at ten, to the sound of the St Saviour's bell tolling merrily. Bride and groom lead the way. Ned, being the largest fellow present by some measure, looks like Hamelin's Pied Piper leading a flock of happy children. Nicholas has bought him a handsome woollen jerkin. It is the first new garment Ned has ever worn, and he carries himself as proudly as if it were pure cloth-of-gold. Passing the Clink prison, he waves regally to old friends temporarily confined there for disorder, who shout their encouragement from the tiny windows. Nicholas smiles vicariously. After all, it was not *so* very long ago that Ned spent his days as a mortuary attendant at St Thomas's hospital for the poor, all but entombed amongst the recently deceased. He could claim to be only occupant of the crypt ever to have risen from the dead. At this moment he certainly looks like a man who's been offered a second chance at life.

Bianca has contrived an almost-new kirtle for Rose, put together from leftover pieces by a clothier in Bermondsey who has donated the farthingale in settlement of his slate at the Jackdaw. The bride is the very picture of a bucolic angel, her black ringlets garlanded with posies, a bloom of contentment on her broad cheeks.

The bride's father having long since passed to a gentler place, Bianca has provided the groom with a dowry: a full cask of the Jackdaw's best hell-cat. In return, the groom's father has provided plump capons for the feast, fresh from his poulterer's shop on Scrope Alley.

At St Saviour's, bride and groom make their vows. Ned stumbles over the words and turns an alarming crimson. In his embarrassment he fidgets with his jerkin, as if troubled by lice. But Nicholas has checked him over in preparation for his later exertions and can guarantee him louse-free.

The ring that Ned places on Rose's finger is made from the handle of a broken tin spoon that someone left at the Jackdaw, re-forged in the smithy by St Mary's dock and cleverly engraved with the words *by no river parted* on the outside and *by this river joined* on the inside – in reference to the Thames, upon which so much of their livelihood depends.

And the wedding feast! There has scarcely been a board like it in living memory. At least none that any common-or-garden Banksider is likely to be invited to. In addition to old man Monkton's capons, there is a side of winter hog smoking and spitting in the Jackdaw's hearth, paid for by a collection taken amongst the customers. Farzad has made a fiery sauce with capsicum, nutmeg and ginger. The sisters at St Thomas's hospital have donated a basket overflowing with winter vegetables from their garden. Timothy – now almost a man and drawing the eye of any number of Southwark's daughters – plays bright jigs on his lute, accompanied by the playhouse musicians. There may be plague across the river, and trade a little poor, but the general consensus is that when Philip of Spain came to England all those years ago to wed Mary Tudor, they should have done it on Bankside, not at Winchester. Yes, he's an enemy now, but look at what he missed.

✠

Just because there's a wedding feast in the taproom, that doesn't mean the Jackdaw has turned its back on the rest of the world. The door is open to all with good intent in their hearts. And to everyone's relief, Solomon Mandel's acquaintances from the three Barbary Company ships moored at Lyon Quay have behaved just as their captain, Cathal Connell, promised. Indeed, like mariners everywhere, they've won admiration for their dancing.

'Marriage is a fine estate, is it not?' asks Connell, as by pure fortune he and Nicholas find themselves in close proximity. 'Without it, we're little better than the beasts.' He is clearly drunk. His voice has a wistful edge to it, as though – by some malign conjunction of the stars and the sea – matrimony is for ever barred to him.

'It can have its price,' says Nicholas, remembering how the loss of Eleanor had almost broken him, led him even to attempt the sin of self-destruction in the dark and turbulent Thames.

Connell misunderstands entirely. 'Aye, well, more fool a fellow for marrying a scold.' He takes another swig of ale, drawing the back of his hand across his mouth. 'Though to be honest with you, I'd take all the scolding that Mistress Merton could give me. What a landfall a woman like that could be to a lusty man. A nice deep harbour and no mistake.'

Inside, Nicholas flinches at Connell's coarseness, but for Ned and Rose's sake he keeps his fists under tight constraint.

'Forgive me for being blunt, but you don't look to me much like a doctor,' Connell continues, a disappointed smile on his face, as though he wishes Nicholas had risen to the bait.

'That's what the College of Physicians like to tell me.'

'You see, *Doctor* Shelby, 'I've known men swear they sailed all the way to China and back, when the truth is they did nothing but hang around the stews on the Bristol quays, tupping the doxies and pissing in the Avon.'

Nicholas looks around the taproom to see if Ned or Rose is near enough to allow him to disengage with a degree of politeness. They aren't.

'Sailors aren't the only tellers of tall tales, Captain Connell,' he says, resigning himself to the conversation. 'You should see some of the cures I've witnessed prescribed by upstanding members of my profession.'

Connell grunts. 'Now, a trading contract is something a simple fellow like me can understand. I ship the cargo. I get paid. Easy. But if I fall ill, and I pay a physician to heal me, only God knows whether I'm to be cured or killed. Not much of an incentive to do business, now, is it?'

The words are weighted with inebriated good fellowship. But there's a barb in Connell's silky brogue. Nicholas decides he doesn't much care for the man Solomon Mandel has brought to the Jackdaw. They seem poles apart: the quiet, contemplative Jew and the salt-flayed, murderous-eyed captain of the *Righteous*.

'Think of it as a mariner might,' Nicholas says, struggling to hide his irritation. 'We're using inaccurate charts. We don't know where the rocks lie. At least, that's my opinion, for what it's worth. The College of Physicians, on the other hand, likes to tell me they've sounded every ocean.'

A thought occurs to him. With the three Barbary Company ships presently at Lyon Quay, is this the man Robert Cecil had intended Nicholas should sail with, on his mission to Marrakech?

'Tell me, Captain Connell, have you by chance been asked to take anything other than cargo on your next voyage to the Barbary Coast?' he asks.

In drink, Connell cannot hide a betraying flicker of suspicion. 'What are you suggesting, Dr Shelby – that I'm in the habit of putting in at Brest to let off a couple of Jesuit priests fleeing the queen's justice?'

'I'm not suggesting that at all, Captain Connell. I simply wondered if anyone asked you to carry a passenger.'

The reek of mad-dog is pungent on Connell's breath. 'I carry certain young gentlemen for a schooling in seamanship, if that's what you're hinting at.'

'I wasn't thinking of apprentices. I was thinking of me.'

'You? Why would Dr Shelby want to go to the Barbary shore? Especially if he has that waiting by his bedroom door?' He nods towards Bianca, the ale causing his head to dip more heavily than he intended. 'I'd be permanently moored with that one, I can tell you. I'd be wearing her ankles for a scarf all the live-long day.'

Nicholas has the sudden desire to smash Connell in the face, to add another raw wheal to all the others that seem to glare at him like contemptuous eyes. But even in drink, Connell is very probably an expert with a blade. And if there was ever a wise time and place to find out, a wedding feast is not it.

'So the answer to my question, Captain Connell, is no, is it?'

Connell's inebriated gaze sharpens. 'Now you come to mention it, I was asked if I could find a berth for someone.'

'Who asked you?'

'Reynard Gault. He's a leading merchant of the Barbary Company. A good fellow to invest with. Has the Midas touch. Knows all the right people.'

'The Cecils, by any chance?'

Connell shrugs. 'Why would *you* want to travel to the Barbary shore anyhow, Dr Shelby?'

Certainly not for Robert Cecil, answers Nicholas silently. Certainly not for saltpetre to make better gunpowder. Certainly not to find out why one Adolfo Sykes hasn't been writing to the queen's privy councillor of late.

'Purely out of academic interest, Captain Connell. The Moors translated all the writings of the ancients into their language. If it were not for them, our knowledge of medicine, mathematics, natural philosophy – all these – would be the poorer. There may be much we can learn from observing how they practise physic.'

'Is that a fact, Dr Shelby? And there's me thinking they were savages.'

'Oh, undoubtedly. Some of the translations back into Latin and Greek are only now being printed in Europe.'

Connell gives a derisive snort. Drops of foamy spittle land on Nicholas's boots. 'Then you'd think the heathens would have more reverence for the God who gave them the knowledge to do it, wouldn't you?'

'As a matter of interest, Captain Connell, when did this Master Gault of the Barbary Company make his enquiry?'

Connell takes a gulp of ale to help him think. 'That would have been three days ago.'

'Three days – are you certain?'

'Reynard Gault isn't often seen around the quays, he's too grand for that. It was three days ago, for sure.'

Three days.

Hot anger surges through Nicholas's blood, followed swiftly by a sense of foreboding. He had refused Robert Cecil's request on Thursday, four days ago. Which means that either Cecil has found a replacement... or, more likely, the serpent isn't yet ready to ease its jaws and let its prey escape.

The flitch of hog has been eaten. The fat is cooling in pots for later use. What Farzad doesn't need for cooking, Bianca will use as a base to hold the herbs in her balms and mastics. Nothing goes to waste. Even Buffle, the Jackdaw's dog, is gnawing the last scraps of gristle off a bone. In the taproom the dancing, the games and the songs have become increasingly bawdy as the bride and groom are prepared for the bedding. But when the door of Bianca's old chamber is finally closed, leaving Ned and Rose to themselves, only a few revellers remain on the landing, serenading the newly-weds with saucy songs of encouragement. Soon even they return to the taproom and its fuggy air of glutted contentment.

In one of the booths, Bianca and Nicholas sit together, replete. He eases loose the points of his white canvas doublet. He puts one arm around her shoulder. It is the first deliberate, unforced touch, and he has made it without design or even prior contemplation.

She leans carelessly into him. He has a natural scent that reminds her of her time in Padua, of the hemp sacks full of herbs and spices in her father's warehouse, warming in the summer sun. She wonders what it would be like to lie with him. The thought has come to her more than once in recent days, hardly surprising given the impending wedding. He's built pleasantly enough, she thinks. Neither London nor the College of Physicians has yet managed to knock the Suffolk yeoman's son out of him. An efficiently rustic lover, she decides – pleasantly free of the elaborate and fake courtesies of a Venetian gallant, but sensitive enough not to take her as though she was no more than a heifer and he the village bull. And so far, thank Jesu, Nicholas hasn't shown any tendency towards milky sonnets and dire poetry, which – she learned quickly upon arrival – is apparently de rigueur amongst all Englishmen who can read and write.

She likes how he escapes her attempts to catalogue him. A more predictable man would have married quickly after his wife's death, seeking to make up for lost time in the practical business of raising sons. A less questioning one would never have blamed himself for losing her, in the first place. He looks like what he is, a tousle-haired, strong-limbed farmer's boy. Yet given the chance, she suspects, he could give a Paduan doctor of philosophy a run for his money. No wonder the aristocratic students at Cambridge called him a country clod-pate, and the College of Physicians thinks him a heretic. A contradiction like that couldn't possibly be boring between the sheets, could it?

And in a way she has already lain with him, in everything but the carnal pleasure of it. She knows his body better than he knows it himself. She remembers that October dawn when they had found him lying in the river mud – one-third frozen, one-third drowned, one-third hanging on to life because it couldn't think of anything better to do. With the help of passing strangers, she and Timothy had carried him to the Jackdaw. There she had stripped him of his sodden clothes, laid him before the fire, washed the water slime from his body, carried him to the attic when he'd thawed a little, and then spent three weeks tending him in his delirium while she wondered who on earth he was, and what had prompted him to throw himself into the river – an act that her Catholic faith tells her is so sinful that God Himself can barely find the compassion to forgive it.

Yes, Nicholas Shelby is less unknown to her than he himself might imagine.

Before she realizes it, Bianca is tilting her head and offering him her mouth to kiss. She feels his body shift in anticipation, waits for his lips to meet hers.

And then she senses a movement at the edge of her vision. She hears a low voice calling, 'Mistress, Mistress—'

Timothy is standing at the edge of the booth, fidgeting, his face on fire with embarrassment. Young Timothy, now almost a man. Timothy, who plucks such sweet tunes from his lute. And who – at this precise moment – is a harbinger of ill news, if ever she saw one.

'Forgive me, Mistress,' he says, staring at Bianca and Nicholas and wringing his hands together, consumed by misery for shattering the moment. 'It's Farzad. I've looked for him everywhere. He's vanished!'

5

Nicholas stands in the lane, the cold night air stinging his face. 'Farzad's probably gone down to the river for some peace. He's worked hard today. He'll soon be back.'

'And did he take his possessions – his second shirt and his knife – for a little tranquillity beside the river, too?' Bianca asks. Her concern for Farzad is making her short-tempered.

They have searched the Jackdaw from the cellar to the attic, every nook and cranny. The only chamber they haven't entered is Bianca's old room. When one of Connell's men – with a leer on his face – suggested it, Bianca silenced him with a single look. On this night, if on no other, Ned and Rose are to be allowed their privacy.

Cathal Connell steps unsteadily out of the Jackdaw's entrance. 'He's soused, that's what he is,' he says, grinning like a traitor's head on a pole. 'Only a young lad – can't hold his ale. He'll be puking into a ditch somewhere.'

'His religion doesn't permit him to take drink,' snaps Bianca, looking Connell up and down. 'Unlike some I could name.'

'What's a Mohammedan doing in a Bankside tavern anyway?' Connell asks, turning his face to the cold night air as though it might sooth his scoured cheeks.

'He was saved from Barbary slavers by an English ship. Off the Ethiope shore,' Bianca explains, looking up and down the lane as though she expects to see Farzad trotting home with his bright smile lightening the dark night. 'They came into the Jackdaw with him one day. He had a cold – English weather doesn't agree with him.'

'He's from Persia,' Nicholas adds, as though a cold was something unknown outside England.

'Which is why I don't believe he's gone down to the river,' Bianca adds. 'Not on a night like this. He wouldn't.'

Connell shrugs. 'Well, it's time me and my fellows were in our hammocks. If we see him on the shore, we'll send him back home with a flea in his ear.'

With the sailors gone and most of the revellers now departed, there are barely a dozen people left to carry out a search of the surrounding lanes, and most of those have difficulty walking a straight line. Southwark lanes at night are dangerous places for the solitary traveller, and there is always the danger of stumbling onto the riverbank in the dark. So Nicholas marshals them into groups of three, each group led by the least inebriated. With Bianca and Timothy in tow, he tracks down the night-watch at their brazier by the bridge and enlists their help.

They search for a good two hours: west into the Pike Garden and the open patches of ground around the bear-pit, east to the Compter prison. They circle the closed-up Rose theatre, which looms in the misty darkness like a monstrous bastion, silent and defended only by ghosts. They wander around the ruins of Rochester House, calling Farzad's name and hoping all the while to hear one of his famously indelicate replies: *The Pope is the spawn of a she-goat and a monkey... the King of Spain wears a woman's farthingale under his gown...* for it is well known throughout Southwark that Farzad learned his first English from the good Protestant sailors who rescued him. Tonight even Bianca would be happy to hear one of his slanders, even though she cleaves to her secret faith and has to hold her tongue when others laugh uproariously.

In the small hours they give up. Though no one says so – for fear of invoking bad luck – each imagines Farzad waiting for them on their return, innocently wondering what all the fuss has been about.

At the Jackdaw Timothy asks, 'Shall we wake Master Ned and Mistress Rose?'

'No,' sighs Bianca wearily. 'Let them sleep. They've earned their joy. Let's not spoil it until we have to.'

✠

The petitioners begin queuing outside the Strand entrance to Cecil House before sunrise. Some have legal suits they want the Cecils to back, some desire the family's patronage, some hope for a hearing at court, perhaps even an audience with the queen herself. More than a few would like a little of the Cecils' largesse, to finance schemes ranging from the practical to the downright mad. They eye each other like the beasts of the wildwood, though they try not to show it, gauging advantage or otherwise by the cut of a cloak, the fabric of a doublet or the quality of a pair of shoes. Their breath forms little clouds of envy or disdain in the pallid air.

The liveried guards at the gatehouse are calling out those with appointments, from a list the clerks prepared the previous evening. Just because your name is on the list doesn't mean you will actually get to see Sir Robert, or his father, Lord Burghley. They may not even be in residence. But if you're called, at least you can wait in the long gallery, out of the cold.

One man to have his name called early is Reynard Gault.

In stature, Gault is commanding. He has in his eyes the hawk's eagerness for a kill. He is a merchant venturer, a rising star of the Exchange. He invests: in Baltic timber, in Muscovy furs, in fish from the seas off New-Found Land. But he invests wisely. He has no time for argosies that sink when they meet the first big wave, or captains without a sound record of success. Speculative adventures to the Indies in search for fabled cities of gold he leaves to fools, and to his Spanish competitors.

And it has made him a rich man. Not yet forty, he has a fine house on Giltspur Street by Smithfield, where he shows visitors a whale's horn that he tells the gullible was taken from a unicorn. He is a leading light in the Worshipful Company of Grocers, having made his original fortune in spices. And being a forward-looking fellow he has recently accepted a prominent position in the Barbary Company. After all, as he likes to tell those who come to him in search of the next big opportunity, the future lies not with princes – Christian or infidel – but with mercantile men.

Once admitted, Gault is delivered into the care of a silent individual with the Cecils' ermine-tail emblem on his coat. To his surprise, Gault is not conveyed to the long gallery where the favoured wait, with varying success, for admittance to the presence chamber, but to an open terrace at the rear of the great house.

Robert Cecil is standing with his back towards a neatly clipped hedge. Dressed in a black gown that hides his twisted trunk, he is attended by a quartet of clerks, all busily taking down notes on wax or slate. He is the smallest man in the group, and for a moment Gault has the impression of a student reciting his thesis to a group of gowned professors. But then Cecil peremptorily waves them away.

'God give you good morrow, Sir Robert,' says Gault, making a low bow.

'And in return, Gault, I shall give you *pepper*,' Cecil says with a smile of congratulation.

'Pepper, Sir Robert? I had presumed you wished to speak to me about the passage you asked me to secure aboard the *Righteous*.'

'It is arranged, I trust?'

'Yes, Sir Robert. But your passenger must be ready before the month is out,' Gault says hurriedly. 'Vessels tied to a wharf longer than necessary are a great burden on the investor.'

'Oh, he'll be aboard, one way or the other. Tell your captain to count on it.'

'And the pepper? You wish me to arrange burden-space? I could offload a part of the *Marion*'s cargo.'

'I don't desire to ship it, Master Gault. I wish to *sell* it. Three hundred tons, to be exact. In chests. Value – ninety thousand pounds, according to the assessment that I and my father, the Lord Treasurer, have made of it.'

Gault whistles at the astonishing figure. He gives a slow, conspiratorial nod, meant to show a fellow venturer that he can read between the lines. 'Spanish pepper, I take it.'

'Portuguese, to be precise – aboard the galleon *Madre de Deus*, seized off the Azores by the fleet of our gallant Sir Walter Raleigh. Currently under guard at Dartmouth.'

Gault knows the story well. Save for the pestilence, tavern talk has been about little else since September last, when – after a bloody battle off Flores Island – the great ship was brought into the Devonshire harbour, her holds bulging.

'I put the guard in place myself,' Cecil continues, 'else the thieving rogues who live in those parts would likely have carried all away in their galligaskins. The queen wishes the cargo sold, to the general benefit of the Treasury. I thought an eminent member of the Grocers' Guild would know the best course for *disposing* of the pepper.'

Gault makes a little bow to show how grateful he is to have been considered.

'To sell such a tonnage at once would glut the market, Sir Robert. The value would plunge before a man might make a profit.'

'Which is why we intend to release it in manageable quantities over a period of years.'

'Very wise, if I may say so.'

'We will need someone to administer the sale, of course,' Cecil says, his brow lifting a little, as if the thought has only just occurred to him. 'Over the years we Cecils have learned many skills. Sadly, grocery is not counted amongst them.'

'Would that person be free to use the monopoly as he saw fit, Sir Robert?'

'I doubt very much the right man could be found to take it, otherwise.'

'Did you have anyone in mind?' Gault asks archly.

'Well, seeing as how you're here... I mean, you're not too pressed with other enterprises at the present time, are you? You could find the time?'

'I'm honoured, Sir Robert,' Gault says a little too quickly, and with the smile of a man who's eaten too much sugar. 'I can think of no better duty for an honest merchant to perform than to assist our sovereign majesty's Treasury in this present time of danger.'

'What a shame more of our gentlemen don't see things so clearly. They seem to think ships and cannon build themselves out of patriotic duty.'

Gault waits patiently for the addendum. When the Cecils make a generous offer, there is always an addendum.

'The Worshipful Company of Grocers, Sir Reynard – prospering, I take it?'

'Very much so, Sir Robert. We are but second amongst all the liveried companies in the city.' Gault gives Cecil a look of immense hurt. 'Of course we'd be first, if the Mercers hadn't cheated.'

'Something about a camel, was it not?' says Cecil, with a sly tilt of his head. 'An incident at the queen's coronation? I seem to recall my father mentioning it. He thought it most amusing.'

Gault's face sours. 'The beast was part of our procession. We thought Her Grace would marvel at it. But we believe the Mercers fed it something that caused it to emit noxious fumes from its fundament. Unfortunately, Her Grace's carriage was directly behind the beast. It was a vile trick.'

'On the camel, the grocers or Her Majesty?' asks Robert Cecil with a twitch of mischief on his lips. He doesn't wait for an answer. 'Let that be a warning, Gault: never trust fellows with an overly vain interest in silks.'

Assuming the audience is over, Gault makes a sweeping bow. But Cecil hasn't finished with him.

'The Grocers' Company licenses the apothecaries in our city, does it not?'

'Indeed it does, Sir Robert. And we are the better for it. Trade does not prosper if charlatans are allowed to devalue the merchandise.'

'And if I were to bring to your attention an apothecary whom I felt was one such charlatan, you would exercise your influence with the Guild to shut them down?'

'Without question, Sir Robert. You have only to tell me his name.'

'It's a *her*, actually.

'A woman? I wasn't aware we licensed *women*.'

'She won her approval solely by the influence of Lord Lumley. He funds the chair of anatomy at the College of Physicians. He was acting on behalf of a certain young physician who wished to advance her. A favour. I didn't object at the time. Perhaps I should have.'

'A female licensed apothecary! Whatever next – doctors in far-thingales?' Gault flicks a hand as though to brush away a fly. 'I shall make it my duty to have her barred immediately, Sir Robert.'

Robert Cecil lays a hand on Gault's arm. 'All in good time. There is no need for haste. Not yet.'

A watery sun sits just above the great houses along the Strand, bathing nearby Lincoln's Inn in a sickly light. 'Look at that,' Sir Robert says absent-mindedly. 'The lawyers get the light before the Cecils. How on earth did my father let *that* happen?'

✠

The kiss has led to a glorious intimacy, just as Nicholas has always known it would. They are lying together naked, coiled in blissful heat. Bianca is kissing his face, whispering endearments to him. He can feel the wetness of her tongue exploring the side of his neck. Why did it take me so long? he mouths happily. Why did I fight against it so resolutely? And then she nips him on the earlobe. A sharp-toothed little bite.

Sitting bolt upright, his head collides with something hard, bringing him rudely awake. Then Buffle launches another joyous assault on his ear. Nicholas groans, pushes the dog aside and crawls out from beneath the table, where he's spent all too few hours of sleep.

The taproom is empty, save for Timothy sleeping on his pallet by the hearth. Bianca, he supposes, is still asleep in the one free lodging chamber. Ned and Rose are presumably still deep in the warm oblivion of love. Climbing stiffly to his feet, Nicholas goes to the door and lets Buffle out into the lane.

In the insipid early-morning light the houses opposite stare back at him like drowned faces. A lad in a broadcloth coat far too large for him is driving a pair of heifers towards the Mutton Lane shambles. If they knew what awaited them, Nicholas thinks, the heifers could simply turn and trample him underfoot. Yet they go uncomplainingly to their fate, compelled only by a small lad with an even smaller stick. Has Farzad fallen for such a simple deception? he wonders uncomfortably.

By the time the search was abandoned – in the small hours – the theories had already begun to bloom. Farzad had run away because he feared the plague would soon reach Southwark. Farzad was sleeping it off under a hedge, or in a doorway, having put aside his religious objections and taken drink during the celebrations. Farzad, almost eighteen and notable for his lustrous black hair and dark complexion, had at last lost his innocence to some pretty Bankside blower and was snoring contentedly in her generous embrace.

And then there were the darker theories, the ones that no one wished to give voice to: that he had left the fug of the Jackdaw's taproom for some fresh air and fallen prey to a particularly violent cut-purse, or that while taking his ease for a moment out in the lanes, he had got into a fatal quarrel with someone who held Moors in the same contempt as he did papists.

Nicholas stretches to ease his aching joints and waits for Buffle to finish her morning patrol. Rose has a fear that the dog will be taken for fighting, and doesn't like her being in the lane unwatched. Lazily his eyes follow her, and so he takes a deeper interest in the scene than otherwise he might.

Around the tavern entrance the boot-marks from the night's search are preserved in the mud. They spread out like the voyage lines drawn on Robert Cecil's globe. Just a few paces from the door, a single track turns sharply right, looping back towards the tavern wall. It is overlaid in several places, suggesting it was made before the search began. Nicholas looks at it for a moment while Buffle barks ineffectually at the departing cows. Are the footprints Farzad's? he wonders.

He dismisses the probability immediately. Dozens of people came and went during the course of yesterday's celebrations. This set of imprints could belong to any one of them. Enough sack and mad-dog had been consumed for a least one person to have had to steady themselves against the wall of the tavern before continuing on their way. Nevertheless, an image of Farzad in his leather cook's apron, his cap at a jaunty angle, stepping out unnoticed into the lane to cool down, compels Nicholas to venture into the lane to take a closer look.

At the point where the solitary imprints reach the wall there is a second patch of churned mud. Multiple footprints lead out into the lane. He can picture the scene: a reveller dancing one last drunken jig in celebration of the happy couple, before being helped home by his companions.

And then he sees it.

Splashed across the old brickwork directly below the chamber where Ned and Rose are at this moment slumbering through their first dawn as husband and wife is a dark stain that holds an awful familiarity for Nicholas. A sudden tightening in his chest turns each breath into an act of protest.

It's not a large stain. But then it doesn't have to be. Once set free, blood finds freedom intoxicating. From his days in Holland, tending the torn and the hacked, the speared and the shattered, he knows exactly how ungovernable blood can be when it's loosed from the body by a blade or a ball. Sometimes it can flow as though it will never stop, yet less than an hour later you're laughing about what a close shave you've had. Sometimes you can die while you're still trying to find the puncture. But splashed on a wall, however small the amount, can mean only one thing: a sudden attack, full of motion and fury.

Now he can see a very different pattern in the mud. The night's events unfold in his mind's eye: a body supported on either side by its assailants as they drag it away from the shelter of the wall.

Not a street robbery, then. If you're going to cut away a purse, you don't take the owner along with it.

Nicholas searches for signs of a blood trail. It doesn't take him long to find them. At regular intervals, dark drops of blood keep company with the confused line of prints that head out into the lane. Some are pristine circles; others have left only a discoloration in the crust. By their distribution he can gauge the stride of the men dragging Farzad's body. It's a long, steady pace. Nicholas has a picture of two men practised at bearing heavy burdens. Men skilled in what they were about.

At the crossroads there is a public conduit. Three women are drawing water, the sleeves of their kirtles rolled up, their plump arms yellowed by the jaundiced sun rising over the rooftops. 'Have you lost something, Dr Shelby?' one of the women asks.

Her companion replies, 'Aye, he's dropped the wedding ring – the one he's going to place on Mistress Merton's finger.'

He thinks his attempt at a self-deprecating smile must look to them like the leering of a madman. He mumbles an incoherent excuse. But they have had their moment of fun at his expense and are once more lost in conversation.

At the crossroads the tracks disappear altogether, churned beyond recognition into the cloying mud. He looks back towards the Jackdaw with a heavy heart. Telling Bianca is going to be bad enough, but the news is going to turn the happiness of Master and Goodwife Monkton into gall.

Refusing to abandon Farzad, if only in his imagination, Nicholas tries each of the other three lanes issuing from the crossroads. All are narrow and overhung with the teetering fronts of tightly packed wood-and-plaster tenements. He goes into the first two only as far as it takes him to determine that the ground is too recently disturbed to show which way Farzad's attackers carried him. Outside one house he thinks he's picked up the trail again, but the dark spot turns out to be nothing but a rusting tin button. He turns, walks back to the crossroads and tries the third lane.

Almost immediately he sees an arc of blood-splatters in the mud. Did Farzad recover enough to struggle? Or is this the place where he died?

To his relief, there are no obvious sign that a body was laid in the mud here. And by now, someone would have found the corpse. A public cry would have been raised.

Looking around, puzzled, but still clinging to hope, Nicholas notices a familiar tenement not far away. It is a house of no distinction whatsoever – certainly no grander than any of the others in a lane where grandiosity is measured by whether or not the sewer ditch outside has a step across it. It is a narrow two-storey timbered house, with little windows criss-crossed by cheap lead and shuttered on the inside. The studs and braces of the woodwork are cracked and faded. Nicholas walks towards it, resolving to speak to the owner. He may have heard something in the night. And being a regular at the Jackdaw – as Nicholas knows him to be – it would be best if he were forewarned.

Reaching the door, Nicholas sees that it bears the marks of numerous lock replacements, though apparently the owner is trusting enough to leave it slightly ajar. A small square of timber nailed above the latch shows the image of a hand, palm forward, the fingers together and pointing down. The once-bright paint is flaked and peeling. *The sign is a talisman, Dr Shelby*, he hears the owner telling him, *a charm against evil. What a pity it doesn't protect a fellow from the flux.*

Nicholas remembers his last visit to this house. He had pre-scribed crushed cinnamon and pomegranate juice to ease the patient's stomach pain, but had stopped short of drawing blood from the veins of the inner arm. 'I think this has more to do with those oysters you ate yesterday than some imaginary imbalance of the humours,' he recalls saying.

As Nicholas lifts his hand to knock, his head tilts downwards in a counter-movement to the raising of his arm. It is unintentional, but it brings into his direct view the dark smear at the foot of the door. He stares at it, an icy flood of disbelief racing through his thoughts.

Surely not here! Not by *this* man's hand.

But when he kneels to get a better look, the nature of the stain is clear to him in all its sanguinary awfulness.

Nicholas pushes against the door. It swings inwards with a rasp of its hinges. He is inside before the wisdom of entering even registers.

A narrow wedge of daylight shows him a low-ceilinged chamber, its limits lost in darkness. The room is cold enough never to have been lived in, though Nicholas knows that not to be true. 'Is anyone there?' he calls softly. 'It's me, Nicholas.'

A moan of pain would tell him there was at least hope. He would settle for that; be grateful for it. But he hears nothing.

He seems to be walking on sand. He can feel his boots sliding on it. Looking down, the light from the half-open door shows him that the dirt floor is covered in a fine dark powder. The pungent smell of nutmeg rises from where his feet have trod.

They have smashed the little chamber as though it were a papist chapel and everything in it an abomination to them. The ash from the brick oven in the corner has been scooped out and cast onto the floor. The torn-up pages of books lie scattered everywhere. Sacks of spices that were once stacked neatly against one wall now loll about like the disembowelled victims of a massacre. The meagre contents of a clothes chest are strewn about, as if the men who did this abandoned their own shadows out of guilt.

Only the simple bed in the corner has been left intact, because they needed a platform on which to perform the more intricate and personal of their efforts.

Nicholas wonders how the neighbours could not have heard the killers going about their business. Then he remembers that many in this lane are regulars at the Jackdaw. They would have been at the celebrations. For the rest, perhaps they were at church. Or visiting friends. Or just so accustomed to the beating of servants, apprentices, dogs, children, whores and wives that a scream or two of torment here and there is nothing to get overly excited about.

In death, Solomon Mandel has a surprising grace about him. His old face bears the stoic certainty of a martyr's, as if the agony of death was little more than a temporary trial to be endured and then forgotten. His beard, matted with blood, is the beard of an Old Testament prophet, not an elderly man with nostalgia for the bread of his childhood. He lies naked and bound, oddly straight, given how they have tortured him. Nicholas marvels at how he has not twisted himself into a posture reflective of the pain he has endured. His white arms are the limbs of an effigy carved in plaster on a tomb. The wrists – bound tightly with cords – lie meek and pious at the groin, as though protecting his modesty.

To Nicholas's shame, the anger that surges in his breast is matched ounce for ounce by relief – relief that the ruined body on the bed isn't Farzad's.

6

Unusually for a public notice raised by the parish authorities on Bankside, the warning tacked to the door of Solomon Mandel's house – within an hour of Nicholas discovering the body – is still there a day later. As warnings go, it is unequivocal. For attempting entry: confinement in the Clink and a forfeit of twenty shillings. For taking away souvenirs from the site of the murder, with intent to sell them to the morbidly curious: branding upon a part of the body to be decided by the magistrate.

'Last murder we had on Bankside, I caught some fellow trying to hawk the victim's boots for a half-angel outside the Tabard,' says parish constable Willders. 'Still had the blood on them. There's some as would sell the corpse itself for an ornament, if they thought they could find a buyer.'

Constable Willders is a short, barrel-chested fellow in a leather jerkin. He wears a perpetual frown and carries his official cudgel slantwise across his chest with the solemnity of a monarch carrying a golden sceptre.

'You know Bankside, Constable Willders,' Nicholas says with a sigh of resignation, 'where there's money to be made…'

Willders points to the little square of wood with its painted hand, set just above the lock, the symbol Nicholas had noticed when the trail of blood led him here. 'What do you make of this, Dr Shelby? Could it be devilish?'

'It's a talisman for protection, that's all. Mandel told me so himself.'

Bianca looks closer. 'I've seen these before, in Padua,' she says, 'on the front doors of the Jewish houses behind the Piazza delle Erbe. My father often took me with him when he went to see his customers there. I think they were mostly Jews who'd fled from Spain and Portugal.'

'I wonder if that's where Solomon Mandel came from.'

'I don't know; he never spoke much about himself,' Bianca says. 'And this being Southwark, no one asked.'

Willders tucks his cudgel under one arm and fishes a large key from his belt. 'I'm not sure Mistress Merton should accompany us, Dr Shelby. The body has been removed, but what remains is not a meet sight for a woman. There's rather a lot of blood.'

Before Nicholas can answer, Bianca says, 'Do I recall rightly, Constable Willders, that last summer you came to Dr Shelby much troubled by an aposteme under your groin?'

Willders stares at his boots. He says nothing.

'Dr Shelby prescribed a soothing plaister, which I applied *after* he had lanced the aposteme and let out the pus. Remember it?'

Willders permit himself the barest nod.

'I can assure you, Constable Willders, compared to *that* experience, whatever is in there can hold absolutely no horrors for me *whatsoever.*'

It's at times like this, Nicholas thinks, as he tries not to grin, that I really do want to take you in my arms and kiss you – whatever Eleanor might have to say about it.

Taking a sudden deep interest in the blade of the key, Willders unlocks the door and leads Nicholas and Bianca inside.

Save for the body, nothing has been moved. The room is still a ruin of upturned furniture and ripped-open spice sacks, the contents cast around like a minor sand dune. The air is heavy and dust-laden. Bianca can smell cinnamon and mace, pepper and nutmeg – and the flat metallic tang of spilt blood. She can see it, too, spread liberally around the now-empty bed, as though someone has smashed a wine bottle over it.

'You've taken him to the mortuary crypt at St Thomas's, I presume,' Nicholas says.

'Aye, and we've sent word to coroner Danby at Whitehall. He's coming across the bridge tomorrow to arrange the inquiry. I suppose you'll want to speak to him.'

'If I must.'

Willders give him a curious look. 'He'll want to hear the nature of the Jew's injuries from your own mouth, Dr Shelby. I would not be qualified to report on such matters.'

'If I know Danby, he's already reached a verdict without lifting his arse off his chair.'

'Do you require further sight of the body, Dr Shelby? Only the parish would like it interred as soon as is decent. With contagion across the river, they want to keep Bankside as clean and tidy as they can.'

'No, I've committed what I saw to paper.'

Bianca says, 'He may not wish to be buried with Christian rites, Constable Willders. Has the parish thought of that?'

Willders seems confused. 'Why would anyone wish for other than a Christian burial, Mistress Merton – unless he had a hankering to wander for eternity in the fires of hell?'

'Because Solomon Mandel was a Jew,' Bianca says. 'Perhaps he would wish to go to God with the appropriate orisons of his own faith.'

'Solomon Mandel was a Christian man, Mistress Merton – whatever else his ancestors may have been,' Willders says with unshakeable conviction. 'He would not be suffered to remain in this realm otherwise.'

69

'How do you know what was in his heart?' Bianca says, trying not to step into the dunes of intermingled spices. 'In Padua, his people lived in their own quarter, practised their religion in their own temples, were buried with their own ceremonies.'

By the look on his face, Constable Willders seems unable to comprehend such a place. 'Padua lies in the lands of the Pope, does it not, Mistress Merton?' he says solemnly. 'We do things differently here in England. There is no place here for a heretic, be he Catholic or Hebrew. Master Mandel will be buried according to God's laws, as revealed by the one true, reformed faith – the queen's faith. If he lied at prayer, he will have to answer for it in the hereafter.'

Bianca invokes a subversive prayer that the summer will be a hot one, and Constable Willders' apostemes will return with a vengeance.

'Would you allow Mistress Merton and I some time here alone, Constable Willders?' Nicholas asks. 'I need to refresh my memory, for coroner Danby.'

'I'll be in the Tabard, Dr Shelby,' Willders says, seemingly grateful to have the responsibility taken off his shoulders. 'Send Mistress Merton with the key when you're done.'

When he's gone, Nicholas retraces his steps around the room. Once again he takes stock of the devastation: the upended clothes chest with its contents strewn in a trail of ripped and tattered fabric, like the banners of a conquered army; the private documents, some written boldly in Hebrew, others in a weaker, English hand; the plain wooden cupboard with its doors hanging off their lower hinges; the humble collection of pewter bowls and plates lying about like grey boulders washed up on a beach. The only thing that seems not to have been scattered like so much chaff in a cruel wind is a Bible lying on a wooden stool by the bed, a battered leather strap holding down a page of the Book of

Matthew: the parable of Jesus feeding the multitude with just five loaves and two fishes.

'I wonder if the killer found what he was searching for,' Bianca says, struggling to keep dark images from flooding her imagination.

'Whether he found it or not, he wasn't alone.'

'How can you be certain?

'One man alone could never have inflicted the wounds I saw on Solomon Mandel's body. There must have been at least three of them: two men to hold him down, one to do the cutting.'

'The cutting?' Bianca's voice cannot mask the horror she is seeing in her mind.

'Strips of skin from his chest. They flayed him.' He shrugs. 'I'm sorry to be so brutal. There isn't another way to say it.'

A glint of metal amongst the debris catches Bianca's eye. She kneels, lifting an object out of the debris, a candle-holder with three curving branches either side of a central pillar. She shakes it, and a cloud of ochre cinnamon-dust hangs for a moment in the air before drifting to the floor.

'Just like the talisman by the door, I've seen these before, too,' she says. 'It's a menorah. They light candles in them during their holy observances.'

She hands it to Nicholas, who turns it over slowly, inspecting the finely crafted metalwork. The cinnamon-dust darkens the engravings like skeins of blood. 'A Bible *and* a menorah,' he says. 'Was Solomon Mandel really a convert to Christianity, or was he practising his true faith in secret?'

'It's more common on Bankside than you might think,' Bianca replies, a weary admission in her voice. Every waking day since her arrival in London she has whispered her own Catholic orisons to God, but only when there's no one around who might betray her.

Knowing the coroner's jury will very likely wish to view the scene of the murder, Nicholas says, 'I think we should preserve this from coroner Danby's eyes. What use would it be – other than to condemn the old man as a heretic?'

With a hint of gentle mockery in her voice, Bianca says, 'For an Englishman, you really are developing a very dangerous habit: tolerance. Does Robert Cecil know?'

He gives her a brittle laugh in reply and looks around for something in which to wrap the menorah. His gaze lands on a length of hemp weave that's been torn from one of the spice sacks. He has the vague notion of keeping the artefact in his chamber at Mistress Muzzle's lodgings, until he can decide what to do with it.

'It seems they set fire to some of his papers,' Bianca says, crossing to the bed. 'They must have done it while they were... while they were doing those unspeakable things to him.'

The coverlet is blighted with a whole delta of dried blood. In one of the pools, she can make out a little cluster of ashes and burnt fragments. They look like dark leaves scattered in a puddle after a storm. Some are no larger than a fingernail. Others are curled and blackened. Only two have survived incineration.

'I noticed them, when I was inspecting the body,' Nicholas says, joining her. 'Perhaps they were burning something before his eyes – tormenting him in some manner.'

Tentatively he begins to work away at the surviving fragments, gentling them free of the pooled blood and ash. It takes him a while, but at last he holds them up for inspection; they have lost little but some charring on the edges.

On one, he sees penned the words ROUGE CROIX. The other contains just six letters – S-U-I-V-A-N – huddled meaninglessly between the charred edges.

'*Rouge Croix* – red cross,' he says to no one in particular. 'Why would Solomon Mandel have a letter written in French?'

'He was a merchant. He traded,' says Bianca, as though he were the dullest country clod-pate imaginable, 'with other countries.'

'Of course,' Nicholas replies, rolling his eyes in self-deprecation. 'So SUIVAN could be *suivant* – following. A follower of the red cross?'

'I'm not sure that translates,' Bianca says. 'But if it does, a follower of the red cross would be an English crusader, would he not?'

'That might explain why they left the Bible where it was, untouched. Perhaps they'd found out that, in his heart, Solomon Mandel hadn't really converted to the queen's religion at all.'

'Then why would he have a Bible by his bed?'

'I don't know. Perhaps for show. He used this chamber for his work, as well as for his rest.'

'So they tormented him for what they held to be heresy, and then killed him?' Bianca postulates. She covers her eyes and shakes her head. When she drops her hands and speaks again, her voice cracks under the weight of such imagined heartlessness. 'If they were *that* affronted, they could have denounced him to the parish. Let the law deal with him. They didn't have to kill him!'

'But I'm not convinced that *is* why they killed him.'

'Then why?'

'Perhaps they were trying to make him tell them something. And whether they were successful or not, they didn't want him alive to identify who was asking the question.'

With gentle reverence Nicholas places the fragments back on the bed, as though he were laying flowers on a grave. Head down, he says, 'I'll let Constable Willders and the coroner know about these. They can tax their minds over what they might mean.'

'And what of the menorah?' Bianca asks.

'I'll keep it with me until I can think what to do with it. Perhaps I'll leave it anonymously at the House of Converts on Chancery Lane. That's where most of the other Jews in the city reside. They can decide what to do with it.' He gives a forlorn shake of his head. 'You know my view, Bianca. I care not how a man – or a woman – prays. Or even if they pray not at all.'

She smiles, her amber eyes brimming with gentle admonition. 'Which, my dearest Nicholas, makes you a greater heretic than any of us.'

7

'**S**helby? The name is familiar to me, but I cannot rightly place it.'

William Danby is the Queen's Coroner. The only reason he is here on Bankside is that the murder of the solitary Solomon Mandel has occurred within the *verge*, an arbitrary twelve-mile radius around the person of the monarch.

It is the day after Nicholas and Bianca's visit to Mandel's lodgings, and Danby has crossed the river to set in motion an inquest. He has brought a little of the court's élan with him. He wears a fine maroon doublet, has garters on his hose and a bottle-green half-cape with fur trim upon his shoulders. He even sports a sword on his hip. But for all his fine apparel, Danby does not look a well man. His grey hair hangs in thin folds over his neat little ruff, and he has a grating cough that seems to have its seat somewhere very deep inside him. Nicholas wonders if he will outlive the inquest that he's come to Bankside to conduct.

'*Shelby*,' he says again, apparently no wiser for the repetition.

'I came to you regarding a young boy pulled from the water by the Wildgoose stairs, back in August of 1590,' says Nicholas softly.

They are in the parlour of Constable Willders's house on St Olave's Street, a few doors down from the hostelry at the sign of the Walnut Tree, and far enough from the river not to be troubled by the smell of tidal mud. In the presence of the Queen's

Coroner, Willders has lost much of his official bombast. He has developed the habit of deferentially tapping his right hand on his thigh whenever Danby finishes a sentence.

'Did you really?' says Danby, passing his cloak to Willders as if the constable were his manservant.

'Yes, Master Coroner. You made the corpse available to Sir Fulke Vaesy for an anatomy lecture at the College of Physicians that I happened to attend.'

'Now I remember you,' says Danby, coughing into his gloved hand. 'You're the fellow who pestered everyone to distraction about the cause of death. You insisted – somewhat argumentatively, if I recall correctly – that the boy had been murdered, even though Sir Fulke told you he had not.'

'I was mistaken,' Nicholas says as humbly as he can contrive.

The lie comes so easily to him that he can almost think it true – that three years ago there never *was* a killer preying on Bankside's most vulnerable. That Ned Monkton's brother Jacob, and the crippled anonymous boy who ended up on Vaesy's dissection table, died wholly natural deaths. That Bianca had never come within minutes of being the killer's last victim. Or that in the years since, Nicholas himself has never wondered what the penalty might be for framing someone for a crime they'd never committed, in order to bring them to justice for several crimes they most certainly had.

Yes, he thinks, it would be all too easy to rub Danby's nose in it. To tell him that murder was *exactly* what it had been. But he cannot. It would open too many doors that must remain locked.

Danby turns to Constable Willders. 'The body has already been interred, I understand.'

'Yesterday. At St George's churchyard, sir,' says Willders. 'There was no family to take it. And the parish thought a swift burial was wise, what with contagion being present across the river.'

'I argued against it,' says Nicholas.

A heave of Danby's chest produces something that is half-word and half-expectoration. '*Wh-hy?*'

If you were my patient, thinks Nicholas, I'd be telling you to go back to your family and ensure your will is up to date. But he says, as civilly as he can, 'I would have liked further time to study the body. And there is no evidence, as yet, that a corpse in Southwark can attract plague from another part of the city.'

'The pestilence spreads in foul air, Dr Shelby, and corpses are a source of such rank miasmas, are they not?' says Danby with a condescending smirk. 'A wise precaution, I would have thought.'

'There is another reason I thought the burial was hurried,' Nicholas says, thinking of his conversation with Bianca.

'And what is that?'

'Solomon Mandel was a Jew.'

Willders taps his fingers against his thigh, as if to say, *We've already had this conversation.*

'How is that relevant, Dr Shelby?' Danby asks.

'There is no place in London given over for the interment of those of his faith. I felt the parish should have sought advice from his fellows.'

Danby seems unconvinced. 'Those few Jews who are tolerated in this city are required to denounce their blasphemy and embrace the one true religion. Under the law – such as it applies to a Jew – Mandel was a Christian. Your concern is wasted.'

'But who knows what was in his heart?'

'Let us hope it was the love of our Saviour, Dr Shelby,' Danby says with the solemnity of an archbishop. 'Like all infidels, the Jew may be redeemed only by his conversion. If he will not convert, then he is damned – in this world *and* the next. The wiser ones know it. Take for an example old Dr Lopez. He is a Jew; from Portugal, I believe. Yet he has converted. And, as a consequence, he prospers. Why, he is even permitted to attend the queen in matters of physic.

No, sirrah, if this Mandel was secretly practising his heresy, being buried in consecrated ground according to Christian rites will be the least of his troubles when he stands before our Lord. You really should read Martin Luther's book on the matter.'

'I'm sure you are right, Master Coroner,' Nicholas says drily, deciding this is neither the time nor the place to start a new disagreement with the Queen's Coroner. Out of the corner of his eye he sees Willders's body relax, like a man reprieved.

'Anyway, the speed of the burial shouldn't hinder the jury's deliberations,' says Danby casually. 'I see you have already made a detailed report on what you observed.' He nods to the sheet of paper on the table, next to the dish of marchpane comfits and the jug of hippocras set down for the important visitor from across the river. 'Have you read it, Constable Willders? Does it accord with your recollection?'

Willders's fingers start to fidget again. 'I could not read it for myself, sir. Dr Shelby read it for me.'

'But does it *tally*, Constable?'

'Dr Shelby is correct in what he sets forth, sir, though I cannot comment on the medical nature of what he has written.'

'But the *scene*, Constable – the scene. Is it accurately described? May a jury rely upon it?'

'Oh, aye, sir. A most discomforting scene, it was. Master Mandel was upon the bed, bound with cords. Dr Shelby showed me where several strips of his flesh had been removed from the breast, with a blade of some sort.' He makes a sideways sawing motion with his hand, as though he's carving a ham at table. 'Like someone had tried to skin him alive, I should say. In consequence, there was rather a lot of blood cast about. In all, it was most disconcerting. I've seen nothing of its like since young Jacob, Ned Monkton's brother, was pulled from the river at the Mutton Lane stairs – but that was before I was made constable.'

'Monkton? Is he relevant?' Danby says.

Nicholas has an image of young Jacob Monkton's body laid out on the Mutton Lane stairs, as empty as a carcass hanging in a Cheapside butcher's stall. At the time, the Queen's Coroner certainly hadn't thought the poor of Bankside relevant for an instant. It would be justice, he thinks, to have Danby walk down to the Jackdaw right now and ask Ned to his face if he thought his little brother had been *relevant*.

'Not in this instance, sir,' Willders says. 'I was merely referring to a past felony. Monkton has no bearing on this one.'

'Could the wounds not have been sustained in what the law refers to as "chance medley" – a hot quarrel?' Danby asks. 'They are quite common here on Bankside, I understand.'

'Mandel was a peaceable old man. He was liked. He had no enemies to get into a quarrel with.'

Willders nods in agreement. 'It's true, sir.'

Nicholas adds, 'Besides, as Constable Willders has told you, he was lying on his bed, naked and bound. Even for Southwark, that's an uncommon way to end an argument.'

'Then to what do you attribute the wounds, Dr Shelby?' Danby gives the breast of his doublet a lawyerly tug with both hands.

Nicholas can't help seeing again the bloody rills sliced into Mandel's flesh. 'That's simple: he was tortured. I think his killers wanted something from him that he didn't wish them to possess.'

Danby considers this carefully for a moment with some noisy sucking of his tongue. 'Have you not asked yourself this, Dr Shelby: that rather than being tortured, he was being punished?'

'Punished for being a Jew?'

'For being a heretic.'

'I *did* wonder,' Nicholas says. 'The killers ransacked his chamber, but they left that Bible by his bed untouched. And I found two fragments of burnt parchment, close to where they killed him. One had the words *Rouge Croix* on it. The other made me wonder if Mandel's killers called themselves "Followers of the Red Cross".'

Danby lowers his head in thought. Willders taps his thigh, as if to encourage him in his wise deliberation. When the coroner looks up again, there is firm smile of enlightenment on his face.

'There *are* those who hold that we should do more than simply condemn Mandel's kind for our Lord's death on the holy cross,' he says. 'Such people say we should actively chastise them for that heinous crime. Not my own view, as it happens – to my mind, the papist is *far* more of a threat to our immortal souls than the Jew. But, as I say, you should read Master Luther's writings upon the matter.' He picks up the jug and helps himself to a cup of hippocras. He doesn't offer any to his host, Willders, or to Nicholas. 'Well, we shall know the truth when we apprehend the perpetrator,' he says confidently. 'I shall speak to the alderman about raising a band to seek him out.'

Willders seems even more surprised than Nicholas by Danby's words. 'Am I to understand that one of the felons has been identified, sir?'

Danby takes a draught of the spiced wine. He swills it around his mouth before swallowing. 'I'd have thought his identity was obvious, Constable Willders. Why else would the Moor abscond?'

For a moment Nicholas can't believe what he's heard. 'The Moor? Are you speaking of Farzad? You think *Farzad* killed Mandel?'

'Heathen passions are of a nature quite alien to a Christian man, Dr Shelby.'

'They were friends! Farzad baked bread for Solomon's breakfast every morning.'

'Who knows how long a hidden enmity might slumber before it is suddenly roused? Have you not seen Master Marlowe's

Tamburlaine performed? The Moor is a creature of exceptionally hot blood.'

Nicholas can only marvel at Danby's conviction. He thinks: so you've read Luther's book and seen Marlowe's play, and now you're well enough versed to decide Solomon Mandel was killed for being a Jew, and Farzad is his murderer. And you accuse *me* of hasty diagnoses!

✠

On St Olave's Lane, Danby takes the reins of his horse from a servant and makes himself comfortable in the saddle, tugging his gloves tight in preparation for the ride back across the bridge. His horse fidgets beneath him, its hooves clattering on the cobbles.

'Farzad Gul did not kill Solomon Mandel,' Nicholas says, trying to remain calm. 'I would stake my life on it.'

Danby favours Nicholas with a smile of faux-courtesy. 'We shall leave that to the inquest to determine. I take it you will wish to be included amongst the jury.'

Nicholas asks quietly, 'Did you know he had a name, Master Coroner?'

Danby looks down, a frown creasing his temple. 'A name? I do not follow you, sirrah. *Who* had a name? The Moor?'

'The crippled vagrant boy I told you about – the body you sent to Sir Fulke Vaesy, for his anatomy lecture.'

'Oh, *him*. He had no name, Dr Shelby. I remember what I wrote in my report: *unknown, save unto God.*'

'His name was Ralph Cullen.'

Danby stares at him, puzzled.

'He has a sister, Elise,' Nicholas continues. 'For months she could not bring herself to speak, because of what had befallen them. But she's alive. I found her. Now she's a member of Lord

Lumley's household at Nonsuch Palace. I thought you might care to know.'

'That is all very interesting, Dr Shelby. But I am not sure what instruction I am supposed to take from it.'

'None whatsoever,' Nicholas says despondently, surprised by the way his throat suddenly seems constricted and his eyes have begun to smart. 'I know he was of no concern to anyone, least of all to the Queen's Coroner. But I wanted you to hear his *name* – if only once.'

Danby turns his horse's head towards the bridge. 'A vagrant is a vagrant, whatever he may be named.' He tightens the reins. 'I recall Baronsdale at the College of Physicians telling me you were a good physician once, Dr Shelby. But he said you could never let the past sleep peacefully. That wife of yours who died, and this vagrant child you seem unable to forget: let them go. That is my advice. What God has ordained for us in His plan is not ours to question.'

Does Danby also take that to include the murder of an innocent old Jew? Nicholas wonders. 'If I take your advice, Master Coroner,' he says as calmly as he can manage, 'will you do a small service?'

'If I can.'

'When you find a moment's ease from the arduous labours of your office, perhaps you can amend your report into Ralph Cullen's death. Write down his name. Then he'll be no longer "unknown, save unto God" – will he?'

✠

'How could Danby possibly think Farzad is a murderer?' Bianca asks, unlacing her boots and wriggling her feet.

She and Nicholas have returned to the Jackdaw after another fruitless search, this time along the riverbank as far west as Gravel

Lane, almost to the Lambeth marshes. They have lost count of the people they've stopped. *Have you seen him? He's an olive-skinned lad with tangled black hair and spice-stained fingers: a Moor, but an honorary Banksider, for all that... Farzad, the Persian boy who can curse the Pope with more invention than all the bishops of England put together...*

'Farzad ran. Therefore Farzad must be guilty,' Nicholas replies. 'Danby prefers his enquiries concluded swiftly, so that he can hurry back to the comforts of Whitehall.'

Ned Monkton and Rose are sitting at a nearby table. Rose is making a tally of expenditure. Ned can write his own name, though never in exactly the same way twice, and he watches his bride with undisguised admiration. 'There's nobody around here Danby could put on a jury who'd support that charge,' he calls out.

'Don't you believe it, Ned,' Nicholas answers. 'There's bound to be an alderman or a magistrate somewhere only too willing to agree with whatever nonsense the Queen's Coroner spouts. If they find Farzad before we do, they'll keep him chained up in the Compter or the Clink until the next Assizes. They might even beat a false confession out of him.'

Rose tosses her head angrily, her black ringlets tumbling about her cheeks. 'Farzad wouldn't survive more than a week in a damp, rat-infested cell,' she protests. 'He can catch a cold on a sunny day.'

'What I don't understand is why anyone would kill a gentle soul like Solomon Mandel in the first place,' Bianca says. 'And in such a cruel way.'

'Because he was a Jew – according to Danby. Some zealot chose to hold him personally responsible for the death of our Saviour on the cross.'

Bianca's amber eyes blaze with a mixture of anger and sadness. 'In Padua, the city used to hold a horse race every year.

The gallants rode their finest stallions, but the governors made the Jews compete on donkeys, just so the crowd could laugh at them. When my father told me of it, I wept for their humiliation.'

'You've known Master Solomon longer than I have, Bianca. When did you first meet him?'

'Shortly after I bought the Jackdaw.'

'That would have been when – some four years past?'

'It was around the time the Moor envoy came to London,' Bianca says, her eyes gleaming at the memory. 'I was in the crowd at Long Southwark, when the procession arrived. I can still see all those fine silk robes, and the strange hats they wore, like onions sitting on their heads. They had faces like hawks, haughty and noble – as if even the meanest of them was a prince. And the colour of their skin – as though they carried the desert sun within their very bodies and it was toasting them from the inside. They were a marvel, Nicholas. As grand as anything I'd ever seen in Padua.'

Her girlish thrill at the recollection makes him smile. He, too, remembers that cold January night when he and Eleanor had joined the expectant crowd on the north side of London Bridge. The Moor party had made landfall in Cornwall and news of its progress towards the city had kept the population on tenterhooks for days. When they eventually rode in, all bathed in flickering torchlight like a caravan sent from a pharaoh's court, they had come attended by the leading members of the Barbary Company, riding escort.

But his own memory of the occasion is coloured not with bright silks, but with pain. That was the beginning of the year in which Eleanor had fallen with child. The year the match was put to the fuse. The slow-burning fuse that would take until the following summer to blow his life asunder.

'He used to buy his chickens from my father's shop,' Ned calls out helpfully. 'Pa said Master Mandel had told him he was born in Portugal.'

'The queen's physician, Dr Lopez, is a Marrano Jew from Portugal, too,' says Nicholas. 'He might have known Solomon. Perhaps he'll agree to talk to me.'

'None of this answers the question: who killed him?' Bianca says. 'Or where Farzad is.'

'Perhaps your Captain Connell might know more about Mandel.'

'He's not *my* Captain Connell, Nick,' says Bianca.

'But Mandel knew the captain well enough to suggest that you invite him to drink here. I don't know if you've looked into Connell's eyes, but if you're looking for a man capable of murder, there's one in there, for sure.'

'You really don't like him, do you?'

'Do you?'

'That's not the point. Connell was at the Jackdaw getting drunk and being uncivil, remember? We saw him leave with his crew, *after* we'd searched for Farzad.'

Nicholas admits defeat. 'You're right. The footprints suggest Mandel was taken from outside the Jackdaw sometime during the wedding feast – either when he went out for air, or perhaps as he was on his way home.'

'So they were out in the lane, waiting for him?'

'That's my guess.' Nicholas gives Bianca a pensive look. 'But whatever Danby says, I don't believe that the murder was a punishment. At least, not for anything Solomon Mandel was keeping hidden in his soul.'

✠

There are buildings in London that seem ideally suited to their purpose. For an inquest into the murder of a solitary old man, thinks Nicholas, you couldn't choose a better one than the deconsecrated church of St Margaret's on the Hill. It, too, appears to be dying a slow and unmourned death. The stained-glass windows have been smashed out and bricked over. Half the graveyard has been dug up and replaced by cheaply built private tenements. Instead of worshippers, the nave now plays host to quarter-sessions of the peace, where the magistrates can dole out brandings and ear-trimmings to the felonious of Bankside. When Nicholas opens the half-derelict door and steps inside, the day after Coroner Danby's visit to Bankside, the sound of his footsteps on the stone floor echoes like a warning whisper: be gone... be gone... be gone...

The nave is empty, the pews long ago sold off or turned to firewood. A cold easterly wind moans outside like the lamenting of a ghostly congregation. He catches the smell of stale sweat, a permanent memory of the prisoners corralled here before transfer to the Compter and the Marshalsea. There is a pile of straw where the rood screen once stood, to provide a measure of comfort for them. It reeks of emptied bladders and despair. If this was ever God's house, He defaulted on the mortgage and handed back the keys long ago.

A murmur of voices reaches him from above. Looking up, Nicholas sees the nave has been cross-beamed and planked over, to make an upper floor in the ceiling vault. He climbs the narrow wooden ladder with a growing sense of dejection.

But when he reaches the source of the murmuring, he discovers that Constable Willders has assembled the jury from amongst the wiser parish notables. Two of them are even patrons of the Jackdaw. Perhaps there's hope for Farzad, wherever he may be.

The only outsider is the clerk that the Queen's Coroner has sent to represent him and record the proceedings. Nicholas wonders if Danby's absence means that Solomon Mandel is destined for the same official anonymity as little Ralph Cullen.

The clerk is a mousy little fellow whose nose twitches in the chill air. He hugs his writing box to his chest, as though he expects some Southwark trickster to steal it away the instant he looks elsewhere.

A table has been set out with a bench on either side. Nicholas takes his place with the others. No one seems inclined to remove his cloak or gabardine. A wicked draught nips at their ankles, let in through the places where Mary Tudor's men were frugal with the mortar when they bricked up the sacristy windows.

'Now that we are all present, I suggest we begin,' says Constable Willders. He closes his eyes, puts his hands together in prayer and misquotes a few words from the Gospel according to St James: 'If any of us here need wisdom, let us open our hearts to Almighty God, and He will provide it.'

Following the *Amens*, Nicholas hears a muttered, 'I hope this won't take long. There's a lovely fire a-roarin' at the Griffon.'

Willders invites Nicholas to read out his report of what he saw at Solomon Mandel's house. He describes briefly how he was able to follow the trail of blood; how he found the door unlatched, and the devastation beyond. Then he recounts the manner in which the Jew died: strapped to a bed, naked, a wound below the left knee – the blood from which accounted for the marks on the Jackdaw's wall and the subsequent trail – and signs on the victim's breast of considerable avulsion.

'*Avulsion*, Dr Shelby? Can you explain what you mean?' asks one of the jurors, a chandler from Winchester dock by the name of Frontwell. 'We are not medical men, here.'

'Forgive me, Master Frontwell. I didn't mean to be obscure. Strips of flesh were cut from his chest. "Sliced" would be a better word, or "carved". Several of them.'

'You mean he was flayed?' askes another juror, his face suddenly taking on an even colder hue than that of the others around this already-chilly table.

'If you prefer it that way, yes. Over an area about the size of my hand.'

'Flayed like the martyred St Bartholomew,' enquires another juror. 'Whilst alive?'

'Yes.'

'That is monstrous,' whispers Frontwell, looking around the ceiling vault as though he hopes to find a morsel of God's mercy hidden somewhere amongst the cracks.

'It is my judgement that Mandel died either by the torment of it or from the blood thereby spilt,' Nicholas says. 'Probably the former. Solomon Mandel was not a young man, remember.'

'But who would do such a thing to him?' Frontwell asks. 'And to what end?'

'I heard that young Moor from the Jackdaw has gone missing,' says a juror whom Nicholas does not recognize. 'An innocent fellow has no cause to flee, does he?'

Nicholas immediately launches a stout defence of Farzad. He tells of the two fragments of parchment suggesting that Christian zealots might have been responsible for Mandel's death, under the banner of a red cross. But he is only partially successful. While the jury stops short of accusing Farzad of the crime, it instructs the clerk to refer the matter to a justice of the queen's peace, so that a proper search can be made and Farzad invited to explain his sudden disappearance – under hard questioning, if necessary. Nicholas alone votes against it.

But doing so does not mean that he thinks Solomon Mandel's murder and Farzad's disappearance are unconnected. Far from it. His greatest fear – one that he does not share with the rest of the jury – is that they are inextricably linked. And that somewhere, perhaps not so very far away, a young Persian lad is waiting in terror for the first cut of the same blade that flayed Solomon Mandel.

Waiting beneath a red cross.

On the walk back to his lodgings, Nicholas stops at St Saviour's church. It is empty, except for an elderly churchwarden in pursuit of a pigeon that has flown in and is now busy shitting on the pews. The man mirrors the bird's agitated flapping as he chases it around the nave. It is a Catholic pigeon, Nicholas decides on a whimsy, sent by the King of Spain to foul a Protestant church. What else can account for the crimson-faced warden's distinctly unchristian curses?

'I'd like to see the subsidy rolls, please – if that's not too much trouble,' Nicholas calls out, giving voice to an idea that has come to him during the inquest. 'You do keep the parish records here?'

The churchwarden breaks off his exertions and comes over. 'God give you good morrow, Dr Shelby.'

'And to you, Warden Dymock. The subsidy rolls—'

Warden Dymock frowns, turning his head towards the fluttering shadow high up in the vault, as though he fears a sudden counter-attack. 'I'm not sure that is possible, without the say-so of an alderman.'

'I'm asking in an official capacity, on behalf of the Queen's Coroner,' Nicholas says, not entirely truthfully.

A smile of understanding from Dymock reveals three missing lower teeth and a little pointed tongue that oozes through the gap, like a snail emerging from its shell. 'Oh, of course – the inquest. I heard about it from Constable Willders. A dreadful business. Quite dreadful.'

'There is something I need to check – for the record, that's all.'

'Well, in *that* case...'

The churchwarden leads him into the vestry and takes a key from a collection on his belt. He unlocks a sturdy wooden chest and lifts the lid. Inside, Nicholas can see piles of wide leather-bound books and stacks of vellum rolls, neatly tied with ribbon. They have the dry smell of old ink: the musty accumulation of a century or more of parish diligence. Given Southwark's general contempt for officialdom, they appear to Nicholas to be surprisingly well maintained.

'Please put them back in the order you find them, Dr Shelby, otherwise I shall never hear the last of it from the aldermen,' Dymock says, turning back towards the nave and his battle with the sacrilegious pigeon. 'Call for me when you've done.'

It takes Nicholas only a few moments to locate the latest subsidy roll, drawn up by the petty collectors to calculate how much tax Bankside might contribute to the Exchequer, should the queen demand a fresh imprest in the war with Spain. He has chosen it because it specifically lists foreigners dwelling in the ward. He runs his finger down the column of residents. Listed against each name is the value of their moveable goods, rents or holdings. Skipping rapidly over the English names, he notes a French grocer named Baudry; a Dutch wax-chandler called Hugelyn; and another refugee from the Low Countries, a joiner who goes by the imposing appellation of Johan Hieronymous van Vestergarten.

And then he sees it. The entry he's been hoping for:

Solomon Mandel, Hebrew; worth assessed at 100 crowns...

So Mandel was comfortably off, despite his humble appearance. Did his killers torture him to find out where his coin was hidden? Nicholas wonders. If they did, they were not local men. Bankside is nothing if not a family, however lawless some of its tribe. The perpetrators of such a brutal crime, committed upon one of its own, could not keep their secret long.

But it is the addendum to the entry, written on the right-hand margin in the petty collector's precise hand, that brings Nicholas up short. After Solomon Mandel's occupation – *spice merchant* – he has added: *The Turk's man.*

8

'The Turk's man,' says Bianca with a frown. 'Solomon Mandel never struck me as anyone's servant. Least of all, that of a Turk.'

It is a bright spring morning, and she and Nicholas are making another footsore trawl through Bankside for a sighting of Farzad. Yesterday was prisons day: first the Marshalsea, then the Compter, followed by the Clink and finally the White Lion. After peering into more stinking cells than is good for the health, they came to conclusion that if Farzad is incarcerated anywhere, it is not by order of the parish authorities.

Today it's the lanes around Bermondsey Street. As always, they choose wisely who to question: day-labourers, travelling tinsmiths, ribbon-sellers, the sort of people who spend their time on the move in search of custom. They even stop known coney-catchers and purse-divers, who with less trade to prey upon, now that the contagion has put an end to public gatherings, seem pleased to pass a few moments in conversation. They've even visited the Flower de Luce, because the landlord there has twice tried to lure Farzad away from the Jackdaw with the promise of an extra thruppence a week on his wages.

'Turk, Moor, Saracen... whoever Mandel's master was, we can assume he's a Mohammedan who's converted to Christianity. He wouldn't be living here otherwise.'

'The queen has a few Blackamoor and Ethiopian servants in her household. I've seen them in processions. Perhaps royal servants have servants.'

'Who are free to eat *kubaneh* bread in a Bankside tavern every morning?' Nicholas says. His face darkens. 'Or *were*.'

'When was the subsidy roll drawn up?'

'It's dated January 1590.'

'A year after the envoy of the Moroccan sultan arrived in the city.'

'You think Farzad was a servant to someone in the entourage?'

'Well, he turned up on Bankside around about that time.'

'Then why did he not return with his master to Barbary?'

Bianca rolls her eyes and says crossly, 'I don't know. Stop trying to catch me out. You're not a lawyer, and I'm not on trial.'

They walk on in silence for a while, following the riverbank. The tide is out, the air heavy with the stink of rotting waterweed.

At the mouth of Battle Creek, they stop to watch a brace of boys in threadbare hose grubbing through the shingle like sanderlings hunting for worms. The place holds an uncomfortable place in Nicholas's memory. This is where – almost three years ago now – the third victim of the Bankside butcher was found, a discovery that allowed Nicholas his first insight into the mind of the killer. He closes his eyes. In his thoughts he sees the body rolling over the side of the little skiff into the dark water. He hears the splash, but when he opens his eyes again he sees only the two urchins, competing to see how far they can hurl flotsam into the current.

'Perhaps I've got it wrong,' he says. 'Perhaps I'm seeking a connection where there is none.'

'You mean between Solomon Mandel's death and Farzad's disappearance?'

'Perhaps he just sickened for his home.'

'Farzad doesn't have a home, Nicholas – other than the Jackdaw. Besides, he'd need more than a second shirt and a knife for a journey to Persia. And he wouldn't have left without speaking to me first.'

'Then maybe he's taken himself off in a fit of jealousy – over Rose marrying Ned. A heart of that age can be a fragile thing.'

'Are you speaking from experience?'

He squirms at her directness. 'It's a passionate age, especially if the passion is unrequited.'

'I'll accept he adores Rose. We all do – when she's not being Mistress Moonbeam with a head full of air. But I never once saw Farzad making mooncalf eyes at her.'

Nicholas senses a deep coldness flowing up through his veins. He wonders if it's this place and the memories it holds. Or perhaps it's just a sudden chill in the air, heralding a shower.

'Who else knows that you let Farzad practise the orisons of his faith,' he asks, 'apart from me, Ned, Rose and Timothy?'

'No one. I'm not a clod-pate, Nicholas. I do know how to keep a secret, if that's what you're suggesting. I've been doing so since the day I landed here.'

'Perhaps Danby was right, and this *is* about religion. If someone discovered Solomon Mandel's conversion was a deceit – that he was secretly practising his old faith – then maybe that same person found out that you were allowing Farzad to do the same.'

'Then where is his body?' Bianca says, more hotly than she'd intended.

'I'm sorry,' he says, giving a shrug of defeat. 'It is a long walk back. We'd best be on our way. It looks as though it's coming on to rain.'

✠

Mistress Muzzle gives a crabby little toss of her head as Nicholas pauses at the door to his consulting chamber. 'You're wet, Dr Shelby.'

'We got caught in a shower.'

From crabbiness to joy in a heartbeat. 'You and Mistress Merton – you've been walking together. Alone.'

'The Puritans don't have the city, Mistress Muzzle. Not yet.'

'Have they found the lad who murdered the Jew – that young Moor who cooks at the Jackdaw?'

'What have you heard?'

'Jenny Solver told me he had committed a foul murder, out of his pagan spite. Jenny Solver says that, in God's eyes, the Moors and the Jews are worse even than the papists. We shouldn't tolerate them in our realm.'

'And when did Mistress Solver tell you this?'

'Yesterday, at church. We were attending Evensong.'

'Then Mistress Solver is speaking through her arse. And you may take that as a physician's professional opinion.' He gives her a cold smile. 'Don't worry, I won't charge her for it.'

Nicholas resists the desire to slam the door behind him. He only partially succeeds. Leaning against the wall, he throws his dripping hat on the floor and begins to unlace his boots. He thinks he might rest his feet awhile and then stop by the Jackdaw for some coney pie.

'And by the way, Dr Shelby, a letter arrived for you,' he hears Mistress Muzzle say from the hallway. 'I've put it on your table.'

Mumbling his thanks, his eyes fall to the folded and sealed square of paper lying beside his potion box.

His heart sinks. A seal that large can only mean the letter is official: another complaint from the College of Physicians about his errant behaviour, or Robert Cecil announcing that his stipend is cancelled because he's refused to go to Marrakech.

And indeed, on inspection, he sees the wax is impressed with the Cecil device. Snapping it open, he curses the Cecils and all their works, in a mumbled stream of invective. Shards of wax scatter across the desk.

To my right worthy and trusted friend, Nicholas Shelby, greetings...

It seems an oddly amiable way, he thinks as he reads, to begin a letter of dismissal. And then his eyes widen in surprise, even as a raindrop rolls down his temple and across the bridge of his nose.

✠

'You're not actually going to attend, are you?' Bianca asks half an hour later as Nicholas sits before a trencher of coney pie in the Jackdaw. 'He's not summoning you out of friendship. There's bound to be another motive.'

'He's not summoning me. He's inviting me. No one turns down an invitation to dine with Robert Cecil. I'm not going to insult one of the most powerful men in the realm, especially as he pays me a stipend to attend his son.'

'What's the point? I don't wish to be rude, but you'll probably be sitting at the very end of the longest table in London. He won't even glance in your direction.'

'Thank you for reminding me of my place.'

'I didn't mean it that way.'

'There are members of the College of Physicians who would consider poisoning their own mothers for an invitation to Robert Cecil's table. Besides, the queen's physician, Dr Lopez, will be there. It's the perfect opportunity to ask him about Solomon Mandel.'

'Nicholas, you're not the sort to find good fellowship in such company.'

'Jealous?' he asks with a lift of one eyebrow.

Bianca's smile is laced with scorn. 'Of dining with a serpent? Never.' She pats him on the wrist. 'But I hope you know where to find a reliable food-taster at short notice.'

✠

It is the Monktons' first spat as man and wife. Not really a spat at all, more an outbreak of tetchiness at the end of a long day at the Jackdaw. And it is over almost before it begins.

Nicholas and Bianca have departed – each to their own self-inflicted solitude – and Rose has just finished inspecting the day's reckoning of victuals sold: eleven coney pasties; seven plates of stockfish; two tubs of oysters; twelve helpings of sprats; and twenty bowls of pottage.

Twenty.

There should be four portions remaining. Rose knows this because she made the pottage herself, at dawn, and she knows through experience the pot contains twenty-four helpings. Not twenty.

The discrepancy is important. With business slack, it is hard enough for the Jackdaw to turn a profit as it is, without giving away food. And Rose has promised Bianca she will be diligent in her stewardship.

Going in search of her husband, she finds Ned in the cellar. He's standing beneath the open trapdoor in the far corner, taking sacks of hops from Timothy, who's out in the yard above. His shirt is open and the auburn curls on his vast chest gleam like gold thread in the sunlight. She admires him at his labour for a while, before asking, 'Have you been over-generous with those watermen friends of yours, Husband? There's pottage missin'.'

Ned puts down the sack as though it were full of nothing but feathers, and wipes one ham-like forearm across his brow. 'No,

I 'ave not, Goodwife Monkton,' he replies, savouring the delight in all the happy implications encompassed by the term *goodwife*. 'I'd not treat Mistress Bianca's gift to us in such a casual fashion. You know I would not.'

'I must have tallied it up wrong then,' Rose says with a diffidence that would astound Bianca, were she here to witness it. She tilts her head to look Ned in the eye – a manoeuvre that deliberately exposes her invitingly silky white neck and a dash of freckles. Coyly, and with a magnificently contrived fluttering of her eyelids, she announces, 'In which case, Husband, I shall likely later have need of serious *correction*.'

Rose is not referring to any correction a magistrate might envision; at least not in his professional capacity.

If at this moment Ned Monkton could find space in his thoughts for anything but his new bride, it would probably be to offer a thousand hosannas to Bianca Merton and Nicholas Shelby for giving him a life beyond that of a mortuary porter at St Thomas's hospital for the sick and destitute of Bankside. As for Rose, she's too busy responding happily to her husband's kisses to consider for a single instant that she might be right about the quantity of missing pottage.

9

Sheltering beneath the sailcloth awning of the tilt-boat, Nicholas watches the private water-stairs below Cecil House loom out of the rain. A Cecil barge blocks the nearest side of the jetty. It rocks gently on the swell, empty and unrigged, the raindrops glinting like jewels on the gilded bulwarks.

The helmsman lets the current carry them past. Then he leans on the tiller and the boat swings around. Rainwater pours over the edge of the awning, cutting off Nicholas's view as though he were standing behind a waterfall. The oars dip twice, rise in unison and then the hull is hard against the jetty. Nicholas barely feels the impact. The jolt comes from above: a flash of lightning. Thunder booms from somewhere very close. Pulling his gabardine about him, he climbs out and hurries towards the Strand entrance of Cecil House beneath writhing black clouds.

Nicholas is not comfortable at grand tables. At Cambridge the gentlemen scholars mocked him for it, imitating his Suffolk burr and asking him if he needed instruction on how to use his knife and spoon, or whether he could tell Gascon wine from country ale. As a consequence, he associates formal feasting more with bloody knuckles than a full belly. But this is not what he has been expecting at all.

The privy dining chamber is panelled from floor to ceiling and softly candlelit. One side is given over to high mullioned windows that stream with rain. Four places have been set on a table large enough for fourteen, a little colony of high-backed chairs, fine plate and silver goblets clinging to an otherwise empty glacier of Flanders tablecloth. It is quite unlike any formal table at the College of Physicians, with old Baronsdale – the president – placed magisterially at the high table and flanked by the senior Fellows, while everyone else sits below the salt in strict order of status. This is more like an intimate gathering of colleagues.

Two men stand talking with Robert Cecil before a fire that crackles in a deep brick hearth. One of them Nicholas recognizes as Roderigo Lopez, the old white-haired Marrano Jew who attends the queen. He wears a formal black physician's gown and starched ruff. The other man is much younger – a mischievous-looking fellow of about Nicholas's age, with long, curly fair hair and a nose that appears to have been broken in a brawl. His beard, worn as close as Nicholas's, looks as though it's been trimmed by a drunken barber. But he's smartly dressed in a well-padded black velvet doublet with braided trim. Nicholas feels underdressed. For the first time in three years he regrets throwing his own doctor's gown in the Thames.

'Dr Lopez, I am sure, is no stranger to you,' says Cecil after Nicholas has made a formal bend of the knee. 'And this disreputable fellow is my cousin, Master Francis Bacon. If you were hoping for the company of another contrarian, you'll meet no one better.'

Cecil directs Bacon to sit beside him, with Nicholas and Lopez on the other side of the table. A Cecil chaplain flutters in to say grace. Expensive wine is poured from even more expensive silverware, by servants who seem to have acquired the knack of being only semi-corporeal. Over his host's shoulder, Nicholas can see Lord Burghley in garter robes peering out on the gathering

99

from within his picture frame, a disapproving look frozen on his painted face. It's a fine likeness, but it makes Nicholas feel even more under close observation.

The food arrives, borne by a procession of liveried lackeys: vinegar fig tarts; a pie stuffed with hind-flank of beef, prunes, raisins and carrots; and salted carp that Lopez – giving his physician's opinion – says is unhealthy for an old man such as himself, but eats anyway, on the grounds it is also good for easing the hot ague.

Save for the discomfort of eating too much, the meal turns out not to be the ordeal Nicholas had expected. The conversation is informal and wide-ranging: how the Privy Council fears Spain might yet send another Armada against England; how King Philip is stalking the Escorial in Madrid in a black rage over the *Madre de Deus*; how a bill has been read in Parliament proposing a ten-pound-a-month fine for allowing a recusant to dwell in your house, and the confiscation of your children if you happen to be one yourself.

Nicholas listens with a sense of mounting intrigue. In the Jackdaw, gossip about affairs of state flows as fast as the mad-dog and knock-down. But it's ignorant gossip. Wild speculation. Downright untruths. To hear from informed men so close to power is intoxicating. Men such as these are not bystanders, help-lessly watching the world unfold. They change its very course.

But some things, Nicholas is dismayed to discover, do not change. When Cecil asks – over a cup of the sweetest sack Nicholas has ever tasted – what new advances might soon be made in the field of physic, Lopez, still with a faint hint of his Iberian heritage in his voice, announces proudly: 'I have been told by Dr Dee, who as you know oftentimes advises Her Majesty on matters of the occult, that soon it may be possible to study the demi-demons that cause some illnesses.'

'How so?' asks Nicholas, struggling to keep the scorn in his voice from showing. This is the sort of nonsense he associates with the midwife who assured him – with equal confidence – that certain holy stones, supposedly anointed with the blood of St Margaret, would help him save Eleanor and the child she was carrying.

'Dr Dee believes these demons may be trapped in certain crystals and thus observed without danger,' says Lopez. 'He also showed me a mirror glass of polished obsidian, by which he claims to see the reflection of those malign spirits that cause pain in a patient's body.'

'And do you believe him?' asks Francis Bacon, sniggering as he chews on a spoonful of bream.

'I have no reason not to, Master Bacon,' says Lopez. 'Dr Dee is a very learned man.'

Robert Cecil stabs his knife in Nicholas's direction as though to skewer an opinion out of him. 'And you, Dr Shelby? Do you also believe that one day we shall carry the cure to all our ills in a crystal brooch, or see the cause of them reflected in a mirror glass?'

I'm not going to call the queen's physician a fool to his face, if that's what you're inviting me to do, Nicholas thinks. Besides, Lopez is not alone in his foolishness; there are more than a few in the College of Physicians who would happily believe what Lopez has just said.

Cecil takes his silence for indecision. 'Come now – I'm sure Dr Lopez would be interested to hear your views. If you were given the power, how would you shake physic by its ears?'

'I'd make the physician get his hands bloody,' Nicholas says cautiously. 'Bring him and the surgeon together in one endeavour.'

'You mean one man performing both roles?' asks Lopez doubtfully. 'But surgeons are not educated in the writings of the ancients. They are artisans – barbers.'

'Master Paré did it in France,' Nicholas reminds him. 'I myself have practised surgery – in the Low Countries.'

'But that was the necessity of the battlefield, Dr Shelby,' Lopez objects.

'I'm a yeoman's son, Dr Lopez. My father drives the oxen, guides the plough and casts the seeds with his bare hands. He reaps the harvest, too. I never noticed anyone in a gown instructing him how to do it from a copy of Cato's *De Agri Cultura*.'

'God's nails, a man of my own mind!' cries Bacon, slapping the table and making the silver plate rattle. 'That's the only way for mankind to progress. The ancients may reason and deduce all they like. But a man of *these* times must discover things for himself. He must take nature in his hand and dissect it with his eyes and his mind. I think of this world as I think of a forest: you cannot know its true extent unless you part the branches, climb the trees, *explore* it. I say enough of dead men's superstition! Are you with me, Dr Shelby?'

'Most certainly, Master Bacon.'

Robert Cecil places a hand over his little breast in a gesture of mock capitulation. 'There is the future, Dr Lopez – in the hands of heretics!'

Bacon grins and takes a draught of sack. 'You see what we are up against, Nicholas? Prophets in our own land, and therefore not to be honoured.'

It is the first time in his life that Nicholas has heard his own thoughts spoken by another. Even his friend Lord Lumley, patron of the Lumleian chair of anatomy at the College of Physicians, possessor of one of the most scholarly libraries in England, has never echoed his convictions so clearly. He feels like a man who's just convinced a hanging judge of his innocence.

✠

'There you have it, Nicholas, in a nutshell. It could not be clearer – to a clever fellow like you.' As he speaks, Cecil rolls his shoulders to ease the discomfort in his twisted back.

They are in his study. Bacon and Dr Lopez are still in the dining hall, engaging in a good-natured argument over whether crystals and obsidian mirrors make a man a prognosticator or a charlatan. The rain has eased. Through the windows Nicholas can see the bushes on the terrace looking like mourners around a grave.

'I fear the excellent food has dulled my wits, Sir Robert. I don't know what you mean.'

'A signpost, Nicholas. A lodestone to show you which course to steer.'

'I didn't know I was lost.'

'God's blood, Nicholas! Spare me the humility. I've digested enough sweetness today already. I'm speaking of your future as a physician. If you put your mind to it, you could bring some of Francis's vision – some of *your* vision – to the College; shake the greybeards out of their complacency; help put men like old Lopez out to pasture. Put an end to superstition.'

'Me?' Nicholas hopes his brittle laugh doesn't sound too insulting.

'Why not?'

'Because the College of Physicians thinks I'm a dangerous heretic.'

'Yes, but you're *my* dangerous heretic now, Nicholas. A physician who lists the Lord Treasurer's son amongst his patients – perhaps even the Lord Treasurer himself, were I to persuade my father on the subject – would have no trouble getting his voice heard amongst the Fellows of the College. Perhaps even our sovereign lady Elizabeth might desire his counsel and his healing hand. Would you not agree?'

'The queen already has more physicians than she needs, every one of them eminent and well trusted.'

'Trusted, yes. All except *one*.'

It's said with just enough latent provocation to have Nicholas answering before he can stop himself.

'And who might that be, Sir Robert?'

'Why, Dr Lopez of course.'

The study seems suddenly robbed of warmth. In Robert Cecil's world, it seems betrayal comes served on silver plate and Flemish linen.

'Lopez is getting old. He doesn't walk far these days. But when he does, it's usually on very thin ice. He intrigues with the pretender to the Portuguese throne, Don Antonio, currently a guest of Her Majesty. Yet he also communicates in secret with those who stole his kingdom from him: the Spanish. He has friends in Madrid. The Earl of Essex is convinced he's a traitor. Whatever the truth, he dabbles in places he should stay out of. At his age, you'd think he'd be more cautious. In my humble opinion, he's as likely to die on the scaffold as he is in his bed. Either way, I suspect it won't be long in coming. *Then* there will be a vacancy.'

'Are you saying that you and Lord Burghley would push for my appointment as his replacement?' Nicholas asks, astonished and more than a little sickened. Suddenly the good food feels like lead in his stomach.

'We Cecils don't push, Nicholas. We *advise*. We recommend. We persuade. In the end, the outcome tends to be the same.' Cecil walks over to the Molyneux globe, still standing exactly where it was the last time Nicholas was here. 'Think of the good you could do for physic. Think of the charitable institutions you could leave behind you, the hospitals and almshouses. Imagine your father's pride when his son wins the family a coat of arms from the College of Heralds – no longer humble farmers, but *gentlemen*.'

From out of nowhere, Nicholas hears Bianca's voice in his head. *Nicholas, sweet, Robert Cecil offers nothing without a reason. There is always a price to be paid...*

'And what exactly do you expect of me in return?' he asks.

Cecil doesn't answer. He simply lays one hand nonchalantly on the lacquered surface of the globe – beside the etched outline of the Barbary Coast.

'Marrakech?' A garrotte of hot anger tightens around Nicholas's neck.

'A few months away, that's all, Nicholas. Maybe less, with favourable winds. Return with knowledge gained, reputation enhanced. Ready to begin the climb to your rightful place as a physician to our sovereign majesty. There are men who would kill for that honour, Nicholas.'

'I told you before, I'm not interested in your commission, Sir Robert.'

'Oh, but you are interested in the *reward*, Nicholas. I can see it in your eyes.'

And to his shame, Nicholas knows it's true.

'There is *one* other factor you might wish to consider.'

Robert Cecil's voice has suddenly turned from a courtier's into that of a blackmailer.

'And that is?'

'Given the present contagion in the city, I have suggested to the Grocers' Company that they root out all persons selling false remedies to the public. That includes apothecaries – especially those of the female sex presently residing in the liberty of Southwark.' Cecil pauses to allow his words to sink in. 'And if the Privy Council were to order the taverns to close – well, I would imagine someone thus turned out of *two* livelihoods would find it very hard to put food in her belly. Think upon it for a while.'

And with that, he leaves Nicholas to the fading rumble of the departing storm and the blank stares of the grey mourners on the terrace.

✠

A private coach rolls into view, drawn by two grey palfreys. It looks to Nicholas like a tester bed on wheels, with four corner posts holding up a wooden roof, and curtains to keep out the weather – or any view the traveller might find distressing. He watches it through the open doorway, the horses' hooves splashing through the puddles, the wheel rims casting a misty wake behind them.

'He's not usually this generous, Dr Shelby,' says Lopez beside him. 'I wonder if he's worried what the queen might say to him, if he lets her old physician catch the ague on a walk home in the drizzle.'

His accent is more pronounced now, Nicholas notices. Perhaps when he's in Privy Council company, Lopez feels the need to downplay his Portuguese origins.

'I'm going to Mountjoy, Dr Shelby. But if you want a lift to the public water-stairs, I'm sure the coachman won't object.'

'That is kind of you, Dr Lopez,' Nicholas replies. 'I've been awaiting the opportunity for a private word with you since I arrived.' He pulls his gabardine cloak tight around his neck and follows the old man into the coach.

As they lurch forward, Nicholas tries to make himself comfortable on the plump, velvet-covered bench seat. The interior smells of ambergris and horse-leather. The roof, barely a foot above his head, is studded with golden stars. How many intrigues have been launched in this confined, damask-lined world?

Should I warn him about Cecil's comments in the study? Nicholas wonders. But what to say? Where to begin? Besides,

Lopez was physician to Francis Walsingham and the Earl of Leicester before he got anywhere near the queen. He can't have lasted this long without developing a nose for intrigue. 'May I be blunt, Dr Lopez?' he asks.

Lopez's rheumy eyes widen in surprise. 'If it's about Master Bacon's new ideas, save your breath, young man. I am not the fellow to champion such wild nonsense.'

'That's not what I wanted to talk about. Have you heard of a man named Solomon Mandel?'

Lopez leans back against the cushions. He studies Nicholas as he might study a patient whose symptoms he's never encountered before. The grey flesh of his furrowed brow is flecked with liver spots. 'Solomon?' he says, speaking the name slowly, as though it belongs in his distant past and requires a little effort to drag it into the present. 'Of course I've heard of Solomon. Do you think there are so many Jews in this city that we're strangers to each other?'

'Did you know he's been murdered?'

Lopez's shock seems genuine. His hollow cheeks give a single quiver of emotion. 'I had not heard of it,' he confesses. 'In Southwark?'

'Yes, by assailants as yet unknown.'

'Poor Solomon. What an end.'

'Was he a friend?'

'I knew him. But we haven't spoken for a long while.'

'You knew he was living in Southwark?'

'I knew he had taken himself south of the river, yes. Beyond that, nothing more.'

'Do you happen to know *why* he left the city to live on Bankside?'

'Why does anyone go there, Dr Shelby? For the whores and the playhouses, I assume.'

'Not Solomon Mandel. Not from what I can gather.'

'Then perhaps he went there to escape.'

'Escape? From what?'

Lopez scratches at his white beard. 'Dr Shelby, I am the queen's physician. That brings certain privileges. I have money. I have some position in this city. I have a nice house at Mountjoy. I am tolerated – even by the queen – with a modicum of civility. Solomon did not have such comforts to shield him from enmity.'

'Coroner Danby believes Master Mandel was murdered because he was a Jew.'

'*Danby?*' A dismissive snort. 'Danby is a fool. You could die in a desert and Danby would claim you had drowned.'

'But on this specific matter could he not be correct?'

Lopez waves one bony hand dismissively across his face. 'He could, Dr Shelby. He could. But let us hope he is not. With plague in the city once more, it will be all too easy for the ignorant to blame their ills on *my* people.'

Nicholas wonders if he should tell Lopez about Solomon Mandel's menorah, perhaps even entrust it to him for safekeeping. But if Lopez has truly converted, he might well find the offer objectionable. And even if he doesn't, being presented with an artefact that could be viewed as heretical would hardly endear him to the giver. So Nicholas decides against it.

The coach stops. Beyond the drawn curtain, Nicholas can hear the coachman's raised voice as he argues with a wherryman. The man seems reluctant to take a fare to the far shore. Nicholas hears Robert Cecil's name mentioned. It secures the wherry, but it will probably double the fare.

'I studied the parish subsidy roll, Dr Lopez,' Nicholas says quietly. 'Solomon Mandel was described there as "the Turk's man". Was he once a servant of some sort – to a Moor?'

'Solomon?' Lopez says with a dry rasp of laughter. 'Solomon was no man's servant. He was an honest merchant, a factor for the Moor traders selling spices to English importers.'

'You mean he was their agent in London?'

'Yes. He kept an eye on their interests: sent them news of how much the Venetians were charging for handling Indies spices, that sort of thing. When the envoy of the Sultan of Morocco came to London in 1589, Solomon was his interpreter – he spoke the Moor's language.'

'So the Turk mentioned in the subsidy roll could be the Moroccan envoy?'

'Or one of his companions. He came with several gentlemen of the sultan's court.'

The curtain is pulled aside and Nicholas sees the river stairs, slick with rain, stretching out into the water. At the far end the awning of a tilt-boat rises and falls, adding to the strange discomfort in his stomach.

'Thank you, Dr Lopez. You've been a great help. I apologize again if you thought me uncivil at the feast. Sometimes I can be a little disputatious. Usually I manage to keep my arguments confined to the College of Physicians.'

Lopez's pale eyes widen in belated recognition. 'Of course, I have it now – you're the young fellow whose wife and child died. The one who threw his practice aside. Now I remember the name.'

'Yes, I am.'

'That explains your desire to overturn the apple cart. I hope it brings you comfort, Dr Shelby. But I fear it will only leave you with more unanswered questions. Take the advice of an old man: stay with what is known.'

Nicholas steps down from the carriage. The curtain closes behind him. A last flurry of rain stings his face. Head down, he hurries towards the waiting tilt-boat, while behind him the carriage rolls away with a funereal rumble of its heavy wooden wheels.

10

Farzad has run away because of something Bianca has said to him, something she cannot remember – and wouldn't have meant anyway. As a consequence, he has drowned. With some wholly imagined insult ringing in his ears, he has stumbled on the riverbank and fallen in. And it's all the fault of her too-hasty tongue, she tells herself in frequent moments of self-recrimination, as if the more guilt she can shoulder, the more likelihood there is of Farzad walking into her shop to tell her it's all been nothing but a silly misunderstanding.

As she unlocks the door to her shop on Dice Lane the morning after Nicholas's visit to Cecil House – making a mental note to have Timothy grease the ancient hinges – she tells herself: *He'll come today. I shall not cry. Nor will I box his ears. I shall confine myself to a simple 'We've been worried about you. Welcome home'* – at least until she's had the chance to embrace Farzad. After that, he'll have to take his medicine like a man.

But to her continuing dismay, when the first visitor of the day enters, admitting a gust of wind that flutters the sprigs of herbs hanging from the rafters, it is not Farzad, but Cathal Connell. For a dreadful moment she fears he's come to tell her the lad's body has been found bobbing on the tide at Lyon Quay.

'So this is where you brew your love-philtres an' your spells, is it?' he says, his scoured face cracking into a grin.

As he moves further into the little chamber, ducking under the larger bunches of borage and wild campion, elder and ele-campane, Bianca sees he isn't alone. A second man follows close on his heels. And when this one turns from closing the door behind him, she sees that he is as different from the master of the *Righteous* as he could possibly be.

Where Connell has the wild-eyed look of famine about him, his companion is well fleshed, commanding even. In contrast to Connell's sailor's slops, he wears an expensive cloak, the fine Muscovy fur trim slicked against the leather. To shame Connell's simple cap, he sports a jaunty banded hat with what might have been an osprey's feather in it – before the rain got to it. Removing the hat, he flicks at the feather with his fingers to coax it back into shape.

Good-looking, Bianca can't help but think. A man so well turned out would have every purse-diver and trickster on Bankside trotting in his wake, were it not for the fact that today they'd half-drown before they could get within striking distance.

'God must be grief-stricken, what with all these heavenly tears pourin' out of the sky,' Connell says, shaking the rain off the cuffs of his sailcloth coat. 'Is He weeping 'cause Mistress Merton ain't wed yet?'

'It's just raining, Captain Connell, that's all,' Bianca answers wearily. 'I fear the courtliness is wasted.'

She still remembers how Kit Marlowe had come sniffing around the Jackdaw – two years ago now, she realizes with a start – pouring the same sickly-sweet treacle into her ears. And look what that got me, she thinks: a conscience troubled by murder.

'On such a jewel, *never*.'

Ignoring him, she asks, 'And who might this gentleman be? He doesn't look in need of an apothecary.'

'Reynard Gault, Mistress,' says the well-dressed one, bending a formal knee to her, 'of the Worshipful Company of Grocers.'

So *that's* it, she thinks, biting her tongue. Ever since Nicholas's friend, Lord Lumley, had convinced the Grocers' Company to issue her apothecary's licence, Bianca has known they would eventually get round to paying her a visit. She's surprised it's taken them so long. Perhaps they expected her to fail. Perhaps they'd simply forgotten they had licensed a woman. Either way, the visit is unwelcome – doubly so at this time.

'Then you are doubly welcome. I am honoured, sir,' she says, trying to wring a drop of politeness from her jaw. She turns to Connell. 'I had no notion you moved amongst such quality, Captain Connell.'

Gault answers for him. 'I also happen to be a leading member of the Barbary Company, Mistress Merton. We are a monopoly founded by the Earls of Leicester and Warwick, and licensed by the queen. It is our mission to expand this realm's trade into the lands of the Moor, to the general benefit of the Treasury.'

With yourself running a close second, judging by your fine apparel, she thinks.

'Captain Connell is the admiral-general of our fleet,' Gault explains. 'When he told me of the existence of a Helen of Bankside, I determined at once to see her for myself.'

'See me for yourself? I'm not London Bridge, or the Tower, Master Gault. I am not a landmark.' She glowers at Connell. 'And as for being admiral-general of – what was it Master Solomon told me: three ships? – well, I can't imagine how Sir Francis Drake lives with the jealousy.'

Connell grins to show he can take a little teasing. 'Drake set off around the world with only five. If I come back from our next voyage to the Barbary shore one-tenth as rich as he, I'll be happy enough.'

Gault begins a slow circuit of the shop, which Bianca finds uncomfortably intrusive. He peers into shelves full of caskets of dried herbs; pulls out bunches of the sea holly she prescribes for low libido; holds up to the light the decoctions of hoarhound she uses to ease discomfort of the menses; sniffs the elecampane roots she grinds into ale for failing eyesight. Wishing him and his cadaverous admiral out of her shop before the customers arrive, Bianca wipes her hands on her apron to signify that she has work to do and says to Gault, 'How may I be of service to you, sir? Only I have some medicines to mix for Dr Shelby.'

'A physician, on Bankside?' he says, halting his inspection. 'How in the name of Christ's wounds does he make a profit?'

'I don't think he does.'

'Then why is he here?'

Bianca ducks down to peer at the grey sky through the little front window. 'Probably for the sunshine.'

'Well, it can't be for the reward.'

'That rather depends on what you mean by reward.'

Connell lets out a desiccated laugh. 'How is Dr Nicholas Shelby, by the way? Preparing for his voyage to the land of the Moor, I take it.'

That brings Bianca up with a start. 'How do you know about that?' she asks, almost dropping the pestle she's taken up, to pound some mullein leaves in a mortar.

'He mentioned it to me himself.'

'When?'

'At the marriage feast. Where, I might add, you outshone the bride like a thousand stars outshine a solitary candle.'

This must be how it feels to be wooed by a corpse, she thinks. 'Well, he's not going. He told me so himself.' She turns her gaze on Gault. 'If there's nothing else I can do for you, there's a little girl on Kent Street with the belly-ache. Her mother will not thank me for wasting time in idle discourse.'

'There is nothing idle about my visit here, Mistress,' Gault says. 'I am visiting the apothecaries to ensure they are prepared for an increase in the number of plague cases, should the weather turn milder.' His voice takes on a harder edge. 'And also to root out charlatans.'

The implication is obvious. Bianca stops pounding the mullein leaves. 'I've been called any number of things, Master Gault,' she says, wondering if there's a law in England against breaking the fine nose of a member of the Grocers' Company with a stone pestle, and whether the penalty might be bearable, 'from a papist harlot to a witch. Mostly by men who felt aggrieved because I would not suffer their courting. But *no one* has ever accused me of being a charlatan.'

Gault settles his hat carefully on his head. It takes a couple of twists before he's satisfied. Then he makes a pretty little bow to her. 'I'm sure they haven't. But there's always a first time for everything, Mistress Merton.'

Nicholas finds Bianca where Rose told him she would be: in her physic garden, her secret place known only to a select few, a walled enclosure between Black Bull Alley and the old Lazar House, close enough to the river to hear it whispering. It is the place where she grows many of the flowers and herbs she uses in her medicines. It is also where she goes when her thoughts become heavy.

The rain has stopped by the time Nicholas crosses the patch of waste ground set between the gable ends of two houses. He pushes open the old wooden door set into the sagging brick wall.

She is kneeling at one of the beds, tending it with the reverence of a novice in holy orders. He watches her for a while in silence, until some second sense makes her look over her shoulder. She stands up, takes off her leather work-mittens and walks towards him.

They meet between the sow-fennel and the pellitory. The spent rain has left so much of itself in the air that her brow gleams with its moisture. An errant wave of her hair has fallen across one eye. He pushes it away, feeling its wet heaviness against his fingers. And then, without either of them having seemed to make any form of conscious decision to jump across the last remaining divide, they are kissing.

And this time it is as unlike their last public embrace – beneath the kissing knot at the Jackdaw – as a single whisper is to a choir in full flood. It is almost bruising. Thirty months of denial ripped to shreds in an instant.

When at last they draw apart, she says breathlessly, 'That was so much easier than the last time, wasn't it? Why did we wait so long?'

'You know why.'

'And do I now take it that Dr Shelby is healed?'

It is the hardest question he's ever had to answer, and the easiest.

'Yes.'

She fixes him with a gaze that demands his honesty. 'Then tell me, how does it feel?'

'To kiss you?'

'To be a free man, Nicholas. A slave to no one?'

'Terrifying – in a good way.'

Something in his expression causes a flicker of doubt to cross her amber eyes. 'Really? Are you *really* free, Nicholas? Can you look at me and say: I, Nicholas Shelby, promise you, Bianca Merton, that I am no longer troubled by ghosts? That I am a free man; free to do – and to love – as I please?'

He wants so much to say yes. But lying to this woman would feel like broken glass on his tongue.

Sensing his hesitation, she pushes him away. 'What is it, Nicholas? What's wrong?'

'It's not Eleanor, I promise you that.'

'Then kiss me again – if you dare to. Prove it to me. Show me that you're free.'

'But I'm not, am I? Nor are you. Look around us: Solomon Mandel is dead; Farzad is missing – perhaps also dead. Then there's the past: little Ralph Cullen, Ned's brother Jacob; Tanner Bell and Finney, those two boys that Dr Arcampora had murdered... And what about the deaths we caused? – Gabriel Quigley; Arcampora and his two thugs, Dunstan and Florin; Sir Fulke Vaesy's wife Katherine... When does it end, this dainty measure we dance with death?'

It's the first time he's seen ugliness in Bianca's face. A scowl of pain.

'Do you think I don't have the same thoughts, Nicholas? Sometimes, just before I'm fully awake, I see those two men falling from the bridge – the bridge I led them to, knowing full well what would happen. I tell myself they had to die in order for you to live. But let us face the truth, Nicholas: we are both murderers now.'

For a while they stand there, like two passing strangers who thought they might have known each other once.

'We must both live with what we have done,' Bianca says at length. 'We must believe it was done for good, not for evil. Then we can be free.' She looks around the garden; draws strength from it, as she always has. 'Enough dark talk, Nicholas. Have we lost the moment – or do you want to kiss me again?'

'More than anything.'

'Then what's stopping you?'

The look he gives her is that of a man who knows he's taking his last glimpse of the world before he loses his sight. 'I have to go away for a while.'

For a moment she doesn't understand him. Is he going back to Suffolk to be with his family? Is he leaving to join his friend John Lumley at Nonsuch, fleeing the city lest the contagion spreads?

And then it dawns on her.

'You're going to *Marrakech*!'

For a moment he cannot speak. The speech he'd prepared on the way from his lodgings has deserted him. It wasn't meant to happen like this.

'How do you know?' he manages lamely.

She clasps her hands over her head, as though a great truth that she's failed to see has suddenly become visible. 'I *didn't*, until now. But apparently Cathal Connell did. He came to my shop. He asked me if you were preparing for the voyage. I told him you weren't going. Obviously I was wrong.'

'I was going to tell you—'

But the anger is already rising in her, hardening her face and making her fingers fidget. 'So *now* I know the truth – this ghost you can't let lie. It isn't Eleanor. It's Robert Cecil!'

'It's not like that!'

'That man brings us nothing but ill, Nicholas,' she barks, the hard accent of the Veneto suddenly blooming to the surface of her voice. 'How much coin has he paid for your obedience this time?'

'He's not offering me money. He's offering the possibility to do some good with my skills.'

'But you *are* doing good with them. There are people here on Bankside who'd be dead, were it not for you.'

'And I rely on Robert Cecil's favour to allow me to continue treating them. He could snatch that favour away in an instant.' He sweeps one hand through the air for emphasis. 'And what then? I could barely earn a living here on Bankside, and only then by treating those who could afford to pay me. Robert Cecil is offering me the opportunity to really cause a stir amongst the College of Physicians. If I did nothing else, helping to put an end to the charlatans who feast on the poor and the desperate would be a goodly legacy, wouldn't it?'

'Charlatans?' She lets out an explosive huff of contempt. 'You sound just like Connell's friend.'

'Who?'

'The very expensively attired Reynard Gault,' she says, her amber eyes glinting with smouldering anger.

For a moment the name means nothing to him. Then he remembers his conversation with Connell at the wedding feast: Gault – the man Robert Cecil had sent to arrange his passage aboard the *Righteous*.

'You've spoken to *him*?' he asks tentatively. 'How?'

'Connell brought him to my shop. Apparently he has some power in the Grocers' Company. Rooting out charlatans, because of the plague. I could have punched him.'

'I swear I hadn't intended you to find out this way,' Nicholas says earnestly, desperate to ensure Bianca doesn't realize that Cecil was behind Gault's visit to Dice Lane. 'I came here to tell you. But you've beaten me to the mark.'

'When do you leave?' Her voice has a skein of ice forming on it.

'In a few days.'

'Are you coming back?'

'Of course! Just as soon as my commission from Cecil is concluded.'

'And Farzad? And Solomon Mandel? Have you forgotten *them* so quickly?'

'Farzad could be anywhere. If he's alive, I don't think he wants us to find him.'

'What if the plague should spread to Bankside? Our need of a good physician will be all the greater.'

'I've already told you: physic has no remedy. I'd be of no more use than the charlatans Gault has his eye upon.'

'What changed your mind?'

The ice in her voice has thickened, he notices. He imagines he can hear it crackling. 'Yesterday at Robert Cecil's table, listening to Francis Bacon, I realized I'm not the only one who doubts the present practice of physic. You should have heard Bacon speak, Bianca. It inspired me. Cecil has shown me a future I had never imagined.'

'He's made you another of his promises, that's what he's done.'

'It is not like that.'

'And you've fallen for it.' She looks away, her anger now alloyed with disappointment. 'Oh, Nicholas! You're worse than a giddy maid who believes a handsome rakehell when he promises her the world – if only she'll hitch up her kirtle for a minute or two. *Jesu*, I thought you better than that!'

Foolishly he tries to stand his ground. 'I owe it to my father, who mortgaged his farm to send me to Cambridge. I owe it to those who need a physician and get only a fraud who quotes false remedies in Latin and robs them of their coin. I owe it to... to...'

'Go on – say it! To *Eleanor*.' Bianca's voice is loud, hard and dismissive. It sets a pair of rooks shrieking in the old hornbeam tree beyond the far wall.

'Alright, yes. To Eleanor, and our child. But it doesn't mean I don't lo—'

'I don't care what it *means*, Nicholas,' she says, cutting him off before he can say the word.

She stalks off to where she left her leather mittens. Crouching down, she puts them on and picks up her garden knife, then stabs it into the wet soil.

'Be gone with you, Dr Shelby,' she calls over her shoulder as he stands there, not knowing what to do or say. 'I'll have no more of you. *Go* to the Barbary shore. Walk the endless deserts of Araby, for all I care. Leave me here to plant something that has at least a *chance* of growing to bud.'

11

St George's church lies just off Long Southwark, close to where the Earl of Suffolk had his great house in the time of the queen's father, the eighth Henry. The mansion has long since gone. There is nothing there now but lowly tenements built up against the cemetery wall. Two days after his encounter with Bianca in her physic garden, Nicholas Shelby wanders amongst the headstones and the crosses in the hazy early-morning sunshine, searching for the grave of Solomon Mandel. Under his left arm is a flat parcel wrapped in sackcloth.

When he finds the spot, Nicholas looks around to ensure he is not observed. Kneeling, he palms aside the freshly dug soil and buries the menorah he took from Mandel's house. He is not sure it is the right thing to do. But in the absence of any other plan, it seems to him at least appropriate.

After a brief, silent prayer for the soul of Solomon Mandel, he heads north towards London Bridge, wishing that all his dilemmas could be as speedily laid to rest.

At the top of Fish Street Hill, Nicholas heads east into Aldgate ward. It is market day here and the lanes are packed. He weaves between customers bound for the fish stalls; dodges out of the way of goldsmiths' apprentices running errands; ducks around haberdashers laden with baskets of braids, ribbons and silk lacings. To his relief, he sees no sign of contagion; no watchmen preventing entry to contaminated lanes; no crosses on doors to warn of disease lurking within. In this quarter at least, the city appears untroubled.

He stops at a food stall on the eastern end of Tower Street. There he buys a slice of manchet bread and brawn for breakfast, served to him by a stout woman with a kindly smile. She leans across the counter to get a better look at him, insisting she recognizes the young physician who used to practise on Grass Street. He tells her she's mistaken. He has long since made himself a non-citizen of this part of the city.

He would prefer to enjoy his meal at his own pace. But his neighbour on the bench is an eel-seller taking a break from the market, his apron smeared with fishy conger-blood that leaves Nicholas's stomach close to turning. He wolfs down his food and hurries on.

He crosses the open ground of Tower Hill, the scaffold standing like an abandoned raft becalmed on an empty sea – a sea that on Robert Cecil's globe might well be labelled *Mare Incognitum*. He pauses in its shadow, staring up at the grim gibbet like a country green-pate recently come to town. It was here, he recalls, that the killer of Ralph Cullen, Jacob Monkton and the others met his deserved end. In his thoughts he returns to that night in the crypt below the old Lazar House, the night Bianca had very nearly become the next victim of the killer stalking Bankside. He had come so close to losing her for ever. Have I lost her now? he wonders.

From that memory it is but an easy jump to an earlier one, from a time before Eleanor's death. Before his fall from prosperous young physician to wild-eyed vagrant. Before Bianca found him.

It is a sweltering Lamas Day, three summers past. A nameless boy-child – at least, nameless then – is lying on Sir Fulke Vaesy's dissection table, awaiting the knife as though he's nothing but a slab of meat to be chopped for the pottage pot. A vagabond child of no importance. An object not for compassion, but for mere instruction. Nicholas is staring in disbelief at the obvious signs of murder. He's wondering why the great anatomist is unable – or unwilling – to see them, too.

Ralph Cullen.

Nameless no longer, thanks to him and Bianca.

But so many doors slammed in his face on the way. So many blind alleys. So much contempt to swallow, from the likes of Vaesy and coroner Danby. He thinks now that had he been a queen's physician with place and reputation, how simple it would have been to get them to listen to him. How many lives could have been saved? If Robert Cecil is offering him the chance to wipe *that* slate clean, simply by enduring the discomforts of a voyage to Morocco, then it is to be grasped – whatever Bianca might think about the contract. How can she not see that he is doing this for her as much as for himself? How can she not recognize his need to do something greater with his knowledge of physic than administer to the poor of Bankside?

Turning his back on the empty gibbet, he hurries on into the city.

John Lumley's London town house stands at the northern end of Woodroffe Lane where it meets Hart Street, close to the city wall. It is a handsome, timber-framed mansion sitting in its own small orchard. As Nicholas approaches, he sees that the path to the house is lined with chests and bundles wrapped in canvas. An empty four-wheeled cart stands nearby. Lumley himself, dressed in black velvet breeches and an unlaced doublet, is instructing four male servants on the technicalities of safe and efficient loading. His long, melancholy face brightens as he sees Nicholas at the gate.

'Your chosen hour is fortunate, Nicholas,' he says in his gentle Northumbrian burr. He rubs his spade-cut grey beard with the back of one hand. 'I had planned to leave for Nonsuch within the hour.'

Remembering Robert Cecil's warning, Nicholas asks, 'Is it the contagion, my lord? Are you abandoning the city? I saw no sign of it on my walk here.'

'Mercy, no, Nicholas. The queen has made it plain she intends to come to Nonsuch during her summer progress. I must needs be ready for her.' A rare smile lightens his brow. 'I can't complain. After all, Nonsuch is hers now.'

To Nicholas's eye, the patron of the Lumleian chair of anatomy at the College of Physicians looks a far less troubled man than when last they met.

'That must be a goodly weight lifted from your shoulders,' he says.

'When I inherited it from my late father-in-law, the Earl of Arundel, it came along with all the debts he owed to the Crown. Now it is returned to the queen, those debts are forgiven. And she graciously allows me to remain there until my span on earth is ended. So it is more than the lifting of a weight, Nicholas. It is the raising of a veritable mountain range.'

'And your library? It will remain intact?'

'All part of the legal agreement. Now I have only my recusancy to keep me awake at nights. And Her Grace seems inclined to allow me even that, so long as I keep it to myself and don't upset her Privy Council with dangerous popish utterances.'

'Then you are that rarest of things, my lord – a man who has outwitted the Cecils,' Nicholas says with a smile, remembering how Robert Cecil had sent him to Nonsuch to spy upon this gentle academic. To expose his Catholicism. To bring him down. Of all the failures in his life, Nicholas is proudest of that one.

'How may be I be of service on this fine morning, Nicholas?' Lumley asks, brushing a strand of grey hair from his high temple.

'I am in need of wise counsel, my lord,' he says humbly.

'Don't tell me you've upset the College again,' Lumley says, almost smiling as he leads Nicholas into the privacy of the orchard.

'Not yet. But I might soon be offered the opportunity to upset them beyond their wildest imagining.'

He tells Lumley of Cecil's offer. Lumley is not a physician, but he knows the College better than most. If anyone can give him an honest assessment of the lure the Lord Treasurer's son has waved before him, it is John Lumley.

'It all comes down to whether you trust a Cecil,' Lumley says, in much the same tone he'd use when asking if you might trust a cornered beast in the bear-ring.

'I know that in the past he has intended you harm, my lord. But I have never yet known him to break his word.'

Lumley considers this for a moment. Then he nods. 'He does have a point, Nicholas. The College could certainly prosper with some young blood in its veins.'

'That is what I believe, my lord.'

'And I *have* heard the rumours about Dr Lopez. He is a man whose time is most surely constrained. It's a shame – I quite like him.'

'I wouldn't wish harm to come to him, my lord – not on my account. Not for this.'

'I don't think you need worry, Nicholas. Going to the land of the Moor for Robert Cecil won't change Dr Lopez's fate one jot. He's like me: a heretic relying upon the queen's favour for his continuing safety. And all the while the wolves of the Privy

Council circle us, their beady little eyes watching for a moment of weakness. Waiting for us to stumble. But *you* – you could do fine work if you were allowed the opportunity. An expedition to the lands of the Moor to bring home knowledge: that could make your name.'

'I remember when I first came to Nonsuch,' Nicholas says. 'You showed me works by their physicians Avicenna and Albucasis. I recall a particularly fine copy of the *Canon Medicinae*.'

'It is amongst the books I treasure most, Nicholas. The Moors' understanding of physic seems similar to ours, much influenced by the ancients. To go there and see for oneself would be a grand instruction, would it not?'

'That's what I thought. Sadly, Mistress Merton doesn't agree.'

Lumley gives one of his long, wintery sighs. 'I had a feeling there was something holding you back.' He grasps Nicholas by the shoulder. 'You must do what you believe to be right. I've said it before: your talents will surely be wasted if they are confined to Bankside. Perhaps it is time for you to re-enter the outside world.'

Nicholas thinks of asking Lumley to intervene with the Grocers' Company, to lift the threat hanging over Bianca's apothecary shop. But the Cecils' influence is far greater than Lumley's. It would only serve to set Robert Cecil against his old enemy once more. And Nicholas will not risk that.

'My lord, if the pestilence spreads while I am out of the realm, might Mistress Bianca seek refuge at Nonsuch?'

'Of course.'

'She has but a few mouths dependent upon her,' he adds, thinking of Ned, Rose and Timothy – Farzad, too, should he ever reappear. 'They would work for their board, of course. They're all young.'

Lumley laughs. 'Nicholas, when the queen and her household descend on Nonsuch, we need more bodies to fetch and carry than Pharaoh needed slaves to build his pyramids. They will be welcome.'

'Then I may go with a clear conscience. Thank you, my lord.'

Lumley lifts a cautionary hand. 'If it comes to it, tell them not to delay. Should the plague increase greatly, no one from this city will be permitted to approach any place wherein Her Grace dwells.'

They walk on through the orchard. Nicholas asks after Ralph Cullen's sister Elise, now safe with the household at Nonsuch. The news is good. She is diligent in her studies, Lumley tells him. When not at her hornbook, she is trilling like a pipit. She is even beginning to turn the heads of the male servants. For Nicholas, hearing of Elise's progress, from the terrified mute child he first encountered, is like opening a door and discovering a warm summer's morning outside, when all you had expected was snow.

When they part, Nicholas takes a different route to the bridge, down Seething Lane to Thames Street. He avoids the scaffold on Tower Hill entirely. I've done all that I can, he thinks. I've had enough of lingering in dark places.

Timothy has been brawling.

By habit a placid lad, more at home with his hands around his lute than around someone's neck, he has responded with unusual violence to an injudicious insult thrown at him in the street.

'You should have found the fortitude to ignore it,' Bianca tells him, when she arrives at the Jackdaw to give herself a break from her duties on Dice Lane.

'How could I, Mistress? They called me Farzad's catamite. They said he was a heathen, and that he'd murdered poor Master Mandel.'

'You know that's not what anyone in possession of their wits believes. Next time, take pity on them for being a goose-cap.'

'Yes, Mistress,' says Timothy unconvincingly.

He's had a lucky escape, Bianca thinks, sending him off to his duties in the taproom while she settles down in the kitchen to tend the only visible wound to his honour: a rent in his jerkin. She cannot blame him. She's sure she would have done likewise, with some added cursing thrown in for good measure. And not simply because of the insult and her concern for Farzad. Nicholas's impending desertion has made her own patience – never exactly steady at the best of times – even more brittle. Indeed, as she darns the woollen jerkin on her lap, she pricks her thumb three times in quick succession.

'Rose, I'm hungry,' she calls out in an irritated voice as she catches sight of her former maid passing the door. 'Have we any manchet bread? A little mutton, too, perhaps?'

'There's mutton in the pantry, Mistress. The bread's there, on the shelf.'

Sucking the bloom of blood from her fingertip, Bianca lays aside her work. 'No, there's no bread here,' she observes, inspecting the bread basket.

'That's odd,' says Rose, coming in to check for herself. 'I'm sure there was some here this morning.' She scratches at her black ringlets in mystification.

'It doesn't matter,' Bianca says wearily. 'Forget that I asked. I'll take a little pottage later.'

'It most certainly does matter, Mistress,' Rose protests in an unusually strident tone. 'It's not the first time things have gone missing around here recently. I could swear by all the saints that someone has been at the pottage pot, too. There's twenty-four measures in it, and several times now I've sold twenty and found it empty. I think we have a thief in the Jackdaw.'

Bianca sighs. 'This is Bankside, dear. I'd be surprised if we didn't. Just try to keep them out of the kitchen, if you don't mind.'

'Perhaps young Timothy has had it without asking,' Rose says. 'He's turning into a right saucy little roister.' And before Bianca can stop her, she shouts, 'Timothy! Haul your lazy carcass in here this minute.'

When he appears, Rose demands to know, 'Where's that piece of manchet bread I left here?'

'Why. Ask. Me?' Timothy says jauntily, playing three descending notes on his lute. 'It's your bread.'

'Strictly speaking, *sirrah*, it's Mistress Bianca's bread.'

'Perhaps your husband had it,' Timothy says with dangerous abandon, 'to keep his strength up for all that *correction* he has to give you.'

For a moment a deep and terrible silence falls upon the kitchen, broken only by the bubbling of the pottage pot on the coals. Then Rose reaches for the nearest knife. She tugs at one earlobe, as if to suggest an ear-trimming.

But Timothy has already fled back to the relative safety of the taproom.

✠

'Is she here, Ned?' Nicholas asks three hours later as he takes despondent sips from his tankard of ale. 'If I ask Rose, she merely looks embarrassed, or starts weeping.'

'She went back to Dice Lane an hour ago,' Ned Monkton answers. 'You should go to her there.'

'I've tried. She won't answer my knock.'

He takes another slow swallow of ale, resisting the urge to down it in one draught because the old dangerous desire is tingling in his fingertips. Once, drink had been his refuge from grief. He knows he dare not hide there again, whatever pain he feels at Bianca's refusal to see him.

'Have courage, Master Nick. You two 'ave seen enough trouble an' come through it not to make amends,' Ned says, his giant frame leaning forward over the bench until the tip of his auburn beard is inches from Nicholas's face. His voice is low. Conspiratorial. 'She'll come around, Master Nick. Look how she cursed *me* when you and I had that quarrel, before we knew one another.'

'You called her a witch, Ned. A papist witch. That was unkind.'

'And you caught me that lucky one – the punch what took me clean off m' feet.' He grins alarmingly. 'Only fellow on Bankside who's ever done that. Knocked down by a little fellow who's been learned at Cambridge! You've no idea how long it took me to regain my reputation after that.'

'The way she cursed you, when I got laid out afterwards, I was half-inclined to believe you, Ned,' Nicholas says with a laugh.

'And now here I am, looking after her tavern for her. It's a long way from the mortuary crypt at St Tom's, spending my days amongst the dead. So there's hope for you, ain't there?'

'I suppose there is.'

'And now I have Rose. *Me*, a married lad. Who'd 'ave thought it? It's easy enough for a gentleman, spoutin' a sonnet to his mistress – a maid goes all milky at that sort of thing. But you try doin' it when you spend your day in a mortuary crypt and you stink of dead folk.'

The fiery-bearded mountain that is Ned Monkton reciting poetry to his beloved is something Nicholas has severe trouble imagining. But the thought makes him smile. And – as he's sure Ned intended – it gives him hope. 'Ned, I want you to make me two promises,' he says.

'Name them.'

Nicholas pulls a folded parchment from his doublet. 'This is a letter I've written to Lord Lumley at Nonsuch Palace in Surrey. If the plague should come across the river, I need to know that you, Rose, Bianca, Timothy – and Farzad, if you can find him – will leave Bankside and seek shelter there.'

Ned gives him a doubtful look. 'The likes of me don't get admitted to places like Nonsuch.'

'John Lumley has given me his word that he'll take you all in. It will be a haven for you, until the pestilence ends.' He repeats John Lumley's warning not to tarry. 'I'm relying on you, Ned.'

'Then you should give this to Mistress Bianca, Master Nick. Perhaps it might mend what's amiss between you.'

'I've told you: she won't see me,' Nicholas says with a defeated shake of his head. 'Besides, you how she can be stubborn sometimes. *More* than sometimes. She'll probably tear it up, just to make a point. So I'm relying on you to get her to take the sensible course.'

Ned takes the offered paper as though it's made of gold leaf. 'You 'ave my word, Master Nick. What's the second promise?'

'This voyage I'm taking – it's not a whim, Ned, whatever Mistress Bianca thinks. If I don't go, Sir Robert Cecil will take her apothecary shop from her. He'll have the Grocers' Company rescind her licence. She doesn't know that. Promise me you won't tell her.'

'I knew there was more to it than meets the eye,' Ned says with a scowl. 'You wouldn't have left her otherwise. What's that crookbacked bastard making you do?'

'I can't tell you, Ned. But this is between you and me. No one else. Swear it?'

'On my life. She'll not hear it from Ned Monkton.' He gives Nicholas a quizzical look. 'So the Barbary shore, then – that's a lot further than the journey you and I made to fix that Arcampora fellow, right?'

Nicholas bites his tongue to stop himself laughing. Ned Monkton doesn't deserve to be mocked. 'Oh yes,' he says, peering into his ale. 'It's a lot further than Gloucestershire.'

✠

To his untrained eye, the letter is impressive. It is written in elegant court-hand on expensive vellum, in English, Latin and Spanish:

> To our right beloved and trusty friend, the princely al-Abbas al-Mansur, King of Barbary, greetings...

'Did *she* dictate this?' Nicholas asks. It is the closest he has come in his life to the presence of the monarch. He cannot deny feeling a little awestruck.

'The queen? Of course not,' says Robert Cecil, sealing the letter with his privy councillor's ring. 'If we relied upon Her Majesty to set us to action, Philip of Spain would be sitting in Whitehall with his feet up on the table, the Pope would be giving the sermon at St Paul's, and Mary Stuart would still have her treacherous head. So we *anticipate*. It's what privy councillors are for.'

'And the other part?' Nicholas enquires.

'If any good comes from it, then it is our task to point out it was all her idea from the start.'

'It sounds like a marriage.'

'Except that the annulment can have fatal consequences,' Cecil replies, with a snort of laughter that makes his little body lurch like a crow with indigestion.

'How am I supposed to pay my way while I'm there? Letters of credit?'

'The Portuguese are paying. Their currency is still accepted by the Moors.' Cecil points to a small chest that sits on his study table. 'There were enough ducats aboard the *Madre de Deus* to send you around the globe a hundred times in some considerable luxury. What's in there should be plenty for your needs.' His eyes narrow. 'I shall expect an accounting, so don't develop any expensive tastes.'

Next come the secret ciphers. Lord Burghley and his crook-backed son have spies in almost every major city from Paris to Constantinople. For their correspondence to remain secure, it must be encrypted. Robert Cecil shows Nicholas the letter-transposition code in which Adolfo Sykes sent his. 'Commit this to memory, then burn the paper,' Cecil tells him. 'If you happen to recover any messages that Sykes was unable to send, use this to read them and make your assessment on whether they should be dispatched with haste or brought back when you return.'

'And if they are urgent?'

'Put them aboard any fast English ship you can find. Tell the master they are urgently expected by the Privy Council, and that he shall have his reward from me.'

'Should I use the same cipher for my own messages, Sir Robert? If anything ill has befallen Sykes, it could already be compromised.'

Cecil laughs drily. 'You're already thinking like an intelligencer. Good.' He asks Nicholas for a section of prose or poetry. 'Something you can remember without having to tax your memory.'

'What about Hippocrates? "Medicine is of all the arts the most noble..." I had to memorise extracts from The Law for my medical studies.'

Cecil makes him write down the first twenty lines. Then he takes up the nib and goes over the text, ringing certain characters, making broad slashes between various letters and words. When he's content, he says, 'See: let us say, for example, that you wish to encipher the word *send*. The first *s* you come across in your extract can be found at the end of *is*. Go back a letter – to *i*. Then forward again, skipping the next five. You arrive at an *l*. So the first letter of *send* will be *l*. The second, the *e* – first found in the word *medicine* – will become an *n*. And so on... Twenty lines will ensure you have a large enough stock, whatever you wish to encipher. Remember: one back, skip five forward. Do you have that in your head?'

Nicholas does. But he also has the awful image of Solomon Mandel's flayed chest there, too. Just because a word is enciphered doesn't mean it can't be revealed.

'Yes, I have it.'

'Good. You have your memory – I have *this*,' Cecil says, tapping the annotated text. 'Of course there may be some wholly innocent explanation for why Sykes's dispatches have ceased. If you cannot find him, or if some ill has befallen him, then seek the Moor courtier I told you about – al-Seddik. He was a gentleman of the sultan's envoy who came here, back in 1589.'

The Turk's man. Nicholas wonders if Solomon Mandel's master had been the Moor al-Seddik.

Robert Cecil picks up a second letter from amongst the many documents on the desktop. 'Give him this. It is from my father, Lord Burghley. They spoke many times while al-Seddik was in London, and he has a little English. He is an ally. This letter commends you to him.'

'Did you write this, too?'

'Of course not, Nicholas,' says Robert Cecil with a frown. 'Deceiving one's queen is one thing. But deceiving one's father...'

Cecil takes both letters and places them in an expensive leather pouch. Pressing the pouch into Nicholas's hand, he says, 'Think how grateful – and generous – Her Grace will be when I am able to assure her that the concord between our two realms is unbroken.'

'But what if I discover it *is* broken? What then?'

Cecil claps Nicholas on the shoulder and offers him a mirthless smile. 'Then we are all relying upon your ingenuity to *mend* it.'

12

'He's keeping something from me, Ned. I know he is.'

Ned Monkton prays silently for a sudden act of God, a loud one with not too many ill consequences – anything that will avert the penetrating stare of those amber eyes.

'He's concerned for you, Mistress, what with the pestilence an' all.'

'Then why is he leaving us?' Bianca asks. 'You're a man; he must have confided in you. Because I'm certain he's lying through his teeth to *me*.'

Ned's squirm of discomfort makes him look like a bear shaking water from his coat after a swim. 'P'raps you should go down to Lyon Quay and ask him yourself, before it's too late. It's not a goodly thing to part with harsh words.'

'So he *did* confess himself to you?'

'No!'

'Then what are the two of you hiding from me?'

There can be no harm in telling her of the letter, Ned thinks. It might even put her off the scent. If she persists with the inquisition, he fears he won't be able to keep to himself Nicholas's story about Robert Cecil threatening to shut her down.

'He's given me a letter, addressed to Lord Lumley at Nonsuch.'

'A letter? Should I know what it says? Or is it more of men's secrets?'

'If the plague comes south, Master Nick wants us all to seek refuge from it there. He says it's arranged.'

Her reply is not what he expects, though with Bianca Merton he long ago learned that it seldom is.

'*Arranged?*' she hisses. 'What are we to him – a bunch of posies to be neatly tied into a garland? Does he not think us capable of our own deliverance?'

'I think he was trying to help, Mistress,' Ned says, bemused at the unpredictability of women. Especially women from Padua.

And then, to his further bewilderment, he sees her eyes begin to moisten. But before he can find even the clumsiest words of comfort, she is already on her way out of the Jackdaw.

✠

As Bianca hurries towards the bridge, anger fights a battle with longing for control over her feet.

It is five days now since the exchange with Nicholas in her physic garden. He has been to the Jackdaw more than once, though she's left Rose in no doubt about her disinclination to see him. This morning, when she awoke in her chamber above the apothecary shop, she thought she saw him standing at the foot of her bed. But it was only the Good Samaritan painted on the wall. Later, at the Jackdaw, she half-expected to see him in the taproom and wondered what she would say to him if she did.

Regardless of what Ned Monkton has just told her, Nicholas clearly does not care one jot for her, otherwise his farewell would have been somewhat more expressive than the self-serving nonsense in the note he'd sent three days ago via Rose. Her eyes hadn't got past *a duty to my patron... improving my prospects of advancement...* before she'd crushed the note in her palm and thrown it in the hearth. Where was the *though it breaks my heart asunder to leave you...?* she demanded out loud, to her empty chamber.

Englishmen, she thinks as she passes the well at the crossroads before Long Southwark – *pah!*

✠

Aboard the *Righteous* there is an air of calm purpose. The tide is on the turn and a westerly wind promises a fair passage down-river to the Narrow Sea. The crew seem cheered by the prospect of having a physician amongst them, and in return Nicholas has pulled his weight with the manhandling and stowing of provisions. His offer to assist with the very last of the cargo is, however, politely declined.

It is delivered in a cart escorted by men-at-arms: six wooden straight-sided coffins, the lids nailed down with iron brads. Each crate bears a wool trader's mark: ?ᶜ – two sickles back-to-back.

Being the son of a yeoman, Nicholas knows cloth comes not in boxes, but in wrapped bolts. He studies the deck planks, feigning ignorance, while Robert Cecil's words ring in his ears: *We send Sultan al-Mansur new matchlock muskets, to defend his realm against Spain and Portugal...*

With Cathal Connell declaring himself satisfied with the preparations, Nicholas wonders why they are not already casting off from Lyon Quay. Is there some arcane maritime ritual that must first be performed? he wonders. Are they waiting for a priest to come and give the voyage God's blessing?

His questions are answered a few minutes later when five lads of about Timothy's age arrive on the quayside. *I carry certain young gentlemen for a schooling in seamanship*, he can hear Cathal Connell telling him at the wedding feast.

In their plain woollen mariner's slops and leather jerkins, they look less like gentlemen and more like servants of the man who accompanies them: a tall, well-turned-out fellow in a velvet doublet. Nicholas puts him at about forty. With the pleasing features of a gallant, his obvious wealth and confidence gleam as brightly as the gold rings on his fingers. His beard is as well cut as his clothes, and the breeze across the deck makes his brown forelock dance as eagerly as the pennants fluttering from the ship's halyards.

'God give you fair winds, Captain Connell,' he says as he follows the five apprentices onto the deck. 'Better yet, may He give you prosperous ones.'

'Aye, Master Gault,' Connell replies with his death-mask grimace. 'For all our sakes.'

Hearing the name, Nicholas looks up from his place by the mainmast shrouds. He sees Gault hand Connell a set of documents, each with a heavy wax seal on a silk ribbon, and hears his reply clearly.

'These are the young gentlemen's. You know what they are, Connell. Keep them safe. A goodly profit depends upon them.'

Connell tucks the documents under his arm and consigns the young lads to his sailing master, a scowling brute with a chef's belly who eyes them up as though he can't decide whether to instruct or boil them.

'Your man's aboard, too, Master Reynard,' Connell says, nodding at Nicholas.

Gault makes a shallow bow in his direction. 'Take good care of him,' he says to Connell, declining to address Nicholas directly. 'I will have to answer to Sir Robert Cecil should any ill befall him.'

Nicholas replies with a nod. Somehow the exhortation does nothing to make him feel any safer.

✠

In the late-April sunshine Bianca stops in one of the few open spaces on London Bridge. She looks out on the river foaming between the arches. This, she recalls, is the very same place where Ned Monkton, with terrifying ease, pitched the living bodies of Dunstan and Florin – Nicholas's would-be killers – into the night, the same falling bodies she still sometimes sees in the moment before she wakes.

Today she sees only the masts of the ships moored in the Pool between Southwark and Billingsgate wharf. And the wherries and tilt-boats criss-crossing the muddy brown water. And three tubby little Barbary traders making their slow way downriver on the westerly wind and the tide. She is too late. The *Righteous* has sailed.

With a longing to catch sight of his face one last time, she wills Nicholas to turn, though she knows full well that at this distance he could not possibly distinguish her from the other folk crossing the bridge. She wonders if he is leaving her in another way, beyond the purely physical. Has Robert Cecil wooed him, filled his head with promises, turned him from one sort of Nicholas into another? That is her deepest fear.

As she watches the three vessels making their way past the grain mills on the southern bank, she wonders if she will ever see him again. The thought of it is like a stab through the heart. But it is the anger in her, still hot, that keeps her from weeping. That I *will* not do, she thinks; not for any man.

Lost in her thoughts, Bianca is unaware of a young maid with a brightly eager face passing behind her, hurrying home to Southwark. Her name is Ruth. She is returning to the lodgings on Pocket Lane that she shares with her husband, after a week away in the company of a beloved but ailing aunt who lives on Fleet Lane north of the river. Passing the slender young woman in the bottle-green kirtle and carnelian bodice who stares so intently out at the river, Ruth starts to feel uncomfortably hot.

By the time she reaches home she will have a fever. She will awake the next morning to find painful swellings in her armpits.

Young and strong, she is in the habit of thanking God for a good constitution. But in a few days she will be dead.

The pestilence has crossed the river.

PART 2

Barbary

13

How does the emptiness not drive a man to insanity?

Save for the *Luke of Bristol* and the *Marion* keeping company three cable-lengths astern – or so Nicholas has been informed, though it means little to a landsman like him – there is nothing to feed the eyes but an endless expanse of grey, turbid water. Nothing to hear but the booming of the sails, the groaning of cordage and the shouts of the ship's sailing master. Nothing against the skin but the stinging salt-wind. And beneath your feet, nothing but a few baulks of oak keeping you from the soundless depths.

Yet the crew go about their toil quietly and efficiently, more at home here than they ever were at the Jackdaw. Standing on the high, boxy sterncastle of the *Righteous*, Nicholas wonders if perhaps they are born with an instinctive hatred of green hills, city walls and church spires. Or are they so in thrall to the wild-eyed Cathal Connell that an empty horizon, seen from a crazily swaying masthead, means nothing to them?

But if Nicholas has learned only one thing since boarding the *Righteous*, it is that for all the uncomfortable loneliness of being out on deck, it is far, far worse below. First, there is the endless pitching and rolling, the ever-present risk of being dashed against unyielding timber. Then there is the smell: the rich stink of damp hide and animal waste, which reminds him of the cow byre at Barnthorpe.

The *Righteous* does not smell because she is dirty, Nicholas has learned, but because in sixty years of seafaring she has absorbed the bodily decoction of all the men who have sailed in her, along with the beasts they have brought with them for milk and meat. No amount of diligent scrubbing can remove it.

And Captain Connell is nothing if not a man of cleanliness and order. He has made that clear from the start. His rules for the voyage have been read out to the crews of all three ships, as not one man in ten can read them for himself: there is to be no cursing on the Sabbath, nor any exchange of ribaldry or dirty tales. All customary services of Her Majesty's religion must be observed at the appropriate hour – unless any ship be in immediate peril and the hands required to save her. Prayers, in that event, are already a given. Helmsmen and navigators are to make hourly observations of tides, current, stars, moon and sun, to be recorded accurately in each ship's log, along with any points of land seen and any phenomena of interest. Finally – and here Connell's voice had risen to a force that carried it clearly above the wind – no sodomy, on pain of death.

This last prohibition, Nicholas has learned, is mostly to protect the young apprentices from the attentions of one or two of their older, more covetous shipmates.

The five lads are quickly shedding their lubberly ways. After only a few days at sea they can take to the rigging as deftly as performing monkeys at the St Bartholomew Fair. When not at their physical labours, they are to be found sitting on the main-deck grating, studying the documents that Gault brought aboard, and which Nicholas assumes are instructions given to tyro seafarers.

Yet as he watches them, he cannot resolve a nagging doubt about the manner of their arrival at Lyon Quay. If they are destined for a life of commerce and discovery in the service of the Barbary Company, why were they not already aboard the *Righteous* when she was being prepared for sea? Why did Reynard Gault wait until the very last moment to bring them aboard?

✠

It is almost nightfall. Rose is waiting for Timothy to return from delivering a final demand to one of the Jackdaw's less credit-worthy customers. She would have sent Ned. He is the ideal debt-collector, with his great size, his fearsome auburn beard and his former reputation for enjoying a quarrel. But now she has seen behind the mask, she knows him to be a kindly soul. He's far too easy a mark for a hard-luck story. He'd probably end up promising to extend the rogue's credit. Besides, the thought of the Southwark doxies making their mooncalf eyes at him on the journey brings out a set of protective claws she never knew she had.

When Timothy puts his head around the taproom door, he looks like someone who expects an imminent beating.

'He's gulled you – hasn't he?' Rose snorts. 'What tearful tale did he spin this time?'

Timothy holds out a handful of shillings. 'He paid up, Mistress. All of it.'

'Then why the look of a guilty man?'

Without a lute to strum, Timothy's hands play an agitated minor chord against his thighs. 'I did it out of love for him, nothing else. I didn't want him to starve.'

'But you have his coin, Tim. What are you jabbering about?'

Instead of giving an explanation, Timothy just looks even more wretched. 'Promise me you and Mistress Bianca will understand. Don't punish him. Don't punish *me*. I *had* to do it. Because of that man Connell.'

'No one who tells the honest truth in the Jackdaw gets punished, Tim; you know that,' Rose says reassuringly. 'Now calm yourself and speak out clearly. What's amiss?'

Timothy looks around the taproom as though he expects an ambush. 'He can't come back, can he?'

'*Who* can't come back?' Rose asks, struggling to curb her impatience.

'That Captain Connell.'

'Not unless he can fly. He's far out on the ocean somewhere.'

Timothy's reply brings her up with a start.

'Only Farzad won't come out of hiding unless he's sure. He made me promise not to say a word until the coast was clear.'

The astonishment floods across Rose's plump face like milk spilt on glass. '*Farzad?* You know where he is?'

Before Timothy can answer, she takes him by the arm and hurries him out of the taproom, mindful that Farzad is still wanted for questioning about the death of Solomon Mandel. But even before they reach the privacy of the parlour, Rose understands where the missing bread and pottage have gone.

✠

Bianca has locked the shop when Rose and Timothy arrive on Dice Lane. It takes her a while to answer Rose's urgent knocking.

'Where is he, Timothy?' she asks as comfortingly as she can manage, after Rose has explained why they've come. 'No one will suffer any ill if you tell us.'

'At the Rose theatre, Mistress. He said it was the best place to hide, what with it being shut up by the parish. I've been taking him victuals to keep him fed, else he would likely have starved.'

'Why in the name of Jesu did he run away?'

Now thoroughly glad to be unburdened of his secret, Timothy becomes almost garrulous.

'At first he wouldn't tell me, Mistress. He said only that he had possession of a terrible knowledge, that he must hide himself away, that if he stayed at the Jackdaw it could harm us all. He said no one must know of it, especially not you, Mistress. He made me swear an oath.'

'And it's to do with Captain Connell?'

'Aye.'

'I know Connell looks like a cruel rogue, but what did Farzad have to fear from him?'

'I asked, but he wouldn't tell, Mistress,' Timothy says. 'He didn't speak of Connell by name until today, when I took him some bread. When I convinced him the captain had sailed several days ago, he said I could break my oath and tell you where he was.'

'How did you find him?' Bianca asks.

'He sought me out, two days after he went missing. I was at the river, buying eels. All of a sudden, there he was.'

'And you've kept this to yourself ever since,' Bianca says with a sympathetic smile. 'I don't know whether to admire you or curse you.'

'Like I said, Mistress, he made me swear an oath.'

The thought of Farzad alone and scared, hiding in the empty playhouse like a half-starved feral cat, brings a sudden tear to Bianca's eyes. 'Does he know about Solomon Mandel?' she asks.

'Aye, Mistress. I told him.'

'Does he also know Master Nick has sailed with Captain Connell?'

'No, Mistress.'

'And is he at the Rose now?'

'Aye. But he's still afraid to come home. He thinks you won't abide his return.'

Bianca suddenly moves closer. Timothy flinches, thinking he's going to have to atone for his sins by suffering a stinging back-hand. But it does not come. To his astonishment, she draws him to her and kisses him on the forehead.

149

'Go straight away to the playhouse,' she whispers, 'and fetch Farzad home. And tell him Rose will have the pottage pot warmed up by the time he gets there.'

✠

A cold breeze spills off the river into the silent lanes of Bankside. The Jackdaw has closed its doors for the night. In the taproom, five figures sit together before the dying fire. Only one of them appears animated.

That is not to say there hasn't been a deal of noisy rejoicing over Farzad's return. But now Bianca, Rose, Ned and Timothy are sitting in appalled silence while Farzad tells them the story of Aži Dahāka – the cruellest man in the world.

'I call him this name after a bad spirit that lived in Persia in the time of my ancestors,' Farzad explains as the embers crackle in the hearth. 'The old Aži Dahāka had three heads and could burn whole villages with his fiery breath. But I must tell you of the new Aži Dahāka. He has only one head. But I think the Devil dwells inside it.'

It is not easy to tell a tale of suffering and death beneath a blazing sun, when you're in a darkened English tavern on a chilly April evening. But Farzad tries his best, even though it is a story he is fearful of raising from the place, deep in his soul, where he has tried so hard to bury it.

It is a hot Arabian day some three years past, he begins. A round score of his extended family is making the *Hajj* pilgrimage, a requirement of their faith. They have pooled their resources to pay for a dhow to take them across the water to Al-Qatif, where they will embark on the long trek across the desert to Mecca. It is early afternoon on the second day at sea and the deck of the dhow is too hot to walk on barefoot. Below is even worse: a fetid dark dungeon where the air is so thick it is like trying to breathe through hot pitch. None of them have been to sea before, and the women – especially his grandmother Abijah – are suffering greatly. Grandma Abijah is becoming delirious. Only the soothing hand of Farzad's younger sister, Sabra, on her brow can calm her. Sabra – or so his father always says – can calm a *hurricano*.

But despite the discomfort, the rest of the party are otherwise in good spirits. The pilgrimage will be hard – they know it. But they will return in a state of grace. And if any should fall along the way, although those left behind will weep, they will be happy, because the departed soul will be guaranteed entry to heaven.

It is Farzad's cousin, Ramin, who first catches a glimpse of a triangular lateen sail shimmering like a shark's fin against the skyline – a corsair caravel, her canvas swollen with wind, twenty oars a side. And she is coming on like an arrow fired from a bow.

'They mean us no ill,' Farzad's uncle, Hassan, says. 'When they see that we are pilgrims, they will let us go on our way.'

But Farzad has already seen the fear in his father's eyes.

And he is right to be afraid. The corsairs turn out to be a band of godless brigands from Khor Fakkan. They swarm over the dhow like ants over a carcass. And they care not a fig for pious pilgrims. They see them only as booty.

The captain of this pack of dogs is a tall, princely man the corsair crew call Tafilalt. This is not his true name, as Farzad will later learn, but the name of the distant desert region from which he hails.

Tafilalt is taller than any man Farzad had yet seen. He carries himself like a prince, his chiselled face lined with wheals of raised skin, as though Allāh – the most merciful, the most compassionate – has stitched him together out of hide left too long in the sun. He does not walk like an ordinary man. He appears to glide as though transported by magic, for Farzad can see no sign of feet between the white robe that he wears and the reflected brilliance of the sun bouncing off the deck planks.

Tafilalt, Farzad quickly comes to realize, is a very bad man indeed. Pity is alien to him. He tells his captives that he has not been born of a woman, but of a stone in the desert. And in this spirit, he announces that they must forget all that has happened in their lives till now: childhood, siblings, parents, marriage, children... everything. If they do not forget, then memory will soon become a torment to them instead of a comfort. From this point on, memories – however cherished – are better cast into the sea and left to sink. They should consider themselves born anew.

They are to be landed at the port of Suakin, on the Red Sea. There they will join a slaver caravan for the long walk across the desert to the western edge of the world – and the fabled slave markets of Marrakech, Tripoli and Algiers. Of those who survive the march, the fittest men will be sold for galley slaves, the less hardy castrated and sent to work as house slaves. As for the women, the young will go for concubines, the older for nursemaids. To prepare them for this enticing destiny, they must each develop a hard outer skin of endurance.

Tafilalt does not expect them to accomplish this by themselves. They will be educated by a man who has taught Tafilalt himself all he knows about piracy.

It is now that Farzad learns that Tafilalt is not the worst man on the ship. Not by a long way.

To his utter bewilderment – because he has never yet met a Christian – the man who is to instruct them all in this new hardiness is not of Tafilalt's race. Not even of his religion. He is an infidel. A man who has come from a distant land to make his living netting human souls from the sea, the way the fishermen at Bandar Siraf haul up the gleaming silver *hamour*. He is a walking white cadaver with a salt-scoured face and wild eyes. Aži Dahāka in human form. The cruellest man on earth. The corsairs call him Conn-ell.

First, this Conn-ell has the pilgrims – young and old alike – clapped in ankle-chains. Then he forces them to squat for hours in the prow of the ship beneath the blazing sun, without water. Those who cannot bear it he chastises, with whispering slashes of a cane. Slashes that begin with the tip pointing accusingly at heaven, and that end with it smacking hard against the deck on the down-stroke.

Grandmother Abijah is the first to lose her mind. Even Sabra's soothing words cannot calm her. So Conn-ell orders the pins removed from her irons and has her thrown into the warm waters off Kish Island, to take her rest as best she might find it.

At this, his sister begins a great and terrible wailing, even though the air is so hot it burns the mouth like melted sugar. Even Tafilalt comes over from his wooden throne on the stern to see what the commotion is about. The wailing only ceases when Sabra too joins Grandma Abijah at her rest.

It takes fourteen days to reach the Bab-el-Mandeb, the stretch of water that marks the entrance to the Red Sea. It is known in Farzad's own language as the Gate of Tears. It is aptly named. By the time they reach it, his cousin Ramin, three aunts and his uncle Hassan have also been cast into the sea because they failed to grow this calloused skin of endurance that Aži Dahāka, the cruellest man in all this world, demands of them.

During that grim fortnight three other vessels are run down and taken: two traders from Manora in Sindh, across the Arabian Sea, and a Christian ship carrying Portuguese merchants. All who survive capture – and more than a few prefer to die, resisting – are inducted into Aži Dahāka's *madrasa*, the school of endurance.

153

For Tafilalt, this is proving a prosperous cruise. Consequently there are few provisions left aboard to feed and water his own crew, let alone forty or so captives. But he has thought ahead. At the Gate of Tears, two other corsair caravels are waiting. And thus it is that Farzad, his father, two uncles and a nephew are transferred with five Portuguese Christians to another vessel.

But the Bab-el-Mandeb can be capricious. The next day a sudden and violent squall separates the little armada. Separated from the others, Farzad's ship is swamped by the heavy seas and abandoned by the survivors among her crew. The only living soul left aboard is Farzad.

With her stern barely above water, she drifts on the current for two more days. To keep out of the sun, Farzad crawls through a hatch into a tiny, steeply tilting space that the water has not reached. And there he stays, his feet against a deck brace, emerging only when the sun slips below the horizon.

The drowned – including his father – come to visit him frequently. They bump against him in friendly greeting as the currents inside the wreck bring them to the surface like fruit bobbing in a cask. He is alone, but unafraid. Being a pilgrim, when the vessel sinks he is certain that he will see again his father, sister Sabra, cousin Ramin, grandma Abijah and uncle Hassan.

It is then that he prays to Allāh, the most merciful, the most compassionate, that his mother too might fail to graduate from Aži Dahāka's *madrasa* of endurance. Because then they will *all* be together in heaven.

When, through salt-scorched eyes, he sees a vessel bearing down on him in the glorious sunset of the second day adrift, he begins to scream, fearing the cruellest man in all the world has returned for him. But the ship is a Christian ship, an English merchant venturer exploring the Arabian Sea, challenging the Portuguese who claim these waters for their own. And she is

safe from corsairs because she carries cannon. Safe from Aži
Dahāka…

✠

Rose is sobbing into Ned's vast chest. Ned himself has that old
familiar, fiery scowl, which warns that his temper is having difficulty constraining itself. Timothy has his arms protectively
around Buffle, as though he fears the dog is in imminent danger
of kidnap. Only Bianca is motionless, though in the firelight the
glistening of her eyes is clear to everyone.

'So I did not come to heaven,' Farzad says wistfully as he stares
at the embers in the hearth. 'I come to Southwark instead. And I
don't know if you can get to heaven from Southwark.'

Ned's voice is like the low rumble of a landslide. 'But you can
go to hell from here, and that's where Connell will be going, if
ever he should show his face here again.'

'Why did you not come to us, Farzad?' Bianca asks. 'We would
have called the constable.'

'There is no constable who can tame Aži Dahāka, Mistress.
When I was insulted in St Saviour's market by some apprentice
boys, they said Conn-ell was here – in London; that he would
know what to do with a Blackamoor like me. Then I saw him *here*.
I feared that if he recognized me, he would kill me – and perhaps
all of *you*. I could not risk such a thing.'

'But you waited until after Ned and Rose's marriage before you
fled,' Bianca says, her voice almost breaking. Rose, her head still
buried in Ned's chest, begins to make a noise like a distressed
goose, her body heaving in dismay.

'Only when I saw he had sailed away did I dare to come out of
hiding.'

'If he saw you, he didn't remember you,' Bianca says. 'Which
means there was no cause whatever for you to go prancing off

155

and toppling all our hearts like skittles.' Her voice is harsher than she intends, but it is the harshness that follows relief.

After what she's heard, Cathal Connell seems the obvious suspect in the Jew's murder, even if he *was* at the wedding feast all night. Perhaps Aži Dahāka has the power to be in two places at once, or to become invisible. She pulls herself up short, recalling the nonsense some people on Bankside have claimed about *her*. Then she remembers Nicholas's warning, that the coroner's jury still wants Farzad questioned. 'Now you are returned to us, my young gallant, you are to stay here at the Jackdaw. Do *not* venture outside. Do you promise me?'

'But I must go outside, Mistress,' Farzad says.

'You have no need, not for a while. I *forbid* it.'

For a moment she thinks he's about to weep. His dark eyes are vast in the light from the embers, a look of desperation in them. 'But I must go out. I must go to Master Nicholas – to tell him that I am home.'

14

Nicholas is drowning. Nicholas is clinging to a sharp rock while the waves pound his body to pieces. He is being eaten by a great fish. He is in the hands of the cruellest man in all this world.

Bianca has lived with the first three images in her head since the *Righteous* sailed, five long days ago. The fourth – conjured by Farzad – is new to her. And having already looked into Cathal Connell's eyes, it is the image now that she fears above all the others.

Unable to sleep, she hears the watch calling midnight, and the answering bell from St Saviour's steeple. Unwilling to abandon Farzad to his troubled dreams, she has rejected her bed above the shop on Dice Lane for a mattress in the Jackdaw's attic, though it has required stern words to keep Ned and Rose in her old chamber on the first floor. So she lies now where Nicholas used to lie when he was here, and wishes he was beside her and not at the mercy of the new Aži Dahāka.

She wonders if Reynard Gault knows what manner of man he employs to command the Barbary Company's argosies. Or if Robert Cecil – if he knew – would be content to have his emissary in the bloodstained hands of such as devil. But being a woman of the Veneto, she knows only too well how merchant venturers can hide away their Christian consciences when profitable trade pouts its painted mouth alluringly at them.

She remembers the time when a Paduan mariner had returned home, ransomed after three years as a slave of the Ottoman sultan in Constantinople. Half the city had turned out to see him arrive. But the rejoicing of his family had soon quietened when they'd seen what captivity and hard labour had done to him. Barely twenty-three, he looked like an old man broken by illness. Her only comfort now is that Nicholas is Robert Cecil's man, and Connell wouldn't dare harm him. She stares at the rafters in disbelief, wondering how on earth it is that she's come to be grateful – yes, *grateful* – to the Lord Treasurer's crook-backed son.

There must be *something* I can do, she repeats in a low murmur, thinking herself like one of those religious zealots who repetitively chant the same line from the holy scriptures. But what? How does a Bankside tavern-mistress and apothecary rescue her almost-lover from peril on the high seas?

She knows what at least half of Bankside would expect her to do: cast a spell, weave some magic. After all, at Ned and Rose's wedding feast, hadn't Connell himself said to her, 'You're the one witch nobody dares hang'?

The answer springs into her mind like a mischievous sprite: cast a charm over Robert Cecil. At daybreak put on your best brocade kirtle, the green one, and the carnelian bodice, have Rose pin up your hair the way that gets Nicholas's eyes dancing in their sockets – *don't think I haven't noticed* – and go to Cecil House. Enchant the little Crab with all your Paduan wiles. Convince him to send the fastest vessel in the queen's fleet to apprehend the *Righteous*, bring Nicholas safely home and clap Connell in chains for a murderer. So what if Aži Dahāka had three heads and could breathe fire? He'd never met Costanzia Merton's daughter, Bianca, had he?

Contented, she closes her eyes and tries to sleep. But then another sprite jumps into her thoughts, this time with a warning wave of its little claws.

What to do about Farzad?

The lad is still the subject of an order requiring his taking up for questioning over the killing of Solomon Mandel. The thought of him languishing in some stinking, verminous hole like the Marshalsea or the Clink, while the law grinds its way to an eventual acceptance of his innocence – possibly months in the future – and then remembers to let him out, has her biting her lip in distress.

No, I will not let that happen, she resolves – not to a lad who has suffered so grievously.

Besides, an hour or two's delay will change nothing for Nicholas. But it could be crucial for Farzad. The charming of Robert Cecil can wait a short while, she decides. First must come the charming of Constable Willders.

✠

A few houses down St Olave's Lane from the Walnut Tree tavern, Bianca passes through an old stone archway and into a passage leading to a churchyard. The brickwork is green with moss. An old brindled cat watches her idly from the cemetery wall, scratches itself and goes back to eating the remains of a pigeon.

An iron-studded door is opened by a small woman with a grey, vanquished face.

'Good morrow, Mistress. Is Constable Willders at home?' Bianca asks as nonchalantly as she can manage.

'Do I take it, from your gentle knocking, that there's no alarum?' the woman asks. 'No call for pursuit?'

'No, I don't think so. I seek only a word or two with the constable.'

As Goodwife Willders ushers Bianca inside, she says in a relieved voice, 'Halleluiah for that, Mistress. I can tell you, if this were *your* door, you'd be dreading every blow upon it. Day an' night, it's "Come quick!" or "Villainy! Villainy!" Not a care whether I'm at my prayers or on my pot. It never stops.' She looks Bianca up and down. 'Take my advice: never marry a constable. Your time's never your own.'

'I can imagine. But all I need is—'

But Goodwife Willders seems to think she's encountered a confidante. 'I swear when we was wed, I was a foot taller. With every bash on this door I've shrunk a notch. I'll be no higher than a little atomy by the time my husband stands down.'

'Is he at home?'

'No, Mistress, but he should be back presently. He's just gone down to our daughter Ruth's place on Pocket Lane with a pot of my broth. Ruth's taken a little poorly, and I make good broth, you see. The night-watch swears by it.' She adopts a stern civic frown. 'A constable's wife must play her part in the maintaining of the queen's peace. Who can tell what riot and disorder my broth has helped quell?'

And Bianca can smell it – a warm, meaty scent pervading the scrubbed little house. She nods appreciatively. 'If she's sick, I could make something up for Ruth, if she wants,' she says helpfully. 'I'm an apothecary. I have a shop on Dice Lane.'

Goodwife Willders looks up at her, the recognition dawning in her weary eyes. '*You're* Mistress Merton!' It is not clear if the statement is an accolade or an accusation.

'Yes, I am.'

'I *thought* you looked a bit foreign. They say you're half-Roman.'

'I was born in Padua, to an English father and a mother from the Veneto. But I'm a loyal Banksider now.'

'They say you're a recusant. A papist.'

There is no detectable malice in what Goodwife Willders has just said. She could be suggesting that Bianca can cook well or run fast. Only the English, Bianca thinks, can insult you with words that sound like pleasantries.

'And I suppose you've heard how I was taken by Robert Cecil to be accused of treason, and came back to Southwark in his own private barge? Over two years ago, that was, and the story still has currency,' she says without thinking, cursing herself for rising to the bait.

'I heard it was the queen's. All painted gold, with crimson silk pillows.'

'And you'll also have heard I'm a witch, I suppose? Would you like me to cast a spell for Ruth's recovery? I don't charge much.'

Goodwife Willders's tired little face puckers. 'I'll thank you not to make such japes in a Christian house, Mistress Merton. Witchcraft is a serious matter. I'll not abide it being spoken of casually.' Then, relenting, she adds, 'Mind, if you could cast a charm to quieten all that hammering on the door...'

'Have you considered removing the knocker?'

As if upon a playhouse cue, the door swings open and Constable Willders steps across the threshold. He looks flushed and troubled, his short body fidgeting with a nervousness Bianca would better ascribe to a Bankside gull appearing before a justice of the peace, rather than a law officer entering his own home. She wonders if he's been dicing or whoring on his way back from his daughter's. Or perhaps he's had more broth than he can stand.

'How now, Mistress Merton,' he says. 'Of all folks, I had not thought to see *you* here.' Dropping his gaze, he spits into his right hand and smears his forelock into a more fetching angle.

'I thought to have a word, Constable Willders, if you will permit me the liberty.'

He seems a little distracted. She's used to men behaving like fools in her presence, wishing only that they would say what they have to say without either bluster or timidity. But she'd thought Constable Willders a more sensible fellow.

He unlaces his leather tabard and throws it over a chair. His shirt looks as though it's been handed down from an ancestor, clean enough, but heavily patched with neatly stitched squares of different cloth. It also seems made for a less corpulent man. 'Have you not brought Dr Shelby with you?' he asks.

'Dr Shelby has gone out of the realm.'

'Has he? Where's he gone – Ireland? He's wasting his time. They're all beyond curing there.'

'He is gone to the Barbary shore, Constable Willders.'

The constable puffs up his cheeks in surprise. 'Has he really? Don't tell me he's turned Turk – become a Mohammedan. I have heard he's not past taking our Lord's name in vain.'

'No, Constable Willders, he has not. He has gone as an envoy for Sir Robert Cecil. He's been sent to forge an understanding with the Moor sultan in the sphere of physic, I think.'

Willders seems impressed. 'I did not know he swam in such fine waters, Mistress Bianca. So how may I help the maid he's left behind?'

'He hasn't "left me behind", Constable Willders. I'm not something he's forgotten to pack in his travelling chest. I've come about Solomon Mandel.'

'Ah, the Jew,' Willders says. 'A matter of record, now. The coroner has delivered his verdict: hot medley – as we all suspected.'

'I remember Nicholas saying as much. But I have new information. At least, I might have.'

Willders thrusts out his chest as if to remind her of his civic position. 'Then I am bound in duty to hear it, Mistress Merton.' He fixes his wife with a haughty stare. 'Madam, please absent yourself. This is business affecting the queen's peace.'

Bianca doesn't fully hear the parting grizzle as Goodwife Willders retires to the kitchen – save for the words *peace* and *bloody knocker*.

'Now then, Mistress Merton, give your statement in all its aspects. And give it truthfully, as an honest subject of Her Majesty,' Willders says pompously when they're alone. 'You *are* honest, I trust.'

'As honest as any here, Constable Willders.'

He seems unconvinced. 'Here being Southwark, Mistress? Or here being... *here?*'

She gives him her best smile. 'Only you can answer that, Constable Willders.'

He wets his hand again and makes another adjustment to his forelock. 'No dissembling, please, Mistress Merton. There is no place for dissembling where the law is concerned.'

'I wish to speak of my kitchen lad, Farzad the Moor.'

'Ah, him. The absconder.'

'Indeed, *him.*'

'And what have you to say of him, Mistress?'

'That he is innocent, Constable Willders.'

'Of the Jew's slaying?'

'As innocent as the holy lamb.'

She waits for a response. Willders inspects the patches on his shirt. 'That *is* what Dr Shelby told the inquest. And if a man cannot put his trust in a physician—'

'If I were to say that I know where Farzad was on the night Solomon Mandel was murdered, and that he is wholly guiltless in the matter,' she continues, 'could it perhaps result in the parish sparing him incarceration? After all, they only want to question him. And I can answer for him.'

'He *is* your servant, I take it?'

'Oh yes, without question,' she says, though in her own mind Farzad – once she'd got used to his parroted slanders against the Pope – has become, like Timothy, more the younger brother she never had than a servant, just as Rose has become not her maid, but her infuriating little sister.

163

'Then you are his mistress and you may speak for him. That is the law.'

'And I say he is innocent.'

Willders studies her awhile. She tries not to notice the spittle gleaming around his forelock.

'You *have* him, don't you?' he says, as though he's just fathomed out a troubling mystery.

Bianca says nothing. She feigns childish innocence.

'Do you know *who* slew Master Mandel? Or should I not tax your honesty further?'

'I have an idea, Constable Willders. But I cannot be sure. The man in question can make an account of himself throughout that night.'

'Then perhaps it is him we should be examining.'

'I'm afraid he, too, is out of the realm.'

Willders rasps his chin with one palm while he considers what Bianca has told him – or hasn't. It takes him a while to reach a conclusion.

'I will tell the parish that the young Moor may be discounted from the felony, Mistress Merton,' he says at length.

'That is good of you, Constable Willders.' She smiles. 'I hope your daughter Ruth is soon restored to health. Please let me know if I can be of help. Anything at all, just send word to Dice Lane.'

Willders says very quietly, 'To avoid any unwanted tumult, may I suggest you keep the young Moor out of sight.'

'I didn't tell you I'd found him,' she says innocently.

'And you, Mistress Merton, didn't *quite* get around to telling me you were honest.'

15

The lines etched into the surface of Robert Cecil's Molyneux globe had looked so constant when Nicholas studied them at Cecil House: thin but unbreakable chains of gold carved into the lacquer, connecting the continents as though anchoring them in place. Follow them, and so long as God calmed the waters and gave you favourable winds, you would arrive in the Newfound Lands, or Bothnia, or Panama. Each line represented a voyage of discovery made by one of England's sea dogs: Hawkins, Drake, Frobisher, Raleigh...

The chain connecting England to the Barbary Coast had seemed to Nicholas barely long enough to require more than a few days at sea. But he has been aboard the *Righteous* now longer than the voyage that took him to the Low Countries, a newly minted physician who had volunteered to serve as a surgeon in the struggle against the Spanish occupation there And out here, in the empty wastes of the ocean, there is no comforting gilded line to follow. There is only the slow concussion of wave after wave, slamming against the ship with a noise that sounds to him like the slow, muffled tolling of a great cathedral bell heard through a wall of sackcloth. Now the tales he's heard the watermen tell when they drink at the Jackdaw have a new and worrying pertinence: the *Squirrel*, lost with all hands in a violent storm off the Azores; the crew of the *John Goodwill*, wrecked on the shores of Bambouk and left there to rot, the poisoned arrowheads still in their bodies; the men of the *Firebrand*, who exchanged a quick death by drowning, when she was wrecked off Hispaniola, for a lingering one, drifting day after day on the open sea aboard a raft only large enough for ten men, until murder became the only way to delay the inevitable starvation of the remaining nine.

But at least he knows he's in competent hands. His distaste for Cathal Connell hasn't weakened a jot. But he cannot fault the man's skill. He handles the *Righteous* with calm proficiency. And he has drilled his men well. Even in the roughest sea they move about the rolling deck as though they've known no other life but this.

Nicholas has even come to like many of them. At first they had been wary of him, being – like all sailors – practical one moment and deeply superstitious the next. Now they seem content enough with the presence aboard of a competent man of physic, a rarity they seem to think will guarantee their safe return to England. He hasn't the heart to tell them to trust to their own knowledge rather than his.

And as an envoy carrying letters from the queen, he is regarded by the crew almost as a courtier, shown exaggerated deference one moment, teased unmercifully the next. Nicholas takes it with a smile. It reminds him of his time with Sir Joshua Wylde's company in Holland.

And he has learned a little of their strange language. He knows the difference now between his windward and his leeward. When someone tells him to get out of the way yarely, he knows they mean quickly. When Connell shouts in his rasping voice to the helmsman, 'Lay her ahold', Nicholas now knows he wants the *Righteous* held on a course close to the wind.

When the sea runs high and the wind howls over the deck, reading his edition of William Clever's *The Flower of Physic* becomes impossible, so then he goes below to muse on what he might do when he reaches Safi, the old Portuguese trading harbour on the coast of Morocco.

At sunset, the *Righteous* goes to sleep. Save for the helmsman and the hands required to man sail and cordage, everyone else takes to their hammocks. There is little dice or card-playing. Connell will not permit any naked flame below the main-deck, for the hold is packed with bales of good English cloth. More than sea serpents and hurricanes, every man aboard has a dread of fire.

Like many English merchant venturers, the *Righteous* is armed. Set on the fore- and sterncastles are an array of culverins, demi-culverins and falconets. These are fired off for practice whenever Connell feels in a belligerent mood. They produce huge clouds of vile-smelling smoke, which even in a strong wind seem to infuse the ship with the stench of sulphur.

'If you encounter a Spanish ship, do you intend to give battle?' Nicholas asks Connell after one such display. The smoke has cleared and the two men are standing on the high, raked stern, watching the five young apprentices studying the documents with the grand wax seals that Reynard Gault brought with him on their departure from Lyon Quay. To Nicholas, they look like schoolboys cramming for a Latin test.

'If she's a galleon, we'll run from her,' Connell says. 'The Dons build them big, but not fast.' He glances aloft, making one of his periodic assessments of the sky. 'If she's a merchant, we'll seize her. We can't expect another *Madre de Deus*, but it will still make us rich men.' He gives Nicholas a sly, conspiratorial look. 'Do you fancy being a rich man, Master Physician?'

Nicholas doesn't answer. 'What about the crew?' he asks. 'There's no room on board the *Righteous* for prisoners.'

'I shall relieve them of their riches, wish them a sweet *Buena fortuna*, and send them on their way,' Connell replies, staring out

167

over the vast expanse of water. He looks to Nicholas as though he's revisiting memories. 'What else would you have a God-fearing man do?'

✠

The hourglass is fixed beside the ship's bell. In calm waters, it behaves itself. But today the sea has spewed up one of its sudden spring gales and the *Righteous* is rolling in a manner that Nicholas finds frankly terrifying. With every sideways plunge, the leeward rail breaches the wave crests, dashing icy water onto the deck. Keeping his eyes on the flowing grains of sand in the glass bulb merely adds to the nausea he feels. But at last it is empty. The mate – a gnarled creature who looks as though he's been hewn from the same forest that the ship's timbers came from – nods. Nicholas rings the bell vigorously eight times. It is noon, as best as anyone can fathom.

In clearer weather the apprentices would check the sun's inclination above the horizon with an astrolabe. But today the sky is a bruised, sullen grey. Sheets of rain drive across the reeling deck, making the planks dark and treacherously slick. And although everyone is clad in oilskin slops and leather jerkins, no one has been truly dry for two days.

Nicholas watches the apprentices throw the knotted log-line astern to calculate the ship's speed. As it runs off the spindle and disappears over the side, they time how many knots have passed, using a smaller, half-minute sandglass. Then the helmsman checks his course against the compass iron. When the mate is satisfied no errors have been made, he reports the measurements to Connell, who plots their position against the course drawn on his goatskin chart. He seems satisfied they are not lost. But for all Nicholas can tell, they could be sailing off the edge of the world.

'You look a little whey-faced, Dr Shelby,' Connell says with a cold grin as Nicholas braces himself against another lurch of the deck. 'If you're going to retch you'd best be facing leeward or else you'll be wasting good vomit.'

Refusing to give Connell the petty victory he desires, Nicholas swallows hard. 'How long do you think this will last, Captain Connell?'

'Not long now. She's mostly blown herself out.'

'Are we making progress?'

'We're not drowned, if that's what you mean.'

'Is that so? I wasn't sure.'

Connell gives him a smile Nicholas has seen before: a smirk of contempt for the outsider. 'In two days we'll be off Cape Finisterre. We can run into Vigo for fresh victuals and water.'

'But Vigo is under Spanish rule,' Nicholas says doubtfully. 'Won't we be in danger of seizure?'

Connell laughs. 'Mercy, Dr Shelby, do you think trade stops just because our queen and the Don king get a little fractious from time to time?'

'But I'm carrying letters from Sir Robert Cecil. If I'm taken—'

'They'll say you're the English queen's spy and hang you,' Connell says helpfully. 'Then that handsome Mistress Bianca will have to turn to a rougher fellow to warm her sheets for her.' He laughs and claps Nicholas on the shoulder. 'Don't trouble yourself. I'll send the *Marion* close inshore to take a look. She's proper handy. If there's a Don galleon at anchor, we can be away before the Spanish can hoist their breeches. Besides, even this far north we're as likely to encounter Barbary corsairs as we are the Spanish.'

'Barbary corsairs?' Nicholas says, adding the thought to his rapidly growing list of seafaring perils. 'They range to these latitudes?'

'Aye, they raid the Portuguese and Spanish coastal villages for slaves. Sometimes they'll take a bite at the French coast, too. And not just the Barbary Moors. Even the Levantine pirates will stick their heads out into the Atlantic if they're hungry enough. But we're safe enough at the moment. In these seas a galley can't row for shit, and they're lubbers with a sail, so they are.'

'But you said the storm was almost blown out. What happens when the seas calm?'

'Then you'd best hope my gunners know their business.'

'But surely the letters I'm carrying to the sultan's court will guarantee us free passage?'

Connell gives a dismissive laugh. 'Number one, there's not one Moor in a thousand as can read English. Number two, a Moor is not just a Moor. They have their own heretics, like we do. Then there's the tribes: a Wattasi wants the blood of a Saadi, who abhors a Turk, who holds an Alevi to be little better than a dog... I could go on, but you'll take my drift. And they *all* hate a Christian. Unless, of course, they have need of him.' Connell propels a contemptuous gobbet of spit over the side of the *Righteous*. 'But don't fret, Dr Shelby. The Moors know me, by reputation if not by sight. Aye, they know the Conn-ell well enough.'

It's said so enigmatically that Nicholas decides to ask Connell what he means. But even as he opens his mouth to speak, he hears a sound as concussive as every demi-culverin and falconet aboard the *Righteous* firing as one. He turns – and sees a huge wave slam against the forecastle.

For a moment he thinks the vessel has run into a cliff of dark-green bloodstone crystal. The *Righteous* seems to stop dead in the water. Nicholas feels his knees give way. Then the wave breaks, roaring across the main-deck and shattering into a foaming mist that momentarily blinds him.

Wiping his eyes free of stinging salt-spume, he looks down from his place on the sterncastle. To his surprise, the *Righteous* is still in one piece. The crew are laughing wildly. Their lucky escape has carried them past terror into a sort of jubilant delirium.

All, that is, except for one of the apprentices, whose body – hurled by the wave against one of the demi-culverins – lies drenched and motionless on the deck like something the sea has spewed up in its passing.

✠

As she walks back from St Olave's Lane, Bianca can still smell Goodwife Willders's broth in her nostrils. It reminds her she hasn't eaten since breakfast. Her stomach yearns noisily for one of Farzad's specialities. But before she can eat, she has an apothecary's work to do. How is parish gossip to spread freely if Jenny Solver doesn't have a basilicon of white pepper, oil of dill, serpillum and euphorbium to keep her migraine in check? How can Walter Pemmel's grumbling be kept bearable if he has no nettle salve to rub on his pustule? How is Parson Moody to read his Bible in comfort if he has no electuary of liquorice juice and eyebright to strengthen his vision? There are trials enough to be endured on Bankside, without Bianca Merton neglecting her duties. So she elects to return to Dice Lane. Eating can wait.

Two hours later, she has almost finished. The hunger has disappeared. But in its place has come an unaccountable weariness.

At first she tries to make light of it. *I have a sound constitution,* she tells herself. *I am not made of meadow-grass. I don't blow over at the first hint of a breeze. It's just tiredness.*

She embarks on a half-hearted stocktaking. She checks the pots and the boxes, the drawers and the jars, sprigs, roots, dried leaves, parings... She is interrupted on several occasions by customers, though when they linger to chat, she feels unusually disinclined to indulge them. Her bones are beginning to ache abominably. If I feel like this tomorrow, she thinks, the journey to Cecil House will have to wait. I feel as though I've fought three rounds with old Sackerson the bear.

Reluctantly she closes the shop. She makes herself a general fortification of fleawort and quince, then retires to her sleeping chamber above. She closes the shutters, takes off her gown, bathes herself with a wet cloth soaked in a distillation of coltsfoot to ease the aches and, when she's dry, crawls into bed.

As she lies there, wincing at the discomfort in her joints every time she moves, Bianca wonders where Nicholas is now. For all the horror of Farzad's story, she cannot imagine he is in danger from Connell, not if he's carrying Robert Cecil's commission. No, charming the Crab can wait upon the morrow. A few hours' sound sleep and she's bound to feel better.

But sleep does not come. The ache in her joints gets worse. Her stomach begins to turn. And even if she could ignore these discomforts, her brain is fizzing with thoughts of how to get closer to Gault, and Robert Cecil. The St Saviour's bell has tolled the hour three times before a troubled sleep finally takes her. But in the moment before it does, the answer comes to her in a sudden flash of clarity.

✠

His name is Edmund Hortop. He is sixteen years of age, a shepherd's son from the Weald of Kent. He has never been to sea before.

All this Nicholas learns from the sailors who carried his broken body from the demi-culverin to the small measure of shelter behind the sterncastle ladder.

Nicholas had yelled at them not to move him, but the howl of the wind had drowned his voice. Now young Hortop is staring up at him with frightened eyes, his face shiny with seawater and sweat, the flesh alarmingly grey.

Nicholas tries to gauge the measure of his injuries. There is no sign of blood, just a raw indentation on his right jaw, which Nicholas ascribes to his colliding with the cannon's iron trunnion. But from his experience as a surgeon with the army of the House of Orange in the Low Countries, he knows an absence of blood is no guarantee his patient might not be mortally hurt.

Nicholas talks to the boy while he unlaces his sea-soaked gabardine. For the first time since boarding the *Righteous*, he feels a measure of authority – no longer an unskilled hindrance to be pushed aside with a shout of *Away, yarely!*

'Where is the pain, Edmund? Can you tell me?'

'It was everywhere, Master,' the boy says in a faltering voice.

'Was?'

'It is better now. It is dying away.' He grips Nicholas by the wrist. His fingers feel like bands of ice. 'Does that mean I'm dying also? I should not like to die in the midst of the ocean, Master.'

'You're not dying, Edmund. You've just received a bad blow. Lie still.'

In Holland he had often reassured a pikeman or a pistoleer, an archer or a matchlock-man, in this manner – knowing full well that he was lying to them. But sometimes comfort is the only medicine a physician can give.

But setting broken bones, cleansing and suturing torn flesh, this is practical medicine he can he sure of. All he has to do is *mend*. And if he can't mend, it will be because the wound is beyond healing, not because he has trouble reciting pages of Galen and Hippocrates in faultless Latin.

Sending one of the other apprentices below to fetch his physician's chest, Nicholas peels the boy's gabardine open and gently probes for broken ribs. The chest seems sound, even if the breathing is shallow and rapid. Hortop remains silent throughout this exploration, staring up at the swaying sky.

The limbs, too, seem unbroken. 'You may have done naught but bruise yourself, Edmond,' he says encouragingly, though a warning voice in his head tells him the boy will be fortunate to have escaped so lightly. He is about to ask Hortop to move his limbs when another wave crashes into the *Righteous*. She rolls sickeningly. Standing over Hortop's prone body, one of the apprentice lads stumbles forward, his boot stamping down hard onto Hortop's right ankle.

Hortop does not cry out. He doesn't even move his leg out of the way.

'Edmund, will you try to move your feet for me?' Nicholas says as the *Righteous* settles herself.

But Hortop remains immobile.

'I cannot, Master. They refuse my will.' His voice is barely audible. Nicholas can see the effort it takes to make the words leave his mouth. He pushes the heel of his palm into the flesh of Hortop's right thigh, halfway between the knee and the groin.

'Can you feel *that*?'

The boy mouths, 'No.'

Nicholas rises and turns to Connell, speaking low so that Hortop will not hear him above the noise of the wind. 'I think the boy is afflicted by a palsy of the limbs. There may be damage to the spinal marrow.'

'Can he be cured?' Connell asks. 'He is worth some amount of money to me.'

Appalled by Connell's callousness, Nicholas struggles to keep a neutral voice. 'The prognosis is not good. For lesser damage, it is sometimes recommended by the ancients that walking on the spine can relieve the pain, or having the body suspended from a frame. But Hortop is not overly discomforted. That worries me.'

'There must be something you can do – with all that learnin' inside you.'

'In extreme cases the French surgeon Paré recommends cutting away the fragments of damaged vertebrae. I tried to do that once, in the Low Countries, with a Swiss mercenary who'd taken a ball in the back. It wasn't entirely successful.'

'What happened?'

'He died.'

Connell considers this for a moment. Then he says, 'I'll send him ashore in Vigo then. The Portugals have hospitals and sisters of mercy. They can have him.'

'Abandon the lad in a foreign land, palsied from the neck down?'

'What else is there to do?'

'Hope that the Moors can treat him,' Nicholas says.

'The Moors?' replies Connell with a contemptuous grunt.

'Their physician Albucasis has written on the condition of paralysis to a greater extent than Christian physicians,' Nicholas says, knowing he sounds like a man losing an argument.

'And if they are successful?'

'He might live. But I fear he will be a great burden to his family when he returns. His father is a shepherd, I understand. He's unlikely to have the money to care for a crippled son.'

Nicholas thinks of the poor vagabonds he's seen on the roads of England, half-starved, clad in rags, begging for food, chased out of towns with the threat of a branding. Many of them were crippled soldiers from the Low Countries, or maimed sailors discharged from the fleet. It might have been better, he thinks, if the wave had carried Edmund Hortop out of this world entirely.

Connell studies the straining sails while he considers what Nicholas has said. 'Safi it is, then,' he says with a shrug. 'Let us hope your faith in heathen physic isn't misplaced, Dr Shelby. For my own part, I'd rather the Devil mixed my medicines.'

✠

The raucous ill temper of next door's cockerel brings Bianca awake. A single shaft of watery grey light falls reluctantly on the bedroom wall. As she sits up against the bolster, her aching joints cry out in protest. She feels no better now than when she went to sleep.

But her hunger has returned with a vengeance. The smell of Goodwife Willders's broth pops into her head. Her stomach begins to rumble. In her present state, she thinks, a good broth might make all the difference.

She wistfully recalls the one her mother used to make for her when she was young: the carcass of a mountain bird – *tetraone* or *fagiano* – boiled for hours with asparagus, parsley and fennel. There had been times when that broth kept her sane: her falling-out with Antonia Addonato, for instance; or that occasion when – aged fourteen – she'd thrown all the feminine wiles she imagined she possessed at Paulo Vianello, the mason's son, only for him to humiliate her in public by telling her to come back when she was a year older, and then only after she'd contrived to grow a pair of breasts. There had never been a trial that couldn't be put in its proper place by that wonderful broth.

Feeling a little better at the mere thought of it, Bianca swings her legs onto the floor, washes from the bowl of well-water in the corner, puts on a clean smock and goes down stairs, infused with renewed purpose.

Admittedly, grouse or partridge might be difficult to find at short notice.

But St Saviour's market will be opening at daybreak, and the fowlers might have caught a few in their nets. And if not, she could always use a capon as an alternative. By midday, she should have the magic completed. Then she'll be in a better state to put on her green brocade kirtle and her carnelian bodice and set forth to enchant the Crab into sending a fast pinnace to fetch Nicholas home from the clutches of the cruellest man in the world.

She is in the process of gathering the other ingredients from her kitchen when Jenny Solver rushes into the shop, her face flushed.

'Am I first in, Mistress Merton?'

'You are, Mistress Solver. I haven't really opened – it's barely daybreak.'

'So there hasn't been a run?'

Bianca looks puzzled. 'A run? On what?'

'Vinegar.'

'No. Should there be?'

'In that case, I shall need' – Jenny Solver starts crossing off her fingers – 'at least a quart of vinegar... tincture of squills... three scruples of wormwood... four drachms of water germander... camphire...'

'Wait a moment, Mistress Solver,' Bianca says, trying to slow her down. 'These are the ingredients for a fumigant: to protect against the pestilence.'

Jenny Solver looks at her as if she's the village clod-pate. 'Why else do you think I'm here at cock-fart, Mistress Merton? It's crossed the river. There's plague on Bankside.'

Bianca's usual habit is to ignore Jenny Solver's gossiping. But something about the look in her eyes says this isn't just rumour. 'How do you know?'

'Parson Moody told me. He buried the first body, late last night.'

Bianca lifts a hand to her mouth. 'No! Who was the poor soul? Did he say?'

'Do you know Constable Willders's daughter, Ruth, the one who married that glover's son? They live on Pocket Lane. Only she'd been across the bridge for a while, see, an' when she come back—'

Bianca feels a wave of cold dread surge through her, taking all the strength out of her legs. She can hear Goodwife Willders's voice in her head: *He's just gone down to our daughter Ruth's place on Pocket Lane with a pot of my broth. Ruth's taken a little poorly...*

And she recalls the way that Willders, on his return, had seemed somehow distracted. He knew, she tells herself. He *knew*. And yet he kept silent. God alone knows how many people might already be infected!

For a moment Bianca thinks she's going to faint. She steadies herself against the table. Jenny Solver is leaning very close to her, her eyes rolling, her lips drawn over her teeth to emphasize the horror of it all. Her voice seems unbearably loud – as if she's shouting into Bianca's face.

'Imagine it: Constable Willders having to confine his dying daughter in a plague house an' all the time wondering if he's tainted himself – an' anyone who's been near him. So if it's all the same to you, Mistress Merton, I'll have that fumigant just as soon as you can manage. Mistress Merton... Mistress Merton... are you alright?'

16

At night Nicholas sleeps in a hammock, rigged in a little alcove where the cases of matchlock muskets destined for Sultan al-Mansur's armoury are stored. On the *Righteous*, that is as close to privacy as anyone – save Connell – can get, a meagre nod to his position as a messenger of the Privy Council. It reminds Nicholas of a crypt in a mausoleum. The only light – until dawn breaks and the hatch forward of the foremast is thrown open – comes from a single horn lantern swaying on a hook from a deck beam. When that happens, the resulting shaft of lurching grey luminosity makes Nicholas fear the sea has broken in. The hatch is open now.

The wind has ceased to howl. The waves have calmed. The first day-watch is going on deck, a procession of grumbling, cursing men clambering sleepily up the ladder to take their turn in the head, the narrow grating beneath the bowsprit – the only place on the *Righteous* a man may empty his bowels, and usually then only shoulder-to-shoulder with his neighbour.

Nicholas takes this daily ritual in good spirit. He is no stranger to enforced communality. In the Low Countries, as surgeon to Sir Joshua Wylde's company, he'd learned to dig a jakes as speedily as any man and use it without complaint, regardless of the stink. Here, at least, a fellow's waste goes into the water, not some stinking ditch or the open drains of London.

But before Nicholas can attend to himself, first he must check on his patient, poor Edmund Hortop.

Yesterday the apprentices lashed the oars of the cockboat together to form a makeshift stretcher, trussed the lad like a rolled carpet and – as gently as they could – lowered him through the hatchway into the darkness below. It had looked to Nicholas as though they were already burying him. 'He's a brave English lad – see, he makes no complaint,' the mate said, though Nicholas could tell Hortop's silence had more to do with his injury than with any courage he might still possess.

Several times throughout the night Nicholas has woken and made his stumbling way by the lantern's light to Hortop's place behind the hatchway ladder, stooping to avoid dashing his brains out on the low deck beams. Kneeling beside the injured lad he has calmed and soothed, talked of the inconsequential, mopped away sweat, moistened the boy's lips. There is precious little else he can do, and he long ago learned that activity, however futile, is a good mask for helplessness where a physician is concerned.

'Will Edmund live, Master Physician?' one of Hortop's friends asked, a rangy lad with the ever-questioning eyes of a child who's lost a parent in a crowd. Nicholas replied with some now-forgotten assurance that he suspects sounded as shallow to the apprentice as it did to himself.

'He *must* live,' another said resolutely. 'He's come all this way. It's within grasping distance now. Courage, Edmund. You'll soon be living like a prince.'

At the time Nicholas had been too tired to question what he meant. But now, as he follows the line of mariners towards the ladder, he recalls thinking that it had seemed an odd thing to say. True, Hortop had come from a humble shepherd's hut, but a life at sea in the service of the Barbary Company hardly seems like a beckoning paradise.

Nicholas reaches the ladder. In the pale wash of light from the hatchway he can see the space behind it is empty. The lad's gabardine coat is lying discarded against a stout timber rib. But Hortop himself has gone.

✠

From hope to terror and back again. Tumbling, always tumbling. One moment Bianca is certain that she's suffering nothing more alarming than a mild ague brought on by too much thinking. The next, she knows in her bones that she has the plague. *I'm going to recover. I'm going to die. Recover... die...*

The only question is: when? In the next hour? Within the day? The pestilence can take you so swiftly you don't even have time to make a Will. Healthy at noon; dead by nightfall. *I'm feeling a little better than I was an hour ago... I'm feeling worse...*

She has closed her shop on Dice Lane. She will not open it, no matter how urgent the call for her balms and tinctures. She dares not risk coming into contact with another living soul.

She understands now why Constable Willders seemed so distracted. He was denying – even to himself – what he had encountered at his daughter's lodgings. She can even allow him a measure of sympathy. What else was a loving father going to do: announce it outside St Saviour's to the general population? *Plague is in my daughter's house! It may have touched me too – and any who have come close to us...*

Thank Jesu I didn't call in at the Jackdaw as I'd intended, Bianca thinks.

She stands in her bedchamber, unpoints her linen smock and lets it fall to her waist. Taking up her mother's mirror glass – one of the few luxuries she brought with her to England – she raises her left arm towards the ceiling and carefully inspects her armpit. Then she transfers the glass to her other hand and does

181

the same on her right side. Returning the glass to her clothes chest, she prods vigorously under each arm with her fingers, just to make sure there is no bubo developing malevolently beneath the skin.

Clean, she decides. *So far.*

Relacing her smock, she tries to remember if she walked or ran to Willders's house, knowing that some physicians hold that exertion can open the pores of the skin, allowing the pestilence in. She is sure she walked.

She prods her stomach, knowing that pain there can presage the disease. It doesn't *feel* sore. And she's still hungry, which is good sign. She places a finger against the vein in her right wrist and feels her pulse. It seems normal.

Going downstairs to the shop, Bianca seeks out the shelf where she keeps a jar of squill leaves soaked in honey and vinegar, a vomitory she sells to customers who've eaten bad meat, or who fear an enemy or a love-rival has tried to poison them. She takes just a small amount – not enough to make her vomit, if she's healthy. If she vomits it could be a sign she's infected.

While she waits, she takes a wooden scoop, lifts the lid off her tub of brimstone and pours some of the yellow powder into a clay bowl. This she takes to the hearth. She heats a fire-iron in the flames for a few minutes, before plunging it into the brimstone. At once the powder begins to produce molten golden beads that give off dancing blue flames and pungent fumes, which make her think she could have done without the vomitory. Eyes streaming, she steps back and waits for the fumes to permeate her lodgings.

She realizes she's used too much brimstone, because eventually she's forced to open the upstairs window. Leaning out to savour the air, she sees the lane is empty. The word has spread, she thinks. I am already an outcast. I'm already dead. It's just that no one has the courage to come and tell me.

An unbearable loneliness seizes her. She begins to tremble. Is it a sign the pestilence is spreading through her body – or just the fear of it? She longs to be able to throw herself into Nicholas's arms. He would understand. He could even help her. He's a good physician, no matter what he thinks of himself.

And then she remembers how they argued in her physic garden the day he said he was taking Robert Cecil's commission: *I've already told you: physic has no remedy. I'd be of no more use than the charlatans Gault has his eye upon.*

She leaves the window ajar and goes back to the shop, the tears in her eyes not entirely the result of the brimstone. There she pours vinegar into a jar, intending to return to her bedchamber and wash herself down with it. There are still a few things she has yet to try. They might help, or they might have no effect whatsoever. It is just a matter of waiting. Waiting for death to make up his mind.

But at least she hasn't vomited yet.

17

'Mistress! Mistress!'

Bianca can hear Rose calling her. She climbs off the bed, catching a whiff of vinegar on her skin. Leaning out of the window, she sees Rose looking up at her from the lane. Behind her, Ned, Farzad and Timothy stand like children around the deathbed of a parent.

'Say it isn't true,' Rose pleads, 'all that nonsense Jenny Solver's been shouting about you being taken with the pestilence.'

'Who's attending to the Jackdaw?' Bianca replies, trying to sound as though she's troubled by nothing more than a mild headache. 'Who's looking after the customers and keeping watch on the takings?'

Rose shakes her head in despair. Her black ringlets sweep rebelliously across her shoulders. She holds up a ring of keys. 'Faith, Mistress, you're not to trouble yourself on that score.'

'You've locked up – securely?'

'Yes, Mistress.'

'And the window in the attic – in Master Nicholas's old chamber?'

'Locked, Mistress,' Rose says in a weary tone. 'It's been locked since he went to Mistress Muzzle's lodgings.'

'But what about trade? We can't live on air, foolish girl. They'll all go to the Good Husband and the Turk's Head.'

'No, they won't,' shouts Ned. 'And if they do, I'll fetch 'em back again.'

Farzad holds out an object wrapped in cloth. Bianca catches the delicious smell of stewed lamb. 'I bring you best *Abgoosht*,' he calls up proudly. 'Is very good for sick mistress.' Then, as his resolves crumbles, 'Please, Mistress Bianca – not to die. I wish not to lose a second mother.'

Bianca has to stifle a cry of her own, at the pain so audible in his voice. 'Leave it by the door, Farzad, sweet. I'll collect it when you've gone,' she calls down. 'Is there any news of the Willders?'

Ned and Rose glance at each other.

Bianca's stomach turns to ice. 'Be honest,' she shouts angrily. 'You'll do me no service by lying.'

Ned's fiery countenance turns into the face of a little boy who's just been slapped hard. 'Dead, Mistress – the constable last night, just after Evensong. Goodwife Willders followed him this morning, at daybreak.' He lowers his head, as though it's all his fault.

For a moment no one seems to know what to do next.

'Does the parish know I was in their company?' Bianca calls down.

Rose hides her fear beneath a veneer of contempt. 'That clacker Jenny Solver ain't stopped squawking about it for a minute, all day. Whenever I ask someone where they heard the news, it's always Mistress Solver what told them. She's taken to her bed in fright.'

'But is she sick?'

'Not according to her husband. He was in for his ale today. Said it was good to have some quiet. Apparently she's squawking like a bishop with the French Gout.' Rose gives an unconvincing laugh. 'But then when is she not, Mistress?'

It's a small encouragement, thinks Bianca. Better than the alternative.

'Come back to the Jackdaw, Mistress,' says Rose plaintively. 'We can care for you there.'

'You know I must not do that, Rose, dear.'

'Then let me come in and attend you. *Please*, Mistress.'

'It's not safe, Rose. It's not safe for any of you to be near me.'

'We don't care,' Rose says defiantly, to a general nodding of heads.

'If I'm infected, you'll leave Ned a widower. Do you want that?'

Rose begins to blubber uncontrollably.

'We just have to wait, and trust to God's mercy,' Bianca says, more calmly than she feels. 'And don't let Buffle out into the street. With plague here now, the parish is likely to slaughter every dog it can catch.'

Rose makes a series of noises against Ned's chest. To Bianca, she sounds like an old drunk with the croup.

Ned translates. 'She says "God can't tell the difference between good and bad any more."'

Rose pulls herself away from her husband's arms. She wipes her nose on her sleeve, takes up a four-square stance of angry defiance and shouts up at the window, 'Why isn't Master Nicholas here to cure you? Why has he left us when we have need of him most?'

✠

Later, in her chamber, by the light of the tallow candle set beside the bed, Bianca reaches out to the hillock that her knees make of the coverlet. Propped there are two documents, the ink now dry, the words no longer deniable. They cannot be smudged into non-existence. They stand. It has taken all her courage to write them, because she knows that if they are read by anyone but herself, she will be dead.

I, Bianca Merton, formerly of the city of Padua, now residing in Bridge Ward Without, in the borough of Southwark, being reconciled unto God in the sure and lasting knowledge of resurrection, do here-within make my will:

To my well-beloved friends Ned and Rose Monkton, I leave the Jackdaw Tavern and all its stock, plate, furnishings, revenues and incomes in perpetuity, even down to their heirs. I do this in the trust that Timothy Norden, taproom boy, and Farzad Gul (a Moor), shall remain employed there for as long as they shall desire, and that they share in one tithe of the said revenues until the end of their days.

To my right beloved friend Nicholas Shelby, physician, I leave my father's books, in the sure knowledge he will treasure them. He knows well the cost to him that wrote them of speaking against the prevailing thought and custom of the day. I leave him also my father's silver Petrine cross – in memoriam of the faith I bore unto the said Nicholas, and in repentance for the words I left unspoken.

Bianca sets down the Will beside the bolster. She takes up the second document. It has taken her longer to write, because the words carry a weight that has made them harder to prise out of her heart.

I know not if you are on land or sea. But you are not here, and it would bring me great ease if you were.

It is no great trial to face death when He stands beckoning at the door. I have kept as faithful to the one true Religion as dwelling amidst heresy will permit, and I know God will take account of that when He determines how long I shall remain in Purgatory. Prayers for the soul are not permitted under England's new faith, I know. But you are not a man who holds much with conformity. So pray for Bianca Merton's soul, Nicholas Shelby.

I know now why you are compelled to remain so restless. You are searching for a truth that will not break, the moment you first step upon its shore. But know this: there is no such continent to be discovered, Nicholas. Not in this world.

I should not have sent you from me with harsh words. When Timothy found you that day, cast up on the shore, I knew you were a talisman, brought into my world by a goodly providence. And so has it proved to be. That I have not told you of my true feeling is my error alone. So I tell you now, Nicholas Shelby, that I love you.

Know this, Nicholas Shelby, that should I chance upon your Eleanor in heaven, I shall make all deference to her and say: The unbreakable truth he seeks was always there in his heart, and I could not sway him from it.

So now, as is the practice of my faith, I shall make my last confession before Almighty God. And I do so with you and Eleanor foremost in my thoughts.

I confess the sin of Envy.

18

'He died in the night,' says Connell casually. 'It's probably for the best. Hortop rests with God now.' He gives a casual nod towards the far horizon.

'You mean you cast his body *overboard*?'

'What else would you have me do?' Connell asks with a derisive shrug. 'I can't have a corpse aboard, Dr Shelby. Even a landlubber physician should know that.'

'Why wasn't I woken?'

'You're more use to me rested. Unless of course you can bring the dead back to life. Can you do that, Dr Shelby?'

'Of course not.'

'Then why the concern?'

'I could have confirmed he was dead.'

'*Confirmed?*' says Connell, his scoured brow rising. It makes Nicholas think of a serpent's skin sliding over its bones. 'Do you think I would have cast him out of the ship for being naught but a nuisance – while he still lived, Dr Shelby?'

'No, of course not, but—'

'I had money invested in that young boy. Why would I let Neptune have him for free?' Connell scans the sky, apparently satisfied by the breaking cloud. 'We should have a goodly sight of the sun soon, to fix our latitude. So I'll attend to my duties, if you'd be so good as to attend to yours. If we have any more calamities aboard, I hope your physic proves more effectual that it did with poor Master Hortop.'

✠

What did he expect of me? Nicholas wonders as he lies in his crypt above the crates of matchlock muskets. The boy's back was broken. I'm a physician, not a worker of miracles.

He closes his eyes. Tries to catch up on lost sleep. The swaying of the *Righteous* has become almost comforting, now that the storm has passed. He rocks from side to side in the darkness, listening to the groaning of the hull and the snores of the sailors off-watch. But a nagging question keeps uncoiling itself in his mind like a worm in a grave: did Cathal Connell *really* have the living body of Edmund Hortop thrown into the sea?

It is a vigorous worm, with teeth that will not let go of Nicholas's imagination. At length he climbs out of the hammock and goes back to the place behind the ladder. The hatch above is still open. But instead of a deathly grey light, sunshine now floods down onto the planks, illuminating a square a yard wide, which moves gently around the deck as the *Righteous* ploughs on through the sea.

Nicholas stands over the spot where he last attended to Hortop. A terrible image jumps into his mind – of the young apprentice, eyes rolling in terror as he realizes what the men lifting his makeshift stretcher intend.

He knows Connell could never have contrived it without the help of several men, and the tacit silence of anyone who might have woken and witnessed what was happening. Which means – if he's right in his suspicions – that he's in the power of a crew of murderers. He wonders what might have happened if he himself had not been in so deep a slumber.

As it sweeps to the motion of the ship, the square of sunlight picks out Hortop's discarded mariner's gabardine coat lying against the bulkhead. Nicholas stoops to retrieve it. It doesn't seem right to leave it there.

As he lifts it up, a folded parchment with the remains of a heavy wax seal still attached lands with a secretive *slap* on the deck. Nicholas recognizes it as one of the documents he'd seen Reynard Gault of the Barbary Company hand Cathal Connell before the *Righteous* sailed – the same papers he'd watched the apprentices studying after the exercising of the cannon, huddled together in deep concentration as though revising for an examination. His memory echoes Gault's words to him now: *These are the young gentlemen's... Keep them safe. A goodly profit depends upon them...*

Nicholas looks up to check the hatchway is clear, then around at the sleeping, off-watch crew. Why he does this, he is not certain. Perhaps it is the thought that some of the men presently snoring in their hammocks within a few feet of him might be the very same men who hauled Hortop up the ladder to his death. Satisfied that he is not observed, Nicholas opens up the single sheet of expensive vellum.

The proximity of the deck beams requires him to stoop a little, his body shading the document. He moves closer to the shifting square of sunlight.

He is looking at a series of interconnected boxes containing elegantly written court-hand. And around the edge of the vellum, a border of what appears to be heraldic coats of arms. He reads the contents of the first box:

```
┌─────────────────────────────────────────┐
│                                         │
│    Sir Clovis de Bassen, warrior of God, │
│    Slain at Acre in the Holy Land, 1190 │
│                                         │
│                   ∫                     │
│                                         │
│        Sir Walter de Bassen –           │
│           Gilda of Arles                │
│                                         │
│                   ∫                     │
│                                         │
└─────────────────────────────────────────┘

┌─────────────────────────────────────────┐
│                                         │
│           Sir Thomas Welland,           │
│           liege man of Edwd. III        │
│            Slain at Crecy, 1346         │
│                                         │
│                   ∫                     │
│                                         │
│      Guy Welland, gentleman, d. 1350    │
│         Brandon Welland, page to        │
│    John of Gaunt, Duke of Lancaster     │
│                                         │
│                   ∫                     │
│                                         │
└─────────────────────────────────────────┘
```

Nicholas frowns, wondering what a shepherd's son from the Weald of Kent might be doing in possession of such a document. And then his eyes fall to a line at the foot of the page.

It is written in a different hand from the text in the boxes. A single sentence. Spelled out in capital letters:

PROVEN BY DUE AUTHORITY OF THE ROUGE CROIX

PURSUIVANT, COLLEGE OF HERALDS

Instantly Nicholas is back in Solomon Mandel's wrecked lodgings, staring at the two fragments of bloodstained parchment that he lifted from the torture bed. On one is written ROUGE CROIX. On the other, the indecipherable SUIVAN.

Could be suivant – following... he can hear himself saying to Bianca. *A follower of the red cross...* And her reply: *I'm not sure that translates... But if it does, a follower of the red cross would be an English crusader...*

Now Nicholas knows they were both in error. He has lived in London long enough to witness her taste for pageantry. He has watched from the crowd as earls and dukes ride past in grand display, their horses caparisoned in silk and cloth-of-gold. He has seen the queen herself, though admittedly from the riverbank, as she was rowed down to Greenwich in a barge that would make Robert Cecil's look like the cockboat of the *Righteous*.

But in his mind now he is observing a procession by one of the city's many grand livery companies. Whether it's the goldsmiths, the brewers, the haberdashers or even the grocers matters not. His eye is fixed upon the fellow leading the vanguard, imperiously commanding the ordinary folk to clear the way. A fellow resplendent in a gilded tabard. A ceremonial appointee, an officer of the College of Arms. One down from a herald in the order of magnificence.

He is a *Pursuivant*.

Suddenly Nicholas hears footsteps on deck approaching the hatchway, and the gruff banter of sailors. He steps away from the sunlight and, with all the calmness he can muster, slips the document back into the folds of Hortop's gabardine.

And even as he does so, he tells Bianca: we were wrong. Solomon Mandel wasn't murdered because a Christian zealot found his religion abominable. He was killed for another reason entirely. A reason that has something to do with Cathal Connell, Reynard Gault and the *Righteous*. And a young lad named Edmund Hortop, whose resting place is now the boundless ocean.

19

There is something unusual about the morning.

Bianca had gone to bed expecting one of two things to happen. Either she would wake to the racket of next-door's cockerel heralding the dawn or she would die in the night.

Clearly I am not dead, she thinks as she wakes. But nor can I hear the cockerel, and already daylight is blooming around the shutters. She wonders if her neighbours have abandoned their lodgings, taken the bird and fled. Or perhaps they're all dead. Perhaps she's the only one left alive on a street of plague houses.

She sits up against the bolster and looks around the chamber, trying to determine what it is that's out of place.

For a start, the Good Samaritan painted on the wall is behaving himself this morning. Today he did not tumble in the moment before she woke. There he is – fixed in paint for as long as the wall lasts, his pious smile unaltered, his robes draped decorously across the feet of the poor beaten traveller lying on the road.

As Bianca leans forward, it hits her: her joints don't ache. She feels fine. Well rested. And the one thing she can be certain of about the pestilence is that – if it's going to take you – it doesn't permit you a morning off in the process.

She wriggles her shoulders. She throws out her arms and flexes her wrists. She kicks off the coverlet and thrashes her legs about, the way Buffle does when you tickle her belly. Nothing aches. She feels fine. She checks under her armpits and around her crotch for buboes. Not so much as a pimple.

Within a minute, Bianca is weeping copiously with relief.

When she regains her composure, she dresses in her work kirtle, goes downstairs, intending to step out into the almost-fresh Southwark air – air that, admittedly, is always a little ripe with animal dung and emptied piss-pots, but fresh enough when you'd doubted you'd ever take a breath of it again in your life.

Jubilantly throwing open the door, she almost knocks a sallow-looking fellow in a leather apron and a labourer's cap clean across the lane. Somehow he manages to keep upright, hugging to himself a pot of red paint, which splashes over his apron as though he's taken a sword-thrust through the chest. He waves the brush in her direction, as though to keep her at arm's length.

'God's nails, Mistress Merton, take not one step forward!' he cries, as though he's come face-to-face with a wild beast.

'Whyever not, Master Coslin?' she asks amiably, recognizing him as a regular at the Jackdaw.

'Why? You ask me *why*?'

'That's what I thought I said.'

He gives her an anguished look. 'Because the parish have sent me to mark these premises as plagued. The lodgings on either hand have been cleared, and I am to paint a cross upon this door.' The anguish turns to guilty regret. 'And *you* are to remain confined within. Forgive me, Mistress. I'm sorry. You was always charitable to me. I shall pray for you. You 'ave my word on it.'

Bianca treats him to a sweet smile. 'That won't be necessary, Master Coslin – the paint or the prayers.'

'Not necessary?'

'No. There's nothing ill with me. It was just an ague. I'm fine. I really am. Never felt better.'

When she's sure he believes her, Bianca goes back inside, takes up the letter she wrote to Nicholas when she thought she was about to die, kneels before the hearth and feeds it to the still-sulphurous embers.

✠

Rose puts a hand to her mouth, forgetting the stack of dirty breakfast trenchers she's carrying. They land with a clatter on the taproom floor. She stares in astonishment at the figure in the doorway, while Buffle – woken from her slumber by the hearth – gulps down the unexpected bounty of scraps.

Ned spills the tankard of ale he is serving to Walter Pemmel – who jumps back from his seat to avoid getting soaked. Timothy stops in mid-verse of 'Thy Heart's Sweet Allure' with a discordant *twang* from the strings of his lute. Farzad says something incomprehensible in Persian.

'Are you not pleased to see me?' Bianca asks, unable to suppress a grin.

And then Rose hurls herself bodily into Bianca's arms. 'Mistress, it's a miracle! God has answered our prayers. You're cured!'

At least that's what Bianca thinks she's says, because Rose's face is buried in her neck. 'It's not a miracle, Rose, dear,' she says, her chin forced upwards by the embrace so that she has a clear view of ceiling beams browned by wood-smoke. 'It was just an ague, that's all.'

Rose draws back, her black ringlets all awry. Her eyes are glistening like a novice who's just seen Christ's face in a cloud bank. 'What charm did you use, Mistress?'

'No charms, Rose. I wasn't infected.'

'But you were! Jenny Solver said so. So did Parson Moody... and Warden Cullicot... and Billy Evans, the stonemason's son... They even sent Jack Coslin to mark your place with a painted cross.'

'I know. I made him spill red paint all over his apron.'

'Did you make one of your elixirs, Mistress? Tell us how, please.'

'Rose, dear, I *wasn't* sick. It was an ague.'

But as Rose demands to know whether the cure contained angelica or tragacanth, wood-sorrel or wormwood, whether it was boiled or distilled and how much of it a body has to take for it to be efficacious, Bianca resigns herself to the inevitable: that her miraculous cure from the pestilence will find its way into the canon of her already extensive notoriety, where it will keep good company with the queen's gilded barge and all the other fancies she cannot correct, no matter how often she tries.

Ned comes over, the fingers of his huge hands working as though he were a small boy with a guilty secret. He tilts his auburn beard at her timorously. 'Mistress, might we speak privily a while?'

'Why, of course, Ned,' she replies, planting a gentle kiss on his left cheek, which has him blushing so that skin and beard are all of one colour.

With surprising agility for such a large frame, he darts upstairs. When he returns, he is carrying what looks to Bianca like a letter. He ushers her to an unoccupied table in a quiet corner.

'Before he left, Mistress, Master Nick gave me this,' he tells her, with all the anxious pride of a man who's been entrusted with a state secret from the hand of the queen herself. 'Perhaps now is the time to take advantage of it.'

In silence, Bianca reads the letter Nicholas wrote commending her, the Monktons, Timothy and Farzad to John Lumley's care at Nonsuch Palace. When she looks up, Ned says, 'He was most insistent. Should the pestilence come to Bankside, I was to ensure we all repaired to Lord Lumley for shelter and board. Master Nick said it was all arranged. All you have to do is present this letter.'

Her response catches him off-balance.

'Is that what he wanted – that we should all run away? Like he did?'

'Mistress, it was done in thought of us, his friends,' Ned says uncomfortably.

'I'm not blaming you, Ned. You have discharged your promise to him. That was proper of you.'

'But the plague *has* come, Mistress. And you have dodged it once already. Should we not do as Master Nick wanted?' A guilty downwards glance. 'I have my Rose to think upon now, Mistress.'

Bianca gives him a sad, apologetic smile. 'Forgive me, Ned. *Of course* you have your wife to think about. You should both go. And Timothy and Farzad. I'll close the Jackdaw. But I can be of use here. Nicholas may say the pestilence is incurable. And he may even be right. But if I cannot cure, then I can at least help.'

'I shall speak to Rose and do as she wishes,' Ned says quietly.

Something about the way he keeps his head down, studying his fingers over the great swell of his chest, tells Bianca he has not given up all his secrets.

'What is it, Ned? What are you keeping from me?'

There is no hiding the struggle going on behind his eyes. 'He didn't do what you said, Mistress – run away.'

'Ned, what is it you're not telling me?'

Ned's huge fingers have begun to drum against the table board. In the past – before he was tamed – that, Bianca knows, was always a sign the Monkton temper was about to explode. But there is no anger in his face now. Only conflict.

'I swore to him I would not speak of the matter to you.'

'But now you believe I should hear of it?'

He nods. 'Because you do him an injustice.'

She lays a hand gently on his arm. 'Then speak, Ned, if that is what your heart is telling you to do.'

He looks at her while he battles with himself a little longer. Then he sighs and says in a rush, 'Master Nicholas only agreed to go to the Barbary shore because Sir Robert Cecil told him he'd have your licence to practise 'pothecary rescinded if he didn't.' He makes a noise like a smithy's bellows. 'There – I've said it. God forgive me for breaking an oath.'

For a while they sit facing each other in silence, Bianca's right hand splayed against her temple. Then she leans back, letting her arms fall to her sides. 'Oh, Ned. I should have realized.' She turns and tilts her head towards the ceiling. If she's looking for something, Ned thinks, she's doing it through closed eyelids.

'And now he's in the hands of that monster, Cathal Connell,' she says, barely loud enough for Ned to hear. 'I know not whether to admire him or chastise him for a fool.'

'What shall we do, Mistress?'

'You, Ned, must do what you think right for you and Rose. I know what I'm going to do. I'm going to beard Robert Cecil in that den of his on the Strand.'

✤

Barely two hours later, having commandeered Rose to help her into her green brocade kirtle, lace her carnelian bodice for her and pin up her hair in as fashionable an imitation of a woman of the better orders as she can manage, and a penny poorer for taking a wherry across the river to save her feet, Bianca stands before the liveried gatekeeper at Cecil House.

'I desire an audience with Sir Robert Cecil,' she says loftily. 'It is a matter of grave import.'

'Are you on the list?'

'I shouldn't imagine so. But it really is a matter of—'

'Grave import. It always is.' The gatekeeper yawns, displaying a jaundiced tongue. Bianca catches a scent that reminds her of the brimstone she burned in the hearth on Dice Lane.

'It concerns Sir Robert's emissary to the Barbary Moors.'

His mouth closes like a trap. 'And who might you be, Mistress, to know aught of Sir Robert's emissaries? Are you a privy councillor, perhaps?' He makes a little piggy snort at his clever joke.

'I am a friend to the said emissary. And I have news of him – news for Sir Robert.'

'Have you really? Who are you?'

Bianca clenches her fists and says, as evenly as she can, 'I am Mistress Bianca Merton. From Southwark.'

She knows at once by his face that she's made a mistake.

'Oh, from Southwark,' he says knowingly. 'Bawdy-houses, bear-gardens, taverns and the playhouse' – another porcine snort – 'oh yes, Mistress, I know all about the matters of grave import there.'

Just my luck, Bianca tells herself: to find my way blocked by a lecherous Puritan.

'I am an honest tavern-mistress,' she says, forcing the words out between a clenched jaw. 'And an apothecary, licensed by the Grocers' Company.'

The gatekeeper swaps porcine for asinine. He gives two sharp brays, like a mule being whipped. 'Aghgh! Aghgh! A pot-wench who sells love-philtres. I know your sort.'

Oh, that I had just one-tenth of the witchcraft Bankside believes I have, Bianca thinks to herself. There would be nothing left of you now, but a smoking dust of expensive kersey and the lingering scent of burnt hubris.

'I really do believe Sir Robert will wish to see me,' she says as calmly as she can manage.

'And why is that, my saucy little Hippolyta?'

Her knuckles land squarely in the languorous curve of his nose, smashing it through to the other side so that he resembles Janus of the two faces. But when she looks at her fist, the knuckles are unblemished and his supercilious face is intact. She takes a deep breath and draws the last shot out of her locker.

'Because Dr Shelby is physician to Sir Robert's *son*, William. And if Sir Robert learns how you have insulted the doctor's intended bride' – how easily *that* came to me, she thinks, as though observing herself from a distance – 'then Bankside's *matters of grave import* will be for ever denied to you, Master Gatekeeper. Because you won't have the coin to pay for them. You'll be dismissed. And penniless. It's your choice.'

After that, her progress into the depths of Cecil House feels like being swept up by a tempest. A series of gentlemen, each more well hosed and cloaked than the last, pass her along so many panelled corridors that Bianca fears she has become lost in a forest of wainscoting, until at last she stands before a small man in a black half-cape and gartered stockings. He wears the resigned look of someone who is expecting to be asked to perform exactly the same task he's attempted a hundred times already, with no pleasing result.

'I am truly sorry, Mistress,' he says with weary honesty. 'I recall Dr Shelby well. It was I who conducted him to Lady Cecil, when Sir Robert feared their son was sick. Had you but been here yesterday, I would have ensured an audience.'

'Yesterday?' she repeats with a welling sense of disappointment. 'Is he not here?'

'Sir Robert has left the city to be with Her Majesty. A precaution, you understand, against the current pestilence. Perhaps you would care to put your petition in writing.'

20

'In the language of the Moor it is called Rass Lafaa: the Head of the Snake.'

Cathal Connell points across the wide bay to a rocky outcrop rising above a tumultuous surf. Nicholas's gaze follows as his outstretched hand then sweeps along the shore, a myriad tiny suns blazing in the wave crests, until it indicates a high stone wall set with round towers. 'And there is the Kasar el Bahr, the Castle of the Sea. The Portingals built it when they had this place, before the Moors threw them out.' The hand lifts again, drawing Nicholas's eyes upwards over gently-rising scrub and olive groves to a line of imposing sandstone ramparts on the skyline. 'And that is the *Kechla*, the citadel. Does it not appear grand to you, Dr Shelby?'

And Nicholas must admit that it does. From the towers of the citadel, intricately patterned Moorish banners ripple in the onshore wind. The afternoon sun paints the ramparts a pale cinnamon.

Suddenly his attention is pulled back to the waterfront and the Kasar el Bahr. A ragged line of white puffs blooms along its battlements. A moment later the deep, reverberating thunder of cannon fire echoes across the bay. For an instant Nicholas fears the *Righteous* is under bombardment. But no waterspouts erupt from the sea around her, no shot tears through the rigging. The smoke drifts away on the wind with the dying thunder.

'That's a grand welcome, an' no mistake,' says Connell appreciatively. He points to the fleet little *Marion*, already moored against the stone breakwater. 'Mind, I did send word we had an emissary of the English queen aboard. Maybe the sultan's sent that rogue al-Annuri down here to shake your hand.'

'Al-Annuri?'

'He's one of the sultan's ministers. A cold bugger. Eyes like a peregrine's. Not the sort of Moor you'd care to cross. But I can't see him coming all this way and wasting good powder on an infidel, mind.'

'The man I'm to meet is named Sumayl al-Seddik,' replies Nicholas, recalling Robert Cecil's instructions. 'He was with the sultan's envoy who came to London some years back. I carry a letter to him from Lord Burghley. He's going to tell me all about Moorish medicine.'

Connell throws back his head and laughs. 'Oh, you'll enjoy that, Dr Shelby. You'll do more eating than learning. Likes his comforts, does al-Seddik.'

'You know him?'

'Of course. Everyone knows old gundigutts. If you pushed him over, he'd roll.' Connell slaps his own lean belly in appreciation of his fine humour. 'Still, whoever ordered that salute, you should feel honoured. They usually keep that sort of welcome for the corsairs when they come home with a bounty of slaves.'

And indeed Nicholas can see a galley beached on the strip of sand, looking for all the world like a trireme from ancient Athens. Her oar ports are empty, the oars themselves stacked nearby.

Noticing the direction of Nicholas's gaze, Connell says, 'You can't traffic with the Moor and not come to appreciate his proficiency in the meat trade, Dr Shelby.'

'The *meat* trade?' echoes Nicholas, a pang of disgust taking away his breath. 'You mean slaves?'

'Aye, slaves, Dr Shelby. European slaves, Protestant and Catholic... Turk slaves... Saracens... fellow Moors of different tribes... Men as black as the finest ebony from the very heart of the desert, who worship gods you've never even heard of. Men, women, children... *Slaves*. The markets are full of them. Here in Safi, in Marrakech, in Algiers, in Tripoli – I've heard it reckoned there's more than thirty thousand Europeans alone sold through those markets. Only the Devil knows the true number. Some are sold to row the sultan's galleys; some to wait in service upon their masters, as we have it in Christian households; some they castrate and set to guard their harems, or to serve them as secretaries. It's rich soil for any fellow with the courage to till it.'

Nicholas wonders if that includes Cathal Connell. He would not be the first, he thinks. He's heard from the watermen who frequent the Jackdaw that Francis Drake and John Hawkins are not above trading in human souls.

'When these fellows aren't raiding Christian ships,' Connell continues, 'they're either working their fields or driving camel caravans. This is where the spice road ends. Strike inland and *one* day – if you live long enough to pass through the High Atlas and more miles of desert than there are stars in the heavens – you'll find yourself in China.' He grins like a skull. 'That's if the giants with one eye in the middle of their foreheads who dwell in the kingdom of Kongo, or the scaly serpents with teeth the size of your fingers that swim in the Nile, don't have you for breakfast first. Welcome to the Barbary shore, Dr Shelby. Aren't you glad you came?'

✠

On the waterfront around the Kasar el Bahr small mountains of merchandise cram the flagstones. Sacks of cinnamon, sheaves of sugar cane, slabs of salt the size of flagstones, chests of saltpetre wait to be loaded aboard the three English vessels, once their holds have been emptied.

The *Righteous* has been warped the last few yards of her journey by gangs of small, agile men who heave on dripping cables until she is moored safely against the great hemp fenders hanging from the quayside. Connell tells Nicholas they are Berber tribesmen from the mountains, earning more by labouring than they ever could herding goats in the foothills of the High Atlas. They grin and chatter as they toil, their glistening skin the shade of old leather soaked by rain.

Nicholas has been picturing this moment since before the *Righteous* sailed. The Low Countries he knows from first-hand observation – not so very different from England. But his understanding of the lands of the Moor has been mostly framed by watching *Muly Molucco* and *Tamburlaine* performed at the Rose, and from reading Pliny's *Natural History* – in the original Latin during his studies at Cambridge, which damn near sent him running back to Barnthorpe and his father's farm.

As he jumps down onto cobbles gritty with windblown sand, he is instantly made aware of his ignorance. Looking around, he sees no despotic chieftains dismembering their enemies with wickedly curved swords, no mountains capped with lightning, no endless deserts of black sand, no men with eyes in the centre of their foreheads or possessing just one huge foot on the end of a single leg... Just a busy little port that could be Dover, were it not for the heat and the colour of the men's skin.

A committee of welcome waits on the breakwater. Some are Moors in long robes that make Nicholas think of Roman togas, the others – judging by their faces and their dress – are Europeans, Jews and Levantines. They have the same cautiously expectant look he's seen in the faces of the merchants and factors who gather on the quaysides in London. They are here to haggle over the newly arrived cargo, and to get themselves the best deal for their own goods when the *Righteous* is empty and ready for the return voyage to England.

Standing apart from the men of commerce is a gang of labourers, ready to do the heavy lifting. They are a sullen group. Of every age from young to greybeard, they are dressed mostly in tattered hose and slops, their chests bare and gleaming in the heat. Save for the fact that most of them are Blackamoors, this could be Galley Quay or Botolph's Wharf on the Thames, Nicholas thinks.

The most alien sight in his immediate compass is a herd of beasts lying hobbled nearby. He takes them to be camels. They wait patiently for their cargoes, their indignant faces reminding him of old Walter Pemmel when he launches into one of his customary tirades against the petty rules of the parish aldermen.

The camels' overseer is a young lad of barely ten. He wears a grubby woollen tunic and shouts first in Spanish and then in English, 'One *camello*, seven English pennies! One half-*camello*, eight English pennies! All very good *camellos*. No lames. Carry cargo very good.'

For a moment Nicholas wonders if by 'half a camel' he means he's also offering them for meat, before it dawns on him that half a camel is a shared load – and the extra expense is to cover the cost of searching out the rest of the load.

✠

In a cool chamber set into the inner wall of the Kasar el Bahr sits a man in a pristine white robe, behind an elaborately carved European table that Nicholas assumes is a relic of Portuguese rule. On his head he wears a voluminous cloth binding that Nicholas can't help thinking looks like a giant onion. The man has a lean, knowing look, as though there's not a subterfuge for avoiding customs duty that he hasn't yet seen through. Studiously ignoring his two visitors, he prefers to study a quill and inkpot set beside two books. One is a simple calfskin-bound volume the size of a large loaf, the other much smaller, but far more extravagantly bound and inlaid with intricate Moorish designs picked out in gold.

'We have to be the first to speak,' whispers Connell in Nicholas's ear. 'To him, we're infidels. Don't ask me to explain the logic in that, but it's his realm we're in now, so needs must.' He beams his skull's smile at the customs official, swings the clay pot onto the table and says, expansively, 'Peace be upon you, Muly Hassan. I've brought you a little of what you like.'

The change is instant. The previously immobile official springs to his feet and begins pumping Connell's now-free hand. When he speaks, his English is surprisingly good. Nicholas guesses it's the result of a lifetime spent mixing with foreign merchants. He wonders if there might be any customs officials in London who can speak the language of the Moor. He doubts it.

'*Wa alaykum*, Sayidi Conn-ell. You have good voyage, yes?' the man says through a broad set of neat yellow teeth. 'Allāh, the most merciful, the most compassionate, filled your sails with a profitable wind, yes?'

'Aye, he did that, Muly Hassan,' says Connell, tapping the taut cloth cover of the pot. 'He must know how much you like English barberry preserve.'

Nicholas watches in stunned silence. Can this Cathal Connell, the bringer of presents of jam, be the same Cathal Connell who might – might – have thrown a palsied English apprentice into the sea while he still lived?

'But I've brought you a present more valuable than barberries, Muly Hassan,' Connell continues, glancing at Nicholas. 'This young fellow here is an envoy of Sir Robert Cecil, a minister of our sovereign majesty Elizabeth. He has letters for your prince.'

'Captain Yaxley of the *Marion*, he tells me this,' says Muly Hassan. He makes a small bow to Nicholas. 'The governor of Safi will make audience with you in the *Kechla* very soon. But first we must make honour to His Majesty Ahmad Abu al-Abbas al-Mansur, the Golden, the Conqueror of the Songhai, Commander of the Faithful. This is required on arrival.'

For a moment Nicholas wonders if he is expected to kneel, or make some other formal salute to the sultan. When Elizabeth passes Southwark in her royal barge – on the way to Whitehall or Greenwich – the salute from the riverbank is usually good-natured cheering and ribald shouts that generally echo Farzad's slanders of the Pope and the King of Spain. But what does a freshly minted envoy do when first setting foot onto a foreign shore? Robert Cecil has omitted to tell him. He looks to Connell for a lead.

But Connell is showing no reverence, other than to drop his bill of loading on the table next to the barberry preserve. He unrolls it. Then he and Muly Hassan pore over the neat lines of handwriting that list in detail what is crammed into the hold of the *Righteous*. Every now and then Muly Hassan makes a tick with his quill on the roll, then puts an entry in the small, gold-embossed book on the desk.

The powerful taking their cut, thinks Nicholas as he watches. The Barbary shore, it seems, has more in common with England than he'd imagined.

✠

With the sultan's tithe agreed and recorded, Connell and Nicholas return to the *Righteous*. The six crates of matchlock muskets are already on the quayside. But there seems to be no hurry to remove the rest of the cargo.

'There's no gain to be had by your hanging around here, Dr Shelby,' Connell tells him. 'At the speed these rogues work, it'll be a while before our holds are empty. And my boys will want some time ashore to take their ease. If you catch my drift.'

He puts out a hand for Nicholas to shake.

'You have my gratitude for bringing me to a safe landfall, Captain Connell,' Nicholas says, wondering if this is the same hand that helped roll Edmund Hortop overboard. It feels like he's clutching a knot of rope that's been dredged up from the ocean floor.

'Don't count your chickens,' Connell says with a laugh. 'Give them the chance, and these heathens will cut out your heart and sell it for a treat, long before you reach Marrakech.'

Glad to be away from Connell, if only for a while, Nicholas sets off up the hill towards the *Kechla*, the old Portuguese citadel on its crest. He has not gone far before a young man in a brown *djellaba* falls in beside him, matching his stride with an easy lope. He has a head of tight black curls and the contemplative face of a poet.

'I am Hadir Benhassi,' he says, as though it's a prize he's been awarded. 'Welcome to Safi. Please, tell me, have you been sent here by the Worshipful Company of Barbary in London?'

Nicholas is looking into a pair of eager brown eyes.

'I fear not, Master Benhassi. My name is Nicholas Shelby. I'm a physician. I've been sent by my queen's minister to study physic in your land. How can I be of service to you?'

Is that a flicker of relief Nicholas thinks he sees on Hadir Benhassi's face? If it is, it's gone in an instant. The lad throws up his hands in a gesture of delight, the *djellaba* sliding down his brown arms.

'I have the honour, *Sayidi*, of being the factor of the Barbary Company here in Morocco. I come from Marrakech to see all is well with Captain Conn-ell's cargo. Three days on a *camello*!'

Nicholas searches Benhassi's face for signs of artifice. He finds none. But if this lad really is the Barbary Company's factor, as he claims, then where is Adolfo Sykes? In his thoughts, Nicholas can hear Robert Cecil's voice: *Three Barbary Company ships have returned to England without a single one of Adolfo Sykes's dispatches. I fear some mischief has befallen him...*

'That's an important responsibility, Master Benhassi,' he says cautiously. 'Do you bear it alone?'

'Yes, *Sayidi*. All alone.'

'In Safi?'

'No, *Sayidi*; in our great city of Marrakech.'

If Hadir Benhassi is lying, Nicholas decides, he's more practised at it than his innocent countenance would suggest.

'Are you returning there, Master Benhassi? Because that's where I am bound. I carry a letter from my queen to your sultan.'

Hadir Benhassi's eyes widen in awe. 'Then you are a most important man, Sayidi Nich-less. And in Morocco, all important men must have a secretary. Do you have already a secretary?'

'I do not, Master Hadir,' says Nicholas, understanding at once how this conversation will end. 'But as I have not a single word of your language, I suppose I should hire one. Might you suggest someone?'

I could do worse, he thinks, than keep this engaging young man close. And what better way to learn – with a little careful diplomatic enquiry along the way – what has happened to Adolfo Sykes. They agree on half a ducat a week.

'Because you are an important man, Sayidi Nich-less, you will need the finest *camello* for the journey to Marrakech to see the sultan,' Nicholas's new secretary says as they follow the dusty track towards the *Kechla*, between trees that look to his stranger's eye like giant dandelions. 'I will get you one. Very comfortable. Only eight English pennies.'

'The lad at the quayside was offering a camel for seven,' Nicholas says, instantly wondering why he's being cautious with Robert Cecil's money.

'You can pay him seven if you wish. But I do not recommend it.'

'Why not?'

'They're not his *camellos*.'

Nicholas smiles. He decides he quite likes Hadir Benhassi – whoever he really is.

They are approaching the high sandstone walls of the *Kechla* and a fine arched gateway set between two high towers. In their shade is a small tented encampment, where men with faces as dark and furrowed as a Suffolk field in winter tend herds of grazing goats. The men wear robes dyed as blue as the sky, and their heads are swathed in broadcloth. The women, garlanded in necklaces of polished stones, sit in circles, chattering gaily as they brew some sort of drink in brass urns.

'Tell me, Hadir, how long have you been the Barbary Company's factor?'

'Since the second *Jumada*,' Hadir says. 'Two months.'

'And the previous factor – was he your father?' Nicholas asks, feigning no more than a passing interest.

Hadir's bright face clouds over. 'Sayidi Sy-kess was very good man to me. But he is dead now.'

Nicholas struggles to keep his face from betraying emotion: he doesn't know of Adolfo Sykes. Never heard of him. Wouldn't know the name if it were painted in letters ten feet high.

'Dead? An old man, was he?'

'No, *Sayidi*. My friend Sy-kess was not old. Was an accident. Very unlucky accident.'

21

Bianca sits in the pews at St Saviour's, a mannered look of submissive piety on her face. It is a mask she adopts whenever she visits a Protestant church. The effort costs her less than the fine for non-attendance. She lets Parson Moody's sonorous voice enfold her like an old woollen blanket that's been left out in the rain. Cloying. Musty.

Moody is telling his flock that the Devil has visited the pestilence upon them because of their own sinfulness. She fancies calling out that she knows of a certain house near the Falcon river steps where the bawd keeps a selection of wickedly pliable canes to employ upon the parson's plump buttocks. But she does not. The arrival of the plague is shock enough for Bankside.

It is two weeks now since she awoke to discover she had escaped its black enfolding wings. The entire Willders family is in the cemetery. In the same plot lie daughter Ruth's husband, the glover, and his twin sisters. The landlord of the Walnut Tree on St Olave's Lane is interred nearby, along with several of his customers, including the tanner Jack Prout and all but one of his family – a grandmother. This ancient survivor has become so deranged by what she witnessed in the closed-up plague house, while her kin died around her one by one, that she now visits the graveyard to be closer to them. There she crawls amongst the tombstones, eating handfuls of earth until the churchwarden shoos her away with a broom.

Walter Pemmel is dead, his old man's whining now for ever cut off, after an ill-advised visit to his son on Pepper Alley. The Lazar House behind Bianca's physic garden has been turned over to the confinement of the sick, although she wonders how much more quickly they might expire if they knew what had happened to *her* in that awful place. The bookseller Isaac Bredwell, Ned's former drinking partner, has been carried off by the sickness and now lies at St Saviour's, along with everyone in his lodging house: twelve in all, including two girls aged three and seven and a six-month-old babe. Ned has managed to find in his heart a measure of sadness for Bredwell, who once tried so hard to turn Nicholas against Bianca when he first came to Bankside in the year of his great grief.

Bianca's attendance at church has little to do with gratitude for her survival. It is a matter of practicality. The parish authorities are wary of doing business with anyone who is not a willing member of a congregation, and so she sits in the pews at St Saviour's and listens to the sermons with as much forbearance as she can muster, trusting that God will understand that in a nation of heretic Protestants, the faithful must sometimes do things they would rather not.

Not that her offers of help have been accepted unanimously. More than a few sidemen, vestrymen and wardens have made it clear they believe a woman cannot possibly understand the complex methods by which the pestilence spreads. Nevertheless, her little apothecary shop on Dice Lane has become the place where the banners of defiance still fly, the place on the battlefield where the survivors can regroup and rearm themselves, refusing to countenance defeat. As a consequence, her physic garden is becoming depleted. She often has to borrow Timothy from Rose and send him across the bridge to the merchants' warehouses on Petty Wales near the Tower to buy dried replacements.

On a schedule that she has organized for the parish, squadrons of women sally forth at dawn and dusk to ensure the lanes and alleys are cleaned of waste and detritus. Even Jenny Solver plays her part, though Bianca suspects mostly to enjoy the opportunity to gossip. These parts of Southwark have never been so clean. Doorways are scrubbed with vinegar; those where the plague has visited with quicklime. The open drains are sluiced with river water twice daily. The Mutton Lane shambles is cleared of blood and scraps at noon and again after Evensong. Middens and dunghills are burned, the debris buried. Fires are lit to incinerate old floor-rushes and the corpses of stray dogs. Buffle is not allowed out and must confine herself to the Jackdaw's yard, except when it is dark. And only then in Ned's company.

Yes, Bianca thinks, things have changed a lot in the fortnight since the pestilence brushed against my cheek, looked into my eyes and then swept on. But one thing hasn't changed. And that's her fear: that everything Nicholas told her about why he was going to Morocco was a lie.

When the sermon is over, Bianca returns to her shop to prepare for the expected lunchtime rush. She checks the brimstone sack. It's well over half-full. Unless there's a sudden increase in demand – and pray to God that won't happen – it should last another three days. She counts off the sprigs of dried borage and meadowsweet, and tops up the oxymel with vinegar and honey. She places the filled pots, vials and twists of cloth into their appropriate boxes, and she asks herself once again if there is something she has failed to think of, in the days since she stood before the secretary in the black half-cape and the gartered stockings at Cecil House.

At his invitation, she wrote a letter to the Lord Treasurer's son, pleading with him to dispatch a fast pinnace to snatch Nicholas from Cathal Connell's grasp. She now imagines the letter languishing in a vast mountain of unread correspondence, because she has yet to receive a reply, or even an acknowledgement it's been safely delivered.

From Cecil House she went to Woodroffe Lane, close by Tower Hill. She had hoped Nicholas's friend Lord Lumley might help her. But Lumley had already decamped to Nonsuch Palace.

The next day she struck upon the idea of taking a wherry to Greenwich or Windsor in search of Robert Cecil. She'd been forced to abandon that idea on the realization that the chances of the guards allowing her to set foot on a royal water-stairs were little better than zero.

In the end she decided the best she could do was let Reynard Gault know what sort of monster he'd employed as admiral-general. So, two days later, she walked across the bridge, up Cornhill and on into the Poultry, in the face of a mischievous breeze that had the hem of her kirtle snapping at her ankles, to the Grocers' Company guildhall on Coneyhope Lane. As she feared, he wasn't there, and the bored-looking doorman refused to tell her where he lived.

As a result, she has spent the days since torturing herself, imagining the very worst of fates for Nicholas. And she holds herself thoroughly to blame.

If I'd known he'd gone to the Barbary shore only to save my apothecary's licence, I'd never have been so abrupt with him, Bianca has told herself on more occasions than she can be bothered to count. We could have come up with an alternative. We could have found a way. But in her heart, she knows that with Robert Cecil, there is no other way.

So it is hardly surprising that it takes all her efforts to remain composed when Reynard Gault, leading member of the Grocers'

Guild and the Barbary Company, walks into her shop with all the insouciance of a tourist from north of the bridge.

✠

'I am inclined to say "God give you good morrow", Mistress Merton,' he says, striking a pose that she suspects is designed to flatter his profile. 'But in these present days perhaps a man shouldn't tempt fate.'

'I'm not at all sure how to take that, Sir Reynard,' Bianca says. She runs a hand through her hair, thinking she must look like a scarecrow in a gale. 'What brings you to Bankside? Are you still searching for charlatans?'

He smiles. A pleasing smile – much to her alarm. 'I've been taking soundings, Mistress Merton. I hear you have become Bankside's bastion against the pestilence. An effective bastion, apparently.'

'I do what I can, sir. It is but little.'

Why is he regarding me with that surprised smile? Bianca wonders. It's as though he's just spotted a bright flower in a bed of weeds and can't decide whether to leave it to flourish or cut it off at the stem and pin it to his expensive velvet doublet.

'They say you had it – the plague.'

'Who says so?'

'People,' he tells her coyly. 'Apparently you worked some magic of physic. And then it was gone.'

They say you can change shape. They say you can drink poison and feel no ill. They say you had the plague and cured yourself. They say you're the one witch nobody dares hang. She's heard them all before.

'I fear I must disappoint you, Master Gault. It was an ague. Nothing more.'

In an instant his handsome face goes from smiling to stern. 'Then to pretend otherwise is a felony. You could lose your licence; even face imprisonment.'

'I haven't *pretended* anything. This is Bankside – tall tales bloom faster than chickweed here. I had an ague.'

'So you claim,' he says, relenting a little. She suspects he has difficulty in holding his certainties up to scrutiny. He seems to her the sort of man who cannot possibly come to any conclusion but the right one. 'How is it that a woman as young as yourself knows so much about precautions against pestilence?' he asks. 'London has not seen it in any great measure for ten years.'

'I was born in Padua, to a mother skilled in matters of natural physic. A great plague came when I was eight. They say we lost some twenty thousand souls across the Veneto. We learned quickly.'

An eyebrow lifts in estimation. 'Then Bankside is indeed fortunate to have you.'

'And here I shall stay, Master Gault. Unlike *some* of my betters, who seem to prefer flight to duty.' She gives him a direct look. 'Are you about to flee the city? I confess I thought you already had.'

'I was in Bristol, Mistress Merton, on a matter of commerce. When I returned, I heard you had come to the Grocers' guildhall asking for me. So, here I am.'

'You ventured into Southwark merely to discover what it was that I wanted? Not to revoke my licence?'

'Why should I wish to revoke your licence, Mistress Merton, when you appear to be bringing credit to the calling of apothecary?' Gault gives her a glass smile that she can see clean through. 'I came because I wanted to speak to you about your preventatives against the pestilence. I may have need of your skills.'

'Have you no apothecaries in your own ward, Master Gault?'

'In Farringdon Without the Wall? Barely a single one who knows a clyster from a compress. Certainly none so comely.'

'You should see me after I've been ladling brimstone, Master Gault.' She shakes her head. 'I'm sorry, but I am a little busy at present to traipse all over the city.'

'Not so busy that you couldn't find time to walk all the way to Coneyhope Lane to enquire after me at the guildhall. Perhaps we should reach an accommodation.'

'I could consider it, I suppose,' she says, admitting to herself that she's always known Gault would give her nothing without expecting payment of some sort.

'Good. I knew you'd see sense. Now, what was it that brought you in search of me?'

Bianca takes a deep breath. 'Cathal Connell – how did he come to the Company's attention?'

His head tilts as he tries to fathom her reason for asking. 'Connell? I engaged him. Good shipmasters are hard to find.'

It's not *quite* an answer. 'Do you know of his past?'

'Of course. I would not engage a man without knowing his reputation. Captain Connell spent some five years voyaging into the seas of Arabia and along the coast of Dalmatia.'

'And his cargoes?'

'All the worthy commodities: sugar... spice... salt...'

'Did you know he also traded in God's own creation?' she asks, her eyes darkening.

'What do you mean?'

'I mean *people*, Master Gault. Human beings. *Slaves.*'

Gault makes a fussy little gesture that speaks of trifles and trivialities. 'The Barbary Company does not trade in slaves, Mistress Merton. In the queen's realm we do not take away another man's freedom, unless her law demands it.'

'I'm not speaking of England. This was during his voyages around Arabia.'

He laughs. 'Are they right about your second sight? Does it let you see as far as Arabia?'

She's known she would have to answer a question like this since she first thought of approaching him. To protect Farzad, she says, 'You forget that I am the owner of the Jackdaw tavern, Master Gault. You can overhear a lot in a tavern. And Captain Connell's crew did enjoy their ale.'

Gault answers with a pout that sours his otherwise pleasing features. 'What Master Connell did, or did not do, when he was in heathen waters is of no concern to the Barbary Company, Mistress. It has no bearing upon his present engagement.'

'A friend of mine has sailed with Connell. Given the captain's past, I'm concerned for him.'

Gault gives her a blank look. 'A friend?'

'Dr Nicholas Shelby.'

'Oh, the fellow Robert Cecil sought passage for.' A glint of comprehension in his eyes. 'I see it now – *he* was the fellow Sir Robert told me petitioned for the grant of your licence.'

'Through Lord Lumley, yes. But now he's gone to the Barbary shore to find out how the Moors practise their physic. He seems to think it will advance his position in the College of Physicians.' The words come so easily to her that she can almost convince herself she believes them, if she wasn't so sure there was another reason behind Nicholas's departure.

'And as a friend, you fear for his safety upon the wild ocean. That's quite understandable.'

'It's not the ocean that worries me, Master Gault, it's the man he's gone with. I would not wish Nicholas in the hands of someone who traffics in human souls. And *certainly* not someone who might have committed murder.'

She watches those unwavering eyes for a flicker of reaction. None comes. Just a laconic 'Murder? That's some charge. Of *whom*, pray?'

'Of Solomon Mandel. A Jew. He was killed near here, shortly before Connell sailed.'

A lazy shake of his head. A forelock falls teasingly over one eye. Gault brushes it aside. 'I fear the name is unknown to me, Mistress. Is there evidence to back your charge?'

She picks up a sprig of hyssop and begins paring leaves into a mortar with a knife, so that she doesn't have to answer. Seeing her hesitate, Gault says, 'Then we must consider him an innocent man.'

'But I'm worried about Nicholas. I had hoped you might somehow be able to... to—' She stops and lets the knife fall to the table. 'I don't know *what* I thought,' she says, her eyes fixed on the hyssop sprig.

For a moment she thinks he's going to reach out and caress her cheek, as though she's a child who needs comforting. She flinches in anticipation. But the touch does not come.

'Be of good cheer, Mistress Merton,' he says brightly. 'I am able to set your mind at rest. Before the *Righteous* sailed, I charged Captain Connell to take all care in the preservation of Dr Shelby's comfort. I told him I would be accountable to Sir Robert Cecil if he did not. Does *that* content your fear?'

And to some measure it does. But as Bianca watches Gault's departing figure through the window of her shop, another fear arrives to take its place.

It is born of a recollection that has just this moment come to her – a recollection of something Nicholas had told her before he left. He'd been describing a conversation in a carriage after a rainstorm, a conversation with the queen's physician, Dr Lopez.

'I told him about the entry I'd seen in the subsidy roll at St Saviour's: *Solomon Mandel, Hebrew; worth assessed at 100 crowns... spice merchant...the Turk's man,*' she can hear him saying now.

And she remembers clearly Nicholas's recounting of Lopez's reply: how the queen's doctor had confirmed that Mandel had been both agent and translator for the Moroccan envoy who had come to London in '89 to such public acclaim.

Which makes her question how it could possibly be that Reynard Gault, an upstanding member of the selfsame guild that had honoured the Moors with an escort of their leading merchants, could possibly pretend he'd never heard the name of Solomon Mandel.

22

It is the first night after leaving Safi, and they have reached a small mud-walled caravanserai set down in a cedar grove.

'We rest here, because robbers haunt the road at night, Sayidi Nich-less,' Hadir explains. 'Very bad men. Will cut your throat and carry away your cargo.' He nods in the direction of an ancient, stick-thin white-robed man of questionable vitality, whose face seems to have been constructed from random strips of very dark clay. The fellow had appeared that morning when the small caravan of six camels had set off from the quayside, bearing the first of the cargo. 'This is why we have Izîl and his musket,' Hadir says.

Izîl grins toothlessly at Nicholas, while brandishing a matchlock firing piece that looks as old as its owner.

'Izîl take this musket in battle with famous Castilian knight,' Hadir explains, 'when we slaughtered the Portugals at Ksar el-Kébir. The Christians' shot could not touch him. Was great miracle.'

Nicholas considers the chances being somewhat slim of Izîl being any more accurate with the matchlock than the Castilian he took it from. But he reckons some protection is better than none.

The camels are unloaded, fed and hobbled. Water is drawn from a well inside the caravanserai and a fire of cedar branches lit. While Nicholas watches the flames take hold, he hears the sound of what he takes to be foxes crying plaintively in the night.

Within minutes, showers of fiery sparks are leaping into the darkness, while shadows race across the inner walls of the compound as the cameleers dance gleefully to the beat of a small tambour. Great clouds of aromatic white smoke rise into the dusk, a signal to every robber and bandit within twenty miles. But the roasted goat's meat is like ambrosia after almost three weeks of eating ship's provisions.

Through Hadir, Nicholas swiftly establishes that the men of this caravan, carrying bolts of fine English cloth towards their sultan's city, have not the slightest notion of where England is. One says it is on the other side of the world, past even distant Cathay. Another confidently asserts it is a land made entirely out of ships, and that the argosies moored in Safi bay are little fragments of it that broke off and went drifting around the world on the ocean currents. The greatest astonishment is saved for when Hadir tells them England is ruled by a queen.

'It's true,' Nicholas says. 'And before her, another queen. Before Elizabeth, Mary.'

At this, there is a deal of serious discussion that he cannot follow. But it seems grave. Every now and then a glance is cast in his direction.

'They want to know if you're a eunuch,' Hadir explains. 'Only eunuchs permit themselves to be ruled by women.'

'Not when last I looked,' Nicholas replies.

Hadir's translation causes an outbreak of joyous ribaldry.

'Where did you learn your English, Hadir?' Nicholas asks between mouthfuls. 'It's good.'

'I learn from my friend Sayidi Sy-kess,' Hadir says. 'He teach me well, yes?'

'Very well. Did he teach you so that you could become his apprentice?'

A flicker of guilt clouds Hadir's eyes. He appears to have a sudden need to study the fingers of his right hand. Nicholas laughs in admiration, as the realization dawns. 'You came to Safi on your own, didn't you? You came to see if you could make your own way as a merchant. That's why you looked relieved when I said I was a physician and not the Barbary Company's replacement factor.'

'I am an honest man, Sayidi Nich-less,' Hadir insists almost plaintively. 'Very honest. I do not steal from anyone. Is against all teaching – even to steal from an infidel.'

'It will be our secret. On one condition.'

Hadir spits a fragment of gristle onto the dark earth. 'Name it, Master Nich-less?'

'You tell me how Adolfo Sykes died.'

At first Hadir says nothing. He stares into the fire until Nicholas convinces himself he does not intend to answer. Then he begins to draw patterns in the dirt with the end of a lamb bone.

'It was after al-'isha prayers, early in Jumada al-Thani – March. I go to his house on the Street of the Weavers as usual. But he is not there. I look everywhere for him. I do not find him.' Hadir raises his hands in supplication to show how diligently he'd searched. In the firelight, Nicholas can see grief written plainly on his face. 'Next morning I hear from a Jewish merchant that the body of Sayidi Sy-kess is found outside the city walls. I run to see. The guard at the Bab Doukkala tells me he must have fallen and smash his head.'

'You saw Master Sykes's body yourself, as it was brought in?'

The gentle face tautens as the mind remembers. 'No man deserves to be food for beasts, Sayidi Nich-less. Not even an infidel.'

'What do you mean, "food for beasts"?'

'Leopards and jackals, Sayidi Nich-less. They don't come close to the walls these days. But perhaps they knew my friend was an infidel, so then they come. I pray to Allāh, the most merciful, the most compassionate, that my friend was already dead when this happen.'

'When *what* happened, Hadir?' Nicholas asks, though somehow he already knows what the young lad is going to tell him.

Hadir seems unable, or perhaps unwilling, to find the English for what he wants to say. But the awful picture is clear in Nicholas's mind as the Moor's fingers make a clawing motion against his own body, like a predator raking a carcass. Or perhaps, as in the case of Solomon Mandel, someone cutting the flesh from a man's chest, in case the secret he was carrying was somehow buried under the skin.

Later in the night, when the others have fallen asleep, Nicholas stares up at the great cascade of stars above his head and recites his thoughts like a man reading a book written in a language not his own, cautiously testing them to avoid mistranslation.

A Jew in Christian London who keeps his faith a secret.

A Christian who keeps a secret watch over Marrakech.

And nothing to bind them together in death, save the apparent similarity of their wounds.

And an Irish sea-venturer named Cathal Connell who thinks nothing of pitching a still-living soul into the depths of the ocean.

And Robert Cecil, who would not rest until Nicholas had agreed to come here.

23

There is a sense of quiet expectation amongst the little caravan now. Yesterday, after the pre-dawn prayers, there had been only the promise of more tedious miles to cover. More discomfort. Another night on the hard floor of a caravanserai. But now, in the sharp light of early morning three days after leaving Safi, Nicholas can detect a renewed purpose. The most taciturn of faces have begun to smile. Even old Izîl, his ancient matchlock musket slung across his back, has found a new animation. He keeps grinning at Nicholas through the toothless cavern of his mouth. Today, inshā Allāh – a phrase Nicholas has heard frequently since leaving Safi, and without which it appears nothing may be imagined or hoped for – they will reach Marrakech.

The road is little more than a narrow track scoured into the dust. It winds through orchards of citrus trees, crosses rivers that died of thirst long ago, loops around ragged hills with crests like shattered flint. It rises over gritty dunes and plunges down wind-swept inclines beneath the bluest sky Nicholas has ever seen. Hadir has given him a cloth turban to wind about his head to keep the sun at bay and the dust out of his mouth.

Several times during the journey Nicholas has feared that the caravan has wandered off the track. But Berber guides don't lose their way, Hadir has assured him; they have been travelling the road from Safi to Marrakech for a thousand years. Nicholas wonders if any of them ever managed to get comfortable on a camel.

He has often caught himself glancing down at the travelling chest slung from the saddle of his camel, as though the letters Robert Cecil has entrusted to him might be conspiring to burst out and fly away on the warm wind, a wind that now carries the scent of oranges on it. He can hear Robert Cecil preparing his reluctant agent for the journey: *One of the sultan's close advisors is benefactor to a hospital in the city...*

As they ride together, Nicholas asks Hadir if he's heard of Sumayl al-Seddik, the man he has come so far to meet. Hadir glances across from his swaying saddle as though he suspects Nicholas of performing magic. 'Sumayl al-Seddik is famous in England, too?'

'No, not famous. But he came to England with your sultan's envoy a few years ago. I bear a letter to him, from our queen's Lord Treasurer, Lord Burghley. It is Burghley's son who sent me here.'

Nicholas can see the calculation in Hadir's eyes. It is not greed. It is not even particularly mercenary. It is simply the look of a young man who's trying to make his way in a hostile world and has just found his companion to be particularly well connected.

'Sumayl al-Seddik is most famous,' he announces proudly. 'He makes much *al-waqf*. You have *al-waqf* in England?'

'You'll have to tell me what it is, before I can answer that.'

'It is how a rich man may be judged mercifully when he stands before Allāh. He must give a part of his treasure to fund hospitals, schools, rest-houses for pilgrims, even *sabils* – our public fountains. When I am a rich merchant, I shall give much *al-waqf*.'

'He sounds to me like a good man. Apparently Lord Burghley thought so.'

228

'Everyone knows of Sumayl al-Seddik. He was at the Battle of Ksar el-Kébir – where Izîl won his firing-piece from the Castilians – fighting against His Majesty's brother, Abd al-Malik, may Allāh rest his soul in heaven.'

'*Against?* You mean al-Seddik was an enemy of the present sultan and his brother?'

'Was fifteen years ago, when Abd al-Malik was our caliph. He had overthrown the caliph who came before him – the dog Muly Mohammed. But the dog made a pact with the infidel Portugals. Together they raised a great army to make a gift of Morocco to the Spanish infidel king.' Hadir glances up into the bright-blue vault of the sky. 'But Allāh willed that the plotters should be cast down. He gave al-Malik a great victory, and Izîl his musket.'

'So the present sultan's brother won.'

'In a great slaughter, Sayidi Nich-less. The Portugal king... the deposed dog Muly Mohammed... all their warriors – all dead.' He gives Nicholas a superior look. 'No woman queen of England could make such a victory, yes?'

'I wouldn't wager on it, Hadir. Our queen's navy has already seen off one attempt to land a Spanish army. And she's not shy with the axe, either – she's already had her cousin beheaded.'

Hadir seems unimpressed. 'Was great victory. But next day al-Malik, he dies also. So then his brother – al-Abbas al-Mansur – becomes *sharif*. Then al-Seddik comes on his knees to al-Mansur and begs forgiveness. His Majesty shows mercy, and now al-Seddik loves him like a brother.'

'Then he's a most fortunate man, this al-Seddik.'

Hadir nods vigorously. 'Most fortunate. Sometimes a new sultan will punish his enemies after a battle. Sometimes he will command that their skin shall be flayed from their living bodies.'

Nicholas wonders grimly if enemies include spies and old Jews.

'How did the present sultan's brother come to die?' he asks. 'Was he wounded in this great battle that he won?'

'No, *Sayidi*. He died of sickness. This is why His Majesty looks with kindness upon al-Seddik – because of *al-waqf*. Al-Seddik gives much gold to the hospital in Marrakech. Also he brings the great Day-Lyal into the city. Day-Lyal is the only infidel physician permitted to attend the sultan.'

Hadir's words strike Nicholas like a bad note played in a sweet tune. 'Day-Lyal is a *Christian*?'

'He is famous throughout our city – he speaks our language, which is most unusual. He is a Frank.'

By Frank, Nicholas presumes Hadir means French. In his mind, Day-Lyal becomes de Lisle. He wonders if Robert Cecil knows the Catholic French have put a man in such a sensitive position in the sultan's court.

'Does English queen permit infidels to attend her?' Hadir asks with a little shudder of disgust.

'She has no Moor physician, if that's what you mean. She has a Jew, but he's been forced to renounce his faith,' Nicholas says, without adding, *And if Robert Cecil is right, he's living on borrowed time.*

Hadir lets out a little bark of contempt. 'The Spanish king must be very weak man to have English woman queen sink his ships and scatter his armies.'

You sound just like Farzad, thinks Nicholas fondly. He laughs. 'We haven't scattered his armies quite yet, Master Hadir. Though we did scatter his fleet when it came against us.'

Hadir poses another of his many questions on the mysterious place Nicholas has come from, and its even more unfathomable ruler.

'Will your queen's sons not turn her out of her palace when they become men?' he asks.

'She has no sons, Master Hadir. She is unwed.'

'Then she is very ugly, yes?'

Nicholas fights back a grin. 'Not at all, Hadir. We call her Gloriana. But she has chosen to remain unmarried.'

'How can she choose this? Why does her father not find her a man?'

Nicholas shakes his head in amusement. 'She's the queen, that's how. And anyway, her father is dead. She inherited the crown from her half-sister.'

'Are *all* English men made like dogs, to cower under a mistress's lash?' asks Hadir, astounded.

'We like to think not. But we suspect she has other ideas.'

'Why do her ministers not find her a husband, or are they all women, too?'

'Believe me, Hadir, they've tried.'

Hadir expels a grunt of bemusement. 'England is a strange place,' he says, a trace of pity in his voice. 'No wonder my friend Sy-kess choose to live here, amongst men.'

And look where it got him, thinks Nicholas as the two men lapse into silence.

The track falls away from a ridgeline towards a sprawling riverbed. Rills of brown water meander between shale and scrub. A long, undulating cry from somewhere behind the caravan sends a heard of goats pelting across their path. Hadir brings his camel to a halt. Nicholas's mount stops, too, though by its own volition rather than by any conscious effort of his. He looks out across the dried-up watercourse.

'Welcome to Marrakech, Sayidi Nich-less,' says Hadir, with the pride of a man returning to the place he loves. 'In the language of the Berbers it is called "The City of God".'

But Nicholas is too consumed by what he is seeing to reply. Cast across the horizon before him lies a pale-red curtain of city walls, shimmering in the heat, towered and turreted, the battlements standing like teeth about to bite the snowy white flesh of the distant Atlas Mountains beyond.

24

The pestilence has returned with a vengeance. The Savoy hospital has closed its doors to new patients, and posted guards on the water-stairs to deter visitors. The chapel's death-bell tolls with increasing frequency. On 28th May, the very day Nicholas reaches Marrakech, the Privy Council – at the queen's insistence – adjourns Trinity term for Parliament and the law courts. Elizabeth has already made it known she intends to retire to Windsor. The exodus foretold by Robert Cecil is in progress. Those who have homes in the country or relatives in distant towns are shutting their doors and departing, either taking their belongings or entrusting them to watchmen and retainers who, quite frankly, would rather be elsewhere. In Southwark, few have such luxury.

When Bianca visits the Jackdaw that afternoon – at about the time Nicholas stands before the walls of Marrakech – she is unequivocal.

'You must go,' she tells Ned and Rose sternly. 'I think we're surviving on borrowed time.' She asks Ned if he still has Nicholas's letter to Lord Lumley. When he says yes, she tells him, 'Take Rose, Timothy and Farzad and go straightway to Nonsuch. You'll be safe there.'

The answer she receives is not what she's expecting. Heads drop. Feet shuffle. All four fidget like scolded children. Refusing a direct instruction from Bianca Merton is not something any of them have ever contemplated before.

Ned speaks for all. 'No, Mistress. We shall not go away. We shall stay here – with you.'

The amber eyes flash a warning. 'What do you mean, *no*?'

It is an odd confrontation: the slender young woman with the olive skin, her feet slightly apart and her chin tilted defiantly, staring down the auburn giant whose frown has been known to clear a tavern's taproom in an instant. In other times, Ned would have the odds stacked overwhelmingly against him. But now he has Rose to make up for his shortcomings.

'I've told my husband my mind, Mistress,' she says boldly. 'We's spoken on the matter at length. If you're staying, *we's* staying.'

If the Earl of Essex had just told the queen he couldn't be arsed to flatter her any more, the silence that follows could not be frostier.

'And so are we,' squeaks Timothy in an unheard-of display of defiance. 'Aren't we, Farzad?'

'Pestilence is nothing to fear,' Farzad says portentously. 'I fear the Pope's farts more.'

Bianca grimaces. She still cannot quite get used to Farzad's casual blasphemies. She takes a deep breath. 'If I'd been master of the ship that saved you, Farzad, I'd have taught you a little more piety. As it is, haven't you and Timothy got a few more hours of unpaid labour to offer Rose, in exchange for all the food you smuggled?'

'We're *not* leaving you, Mistress,' Ned says bluntly. 'Cast a spell on us if you want. Curse us, in that Eye-tallien you speak. But we've made up our minds. We're staying. Aren't we, Wife?'

'Yes, we is, Husband,' says Rose with a defiant shake of her black curls.

And with that, Ned produces Nicholas's letter to John Lumley from his jerkin – where he's stowed it in expectation of this very moment – and tears it into quarters. 'There, Mistress,' he says. 'Have we settled the matter?'

✠

Bianca's face remains constrained until she has left the Jackdaw. When she knows no one can see her from the tavern windows, she allows the tears that have been welling in her eyes to trickle down her cheeks. No one she passes takes any notice. Tears are commonplace on Bankside now.

As she walks back to Dice Lane, she wonders how long the pestilence can be kept at bay. Yes, the open drains are free from human soil and smelling more tolerable than they have been since she arrived; middens and cess-pits no longer foul the air; and only the vaguest scent of butchered meat hangs over the Mutton Lane shambles. But how long can the defences hold? She wonders why the city across the river has not been as diligent. Then she remembers what Nicholas had told her about physicians: how you could put ten of them around a patient's bed and come up with twelve different diagnoses, and the patient would probably be dead by the time they stopped arguing. Thinking of him now turns her mind to the letter she wrote to him when she believed she was infected and dying. Never in her life before had she committed such intimate thoughts to paper, made them real, given them a weight that her fingertips still remember.

She tries to imagine where he is now, but whenever she pictures him, it is always in the shadow of the cruellest man in the world. All she has to comfort her is Gault's promise that he'd warned Connell to take good care of his passenger. But now she knows Gault has lied to her about Solomon Mandel, she doesn't trust *him* much more than she trusts that Aži Dahāka in human form.

And there are plenty of other fears to torment her – fears that have sprouted like weeds from the fertile soil of her childhood imagination, from the moment Nicholas told her he was leaving.

In Padua she had often seen merchants and sailors from Araby, dark-skinned, saturnine men who wore clothes unlike any Italian and seemed to have been forged out of the very sand and rocks of their distant, arid deserts. When she was young they had frightened her. She had ducked behind her mother's skirts whenever they'd looked at her. This was because she'd heard the tales of how the Turk corsairs raided coastal villages in Sicily and around the Ionian Sea, carrying off men, women – even children like her – to a life of slavery in their galleys or their harems. It had taken all her father's efforts to assure her they wouldn't bother to march all the way inland to Padua. Even then, she'd refused to go to bed unless she could take a small kitchen knife to place beside her pillow, next to her favourite cloth doll, Caterina. If a Turk should unexpectedly burst in, she had decided to sell both the doll and herself dearly. No amount of persuasion by her mother could encourage her to leave the blade in the kitchen. It was only on her ninth birthday that she relented, when news arrived of the smashing of the Ottoman fleet at Lepanto by galleys of the Italian and Spanish Holy League. Then, with the solemnity of a general bringing home a sacred trophy that had cost much brave blood, she'd returned it to the kitchen, cutting a finger in the process and earning a weary rebuke from her mother: 'Now do you see where the greater danger lay?'

The greater danger.

That must have been how Nicholas had seen the choice Robert Cecil offered him, she thinks: face God-only-knows what dangers in the land of the Moor or see the Grocers' Guild revoke a certain person's apothecary licence. So, to protect her, he had chosen to put himself in the care of the cruellest man on earth and set off for a land where – or so she imagines – sleeping with a knife beside your pillow is probably the very least of the precautions you ought to be taking.

Her mood swings violently between loving Nicholas for the way he wanted to save her from hurt, and hot anger that he'd allowed himself to become a pawn in Robert Cecil's machinations. And on each swing, the pendulum bumps against her guilt at sending him on his way with a cold face and an unforgiving heart.

When she arrives in Dice Lane, she sees a small crowd waiting outside her shop. Even Jenny Solver is there, beaming all over each of her two faces, pretending that only days ago she hadn't fled in such haste that anyone would think she'd discovered the Devil serving behind the counter. Bianca wonders how she'll get all the balms, tinctures and distillations finished before nightfall, because they'll all want to gossip.

She reminds herself she's almost out of brimstone. She'll have to go across the river to Petty Wales soon, to an Italian Lutheran merchant she knows there, who imports it from Sicily via her cousin Bruno in Padua. In return for Bianca paying a good price, the merchant sends her letters to Bruno along with his orders. Thus she receives news of old friends, like Cardinal Fiorzi – currently enjoying a serene retirement with Mercy Havington. She knows, for instance, that Samuel – Mercy's grandson – has made a name for himself as a gardener in the cardinal's estate, that his falling sickness has abated and that he is to marry a sweet maid named Alessandra.

As Bianca reaches her door, a young lad pushes forward, drawing angry looks from the waiting customers. Simply dressed in woollen hose, jerkin and apprentice's cap, he seems to think himself more important than he has a right to. 'What's the matter with *you*?' Jenny Solver asks petulantly. 'Wait your turn, like the rest of us.'

Ignoring her, he presses a folded paper into Bianca's hand and disappears in the direction of the bridge.

It is only when she has closed the shop again – an hour after nightfall, when the last customer has been served – that Bianca has the opportunity to study the message.

She'd assumed it was a prescription, perhaps from one of the barber-surgeons at St Thomas's hospital for the poor. But it isn't. It's a letter from Reynard Gault, written in a sweeping hand as ostentatious as the man himself – so much so that the lines have to curve downwards at the end to prevent themselves tumbling off the page:

> To Mistress Merton, my greetings and most respectful compliments. Mindful of your undoubted skill at physic, coupled with the mercy Almighty God has shown unto you of late, I desire you to repair to my house on Giltspur Street at Smithfield, at your earliest convenience. I find myself in need of your competence, to protect myself and my interests from this present dreadful winnowing. In addition, I have a confidence to impart that may be advantageous to you.
> Your True Friend whilst I breathe,
> Rynd Gault

She reads it three times, gaining much pleasure from the fact that the popinjay who'd had the gall to imply to her face that she was a charlatan now has need of her. But when she lays the letter aside, she's still none the wiser. What confidence could he possibly have to share with her that would be to her advantage?

Unless, of course, he knows more about why Robert Cecil sent Nicholas to Morocco than he's admitting.

Or he's suddenly and uncharacteristically found the need to unburden himself of the sin of lying – about knowing Solomon Mandel.

25

The Bab Doukkala. Hadir gives Nicholas the name so quickly he can barely catch it.

It is unlike any city gate he has ever seen: a concentric nest of archways decorated in arabesque carvings and tiled in vivid colours: blues as brilliant as the sky and yellows as fiery as the sun, interlaced with weaving threads of silver. On either side, two forbidding towers of red mortar command the approach. From the battlements, bored sentries look down upon a throng of trades-men, farmers, potters, weavers, spice merchants, all touting for business as vocally as any at St Saviour's market on Bankside.

Bringing the camels to a halt, Hadir calls a friendly greeting to a guard in a chainmail apron and a conical helmet wrapped in white cloth, who shelters from the sun in the shadow of the gateway. He has a wickedly curving scimitar at his belt, and a matchlock considerably newer than Izîl's over his shoulder. The two exchange what Nicholas takes to be pleasantries, delivered at the same impenetrable speed. As Hadir speaks, the guard studies Nicholas in frank disbelief. Then he shrugs, dispatches a boy squatting in the shade of the left-hand tower to carry the news of their arrival to some destination unknown and, with a private joke to Hadir and a final shake of his head, nods them on their way into the city.

'He said England must be a poor land if their envoys look so unremarkable,' Hadir tells Nicholas cheerfully. 'When the sultan sends an ambassador, he sends him robed in silk and bedecked with jewels, bearing a whole caravan of gifts.'

Nicholas gives Hadir a tight smile to show he's not offended. 'My queen would rather spend her coin on fighting enemies,' he says, in what he hopes is a suitably imperial tone. 'And if there's any flattery to be dealt, she prefers it to be imported.'

In a garden shaded by the towering red city walls the camels fold themselves onto their knees like discarded empty wineskins. As his mount sinks beneath him, Nicholas tries to remember what he's learned in the past three days. Hadir has told him that Christians are only allowed into the city by the express permission of Sultan al-Mansur; they must live together in a quarter named the Aduana; the Jews reside in the el-Mellah district to the east of the sultan's great palace, where they help the cogs of trade between Christian and Moor turn with as little friction as possible; and each community is allowed to practise its own faith and custom in peace. But Hadir has not managed to teach Nicholas how to dismount from a camel with any semblance of dignity.

As if to rub salt in the wound, he spots in the corner of the garden a clutch of women regarding him with amused interest. They are clad in brightly dyed gowns and headdresses adorned with long ribbons studded with metal discs that flare in the sunlight. One of them, younger than the others, stabs an elbow into a neighbour's side and the two women laugh conspiratorially. It makes him think of how Bianca and Rose like to prick his occasional lapses into pomposity.

He makes the best fist of it that he can, trying not to wince as the muscles in his thighs protest when he swings his right leg over the pommel and slides off like someone slipping down a muddy bank.

A man of Izîl's age appears, armed not with an ancient matchlock but a round silver tray, on which stands an array of glass cups and a jug with an intricately etched lid. He lifts the jug and, from shoulder-height, pours a stream of dark liquid into the cups without splashing a drop.

'It is *atay*,' Hadir tells him. 'The leaves come from China. The sugar and the mint are ours. The result is from heaven.' He lifts his glass. 'You must drink thrice while the leaves brew. The first drink will be as sweet as life. The second as strong as love. And the third as bitter as death. Is custom!'

Grateful to have his thirst quenched, Nicholas drinks. The *atay* is sweet and fragrant. Piping hot and deliciously refreshing, it has the aromatic tang of mint.

Over the rim of his cup, he sees Hadir watching him. His expression keeps shifting between pride and expectation. But the eyes, wide and brown, brim with a hope forged in the furnace of disappointment.

'What is it, Hadir? Is something wrong?'

Hadir shuffles on his haunches. 'Is a long way from Safi to Marrakech,' he says, as though the thought has only this minute occurred to him.

'Yes, I'm glad it's over.'

'And the road is dangerous. Many bandits.'

'Yes. I'm glad we had Izîl and his musket.'

'Izîl's musket very powerful. He makes good black powder with best saltpetre. Kill all bandits.' He makes an explosive puff with both mouth and hand.

'Thanks be to God, he didn't need to,' Nicholas says.

Hadir suddenly looks very serious. 'But saltpetre very costly. Izîl has wife and five children.'

Even in the heat, Nicholas feels his cheeks bloom with embarrassment. 'Of course. I understand.'

He crosses to where his camel is resting, its mobile mouth munching on the sparse vegetation. Unlocking his travelling chest, he takes out a ducat from the Portuguese coins Cecil has provided and returns to Hadir. The lad has watched his every move, but his feigned astonishment would put to shame the best of actors at the Rose theatre of Bankside. You're well on your way to becoming a seasoned merchant, thinks Nicholas with a smile.

After that, it is simply a matter of waiting while a succession of officials appears, each apparently more important that the last, judging by the volume of the shouts they hurl at their growing number of attendants. It is only when a man in a white turban, which shrouds his face and hangs in plush folds around his neck, arrives that the mood in the garden changes. The dispenser of *atay* disappears, along with the women. And this time there is no shouting. Nicholas notices Hadir's hands are trembling. The lad seems about to drop to his knees in supplication. Nicholas wonders if protocol requires him to follow. But the man reaches out and stops Hadir with the gentlest of touches on the left shoulder.

He is clearly a man of great importance, though simply dressed in a white silk robe with a narrow jewelled sash across the breast. Nicholas guesses he is in his middle thirties. The well-barbered black beard lies against the gleaming drape of the turban like dried blood splashed over white marble. He carries himself with an almost feminine grace. His dark eyes are quick and perceptive, the brows jet-black and gracefully arched. The face, sundered by a long curving nose, could almost be tyrannical, were it not for a mouth that seems ever about to break into an indulgent smile. The man addresses Nicholas directly: in Italian.

Caught off-guard, Nicholas confirms that he is indeed the envoy sent by Minister Cecil. But his own Italian – learned mostly from Lutheran mercenaries in the Low Countries, the rest from Bianca, and none of it diplomatic – is soon exhausted.

Rolling his dark eyebrows at Nicholas's discomfort, the man tries Spanish. Nicholas grimaces apologetically.

Giving up, the newcomer fires a stream of instructions to the quaking Hadir. A single snap of his fingers brings forth a scurrying minion bearing a heavy key a foot long. This is solemnly entrusted to Hadir as if it were part of the crown jewels. Then, his astute eyes lingering for a final – and clearly disappointed – appraisal of the newly arrived English envoy, the man in white shakes his head in disbelief and departs, his silent attendants gliding away in his wake. Hadir watches him go like someone who's just had a close shave with death.

'I have seen him, but never do I speak with him,' he whispers, clearly in awe.

'Were we in the presence of Sultan al-Mansur?' Nicholas asks.

He might as well have asked if they'd just been visited by the Holy Roman Emperor, given the laugh his question elicits from Hadir. 'No, Sayidi Nich-less. The sultan would not leave his cushions to greet an infidel!'

'Then who was that?' Nicholas asks, wondering if it is the fate of all envoys to be insulted by their hosts.

'That was His Excellency Muhammed al-Annuri, the sharif's most trusted minister.'

Cold bugger, Nicholas can hear Cathal Connell saying. Eyes like a peregrine's. Not the sort of Moor you'd care to cross.

'Did he know who I was?'

'Of course. The governor of Safi sends a message ahead.'

'And the key?'

'His Excellency says I am to take you to the same house the sultan gives to my friend Sy-kess. I am to see you well lodged there. Then, when the sultan wishes to see the letters you bring from the England queen, he will send word for you. That is good, yes?'

'How long do you think I'll have to wait?'

Hadir shrugs. 'His Excellency al-Annuri does not tell Hadir. Hadir is less than the dust on his sandal. He will send word when the sultan is ready.'

'In that case, once I've had the opportunity to sleep a while, I would ask a favour of you, Hadir.'

'You have but to name it, Sayidi Nich-less, and it will be done – inshā Allāh.'

'I would like to visit Master Sykes's grave. Is that possible?'

A happy grin, but a hesitation nonetheless. Slight, but noticeable. 'Is easy, Sayidi Nich-less. Is in the Aduana quarter: in the Christian cemetery. I take you there later.'

'And then I'd like to see the place where he had—' Nicholas pauses. How much does Hadir suspect about Sykes's death? he wonders. Is there perhaps the possibility that the new, self-appointed factor for the Barbary Company knows more than he has so far admitted? 'I'd like to see where Adolfo Sykes met with his unfortunate accident.'

'Why does Sayidi Nich-less wish these things? He was not your friend.'

Nicholas puts on the smile he keeps for distrusting patients. 'Master Sykes died here in the service of my country. The least I can do is to mark his passing.'

Hadir contemplates Nicholas's answer for a moment. 'It shall be done as you ask,' he says, nodding wisely. 'But first we go to your lodgings. Sharif al-Annuri says I must stay close with you always – like a shadow.'

And to help Hadir in this important task, Nicholas notices, the imposing Muhammed al-Annuri has thoughtfully left behind two taciturn young men of fighting age, clad in white robes, a scimitar at the belt and a threatening aloofness about the eyes. The sort of men you'd employ if you wanted to protect a precious possession.

Or to guard a valuable prisoner.

✠

As they step out from the shade of a winding lane and into the merciless glare of the sun, Hadir announces they have almost reached the house on the Street of the Weavers. Shading his eyes, Nicholas looks ahead.

He is standing at the rim of an open, circular space. It is large enough to stage a decent May Day fair – fire-eaters, jugglers and performing bears included. But there is no scene of bucolic entertainment to meet his eyes, no courting couples sneaking off into the woods while their parents watch a morality play, no archery contests, no one dressed up as Queen Elizabeth smiting the village clod-pate, disguised as Philip of Spain. Some other purpose is being enacted in this open furnace. It takes Nicholas a while to comprehend what he is seeing.

It is a market. But the merchandise on sale is human. Small clusters of people – some naked, almost all with shaven heads – stand cowering as though they've been caught in a storm and have nowhere to shelter, no alternative but to brace themselves for the downpour. The stink of confined human bodies hangs in the air like a hot fog.

As his eyes adjust to the light, he sees that many are Blackamoors, but not enough to make the scene uniform. There are numerous white faces, too. Prospective buyers walk amongst the huddled groups, inspecting the wares for breadth of back and conformation, while the merchants beat their stock into pleasing postures with lengths of cane.

How does a human soul not break when it finds itself in such a place as this? Nicholas wonders. What hopes and plans did these people have, what ambitions, before ill fortune tore them to pieces? Surely, he thinks, when God created people, He never intended that they should be of no more value than a stool in a bedchamber, or a cart in a barn – just another possession. He remembers the despair that had engulfed him when his own life had been ruptured by the deaths of Eleanor and the child she was carrying. If it had not been for Bianca, he would have given in. Perished. What possible hope of redemption can these poor souls have?

Thinking of her brings an overwhelming loneliness flooding over him. He pictures her at her bench in her apothecary shop, mixing her cures with one hand while she pushes those heavy, dark tresses back from her forehead with the other. He sees her in the Jackdaw, herding the errant Rose, the girl she likes to call Mistress Moonbeam; hears her putting Walter Pemmel in his place, her voice gentle but implacable. In his mind, he even can smell her: the rosewater she likes to splash on her neck, and which is one of her few extravagances. And he wonders if she has forgiven him yet for leaving her.

'Are there no slaves in England?' asks Hadir, seeing the expression on Nicholas's face.

He is about to reply with an emphatic No. To protest. To insist that all Englishmen are freeborn. But then he remembers the English indentured servants who are tied through contract to their masters, the day-labourers who carry like mules for pennies, the Bankside doxies who sell their bodies in the stews, and the vagrants and vagabonds forced onto the road through destitution. So he confines his answer to a bland, 'Where have they come from, Hadir?'

'Everywhere,' Hadir tells him. 'Some come across the desert from Arabia. Some from Africa. Some are captured at sea by our corsairs. Some are captured in battle. Some are sold by their own families. An important man is judged by the slaves he can count. Hadir shall find you many slaves.' A conspiratorial dip of the eyes. 'Women, too, for concubines. Tomorrow Hadir will take you to the market so you may choose your own slaves. I tell you which dealer to trust. You must have cook and washerman. And a fellow to carry a sun canopy for you.' He places a hand over his head to illustrate the necessity.

'I'd rather you find me willing servants I can pay,' Nicholas says.

'Sayidi Sy-kess was the same,' Hadir laments, rolling his eyes at the strangeness of the infidel mind. 'This is what comes of having a woman sultan!'

✠

From the outside, the house on the Street of the Weavers resembles a squat, defensive tower raised to guard some wild and disputed borderland. The plain walls are made of compacted mud and pierced by nothing that could ever claim to be a window. With the key al-Annuri gave him, Hadir opens a door carved with intricate arabesque designs. Nicholas follows him inside. Ducking under a low lintel, his sun-soaked eyes register little but darkness. He smells cedar, cinnamon and hot plaster.

And then he steps out from a cloister of graceful arches into an inner garden bathed in sunlight. There are olive trees in the garden, and a fountain set upon a mosaic plinth. There are strange shrubs with spikes instead of leaves. There are tiled paths that quarter the flowerbeds. Looking up, he sees the cloister has an upper gallery where little windows peer down in approval of his captivation, and sparrows sing beneath a square of brilliant blue sky.

'Sultan al-Mansur is a generous man,' Nicholas says admiringly under his breath to no one in particular as he looks around his temporary new home.

Hadir leads him back into the cloister and up an enclosed staircase. They emerge onto a roof terrace that runs around all four sides of the house, affording a magnificent view over the city. On one side he can see the tower of the Koutoubia mosque rising into the sky, on another the vast walls of what he takes to be Sultan al-Mansur's palace. He lets his gaze expand out beyond the city, across distant groves of date palms to the hazy horizon and the snow-capped curtain of the High Atlas.

'It is beautiful,' says Nicholas. 'Until I came here, I had never seen a mountain. We don't have them in Suffolk.'

Hadir's outstretched hand draws his gaze back towards the palace. It looks to Nicholas like a castle set down inside the city. While it lacks the ravelins, bastions and tenailles of a modern European fort that create a killing ground for any attacker, it looks formidable enough, though he suspects it wouldn't take long for an artillery train to batter down the sandstone walls. Wooden scaffolding reveals where construction work is still going on.

'The *sharif* make all this with gold taken from the Portugal infidel,' Hadir tells him confidently, as though the sultan has been pleased to confide this fact to him personally. 'And Portuguese slaves to build it. Take many slaves.' He turns back to the roof terrace and with sadness in his voice says, 'This is where my friend Sy-kess tell me many times of the English queen, and how it is to live in her country. Here we eat together when the sun goes down. Here I learn how to speak England.'

'You admired him, didn't you?'

'Sayidi Sy-kess was a kind man. I like him, even though he was *berraniyin*, like you.' He frowns as he searches for translation. 'From outside.'

'An outsider.'

'Yes. An outsider.'

You couldn't have described me better, if you were the president of the College of Physicians, Nicholas thinks. He walks to the street side of the terrace and looks down. Al-Annuri's two armed men are still there, sitting in the shade of a date palm within easy striking distance of the front door, and looking like two wolves who've cornered a lamb in a thicket and can't be bothered expending the energy to go in after it. At least, for the present.

26

Nicholas wakes to the morning call to prayer, a lyrically resonant song of unshakeable faith echoing from the Koutoubia mosque. He lets his head fall back on the pillow, feels the warmth of the sun flooding through the little window. And then he remembers: he is lying in a dead man's bed.

By his judgement, in a week it will be Whitsunday. He looks into the future and imagines Bianca at the Jackdaw, supervising the celebrations, chivvying Rose and Timothy about their tasks. The taproom will empty as the Morris men pass by, stamping, clacking and trilling their way towards Bermondsey Street. Farzad is to be crowned Summer King this year – a role he will play to excess, insulting the Pope and the Spanish king to riotous applause as he's enthroned on an upturned tub in the taproom.

Thinking of Bianca now, his memory offers him the occasion the night-watch caught the two of them together at the corner of Black Bull Alley, sneaking back from hiding the enciphered letters that had unlocked the Samuel Wylde conspiracy. She pushed him up against the wall of the chandler's shop to make the watch think they were lovers enjoying a secret tryst. What had stopped him from kissing her then? Guilt at the thought he might love another woman, after Eleanor? Or the ring-bolt in the wall that was pushing on his spine like an implement of torture?

Remembering how her body had felt against his, Nicholas understands now that it was neither. It had been his own timidity.

It had been the fear of what kissing her would unleash. He curses himself now for not being brave enough to seize the moment. Why did I have to wait for Ned and Rose to bring us together beneath the lover's knot in the Jackdaw taproom? he asks himself accusingly.

Hadir's voice, calling down from the roof terrace, breaks into his thoughts.

'Did you sleep well in God's city, Sayidi Nich-less?' he asks when Nicholas joins him.

'Very well, Hadir, thank you.' *The sleeping was fine. It was the waking I found disconcerting.*

Hadir has conjured a breakfast of dates, freshly baked bread and preserves made of fruit that Nicholas cannot identify. He pours piping-hot *atay* into a glass cup. The scent of mint blows through his mind like a bracing winter wind.

When the meal is over, Hadir insists on trimming Nicholas's beard with a sharp knife. 'Sayidi Sy-kess like his beard short,' he tells Nicholas. 'My father was barber, so I do this for him.'

Nicholas is happy to submit. After almost three weeks aboard the *Righteous* his beard has become unruly, and he prefers to wear it close. Besides, he thinks, it would be better if Sir Robert Cecil's envoy to the court of Sultan al-Mansur didn't arrive looking like a country poacher.

'Tell me, Hadir, does the new factor for the Barbary Company have the records of the old factor in his safekeeping?'

'Of course, Sayidi Nich-less.' A hurt look – *What manner of incompetent fool do you take me for?* – followed by a glint of suspicion. 'Why do you wish to see them? You are a physician, not a merchant.'

'Do you read English as well as you speak it?'

'No, *Sayidi*. I cannot read it at all.'

'Then what if there were letters amongst his papers that should rightly be returned to England?'

251

Hadir considers this hastily contrived explanation for a moment. Apparently it passes inspection. 'I shall fetch them, *Sayidi*.'

Squatting in the shadiest part of the terrace, Nicholas reads through Adolfo Sykes's tally books and records, which Hadir has brought from a storeroom. They appear meticulously kept. Nicholas can imagine not a single bolt of imported English cloth has been unaccounted for, not a bushel of exported sugar or slate of salt overlooked. Whatever the reason for his death, it wasn't poor accountancy.

'Come, Sayidi Nich-less, we have work to do,' Hadir says when Nicholas has finished. 'Now Hadir find you servants!'

'I told you, Hadir, no slaves. I will not buy a man – or a woman, for that matter – as I might purchase a new pair of boots.'

'No slaves, no slaves,' Hadir promises with a weary sigh.

Leaning over the terrace wall and looking down into the street, Nicholas sees al-Annuri's two men lounging under a date-palm tree. He wonders if they've been there all night.

Am I a prisoner here? he wonders. Does my liberty depend upon the continuing indulgence of Muhammed al-Annuri?

When he steps out of the door with Hadir, his fears are confirmed. One of the men gets up, brushes the dust off his white robe and follows them at a discreet distance with all the feigned innocence of a Bankside purse-diver caught in the act.

At the end of the Street of the Weavers is a patch of open ground dotted with olive trees. In their shade sprouts an undergrowth of conical tents. Huddled around each, Nicholas can see families taking their ease in the warm morning air. Their stoic faces tell of people who live or die by what they can scavenge from the earth after richer folk have had their turn; people who must daily ask God if they should starve, die of thirst, or – *inshā Allāh* – survive. The women, their faces darkened by the rims of broad felt hats fringed with trails of beads and medallions, gossip as they keep watch over earthen cooking pots. Children stand guard over grazing sheep and camels. The men wear cloth hoods dyed as blue as the sky.

'Berbers,' Hadir tells him. 'They live in the empty desert beyond the mountains. It is told that before they learned of Allāh, the most merciful, the most compassionate, they worshipped nothing but rocks.'

Hadir delivers a rapid fusillade in his language to the nearest group. Nicholas stands uncomfortably as the faces lift to regard him with varying degrees of interest. To some, he is clearly a creature of fascination. To others, of no more import than the stones on the ground.

A glance over his shoulder tells him al-Annuri's watchman is observing the proceedings from the shelter of the last house in the street, squatting nonchalantly against its earthen wall as though he has all the time in the world. Nicholas thinks: Robert Cecil's watchers could learn a trick or two from you, when it comes to brazenness.

Within minutes Hadir has acquired a cook, a boy to fetch water and a girl of no more than ten to do the infidel's washing. The cook is an ancient woman with wise eyes and a smile that all the years of a female Methuselah has not managed to dim. She grins at him maternally. The two children regard him with eyes the size of Cecil's Portuguese ducats. As Hadir moves on to the next group, Nicholas realizes that if he doesn't call a halt, Adolfo Sykes's former house on the Street of the Weavers will have more servants in it than Greenwich Palace.

'My needs are simple enough, Hadir. Let's not trouble these people any longer.'

'But you are ambassador of English queen!' Hadir cries, like a hungry man dragged away from a feast.

'I'm not an ambassador; I'm a physician. This will do.'

With his newly acquired household in tow, Nicholas heads back towards the house. As he passes al-Annuri's watchman, he says cheerily, though without any expectation of being understood, save by his smile, 'Good morrow, sirrah. I hope you slept well last night, under your tree. I'll ask Hadir to send you and your companion some breakfast.'

The man does not react. He stares clear through Nicholas, as though his eyes have been put out. But no sooner has Nicholas passed by than he's padding along in the wake of the man he's pretended not to see.

✠

The sound of the altercation becomes audible long before Nicholas reaches the house. Not so much an altercation, he thinks, as the sound of an angry schoolmaster berating a lazy pupil.

Beneath the date palm that has become their sentry post, the second of al-Annuri's watchmen is standing, head bowed, before a rotund little man in a brightly striped robe. The man is in full flood. His raised voice has a high-pitched sweetness about it, quite at odds with the invective it delivers, punctuated by aggressive stabs of a chubby forefinger.

The guard is taking this tirade without protest, even though he's a head taller than his tormentor and half his age. Close by, a younger man in a plain cloth robe, his bald head gleaming in the sunlight, looks on with amused interest.

As Nicholas approaches, the little man turns towards him. The invective stops in mid-sentence. The face softens. He becomes a wholly different character altogether: smiling, avuncular, a soul whose sparkling brown eyes hold malice towards no one.

'At last, the esteemed English physician returns from his first adventures in our noble city,' he says in his high, dancing voice.

A flick of his fleshy hand, a sudden, short reversion to his former angry self, and al-Annuri's guard slinks away to join his companion, who has stopped a little way down the lane. Their brief exchange reminds Nicholas of a pair of troublemakers who've just been thrown out of the Jackdaw by Ned Monkton. They seem to be debating whether to go back and try their luck with their fists. But then they appear to think better of it, setting off in the direction of the Berber encampment with the edgy swagger of the publicly defeated.

The little man fixes Nicholas with a benevolent smile that fractures his curly white beard like a fall of sunlight on snow. 'And I am Sumayl al-Seddik, minister to His Majesty Ahmad al-Mansur, beloved of Allāh, conqueror of the Songhai, lion of Timbuktu. I am charged by him to bring you greetings.' He extends a plump little hand for Nicholas to shake. 'I must ask your forgiveness for the insult,' he says, nodding towards the departing guards. 'That desert scorpion al-Annuri has no honour – that he should set watchdogs on our foreign guests as though they were nothing but bandits and thieves!'

'In truth, sir, I felt a little sorry for them – having to follow me around and sleep under a date palm.'

'They are nothing. Less than the dirt beneath your shoes. Al-Annuri is a dog. He knows only how to make people fear his bite.'

Remembering how Hadir's hands had trembled when al-Annuri appeared in the garden beside the walls, Nicholas says, 'I don't want them punished, sir. I was becoming a little fond of them.'

Al-Seddik finds this amusing. 'I'd forgotten how sentimental the English can be. Fear not. They will know how to bear it. A mule cannot live long if he does not become accustomed to the cane.' His eyes observe Nicholas with interest. 'So, you are the

English man who has come to study medicine in our land? I hear of your arrival from the governor of Safi.'

'I am, sir,' says Nicholas. 'My name is Dr Nicholas Shelby. I carry a letter for you, from Lord Burghley, who wishes to be remembered to you. I am here by command of his son, Sir Robert Cecil.'

'So the queen has knighted him at last,' says al-Seddik with a chuckle. 'I trust that made him happy.' He indicates the man beside him. 'And this splendid gentleman is Dr Arnoult de Lisle. He is privileged to hold the position of physician to His Majesty. We thought we should both come to bid you welcome.'

De Lisle offers a reserved nod in lieu of a greeting. With his skin burned a dark brown, he could easily pass for a Moor. His iron-grey beard, cut close, adds a bladed edge to a face that has a keen intelligence about it, bordering on the haughty. He seems like a man not overly given to the tolerance of slower minds. Nicholas puts him in his late thirties.

'I'm honoured by your presence, Masters,' Nicholas says in what he hopes is a suitably deferential tone for a newly arrived envoy.

'Professor de Lisle is reader in Arabic at the Collège de France, appointed by King Henri himself,' al-Seddik says with a gracious nod to the younger man. 'He is also one of his nation's finest physicians. He speaks our language as if it were his own. And English, too. We are fortunate to have him in our humble land.'

De Lisle gives the merest wince of a smile, as if to show humility in the face of undeserved abundance. As he reaches out to shake Nicholas's hand, the robe slips from his wrist. Heavy gold bracelets, Nicholas notices. De Lisle had done well in the sultan's service, it seems.

'This letter, from milord Burghley: may I see it?' says al-Seddik.

Nicholas hesitates. What is the protocol for playing host to a sultan's minister – or a sultan's physician, for that matter? He adds the question to the growing list of things that Robert Cecil has failed to tell him.

Hadir comes to his rescue. Within what seems like moments, Nicholas is sitting on the cushions on the roof terrace while Hadir pours *atay* for the guests. The Methuselah woman from the Berber encampment serves the dates and nuts left over from breakfast.

'You have the gauge of us already, Dr Shelby,' al-Seddik says admiringly. 'We are simple folk and are at our most contented with simple pleasures.'

A glance across the roof at the magnificence of the sultan's palace tells Nicholas that al-Mansur's minister, for all his avuncular charm, is being disingenuous.

'I have to compliment you on your command of my language, sir,' Nicholas says. 'It is a great comfort to a stranger in your land. Did you acquire it while you were in England, with His Majesty's envoy?'

'I had a little of before I went, from the English merchants here in Marrakech, and from Dr de Lisle. But I'm an inquisitive fellow, and our delegation went to your London playhouses more than once.' Al-Seddik smiles at the memory. 'An extraordinary affair – to see young boys pretending to be females, and weak men with proud bellies taking the parts of heroes. How you English contrive to deceive each other!'

Nicholas hands over Burghley's letter, which al-Seddik tucks away in his satin robe. 'I also carry a letter of greeting from Her Grace, Queen Elizabeth, to Sultan al-Mansur,' he says. 'When may I hope to present it?'

'I will arrange an audience,' al-Seddik tells him. 'It may take a while; the *sharif* is much concerned with the work taking place on the el-Badi Palace. In the meantime, my tent shall be your tent. You will feast with me tomorrow afternoon, after the *al-zuhr* prayers. I shall send Dr de Lisle to fetch you. Does that please?'

Nicholas confirms that it pleases greatly. He follows al-Seddik and de Lisle down the dark stairway and out onto the Street of the Weavers. When his eyes recover from the transition from light to darkness and back to light again, he sees al-Annuri's guards have not dared to return to their place beneath the date palm. The street is empty, save for a child leading an old blind man, stick-thin and hollow-cheeked, towards the Berber encampment.

'This house, sir...' Nicholas begins tentatively.

'It does not satisfy?'

'On the contrary, it's perfect.'

The faintest lift of one white eyebrow. 'So, then?'

'I understand the previous tenant was the factor of the Barbary Company here in Marrakech.'

'Adolfo Sykes, yes.' A sudden look of remorse as al-Seddik comprehends. 'Of course! Forgive me, Dr Shelby. An unforgiveable error. You should never have been lodged here, not after Master Sykes's sad demise.'

'It's not that. It is a very agreeable house,' says Nicholas, aware the ground beneath his feet suddenly feels as though it's made of eggshells. 'I merely wondered why it had been chosen. It is not in the Christian quarter.'

'Does that offend you?'

'Not at all. It's simply that I understood the Aduana district was where visitors from Christian lands were quartered.'

'There was nowhere vacant in the Aduana that was as comfortable,' al-Seddik assures him, beaming with goodwill. 'Besides, this is a large city. We like to know where to find our most honoured guests.'

And as Nicholas watches him go, a jovial little puffball wrapped in silk, Arnoult de Lisle's angular frame loping along beside him like a servant trying to anticipate his master's whim, it occurs to him that there are subtler ways of keeping watch on someone than sitting outside their door in the shade of a date palm.

27

The lanes leading to Smithfield are emptier than when last Bianca came this way, the taverns quieter even than those on Bankside. At this rate, Whitsunday will be the quietest she's known since coming to the city. In happier times the maypoles would be festooned with ribbons fluttering on the breeze. The Summer Kings and Queens would parade in their makeshift finery. Courting couples would slip away to hide beneath the washing laid out on the hedges to dry in the early-summer air. But now the maypoles stand forlornly naked. Even where public gatherings are not forbidden, people have lost their appetite for a crowd.

Whitsuntide. She still can't get used to the term. She prefers to call it by its Catholic name – Pentecost – but only when she's amongst those she trusts. Use it elsewhere and she knows she's likely to mark herself as, at best, a recusant. At worst, a heretic.

As she walks towards Giltspur Street, Bianca imagines how she would spend this coming Whitsunday, if Nicholas was here. She might persuade him to dance a measure or two with her in the Pike Garden on Bankside, even though he has said more than once that dancing occupies much the same place in his mind as tooth-pulling. But she would have found a way, she thinks.

She imagines it now: his body beginning to relax and that reluctant smile of enjoyment fighting its way onto his face. She can feel his hands clasping her waist a little more tightly, his body pressing somewhat closer than is strictly necessary for those with Puritan sensibilities.

And then she imagines Robert Cecil scuttling up and demanding Nicholas's presence elsewhere.

She wonders where Nicholas is now: basking in some sun-drenched kasbah, more than likely – stretched out on silk cushions, listening to exotic tales of Arabia whispered to him by some kohl-eyed beauty, while a eunuch in a silk kaftan plucks the strings of a lyre and makes that strange discordant music she'd sometimes heard on the Ruga dei Spezieri in Venice, where the Ottoman traders had their shops.

An apprentice boy shatters her musings as he pushes rudely past. Bianca unleashes a stream of Italian invective at him. Surprised, he glances over his shoulder and shouts, 'Fuck off back to Spain, you papist trull!'

She wills him to fall flat on his face in the nearest pile of horse dung. But for some unaccountable reason, today her ability to cast charms appears not to be working.

Reynard Gault's house stands alone in a patch of open ground beside the complex of bakehouses that provide ships' biscuits for the royal fleet. It is newly built. The oak beams are as pale as the moment they emerged, ridged and tufted, from the sawmill, the plaster pristine.

In the spacious hall, a maid takes Bianca's overgown and bids her wait. Looking around, she notes the flagstones are so spotless they could have been quarried yesterday. She can smell linseed on the new half-panelling, and fresh paint on the strapwork below the plastered ceiling. The house is like a gift he's bought himself on a whim.

Above the wide hearth hangs a portrait: a younger Gault looking out on the world with unshakeable confidence – even a little avarice – and dressed in a breastplate and sash, his left hand resting fetchingly upon a bejewelled sword hilt. At his back, verdant acres roll towards misty mountains.

'It's by Master Hilliard,' the real Gault says from behind her shoulder. 'Cost me a duke's ransom. I had him change the background, to remind me of Ireland.'

'You fought there?' Bianca asks causally, trying to not to show how much he's startled her.

'Gracious, no! I'm no warrior,' he says with over-egged humility. 'I'm a humble merchant. I was born there. In Leinster.'

'But the sword—'

'You know what these court painters are like. They flatter to ensure they get paid.'

But you didn't object to the pretence, did you? she thinks. Perhaps convenient omission is in your blood. Perhaps that's why you pretended not to have heard of Solomon Mandel. 'I had not realized you were Irish,' she says pleasantly.

'My family has a little land in Dundalk. Sheep, for the most part. We export the bulk of our yarn to England. The rest we sell to the Moors. Hence my position in the Barbary Company.'

Bianca turns away from the painting. 'That is all very fine, Master Gault, but I really do not believe you summonsed me here to discuss sheep. What is it that you want from me?'

He appraises her, like an abbot trying to decide if he's been sold a fake holy relic. Then, apparently satisfied, he says, 'Mistress, come with me.'

Gault leads her to a neat chamber, bare except for new wainscoting and six French fruitwood chairs with needlework upholstery that look as though they've only just been delivered. Through a leaded window she sees a courtyard garden and newly planted honeysuckle that hugs its canes like neatly ordered columns in a ledger. At the centre of the garden is a square of gravel. Two lads of about Farzad's age, dressed in uniform grey kersey jerkins, are at sword practice. Three others sit around watching them and shouting encouragement, their voices almost mute beyond the glass.

'Your sons?' Bianca asks, even as she knows they cannot be, given their similarity in age.

'Mercy, no. Our Lord has not yet bestowed such blessings upon me. They are good lads from my lands in Ireland.'

'You teach your servants how to kill with the sword? I had not realized Ireland was such a lawless place.'

He laughs at her misunderstanding. 'It is, Mistress. Very lawless. But these lads are not learning how to kill; they are learning how to live.'

'You're turning them into gallant little English gentlemen?' she suggests with a hint of sarcasm. In her experience, English gallants are no less reluctant to brawl with the sword than those who had paid court to her in Padua. At the Jackdaw she's had Ned and Nicholas eject more than a few.

'After a fashion, yes,' he admits. 'I have apprenticed them to the Barbary Company. I take the brightest from my Leinster estate in Ireland and offer them a better life than breaking their backs on the land.'

'How generous of you, Sir Reynard. I'm sure they're very grateful.'

'These fellows are almost ready to begin the next chapter in their studies,' he says.

'And what will that be – fist-fighting and vomiting in tavern doorways? Insulting young maids? Knocking the hats off foreigners?'

He looks hurt. 'You do them a disservice, Mistress. When Captain Connell returns, these fellows will go aboard his argosies to learn navigation and seamanship.' He gazes proudly at the lads in the courtyard, as though he's admiring a bank of fine flowers he's watched grow from seeds. 'These young fellows are the next generation of English merchant venturers. Would you have them go out into a dangerous world without the means to defend themselves?'

'I suppose not,' she says, recalling the hard, sunburnt men she'd seen preparing to set sail from the Venice *Arsenale* on their voyages of discovery and plunder.

'The Dutch are already in the Indies. The Spanish and the Portuguese have Hispaniola and the Americas. Trading with the world against such competition will require men of resolve and courage.'

'And you don't want them dying of the plague before they start,' she says.

A leaden seriousness comes over his face. 'I have put a great deal of time and effort into these lads. They are not the first. There will be many more to come. They are the future of this realm. I would be remiss if I did not do all in my power to protect their well-being.'

More likely your investment, Bianca thinks. 'May I be blunt with you?' she asks.

'I would expect naught else.'

Given the painting, she suspects he's not the type to receive mockery with a self-deprecating smile and a shrug. So she chooses her words carefully.

'You have to understand, Sir Reynard, that Bankside is a place where you'll hear ten rumours to one truth. There's less fiction heard on the stage of the Rose theatre than on the streets. The stories of my escape from the pestilence are just that – fiction. I *didn't* have the plague. Yes, I can make you any number of preventatives, but none are certain. Your best course is to keep your house clean, free of rats, and to pray. Or you could send the boys to the country.'

'That is not possible,' he says, studying her as though he's trying to gauge what counter-offer to make.

'I didn't have it,' she insists. 'It was the ague. Nothing more. I think I must have been working too hard.'

'You may deny it all you want, Mistress,' he says with the conviction of a man who cannot bring himself to deny his own certainties. 'But there are queues at your shop door. The parish authorities heed your advice. And the pestilence is more contained in Southwark than here. Will you help? I will make it *very* worthwhile.'

I could do with the money, she thinks, given the decline in trade at the Jackdaw. It can't hurt to provide a few more distillations and a bag or two of brimstone, can it? And if I am to find out why this man has lied to me about Solomon Mandel, what better way to begin than to make him dependent upon me.

'Very well, Master Gault. I will do what I can.'

'I will send one of my lads to Dice Lane. Will tomorrow suit?'

Bianca laughs. 'You may purchase my preventatives, Master Gault, but you may not purchase *me*. You will have to wait your turn – at least a week. It could be more; I give priority to those without the means to buy their way to the head of the queue.'

He seems to take this as an opening gambit. 'Come now, is my coin not good currency on Bankside?'

'As long as it's not clipped, it's as good as any.'

'Three days, then.'

'I've told you: you will have to wait your turn. I will send you word when I am done. And you must understand, I cannot promise to cure anyone of the plague.'

He shrugs, giving her the sort of smile she imagines he reserves for the celebration of a profitable agreement. 'Very well. That wasn't so irksome, was it?'

And then, to her shock, he seizes her by the arm and pulls her to him. For a moment she thinks he's going to kiss her, perhaps

265

even force himself on her. She grabs a fistful of satin doublet, partly to stop herself stumbling, partly to hold him at bay.

'There is more I desire of you than just medicine, Mistress Merton,' he says huskily.

She remembers her mother's frequent exhortation: when someone is about to threaten you, go on the offensive. Stand up straight. Look them directly in the face. Then – when they're transfixed by your God-given amber eyes – one sharp knee in the *coglioni* should make them see reason. For the moment she takes the advice only as far as looking Gault in the eye.

'This, sir, is *ungallant*,' she spits.

His eyes are all over her, but it is uncertainty rather than lust that drives them. He releases his grip a little. 'Do not bait me, Mistress. Tell me the real reason why Robert Cecil wanted your friend Dr Shelby aboard the *Righteous*.'

Bianca stares at him. 'Nicholas?'

Gault releases her arm. 'If that is the name he received at the font, then yes.'

Bianca steps back, kneading the place where his fingers have pressed skin against bone. 'Is there a *real* reason? I was rather hoping you might tell *me*,' she says.

Gault stares at her. 'Don't play a saucy match with me, Mistress. Tell me the truth.'

'I know that to persuade Nicholas to go to Morocco, Robert Cecil offered him some pretty comfits, which I have to say, with all sadness, the silly addle-pate fell for. Then, as a precaution, he enlisted your help to have me shut down, if Nicholas saw sense and changed his mind. Why would Cecil go to such lengths – all for a scholarly wish to learn how the Moors practise physic? You tell me, Master Gault?'

She thinks she sees a glint of admiration in his eyes. 'How did you discover this – guesswork? Second sight?'

To protect the pact Nicholas made with Ned, she says, '"Deduced" might be a better word. I know Sir Robert of old.' She senses an errant strand of hair threatening to slip over one eye. She pushes it firmly back beneath her coif. The movement forces her chin to tilt upwards and her throat to curve towards him. It gives her a sudden sense of vulnerability.

'Well, Mistress, you may *deduce* all you like. I deny it, of course.'

'I think Robert Cecil offered you some incentive, some boon, if you agreed to have my licence revoked. Is that how it went? What was it – gold?'

Gault stares at the ornate ceiling, a wry smile on his lips. 'Pepper, actually.'

'Pepper? You agreed to take away my livelihood for *pepper*?'

'A very great deal of pepper.'

'But why?'

'Sir Robert didn't see fit to make free with his motives, Mistress.'

'But you think there was another reason why he wanted Nicholas to go, or else you wouldn't have been so saucy with me just now.'

'Did Dr Shelby not confide in you?'

'Only that Cecil was sending him to learn about physic in the land of the Moor, if that's what you mean.'

'Nothing else?'

'No. Nothing. We're not *married*.'

His smile is like the one her uncle Salvatore used to give her when she turned fourteen, before her mother banned him from the house – half-cruel, half-covetous.

'But why choose him? Why not one of the senior fellows at the College of Physicians? Or old Lopez, who serves the queen?'

'I don't know,' she says crossly. 'Perhaps Sir Robert thought they were too old to attempt the journey. I assume it was because Cecil trusts him. Nicholas – Dr Shelby – is physician to his son.'

267

Gault crosses to a sideboard and pours two glasses of wine from a silver jug. He offers her a glass. At first Bianca is inclined to refuse it and leave as quickly as she can. Gault sober is unpredictable enough for her tastes. But that would be to admit defeat. Besides, a glass of sack might steady her nerves. When she tastes it, the tavern-mistress in her calculates you couldn't buy a bottle from the Vintry for less than five shillings.

'May I be plain with you, Mistress Merton?' Gault asks, raising his glass.

Here it comes, she thinks. There is another reason Nicholas has gone to the Barbary shore, and I'm the only sap who doesn't know it. Gault has been playing me. And now he's going to reveal the truth – on the condition that I agree to lie with him. He thinks I can be bought for five shillings a bottle.

'If you must.'

'You are a recusant, are you not? A *Catholic*. In Robert Cecil's eyes, a heretic.'

The bald statement isn't at all what she's expecting. 'I suppose you heard that when you were asking about me on Bankside.'

'It was mentioned.'

'By who – Jenny Solver? If you're going to threaten to tell Sir Robert Cecil, don't bother. He already knows. We have an understanding.'

Gault doesn't even attempt to disguise his surprise. 'An understanding – you and Cecil?'

'If you heard rumours that I was a recusant, no doubt you will also have heard how I was taken to Cecil House to be examined – and returned in Robert Cecil's private barge.'

'I do recall such stories.'

'Well, they're true, Master Gault. Robert Cecil and I have reached an accommodation.'

'An *accommodation*?'

What hurt can it do, she wonders, to embellish rumour with a little fantasy? The more exotic she is to him, the more carefree he may be with his secrets. 'Yes, Master Gault – an accommodation. I don't cast a spell to dry out his seed; he leaves my name off the recusancy rolls.'

To her joy, Gault actually shudders. 'That is *witchcraft*,' he whispers.

'Well, it would be – if I'd done it. But I'm pleased to say that Lady Elizabeth gave birth to a healthy young son.' She gives a little what-might-have-been shrug. 'Let us all give thanks that I don't have to pay a recusant's fine, and the Cecil heir wasn't born a walnut stone.'

Gault watches her as though he can't quite fathom what manner of creature she might be. There is admiration in his eyes, and more than a little caution. He seems to be struggling to decide how far he can trust her.

'So you see, Master Gault,' she continues, taking advantage of his indecision, 'if you're thinking of threatening to denounce me as a heretic, you're wasting your time. It won't make me any the more compliant. I am the one witch no one dares to hang. And if my Nicholas should fall to any ill at the hands of that monster Cathal Connell – the man *you* entrusted him to – then dry seed will be the very least of your problems.'

28

It seems a poor place to die. Barely a ditch. Little more than a scraping in the burning dust where lizards run and scorpions arch their stings. But then, thinks Nicholas, Adolfo Sykes probably didn't die here. The Doukkala gate is barely fifty yards away; the sentries would have heard the screams.

He has a picture in his mind of a dark night and a waggon leaving the city; a contrived stop for the driver to relieve himself in the ditch, while his companions roll the body out from under its coverings. He pictures it landing in a twisted heap, the sound barely audible above the whistling of the waggoner. No more enciphered dispatches for Robert Cecil.

He glances back at the Bab Doukkala, shading his eyes against the glare of the afternoon sun reflecting off its tessellated arches. He's glad Hadir has provided him with a Berber's blue headscarf. As well as protecting him from the sun, it also has the benefit of shading his European features from passers-by, who might otherwise question what an infidel is doing inspecting a patch of ground just outside their city walls.

Why take the risk of dropping the body so near? he wonders. Why not somewhere further along the Safi road, well out of sight? Did they not care about the guards?

Nicholas can see one of them now, lounging against the battlements in bored contemplation of the road. How much harder would it be to stay vigilant at night, whiling away the long hours on guard duty? He can well imagine a sentry succumbing to the tedium and finding some other means of passing the time than watching a cart disappear into the darkness.

'Are you certain this is where you saw the body?'

'No, *Sayidi*. Bachir sees it.'

Nicholas's hopes sink. A friend saw it. A friend of a friend. A friend told me that someone *he* knows saw it... 'Bachir? But I thought you said *you'd* seen the body.'

'Was my friend Bachir,' says Hadir, nodding vigorously. 'The guard you saw me greet, when we arrived from Safi. Was market day. He said when the sun comes up, he sees Sayidi Sy-kess by that bush there, the one that looks like a *camello* taking a shit.' He nods towards an acacia shrub barely five paces from where Nicholas is standing. 'Bachir tells the guard commander. The guard commander say he don't want no dead infidel spoiling market-day business.'

'But you told me *you* saw his wounds – the ones you thought had been made by a wild beast.'

'I was inside the gate when Sayidi Sy-kess was brought in on the cart of Ibn Daoud. I know Ibn Daoud, also. "Hey, Hadir, come see the heathen Englishman," he calls to me. So I go and see. It is very bad for me. I liked Sayidi Sy-kess very much.'

'I know this is hard for you, Hadir, but can you recall if there was much blood? Did the wounds look freshly made?'

Hadir winces. His face is not made for dark thoughts. 'Was little blood, most only here.' He splays his fingers down the sides of his ribcage. 'Maybe the beast who killed Sayidi Sy-kess drink it all.'

'You knew Master Sykes well, Hadir. I presume you knew his routine. What reason would he have to be outside the city walls at night?'

The boy might be an astute trader, but where his friend Adolfo Sykes is concerned, he hasn't yet learned to dissemble. 'I do not let myself ask this question,' he says, his composure crumbling.

271

'Why not?' Nicholas asks, though he suspects he knows the answer.

'Because it means it was not an accident. It means my friend was kill-ed – but not by wild beasts.'

'Did Adolfo Sykes have enemies?' Nicholas asks as gently as he can.

Hadir shakes his head. 'He was a *good* man. No enemy!'

Nicholas thinks, I would have said the same thing of Solomon Mandel, if anyone had asked me. He remembers what Hadir had told him on the road from Safi, how Sultan al-Mansur had forgiven his old foe al-Seddik: *Sometimes a new sultan will punish his enemies after a battle. Sometimes he will command that the skin shall be flayed from their living bodies...*

He looks again at the patch of dirt Hadir has led him to. A small scorpion emerges from the meagre shade of a rock and sets off in a slow scuttle towards the nearest acacia bush.

'I've seen all I need to see here,' Nicholas says. 'Now show me where your friend is buried.'

✝

A twenty-minute walk brings Nicholas to the Aduana quarter, a district of warehouses and private dwellings where the Christian community of Marrakech plies its trade with its hosts across a mud-brick frontier ten feet high. In the heat, Nicholas feels as though he's walked from Bankside to Barnthorpe without resting on the way.

To his relief, it is shady in the lanes of the Aduana. But the shadows cannot dim the colourful garb of its inhabitants. Instead of soberly dressed Woodbridge merchants or the dark-gowned worthies he's seen in the Exchanges in Antwerp or Rotterdam, here the factors and the middlemen, the sellers and the buyers are draped in vividly coloured clothes. He sees silk gowns, linen ponchos, brilliantly dyed cloth coats, pantaloons and galligaskins of every hue under the sun. From Hadir, he learns these are Christians from Andalucía, Constantinople, Alexandria, from the Balkans and the Levant, some even from Persia. Hadir exchanges greetings with many of them. Nicholas begins to understand now why Cecil House is so full of busy, serious-faced clerks hurrying to and fro. If Adolfo Sykes was but one single agent in the Cecils' vast network of intelligencers, the reports flowing into Cecil House must give Lord Burghley and his crook-backed son an almost god's-eye view of the known world.

The Christian church in the Aduana is a mud-brick building almost indistinguishable from the others in the lane, save for an iron three-bar cross of Eastern design above the entrance. In the adjoining graveyard, Nicholas walks amongst a score of dirt mounds, each bearing a simple cross. Adolfo Sykes's resting place is the newest. The stone still bears the recent marks of the mason's chisel, and the wind has not yet softened the dirt mound beneath it. Though he has had cause in his life to question the deity to whom this little plot is sacred, Nicholas stands for a moment in silence and offers up a prayer that Adolfo Sykes's suffering is at an end.

'Why does Sayidi Nich-less wish to see the grave of a man he does not know?' Hadir asks, his gentle brown eyes focused on the grave, as though he's embarrassed by his own question.

Not wanting to ensnare himself in a hasty lie, Nicholas takes his time replying.

'A friend of his, in England. He hadn't heard from Master Sykes for some time. When he learned I was coming here, he asked me to seek news of him.'

Hadir looks him in the eye. 'Is this friend you speak of the minister of the English queen? The minister who sent Sayidi Nich-less here to study our medicine?'

'Just a friend,' Nicholas says, before making a discreet bow and turning away from the grave.

An innocent question? he wonders. Or has Hadir Benhassi started drawing his own conclusions about my visit to the grave of Adolfo Sykes?

✠

When Sumayl al-Seddik had told him 'my tent shall be your tent', he was being somewhat modest, Nicholas discovers the next day.

The minister's mansion is near the el-Badi Palace, close enough for the rotund little courtier to answer the sultan's whim without working up an undignified amount of perspiration. Like most fine houses in Marrakech, its external walls are an unremarkable, unadorned expanse of mud-brick. Only when he is inside does Nicholas see the beauty – and the wealth – on display. He sits with his host and Professor de Lisle on cushions in a fragrant garden, shaded from the worst of the sun beneath a row of fig trees. Musicians serenade them with strangely enticing music played on lutes with extravagantly long necks. A spicy fish pottage is served. 'We call it *shebbel*,' al-Seddik tells him. 'It is similar to your English salmon.' But Nicholas cannot think of any salmon he's ever eaten that was plucked by hand from an ornamental cistern full of water piped down from the Atlas mountains. The dish is serviced to him by a black slave more than six feet tall, as handsome as an angel, and purchased – as his master is happy to explain – at huge expense from the most exclusive slave merchant in Timbuktu. His companions, not one of them less imposing, cast cooling water scented with ambergris from brass censers over the diners. The plump little courtier, Nicholas decides, has a taste for the exceptional.

The meal is commenced without formal prayers, Nicholas notices. Al-Seddik simply mouths his own grace before tucking into the food with his bare fingers.

As they eat, Nicholas learns where this great wealth comes from: interests in gold mines, in tanneries, in slaving ships. And al-Seddik is humble in his gratitude for his good fortune. 'I am a simple man, with simple tastes,' he assures Nicholas on more than one occasion. 'Why Allāh, the most merciful, the most compassionate, has chosen *me* for such favours, I cannot imagine, other than that I might contribute much al-*waqf* to my fellows. The Bimaristan al-Mansur hospital will ensure that I may continue to thank Him long after I have passed into heaven.'

Nicholas cannot stop himself smiling as he thinks of what old Baronsdale, the president of the College of Physicians, would make of this, with his parson's rectitude and stern frugality.

The talk turns to physic, de Lisle translating the more arcane matters that al-Seddik's otherwise excellent English cannot encompass. Nicholas discovers that the Moors practise medicine much as the Europeans do, using the same Galenic and Hippocratic texts from antiquity. Plague, he learns, is as much a tribulation here as it is in London, though London is happily spared the malignant ills caused by eating too many musk-melons and apricots, which al-Seddik terms *fruit-fevers*.

'Tomorrow, Dr Shelby, you must visit our Bimaristan,' al-Seddik says, as though he's kept the best dish till last. 'I think you might find it a little different from your hospitals in England. A procedure is to be performed that may interest you. Have you perhaps witnessed a... a...' He struggles to find the correct English. 'Help me, please, Professor – an operation on the *qassabat al-ri'a* – the pipe of the lung?'

'The windpipe,' says de Lisle in a superior voice. 'The procedure to be performed is a laryngotomy.'

Nicholas's eyes widen in surprise. To his knowledge, the procedure has been performed successfully only once in Europe, and that almost fifty years ago. Al-Seddik might just as well have invited him to watch a hanging or a burning – because the subject's chances of survival could hardly be worse.

29

'It's nothing but a sentence of death,' Bianca tells Jenny Solver, barely able to keep the tears of pity from pooling in her eyes. 'They might as well drag the poor souls to Tyburn and hang them. It would be quicker and a deal more merciful.'

'I heard it from Alderman Goodricke's maid,' the other woman replies, with the customary joy of an inveterate gossip, 'so it must be true.'

Bianca shakes her head in disbelief. 'A wooden house, thrown up on the Pike Garden, to imprison all who have the sickness? It's positively heartless. They should be treated in their own homes. If they must die, let it be in the bosom of their families.'

'It's better than having them wandering the streets, passing on contagion,' Jenny Solver says with a busy flick of her hair.

But Bianca will not have it. 'It's a tragedy the monasteries have all been pulled down,' she says. 'They could have sought shelter there. When we had the plague in the Veneto, the holy houses were a place of refuge.'

Taking the pot of medicine Bianca has prepared for her – a decoction of drop-wart to get her urine flowing properly – Jenny Solver purses her plump lips in objection. 'Then we'd have *two* plagues, Mistress Merton: pestilence *and* papistry.'

Fuming, Bianca watches her leave. I should have put pepper in it, she tells herself – that would put a stop to your gossiping for a while.

Once alone, her thoughts turn to Reynard Gault. She has yet to prepare the preventatives she'd promised him. She wonders if he really needs them, or if it was – as she suspects – simply a way of drawing her closer to him, so that he can discover what he *thinks* she knows about Nicholas's journey to Barbary.

She has concluded – if there had ever been any doubt – that she does not care for Reynard Gault. There will be no fetid, temporary communal sick-houses thrown up for the likes of him. His kind have comfortable homes in the countryside to flee to. Men like Gault can distance themselves from the pestilence. They can buy themselves a measure of safety. Here on Bankside, people do not have that luxury.

For a moment she considers letting him stew, only attending to his request when she's exhausted every reason to delay. But then the old, familiar worm of curiosity starts to squirm. She knows in her heart Gault wants more from her than medicines.

She can feel now, as she recalls their exchange in his fine new house, the insistent pressure of his fingers squeezing her arm in a manner quite at odds with the gallant's mask he wears. His sudden reaction still makes her shudder, even now. She wonders, not for the first time, what brought about such a sudden parting of the curtain, allowing her to see a darker world beyond. His desire to know why Robert Cecil sent Nicholas to Morocco burned in his eyes like a fever. For a moment, she feared he was going to try to beat out of her a secret she didn't possess.

Which means Nicholas has lied to her; there *is* something more to the commission he's undertaken for Robert Cecil than the mere desire for knowledge. *Nicholas*, she hisses to her empty, silent shop, *what have you got yourself mixed up in? Haven't you learned your lesson yet, that nothing good can come of dealing with the Crab?*

But as she begins the task of gathering the ingredients to make Gault's preventatives, spooning sweet-smelling powders from clay pots, taking up sprigs of herbs, pouring oils from little pewter pots into a stone mortar, the fear begins to gnaw at her heart that this time Nicholas has placed himself in a danger too distant for her to come to his aid.

She thinks again of going to Robert Cecil at Windsor and confronting him. But she knows she wouldn't be allowed anywhere near him, certainly not now that the pestilence has come to Southwark. They'd slam the town gate in her face.

No, she thinks, the only way to find out what Nicholas has got himself embroiled in is to pay reluctant court to the one man who seems to want to know as badly as she does.

Arnoult de Lisle arrives next morning after the *al-fajr* prayers, to conduct Nicholas to the Bimaristan al-Mansur. The Frenchman is dressed in the Moor fashion, in a cream linen *djellaba*. With his tanned face, it is all too easy to take him for a native of Barbary, expect when he speaks. His French accent is cultured, his English fluent.

Professor de Lisle is reader in Arabic at the Collège de France, appointed by King Henri himself, Nicholas can hear al-Seddik telling him. He wonders what other talents de Lisle might be keeping hidden: subversion of the alliance between the Moroccan sultan and the English queen, for instance.

The walk to the Bimaristan takes them across a broad public square thronged with people. The sun beats down on merchants selling oils, honey, parsley and oregano; troupes of wrestlers; jugglers and snake-charmers; young boys with solemn faces and bells on their wrists, performing energetic dances to the applause of the crowd. There are men sitting on stools who turn spindles on foot-lathes, fortune-tellers, acrobats, professional storytellers, even a display of severed heads stinking and plum-dark on their poles, reminding Nicholas of the traitors' heads that grace the top of the gatehouse on London Bridge. Were it not for the heat, it could be Bankside on any May Day.

But when he enters the Bimaristan al-Mansur, Nicholas wonders if perhaps the Frenchman hasn't led him to one of the sultan's palaces by mistake.

It takes Nicholas a while to grasp the full magnificence of what he's seeing. He stares in silence around the high vaulted chamber of gleaming white marble; at the slender pillars whose spreading crowns seem made of stone lace; at the intricate patterns of blue, red and gold tiles beneath his feet, each one no larger than a pebble; at the glittering water flowing from a fountain in the shape of a six-pointed star laid on its side and set upon a stepped dais. It is unlike any hospital he has ever seen. He imagines the patients must think themselves already in heaven.

Sitting on the lowest step of the fountain is an old man in a white *djellaba*. He plucks strange notes from a stringed instrument with a long neck, which looks too fragile to produce such calming music. His face seems unmoved by the beauty of the sound he makes. He could have been sitting here for a thousand years, Nicholas thinks, his music soothing back to health countless generations of the sick.

Al-Seddik appears, his white beard jutting out beneath his gleaming smile of welcome, his round little body wrapped in pale-blue silk – a plump damson in bejewelled slippers.

'It is our tribute to Allāh, the most generous, the most bountiful, for his gift of physic,' he says proudly, one downy forearm wafting carelessly to encompass the magnificence.

'It's beautiful,' says Nicholas, almost lost for words. 'Very clean.'

'For hygiene,' al-Seddik tells him. 'This is the command of the great al-Abbas al-Majusi. A Christian may know him better as Haly Abbas. You have heard of him in England, perhaps?'

'I studied a translation of his *Complete Art of Medicine*, at Cambridge,' Nicholas says. 'Not entirely with success; my Latin is a little shaky.'

'We have a copy in our library,' says al-Seddik proudly. 'It is an original – six centuries old.'

Nicholas purses his lips to show how impressed he is. He's not even sure there *were* physicians in England that long ago. 'I'd like to see it,' he says, thinking of John Lumley. 'A friend of mine has a translation of Avicenna's *Canon* in his library – printed in Paris more than a century ago.'

Al-Seddik beams with pleasure. 'Ah, the great Ibn Sina! We have an original of the *Canon* – the *al-Qānūn Fi al-Tabb* – too.'

'An original?'

'Of course.'

'Six hundred years old?'

'Give or take a few decades,' al-Seddik says, clapping Nicholas on the arm in friendly commiseration. 'Personally, I prefer al-Majusi. His method for siting hospitals was the guiding principle when this location was chosen.'

'That must have been the part where I had trouble with the Latin.'

Al-Seddik laughs. 'The builder of a hospital must lay out pieces of meat in the places he is considering.'

'Meat? As an offering?'

'We are not heathens, Dr Shelby,' al-Seddik protests amiably. 'The builder should choose the place where the meat lasts longest before spoiling. This indicates a location conducive to healing. It suggests good air.'

'In London it's hard to escape the smell of spoiling meat wherever you live.'

'Do you also have fountains in your hospitals?' al-Seddik asks, dropping a coin for the musician.

'Only if the barber-surgeon accidentally cuts through an artery,' Nicholas replies. He takes another look around the hall of gleaming stone. 'Surely only the richest can afford treatment in a place like this.'

'On the contrary. Thanks to our system of *al-waqf*, where rich men give a portion of their treasure, anyone may come here. Man; woman; sultan or pilgrim; even slaves are treated here.'

'And the procedure you wish to show me – Professor de Lisle says it is a laryngotomy.'

'Given its rarity in Christendom, I thought you would find it of interest. Come.'

Al-Seddik leads them through more cool high-vaulted chambers to a large room in the heart of the Bimaristan. At its centre is a waist-high platform, tiled with the same intricate patterns that cover the floor, each tiny square so polished that Nicholas thinks he could be standing in a treasury full of rubies, emeralds and topaz. Set into the ceiling is an opening – again in the shape of a six-pointed star – and beyond it an awning on the roof to keep out the worst of the sun.

But it is the man lying on the platform that draws Nicholas's gaze. Clad in a simple cloth shirt that comes almost to his knees, he seems to be in the grip of a trance. Surrounded by such beauty, he would make Nicholas think of a dead pharaoh in his tomb, were it not for the slow, desperate sawing of his breath.

'The patient is slowly suffocating because of a tumour in his throat,' al-Seddik tells him.

'Do you expect him to survive the procedure?' Nicholas asks, knowing the chances are slim.

'*Inshā Allāh*. In England I think you say, "If God wills it".'

'It has been performed successfully only once in Europe – by Signor Brassavola, in Ferrara,' Nicholas says. 'And that was before my queen ascended the throne. We hold it to be too risky a procedure to attempt.'

'Then this fellow is most fortunate that he is not a Christian,' al-Seddik says mischievously. 'His chances are good. We have been performing it since the great Ibn Zuhr first attempted it on a goat, four centuries ago. Surgeon Wadoud is very competent. But in the end, it will be up to Allāh to decide if he lives or dies. So it is with us all.'

Squatting along one side of the chamber is a line of assistants, all dressed in similar linen robes. Some carry wooden writing tablets with concave ends that fit comfortably across their thighs. As Nicholas watches them, a young woman enters, dressed in a pale gown sewn with silver thread, a green linen scarf covering her hair. She has huge brown eyes like Hadir's, and the same quiet thoughtfulness. She walks slowly around the patient, pausing frequently to deliver what Nicholas takes to be observations in a gentle, reflective voice. Above the rasping of the patient's breath, he hears the sound of chalk sticks on wood as the assistants record her words. He approves, thinking of how many times in the Low Countries he could have done with properly written notes in advance, how many wounded men such preparation might have helped him save. It is only when the woman claps her hands – and an assistant gets up and presents her with a scalpel – that Nicholas realizes the woman is Surgeon Wadoud.

'You appear surprised, Dr Shelby,' al-Seddik says with the faintest hint of a smirk.

'I admit I wasn't expecting it.'

'How strange. You Englishmen have a queen to rule over you, yet no women physicians to cure you.' Al-Seddik makes a little huff of satisfaction. 'Allāh has blessed us with clever women doctors for centuries. Take the man who first perfected this very procedure, Ibn Zuhr – two of his daughters became royal physicians. It is our usual custom to confine them to caring for their own sex, but when a doctor is as skilled as Surgeon Wadoud, we would be foolish not to make use of the skills Allāh has given her.'

There is a brief exchange between al-Seddik and the woman, during which she glances at Nicholas as though his presence is a matter of complete indifference to her.

'Surgeon Wadoud is content to have a Christian physician observe her skills, for the greater glory of Allāh, the most merciful, the most bounteous,' al-Seddik says. 'I suggest the description of the procedure is best left to Professor de Lisle, given his medical expertise and his command of our language.'

The superior look on de Lisle's face would not be out of place at the top table of a College feast on Knightrider Street, Nicholas thinks.

The Frenchman translates while Surgeon Wadoud makes what Nicholas takes to be her opening address. She circles the patient with a sinuous, confident grace.

'The procedure is customarily performed with the patient in a sitting position. Madame Wadoud does not agree with this. It is better that he should be prone.'

'To bring the trachea close to the surface, I presume,' says Nicholas.

'Exactly. And the patient must be calmed to the point of sleep with the juice of poppy and mandrake, or it is likely that he will struggle. If he does, there is too great a risk of severing the carotid arteries, leading to death. The sedative must be carefully mixed, or the patient may die before the procedure can begin. If performed correctly, there should be little loss of blood.' He pauses to concentrate on what Surgeon Wadoud is saying. When he has it in his head, he nods. 'Madame Wadoud explains it is wise to have close by a paste of spiders' webs and rabbit hair mixed in egg-white – lest a mistake is made and the patient bleeds profusely.'

Nicholas nods to show he has absorbed this crucial information.

'Also, she has taken the precaution of consulting a horoscope to ensure the stars are propitious.'

Nicholas can hear Elizabeth Cecil's accusing voice in his ear: *Is it true you abjure casting a horoscope before you make a diagnosis?... that flies in the face of all received wisdom...* He says to de Lisle innocently, 'Let's hope that Capricorn was in the ascendency then.'

De Lisle looks at him blankly. 'Capricorn?'

'The horned goat. Master Ibn Zuhr learned this procedure by practising on a—' He pauses. 'Oh, never mind.'

Surgeon Wadoud advances on her patient, the long iron scalpel held between her slender fingers like a quill. Save for her mouth, her face is immobile, determined yet utterly calm. Nicholas has never witnessed such controlled beauty. De Lisle translates her brisk commentary.

'Also, Surgeon Wadoud has ensured that to favour the outcome, a square of magic numbers has been provided,' he says as one of the attendants holds up a wooden square about the size of a large book. Written across the top are five lines of Moorish writing. Beneath, in each square of a chalked grid, is drawn a symbol that Nicholas takes to be a number.

'At the top is a charm,' de Lisle continues, 'to strengthen the courage of the patient. The numbers in the grid add up to the same sum, no matter which way you do it – up, down or across. The Moors hold this phenomenon to be magic.'

With an unexpected pang of pain, Nicholas recalls how the midwife tried to stop Eleanor's descent towards death, putting her faith in holy stones that she claimed had been washed in the blood of St Margaret. It occurs to him now that while their hospitals might leave England's in the shade, the Moors share the same reliance on mystic hogwash.

Surgeon Wadoud snaps her fingers. An attendant places a rolled cloth beneath the patient's neck, arching the throat as though preparing him for an execution. The tortured breathing becomes deeper, slower. Now Nicholas can see what's causing the man to slowly suffocate – a large swelling on one side of his neck, just above the Adam's apple.

Wadoud places her free index finger on the man's throat and nods an invitation to Nicholas to do likewise. The flesh is still damp from washing, he notices.

Wadoud guides his fingers until Nicholas can feel the ring of cartilage above the trachea. Her touch sends a pulse through his body. Her face is very close to his. He can smell the rose oil on her skin, reminding him of Bianca. She gives him one short glance with her extraordinary eyes and presses his fingers down on the patient's throat, saying something to him in her language. It could be an instruction. It could be a lover's endearment. Nicholas forces himself to concentrate.

'Keep pressing, and watch closely,' de Lisle translates at his shoulder.

Surgeon Wadoud moves her index finger to a spot midway between where Nicholas is pressing and the top of the patient's sternum, talking all the while.

'The cut must be made on the centreline,' de Lisle says as the scalpel tip touches the flesh like a jewel placed against a lover's throat. 'Or else when the reed is inserted, it can slip under the surrounding tissue. And it should be vertical – with enough force to penetrate the trachea – thus.'

Surgeon Wadoud's scalpel slices downwards into the patient's throat. His body gives no more than a brief tremor.

For a moment she leaves the blade there, as though she's testing the centre of a joint of meat to see if it's cooked. When she removes it, the pink edges of the wound draw back like morning-glory petals opening to the rising sun. Just as she'd promised, there is little bleeding.

An assistant produces a short length of reed, neatly trimmed at each end. He rolls one end in honey smeared on a small trencher and hands it to Surgeon Wadoud, who deftly inserts it into the open wound, inspects the results of her labours, nods to show she is content and steps aside.

Two more helpers hurry forward to anoint the wound with a balm of oliban, aloe and myrrh, sprinkling it with red iron oxide. They bandage the patient's neck with clean linen, leaving the tip of the reed exposed. Nicholas notices the rasping sound of his breathing has been replaced by a soft whistle with each exhalation. If Surgeon Wadoud is pleased with her efforts, the deep-set eyes do not show it.

De Lisle says, 'Now there is a chance he will live – God willing – while his tumour is treated with...' a quick exchange with Surgeon Wadoud to get the correct words, 'regular cupping to draw out the black bile. The wound should be washed daily with water and honey. Provided that he is fed only cold broth, he should recover his speech.'

'Such a simple procedure,' says Nicholas, impressed. 'We could have made use of it in the Low Countries.'

'Aside from the risk of severing the carotid artery, there is also the danger that the wound becomes foul. The trick is in keeping it clean.'

'That would put us at a disadvantage,' Nicholas agrees. 'It could be a while before we get marble and fountains in our hospitals.'

Surgeon Wadoud receives Nicholas's expressions of thanks and admiration with what appears to be supreme indifference. But al-Seddik is visibly excited.

'After the work must come the play, yes?'

The minister makes it sound as though he's performed the laryngotomy himself. He beams with self-congratulatory pleasure.

'I have arranged a visit to the hammam, the bathhouse.' He lays a regretful hand across his ample breast. 'Sadly, it is not permitted for someone who is not a follower of the Prophet – peace be upon him – to bathe amongst the faithful. So I have arranged for Professor de Lisle to take you to the hammam in the Aduana, where the Christians bathe. Then we shall all feast together at my house. You can tell me how Lord Burghley and his son are faring in their dealings with your queen.' He takes a final look at the patient wheezing gently on the table and sighs. 'It must be difficult for such clever men to have to step so cautiously across the shadow of a woman who can end their lives on a whim.'

And just for a moment Nicholas's isn't certain whether the woman he's referring to is Queen Elizabeth or Surgeon Wadoud.

The hammam is a nondescript building set deep in the Aduana, with nothing to show its purpose other than a faded hand brandishing a strigil painted beside the entrance. Nicholas is unsure what to expect; the queen's father shut down the Southwark bathhouses long before he was born, for being dens of vice and lascivity. And he's not asked Arnoult de Lisle, for fear of looking like a country green-pate.

At the doorway the Frenchman gives way to a departing customer, a man who stops Nicholas dead in his tracks for reasons that go far beyond mere courtesy.

He is a studious-looking fellow of about thirty, whose benign, freshly cleansed face glows with rapturous contentment, though whether from piety or from the exertions of the masseur it is hard to tell. What concerns Nicholas is his dress: the black gown and broad-brimmed hat of the Society of Jesus – the Jesuits. Nicholas tries not to stare.

To the Cecils – indeed, to the Privy Council and the queen herself – a Jesuit is a wasp to be stamped upon, before it has a chance to sting you. It is the Jesuit order that sends papist agents into England to plot against the woman they consider a heretic. If they are here in Morocco, Nicholas thinks, who knows what mischief they could be about. What will Robert Cecil expect him to do, he wonders: follow the Jesuit home and garrotte him in a dark alley?

De Lisle greets the man in French, and Nicholas hears the physician mention his name. The priest looks his way and makes a polite little nod. Unsmiling, Nicholas returns it. Then, sparing him further consternation, the Jesuit goes on his way, clean in body if not in religious conviction.

Once inside the hammam they are greeted by the owner, a large, glistening fellow, whose smile of welcome reveals a row of extraordinarily uneven teeth. His tunic is stained with cleansing oil and his heavy hands have the calloused palms of a vigorous masseur. He's a Melkite Christian from Aleppo, de Lisle explains, though it means little to Nicholas.

After Nicholas and de Lisle have undressed, wrapping themselves in silk towels for modesty, they are ushered into a warm antechamber where *atay* is served. When they have drunk, they move on into a broad, hexagonal space with a domed roof and a circle of pillars. It is as hot here as it is outside, under the full glare of the sun. But the air is steamy, thickly laden with the scent of foreign unguents. On wooden benches a score of bathers sit, conversing in almost as many languages, their voices echoing off the dripping plaster walls: business talk, by the earnest tone of it, offers and counter-offers, protests at an inflated asking price, laughter as hands shake on the deal. From somewhere beyond a doorway arched in the Ottoman manner comes the slap of fists pummelling flesh, and the groans of tortured ecstasy that escape the mouth when muscles suddenly unknot.

As they take their places on a vacant bench, Nicholas feels the sweat streaming down his body. For a moment he feels light-headed. De Lisle leans closer and, with a knowing smile, says casually, 'You need have no fear. Fra Cyprien is a negotiator.'

Caught off-guard by both the atmosphere and the Frenchman's words, Nicholas feigns innocence. 'You have me at a loss, sir. I know of no such person.'

'The Jesuit. I saw the look on your face – like a man who's noticed he's about to step on a scorpion.'

Nicholas gives his host a grim smile. He feels a pool of perspiration overflow his top lip. 'We have a certain distrust of Jesuits in my country.'

'And so you thought he and I might be in league, yes?'

Nicholas's reply feels like the most transparent thing he's ever said. 'Of course not. Why would I think that?'

De Lisle claps him wetly on the shoulder. 'You can relax, Dr Shelby. Fra Cyprien has come to Marrakech to arrange a ransom. It is a regular occurrence.'

'A ransom? For whom?'

'Did you not see the slave market when you arrived? Fra Cyprien has come to negotiate the return of a fellow Catholic taken by Moor corsairs. They stopped his ship off Sagres last September.'

Amongst the echoing voices, Nicholas thinks he can hear Cathal Connell's: *You can't traffic with the Moor and not come to appreciate his proficiency in the meat trade, Dr Shelby...*

'The man's family can afford one thousand marks,' de Lisle continues. 'The slave owner wants fifteen hundred. Hopefully, Fra Cyprien will negotiate a compromise. A slave's value is sometimes greater than his worth as a mere beast of burden – if he has resources to call upon.'

'And if there is no agreement?'

'Then Fra Cyprien will return home a disappointed man. And the poor Catholic will remain a slave – unless he can find someone else to pay the ransom.'

It seems a plausible explanation for the Jesuit's presence, Nicholas thinks. The only question in his mind is: is it the truth?

When they have taken enough ease in the heat, the two men pass into a chamber where attendants ladle cold water over them from polished bronze bowls. From there, it is but a few steps to the alcoves from which Nicholas had heard the groans and cries emanating. He and de Lisle stretch out on stone plinths while the masseurs go to work, showing neither man much mercy.

Giving himself up to the unfamiliar mix of agony and ecstasy, Nicholas notices an attendant moving amongst the plinths. The man is dispensing oil from a clay jar to the masseurs. He moves with a strange lopsided gait.

'See? That's what can happen if you don't have a rich family and a Fra Cyprien to call upon,' says de Lisle, once again catching the focus of his guest's gaze.

'An accident?'

'Castration,' de Lisle says brutally. 'Marcu is from Sicily. The poor fellow came here in payment of the *devshirme*. He was then unwise enough to attempt an escape.'

Nicholas gives de Lisle a blank look. 'The *devshirme* – what is that?'

'The blood-tax. Every year young men from the Christian coastal villages around the Mediterranean are given up by their families to the Moors. In return, the corsairs spare those same villages from destruction. The boys have a simple choice: renounce their Christian faith, become a Mohammedan and serve the Moors as warriors – or die.' A sad shake of the head. 'Being poor, they have no need of a negotiator like Fra Cyprien. They have nothing with which to pay a ransom.'

'It's not much of a choice, this blood-tax,' Nicholas says, suppressing a groan as the masseur harrows the flesh between his shoulders.

'On the contrary. It can be a good life, better than the one they left behind. They are enlisted as janissaries – the sultan's elite warriors. They are fed well. They have status. They can take their own slaves in conquest. All they have to do is forget that their immortal souls have been damned by apostasy.'

Nicholas glances again at the hobbling, butchered Marcu. 'If someone was threatening to do *that* to me – or worse – then I might consider turning my back on the Almighty,' he says. 'Few of us have no limit to the courage in our hearts.'

De Lisle turns his head and smiles. 'Never fear, Dr Shelby. No one will ask *us* to pay the blood-tax. You and I, we are useful to powerful men. Best we keep it that way, eh?'

✠

Nicholas's education continues the following morning. It continues in much the same vein for almost a week. By day, he spends his time in the Bimaristan al-Mansur, with Arnoult de Lisle and Surgeon Wadoud as his guides. He tours the wards, which Surgeon Wadoud calls iwans, and speaks through the Frenchman to the patients. He visits the iwan where maladies of the eye are treated, and the ward reserved for women, though he is not permitted further than the delicately arched entrance. He sees where those who are sick of mind are cared for, and it is as unlike London's Bedlam – where the mad dwell in a misery that is by no means confined to the spirit – as he can possibly imagine. When he lingers in the spacious gardens, watching the recuperating patients sitting in the shade of the orange trees while they recite passages from holy texts in gratitude for the wisdom that Allāh has revealed to his physicians, he cannot help wondering what old Baronsdale and the fellows of the College in London would make of it all.

Sometimes he catches Surgeon Wadoud glancing at him with cool interest, as though she cannot quite fathom the foreigner who has appeared in her domain. She seems disinclined to ask him about physic in his world. But then what would he tell her – that far from benefiting from a system like *al-waqf*, English hospitals have scarcely prospered since the queen's late father threw down the monasteries and forced the sick to search for relief elsewhere? What could he offer her that would match the fabled Bimaristans of Damascus, Cairo and Baghdad, which she tells him have existed for almost a millennium?

On the seventh day Sumayl al-Seddik arrives to escort him to the Bimaristan's library, where Nicholas is permitted to view the ancient texts by Ibn Sina, al-Zahrawi and Ibn al-Nafis. He looks on in awe as de Lisle translates the Moorish writing, lines of strangely sweeping curlicues that remind him of wave-crests blown on a summer wind. He learns about the importance of foods to aid recovery: foods that heat, and which the Moors call *garmi* – goose and duck and the flesh of a male goat, peaches and olives; and foods that cool, which are termed *sardi* – female goat meat, melons, figs and pomegranates. He learns the classifications of an irregular pulse by the animalistic names the Moors use: gazelle, ant and rat-tail; and the fifteen different varieties of pain.

By now he has begun to feel a measure of guilt. If he was back on Bankside, tending to the sick at St Tom's as his professional self has told him more than once he should be, he'd have precious little to offer them in comparison. But most of all, he feels like a thief who's been given the key to a vast treasure store.

'Is there news of when I might present my letter to the sultan?'
he asks al-Seddik when his tour of the library is over.

The Moor rubs one hand over his silk-sheathed belly, as
though in anticipation of another good meal. 'Soon. Very soon.
Inshā Allāh.' He gives Nicholas a diplomat's smile. 'It is a little
like heaven: one trusts one will get there one day, but there is no
certain way of knowing quite when.'

✠

When Nicholas returns to the Street of the Weavers a short while
later, the mud-brick walls still shimmer from the heat of the sun,
even though it is almost evening. The lane is deserted, its only
occupant a scrawny grey cat playing idly with a half-dead lizard
beneath a date palm.

Approaching the house, he sees that Hadir has left the door
open in anticipation of his return. He steps through the low
entrance and into the cool darkness of the interior passage.
He stands still for a moment, breathing in the scent of orange
blossom from the trees in the central courtyard. Then he calls
out to let Hadir know he's arrived.

Three times.

Each without an answer. The lad must be asleep somewhere.

But why has no one else come? Where is the Berber Methuselah
woman who does the cooking? Where is the boy who fetches
water, and the young girl who does the infidel's washing and
still hasn't stopped staring at him with those immense brown
eyes? All he can hear is the twittering of the sparrows as they dart
around the upper gallery. He steps out into the courtyard.

They have planned the ambush to perfection: two figures,
moving unnaturally fast from the blurred edges of his vision,
so indistinct they could be apparitions. In a moment of startled
comprehension, Nicholas realizes they have waited patiently for

the moment when moving from darkness into dazzling sunlight makes the victim almost blind.

They strike so swiftly that Nicholas has little chance to defend himself. Before he can even think of resisting, one of them has his head in an armlock that forces him to close his eyes or stare directly into the sun. Inside a hot orange mist, the blood vessels in his eyelids become a dark spider's web ensnaring him. The arm about his neck tightens. Nicholas begins to gasp for breath, clawing with frenzied fingers at the suffocating weight crushing his windpipe.

Before the blackness takes him there is a brief moment of dreaming. The merest flash of a fantasy. Bianca Merton is crouching over him, moving her lips towards his upturned throat. She is preparing to put Eleanor into her rightful place in the archive of his past. And this time there is no kissing knot, no audience in the Jackdaw's taproom to make a mockery of it. His neck arches. Waiting. Waiting for the moment he has denied for so long.

But when her tongue touches his throat, it is not the hot kiss of long-delayed consummation that he feels. It is the icy thrust of Surgeon Wadoud's scalpel.

30

'Bastarda!' Bianca barks under her breath as the pestle flies out of her hand and rolls across the tabletop. She steadies the mortar before it can follow, and retrieves the pestle in the very last moment before it crashes to the floor. Then she blames Reynard Gault for being the cause of her clumsiness.

She has spent the last hour preparing the pomanders of rose leaves, tragacanth gum and camphor for him to hang about the necks of his investments, should the pestilence ever have the temerity to stick its nose around the front door of his new-toy house in Smithfield.

She thinks again of her visit to Giltspur Street, and how she'd left with the distinct impression that Gault was as interested in what Nicholas might have told her about his mission for Robert Cecil as he was in her physic. Now she is more convinced than ever that Nicholas has not told her the whole story. As a consequence, Bianca fears for him more than ever. And though she will not admit it, she knows that is the real cause of the pestle taking on a wilful life of its own.

And there is something else troubling her. It is the lie Gault told her about not knowing the name of Solomon Mandel.

Was he somehow involved in the Jew's death? she asks herself, as the leaves she is pounding release their heady scents. Why else would he have lied to her?

She wonders how she might prove that Gault knew Mandel, or at least met him, as she suspects. Perhaps the Barbary Company has a record of the events surrounding the Moor envoy's visit to London – the visit that was welcomed by its leading merchants. She shakes her head as she imagines the welcome she'd get if she turned up at the guildhall and asked to see it. Besides, Gault would be bound to hear of it.

She is about to resign herself to defeat when her eyes alight on a small earthenware pot, sitting all by itself on the window ledge by the street door, softly lit by the late-afternoon sun. It contains ointment for Parson Moody's tired eyes. She is expecting him to call today and collect it, if he can find time away from the growing number of funerals that he must conduct.

Of course. Parson Moody!

Chiding herself for not having made the connection when she was preparing the ointment, she almost drops the pestle again. Her jaw stiffens with satisfaction. Parson Moody is the priest at St Saviour's where the parish records are stored, the same records that include the subsidy roll that enabled Nicholas to learn that Solomon Mandel was the Turk's man.

And Southwark was where the entourage of the Sultan of Morocco's envoy entered London, after its landfall in Devon in 1589.

Grinning like a crazed woman, Bianca wields her pestle victoriously in the air, as if she has just battered an assailant into submission. Because it has dawned on her that if she's learned only one thing about Englishmen like Reynard Gault since arriving from Padua, it is this: when it comes to matters of great civic occasion, they would rather walk naked through the Royal Exchange than have their names left out of the record.

✠

She arrives at St Saviour's to find Parson Moody preparing for Evensong. He is flustered. He's only just returned from burying the entire Molestrop family: husband, wife, one full set of grandparents and an unmarried daughter of sixteen, all of whom were only permitted to leave their plague house behind the pike ponds when they had been dead long enough to satisfy the parish collectors.

'I do not know why God punishes the innocent so,' Moody says harshly, wiping his brow so that his brimmed hat tilts back over his temple. 'We pray. We abjure from sinfulness as best we can. And then we pray some more. It makes no difference. What His plan for us is, I cannot imagine.'

'I've brought the medicine for your eyes, Parson Moody,' Bianca says, handing him the pot.

'You are a good woman, Mistress Merton,' he says with a priest's unassailable smile. '*Whatever* some in this parish may say about you.' He pats her arm. 'I want you to know I never believed the wilder speculations.'

'I'm glad to hear it.'

'Is there news of when Dr Shelby might return? I had not imagined he would abandon us at such a time as this.'

'I don't believe he has abandoned us, Parson Moody. Had he known the pestilence would increase, he would have stayed.' As a defence, she thinks, it's not entirely watertight. 'Besides, there is little a physician can do that we are not already doing ourselves. Nicholas said as much before he left.'

'Then that simply reminds us that we sinners are all dependent upon God's continuing grace.'

She nods sagely, if only to make him feel better. 'I would ask a question of you, Parson Moody. Will you spare me a moment of your time?'

'And what question is that, Mistress Merton?' he replies as she follows him into the coolness of the church.

'When Dr Shelby was called to the inquest into Master Mandel's brutal murder, he came here to ask if he could inspect the parish records, to see if he might find out a little about Solomon's past.' She can hear her words echoing faintly off the ancient stones. 'Before he left, Nicholas asked me if I would continue his investigation.'

'Is that so?'

'As you know, Solomon's murderer has not yet been brought to justice.'

'I thought that young Moor of yours was a suspect.'

'Farzad? No. I can vouch for Farzad. It couldn't have been him. Even Constable Willders knew him to be wholly innocent.'

'I'm glad to hear it. We have so many foreigners in the city these days, I sometimes marvel that more of us are not murdered in our beds.'

'I would remind you that I am also a foreigner in this land,' Bianca says emphatically. As soon as the words are out of her mouth, she regrets them. This is no time to alienate Parson Moody.

'Are you really?' he asks, as though she'd told him she was a mermaid. 'Oh yes – Italy. I remember Mistress Solver telling me you had an Italian mother and an English father.' He looks at her with unshakeable conviction. 'So, really, you are one of us. Barely foreign at all.'

She wonders what that smile might look like if she told him she was also a Catholic. But perhaps he already knows. Perhaps Jenny Solver told him that, too.

'How long have you been here at St Saviour's?'

'Fifteen years.' From his voice, it could be a gaol sentence.

'A long while.'

'I *could* consider it a failure. Bankside is no godlier today than when first I arrived. The playhouse and the bear-pit are still dens of vice. There's barely one man in three practising an honest profession. And as for the lasciviousness of the women – not including yourself, of course...'

'Of course,' she echoes, stifling a grin as she thinks of the bawdy-house near the Falcon stairs she knows he likes to visit.

'Fifteen years battling Satan from the depths of such a moral cess-pit might have broken a man with less faith in his heart.' He glances reproachfully towards heaven. 'Now, Mistress, what was it you wished to ask of me?'

'Can you recall the occasion of the visit to London by the envoy of the Sultan of Morocco? It was in '89 – January, I think.'

'I would be a poor fellow if I could not. A most impressive sight. All those faces burned by the desert sun. How those Moors must have marvelled to see civilization up close.'

'Do you recall who was here to greet them?'

'The Lord Mayor... most of the Corporation of the City... Lord Burghley... I cannot be exact, but certainly many notable men, for sure.'

'Do you happen to know if the parish records contain any report of the event?'

'Oh yes, I drew it up myself – for the aldermen,' Parson Moody says proudly.

'Might I see it?'

A look of unbearable sadness clouds his face. 'I am *so* sorry, Mistress Merton, but that will not be possible.'

'Why not?'

'They are confidential records. And you are a woman. I am sure you understand.'

'But you let Dr Shelby see them.'

'That's different. *His* request was on behalf of Coroner Danby.'

'That's a pity.'

'I wish I could be more helpful. I really do.'

'No, you've been most generous with your time, Parson Moody. I'm sorry to have troubled you.'

'Is there aught else I may do for you, Mistress Merton?'

'No. Nothing.'

'Then thank you again – for the ointment.'

Bianca raises her voice just enough to get a good echo back off the church walls.

'Twice a day,' she says sweetly.

Parson Moody seems puzzled. 'Forgive me – you have me disadvantaged...'

Bianca dabs at the corners of her eyes. 'I recommend you apply it twice a day. A small amount should do the trick.'

'Ah, of course.'

'Then you'll be able to see your way to the Falcon stairs without difficulty. After Evensong, isn't it? Every Wednesday. Or is it Thursday? I forget which. I'll have to ask the bawd – Mistress Jennings. I'm sure I've seen her in your congregation.'

✠

Five minutes later Bianca is alone in the vestry, a pile of parchment rolls and leather-bound books on the table before her. Through the open door she can see Parson Moody prostrate before the altar, deep in prayer.

It takes her some time to find it, but when she does, her heart begins to race. It is a description of the event recorded for posterity and the aggrandisement of the parish – how the sultan's envoy was met on Long Southwark by the Lord Mayor and the Corporation of London.

And amongst all the dignitaries, one humble translator, Master Solomon Mandel, a trader in spices between England and Morocco, with skills in the language of the Moor.

And forty leading lights of the Worshipful Barbary Company of London. Including one Reynard Gault, merchant venturer.

At which point the strength in her legs seems abruptly to desert her. She has to reach out a hand to the table in order to steady herself. She stares at the neatly inked script, unable to believe what she has seen.

She reads the line again, just to be sure:

Reynard Gault. Merchant venturer.

Who is attending not merely in his commercial capacity, but in a more formal role – as representative of the English College of Heralds, in which august body he is proud to hold the purely honorary position of Rouge Croix Pursuivant.

PART 3

Blood-Tax

31

'Why have you come here?'

The heavily accented voice has asked the same question since Nicholas's consciousness first began to emerge from the dark cave to which near-suffocation had dispatched it.

He is sitting against a rough wall of pitted grey masonry, in a plain narrow storeroom in the house on the Street of the Weavers. The early-evening light spills through a small grille set into the ceiling, casting an irregular shape at the foot of the far wall. He cannot move his arms. In his befuddled state he thinks he's still aboard the *Righteous*, and the figure standing over him is Cathal Connell, come to pitch him into the ocean before he regains the use of his limbs. Then he realizes his hands are bound behind his back.

'Why have you come here?'

The voice is clearer now, though still slightly muffled. Nicholas realizes it is not the man standing guard over him who is speaking, but a figure sitting cross-legged just out of striking distance. His face is covered by a cloth *kufiya*, save for the eyes, which fix Nicholas like a hawk's. At his back Nicholas can make out three other men, standing in silent watchfulness. The *kufiya* speaks again.

'Dr Shelby, if you wish this place not to be a charnel house for your bones, tell us why you have come to our city – the *true* reason.'

A young voice. Someone in their early twenties. The English is not that of a native speaker, nor does it have the accent of a Hadir or an al-Seddik. Somewhere to the east of Italy is all Nicholas can manage. He remembers something de Lisle told him earlier at the hammam: *The blood-tax... a simple choice: serve the Moors as warriors – or die...*

Is that who these people are, Nicholas wonders: janissaries?

'I am an envoy from the queen of England,' he says, in his best imitation of an outraged diplomat. 'I carry a letter from the queen to the sultan. It is your duty to let me go. And if you've harmed anyone in my house, you will pay for it dearly.'

The reply has a note of disappointed familiarity to it. 'How many times has my master heard those words *let me go*? In the slave markets, in the galleys, in the prisons, always it is: *please* let me go. But a man who begs in such a manner is not a true man at all. He is no more of a man than one who is ruled by a woman. Wouldn't you agree – *infidel*?'

'Who are you? Why have you abused the envoy of a friendly nation in such a manner?'

'I am at the service of His Excellency Muhammed al-Annuri,' says the *kufiya*, clasping his hands together as though about to pray. Young fingers to go with a young voice, Nicholas observes. 'It is a name you should learn to fear.'

Nicholas is under no illusions. If these are the men who tortured and murdered Adolfo Sykes, then his bluster will last only until they draw the knife.

'What does he want from me? If I have transgressed some custom or other, I apologize. It was through ignorance. Nothing more.'

A short silence – graciously given to allow him time to consider the inadequacy of his statement.

'I will ask you again, Dr Shelby. Why have you come to Marrakech? My master wishes to know.'

'I told you. I am an envoy. Also, I have come to study physic in your land. In all civilized lands that would entitle me to safe passage. So now let me go.'

The man sitting before him seems unconcerned by royal letters expressing friendship, or even the diplomatic conventions of civilized lands. 'I do not believe you,' he says. 'I think you are a spy. It is His Excellency al-Annuri's task to root out spies. To crush them between his fingers like lice.' He snaps the tip of his middle finger across his thumb to show how it is done. 'Why did you visit the place where the infidel Sykes met his death? Why did you then visit his grave?'

It does not surprise Nicholas to learn that he was followed to the church in the Aduana. Cecil's watchers in London do it to foreigners all the time. He falls back upon the fiction he told Hadir.

'I was asked by someone in England to bring them news of him – a friend of Master Sykes. I would hardly call that spying.'

'I do not believe you,' says the *kufiya*.

'It is the truth.'

'I think you have come to replace him.'

'Why should you think that? I'm not a member of the Barbary Company, I'm a physician. I don't know the first thing about wool, other than how to darn a hole in it.'

The body of his questioner tilts towards him, as if a great confidence is about to be revealed.

'The infidel Sykes was spy. He sent intelligence to the English queen. You have been sent to continue his work.'

'He was just a merchant,' says Nicholas. 'If he was sending anything to England, it was probably information about trade. That's not sedition. All merchants do it.'

Another long pause, while the *kufiya* considers this.

You're feeding me rope to hang myself, thinks Nicholas. He wonders how long he can keep his head out of the noose. Or his breast away from the knife.

'What is in the letter to our sultan? Have you read it?'

'Yes – in England, before it was sealed.'

'And its contents?'

'An expression of greetings and continued goodwill. And a line or two commending me to His Majesty the sultan. I know Her Grace is eager to maintain the friendship between our realms, and to assist His Majesty in defending Morocco against the Spanish king. If you don't believe me, it's in the chest in my chamber. Read it. But you'll have to explain to your sultan why someone else had first sight of a privy letter.'

The *kufiya* leans forward again. Nicholas thinks he sees the first flicker of uncertainty in those anonymous eyes.

'What do you know of the death of Adolfo Sykes, Physician?'

'Nothing. I was told it was an accident. Why do you keep asking me about Sykes? I've never even met him.'

'This friend in England who asks after the infidel Sykes – what is his name?'

'Does it matter?'

'The *name* of this friend.'

The *kufiya*'s hand rests gently on the hilt of the curved dagger he wears at his belt. Nicholas has another awful vision of Hadir's blood soaking into the plaster of the roof terrace, long ribbons of flesh stripped from his young chest.

He reasons that if al-Annuri already knows that Sykes was Robert Cecil's agent, then telling his interrogator it was Cecil who sent him could prove as fatal to a physician as it could to a factor of the Barbary Company. So he pulls out of the air a convenient name from his past, one that will suit his professed reason for visiting Marrakech.

308

'Fulke Vaesy,' he says.

'Who is this Vaesy?'

'He was a medical man. I studied under him some years ago. He was learned in anatomy – at least, he thought he was.'

'And how does this Vaesy in England come to know Adolfo Sykes in Marrakech?'

'I haven't the slightest notion. I was just asked to pass on his remembrances, that's all. It's not a crime. And it's certainly not spying.'

The *kufiya* holds a brisk impromptu discussion with the men standing in the shadows behind him. Nicholas guesses that whoever their master is, he is not in the chamber with them.

'What is your relationship with Minister Cey-cill?'

Nicholas's heart sinks.

'I am physician to Sir Robert's son.'

'And his father, Lord Burg-ley?'

'I have no relationship with Lord Burghley. I'm simply carrying a letter of remembrance from him to Minister al-Seddik. They met in London.'

Another brief discussion, more hesitant than the first. It occurs to Nicholas that these men have been schooled in what to ask. Faced with answers they did not expect, they are uncertain how to proceed. Nicholas seizes his opportunity.

'His Majesty al-Mansur will not look kindly upon those who harm an envoy from his trusted friend, Queen Elizabeth. In my realm it is customary to flay those who dishonour an emissary from an allied nation. Then we behead them. I suggest you tell His Excellency al-Annuri that.'

The *kufiya* studies him intently for a moment, as though trying to reach a conclusion.

'How long do you intend to remain in our land, Physician?'

309

Nicholas feels brave enough now to step up the bluster. 'After this outrage, for as short a time as possible!'

The *kufiya* gets to his feet. 'That would be most wise.' He walks over. Nicholas braces himself for a brutal kick in the ribs.

It doesn't come.

'Sultan al-Mansur is a busy man,' the *kufiya* says. 'He does not have the time to ensure the safety of every infidel who comes into our realm, not even those who are envoys of the English queen. Take my advice: go home at the earliest opportunity. You would not be the first man who has come here only to disappear into the slave market.'

They leave him sitting against the wall. When they close the door, he hears the sound of a key turning in the lock. As their voices fade away, Nicholas's legs begin to tremble. He slides himself into the patch of light, hoping that the heat of the dying sun will thaw the cold tentacles of fear writhing in his stomach.

✠

When Hadir unlocks the door and enters the storeroom there are tears in his eyes. 'Thanks be to Allāh, the most merciful, the most compassionate – you are alive!' he cries. 'I thought you dead, like Sayidi Sy-kess.'

'Where is everyone? Are they safe?'

'All safe. But these men who came here, they said if we did not leave the house and stay away until after the *al-maghrib* prayers, they would kill us all. Starting with grandmother Tiziri.'

For a moment Nicholas wonders who Hadir is talking about. Then it dawns on him: he has no idea of the names of his Berber servants. But he is immeasurably relieved they are alive.

'They claimed they were al-Annuri's men,' Nicholas says. 'They wanted to know if I was a spy. I suppose, after Minister al-Seddik chased away his watchers, he decided to forgo diplomacy. Are they enemies, al-Annuri and al-Seddik?'

'To Muhammed al-Annuri, all men are enemies. Except his master the sultan.'

Hadir fetches a knife and cuts through the bindings around Nicholas's wrists and ankles. As he follows Nicholas out of the storeroom he says plaintively, 'Half a ducat a week – it is not suitable for work such as this.'

✠

That evening grandmother Tiziri the Methuselah woman, Gwata the boy who fetches the water, and his sister Lalla who does the washing do not hide themselves away. They eat with Nicholas on the roof terrace. Hadir explains that tomorrow a holy month of fasting begins, and the meal must be savoured; Nicholas, as an unbeliever, may eat and take water between sunrise and sunset if he wishes, but only grandmother Tiziri may take sustenance, because of her great age.

The Berbers listen wide-eyed as Hadir translates vignettes of life in England. There is much laughter when Lalla announces that she will be the second Queen of Morocco, after grandmother Tiziri has tired of the luxury.

The good companionship is dented only by Nicholas's deep-seated fear: that Adolfo Sykes unearthed something in this city that cost him his life. And that *someone* suspects Nicholas has come here to finish what he began.

After the dishes are cleared away, he goes down to the courtyard and lingers awhile, savouring the coolness of the evening air and the scent of orange blossom while he tries to make sense of the day's events. He sees again Surgeon Wadoud at work and stores away what he has learned, though he's sure if he ever attempts the same procedure back in England the College of Physicians will very likely impeach him. He remembers the gelded slave Marcu, and the pink, rapturously optimistic face of Fra Cyprien – who may, or may not, negotiate a captive's return to his family for somewhere approaching fifteen hundred marks. He thinks of the *kufiya*'s warning about how a man may disappear into the galleys without trace, if he doesn't take sensible advice and go home at the earliest opportunity. And of Adolfo Sykes, a man he has never met, but to whom he feels he owes the duty of commemoration.

And he yearns to be back in England, making love to Bianca Merton, and not here on the Barbary shore where beauty and butchery wear interchangeable faces.

✠

The square of sky above the courtyard is a luminous mauve, the first stars emerging tentatively from the haze left by the heat of the day.

'Sit with me a while, Hadir,' Nicholas says, sinking down against the trunk of an old pomegranate tree. He has known this moment was inescapable from the time he first put his trust in the young Moor. 'I have to be honest with you. While I *am* a physician, and I *have* come to Morocco to learn about your people's physic, I have also been sent here to find out what happened to your friend, Adolfo Sykes.'

Hadir, squatting down beside him, seems to sag like a man freed from a heavy load. 'I know this since you ask me questions by the Bab Doukkala. I think then that this *berraniyin* who has come from England is more than he says.'

'Well then, this *berraniyin* doesn't believe your friend died of an accident and was then mauled by wild beasts, any more than you do.'

Hadir nods miserably.

'How long have you suspected?'

'Since my friend Sy-kess decided he must hide the letters he was planning to send to England,' Hadir says, pointing across the courtyard.

Set into the wall of the opposite cloister is something Nicholas has not noticed before: a talisman to ward off ill fortune and evil spirits. A talisman in the shape of a plaster hand, the fingers pointing downwards. Just like the one beside the door of Solomon Mandel's house on Bankside.

32

The dimpled wall of the little cloister is bathed in soft evening light. Nicholas studies the talisman in which both Adolfo Sykes and Solomon Mandel had so misguidedly placed their trust. The stone hand seems firmly cemented to the masonry, its fingers pointing downwards towards the tiled floor.

'Let me, *Sayidi*,' says Hadir. 'My friend Sy-kess show me how.'

Hadir cups the talisman with both hands, curling his slender fingers over the stone to get purchase. In Nicholas's mind, it is the hand of Adolfo Sykes he clasps, greeting his mentor after a hard day spent trading in the Aduana.

After a moment's careful manipulation, Hadir slowly pulls the talisman away from the wall. It makes a rasping sound as it slides out, revealing the slug of stone that held it in place. Triumphantly Hadir lifts it away, revealing a dark recess some three inches square.

Nicholas squats down and tries to see into the hole, but the fading light and the ceiling of the cloister make it impossible. He is about to put his fingers in when Hadir stops him.

'Sometime scorpion make his home in a place like this. Is not good to touch.'

An oil lamp is obtained from grandmother Tiziri. By its light, Nicholas peers again into the cavity. There is no scorpion. But nor are there any letters. The space is empty.

'Perhaps Sayidi Sy-kess already send the letters to England,' Hadir says with a shrug.

'But why did he need a hiding place? Who was he hiding them from?'

'I do not know, Sayidi.'

'Did he tell anyone other than you about this hiding place?'

'He made me swear an oath not to speak of it. And I did not.'

'Did Master Sykes have many visitors here? Could someone else have found the niche?'

'Sayidi al-Seddik, he comes sometimes. And Day-Lyal, too. Also many merchants from the Aduana. But my friend Sy-kess, he would not want anyone to know of this place. I am sure of that.'

Nicholas returns to the pomegranate tree and sits down in the shadows, leaning back against the gnarled trunk. Hugging his thoughts to his body, he discovers tiny fragments of grit from the floor of the storeroom still stuck to his elbows. He hears the scraping of masonry as Hadir replaces the talisman in the wall. It sounds to him like a tomb being sealed up.

Imagining himself their judge, he pictures the faces of the three men most likely to want to decipher and read the messages from Robert Cecil's agent in Marrakech. First amongst the guilty is Muhammed al-Annuri, with his assassin's smile. Even though his master the sultan is England's ally, the minister himself has already proved he's not above putting her envoy under harsh questioning. Then there are the two Frenchmen: Arnoult de Lisle and Fra Cyprien, Catholics both. Perhaps they are all guilty – a triumvirate of conspiracy.

He breathes in the scent of orange blossom, watches the birds flitting in and out of the courtyard, darting along the upper gallery. The sparrows have made way for the swifts that come with the evening. They wheel and swoop, diving so fast they seem about to dash themselves to oblivion against the walls, yet break away at the last moment to go soaring back into the darkening sky.

When it hits him, the answer is so obvious that he wonders why he hadn't realized it before. Adolfo Sykes didn't send the final letter of his life on this earth to Robert Cecil. He sent it to Solomon Mandel.

Seals can be broken and artfully replaced. Letters can be read by those for whom they are not intended – even encrypted ones, if you're clever enough. Which means that Adolfo Sykes did not trust Cathal Connell to carry his last dispatch to England.

'Hadir, did any other English ships depart around the time the *Righteous*, the *Marion* and the *Luke of Bristol* last left Safi?'

From the cloister Hadir replies, 'No, *Sayidi*. None that I know of.'

Nicholas allows himself a tight grin of satisfaction as the realization hits him: *You didn't send the letter, did you? They thought you did, but it's still here. You've hidden it somewhere else, because in the end you didn't even trust the talisman to protect it. The only question is: did you keep your secret when they began to carve the skin off your chest?*

Nicholas climbs to his feet and walks back towards the hand-shaped talisman, trying to force order upon his racing thoughts. Hadir watches in bemusement, as though the new occupant of the house on the Street of the Weavers is engaged in some unfathomable ritual that only infidels of questionable sanity might practise.

As he steps onto the tiled floor of the cloister Nicholas feels something give way beneath his feet. He looks down. Just enough light remains for him to see that where he has placed his foot, a tile has cracked neatly in two.

But he's sure it didn't break when he stepped on it. There had been no sound. The tile hadn't snapped, it had yielded. It must already have been broken.

He retreats a pace, kneels and lifts the two halves of the tile, hoping to uncover a second hiding place. He finds nothing beneath but compacted earth.

Only when he returns the two pieces of tile, rises and looks again at the talisman on the wall does Nicholas see that they are in perfect alignment. The fracture is aimed directly at the downward-pointing middle finger of the stone hand.

Coincidence? Or something else – a sign?

Nicholas steps back onto the tiled surface of the cloister. He turns his back to the stone hand, and in his imagination extends the line of the fracture out into the courtyard.

He sees nothing out of place. There is no second talisman set into the opposite wall, no matching broken tile. But he cannot shake off the conviction that the ghost of Adolfo Sykes is standing beside him in the fragrant dusk, encouraging him, willing him not to stumble off the path he has laid for him.

What have I missed, Master Adolfo? Nicholas asks himself, his mouth mutely forming the words. He is quite unaware of Hadir staring at him, or of grandmother Tiziri in the kitchen doorway watching with bemusement the strangeness of the *berraniyin*.

He lets his gaze lift to the upper floor.

Running along the rough plaster wall, just below the line of little windows, is a fine wooden frieze, carved and painted with intricate arabesque symbols. Made of individual pieces a couple of yards long, it extends right around the courtyard.

Nicholas stands directly over the broken tile. He raises the index finger of his right hand and holds it out before his eyes, as though it were an arrow he was about to loose from a bow. Squinting down the imaginary shaft, he sees that it's aimed directly at a spot where two sections of frieze join, about a foot and a half to one side of his chamber window.

And as he stares into the gathering dusk, a single swift emerges from behind the carved decoration. It tilts its head in his direction, as though seeking his approval, and sails out into the approaching night.

33

On Bankside, in the same dusk, Bianca Merton reflects upon a day that brought news of two departures from the city, both – in their own way – troubling.

The queen has moved her court from Whitehall to the relative safety of Windsor. Mere coincidence, says the official line; nothing unusual. Elizabeth has simply decided to commence her summer progress through her realm a little early.

But ordinary folk know better. A summer progress does not require a guard set on the Windsor road, turning back all who have recently dwelt in pestilential London.

On Bankside, where hurried departures – prompted by the anticipated arrival of bailiffs, creditors or vengeful husbands – are commonplace, the news has been greeted with little more than passing comment. Today, the talk has been mostly about that golden roaring-boy Kit Marlowe: slain two days ago in a brawl in Deptford.

It was an argument over lewd and forbidden love between men.

He was killed because he was a secret papist.

He was stabbed because he was a spy... because he was a heretic... because he hadn't paid his share of the reckoning at Widow Bull's lodging house... because he'd got into an argument with an aficionado of the playhouse who said he ought to stop writing such leaden prose and make way for that new fellow, Shakespeare...

After paying a Bankside ragamuffin thruppence to carry the message to Raymond Gault that his preventatives are ready, Bianca stops by the Jackdaw to help Ned and Rose deal with a delivery of imported malmsey from the Vintry across the river. She receives the news of Marlowe's death with more than passing interest. It does not come as a surprise.

She remembers how – two years ago – he had turned up at the Jackdaw unannounced. The carpenters were in at the Rose theatre making repairs, and he needed somewhere to rehearse his play *The Tragical History of the Life and Death of Dr Faustus.*

She smiles at the memory of how Marlowe's arrival brought out the first real signs in Nicholas that he harboured feelings towards her that were more than just brotherly.

Marlowe had seemed such a larger-than-life character – an achievement in itself on Bankside, where edgy flamboyance is common currency. His presence had sent Nicholas almost mad with jealousy. But in the end, Nick – good, dependable, courageous Nick; Nick who could always save himself from perfection by a joke, or an act that had everyone wondering if perhaps there wasn't a small whiff of sulphur lurking behind the solid yeoman's decency – had been right: Kit Marlowe had brought in his wake nothing but tribulation for both of them. She wonders now how he would take the news.

She also wonders in a candid moment, as she helps Rose clear away the trenchers, if she might ever have lain with Kit, if he hadn't been more interested in dice, boys and tobacco. Perhaps she might have. But it could never have been more than a brief taste of exotic but dangerous fruit. Nicholas would have won on every throw of the dice.

Thinking of Nicholas now, she imagines he would be astounded to know what she has discovered about Reynard Gault. She is intensely proud of herself for having identified him as the Rouge

Croix Pursuivant. But she is still no closer to understanding why Gault lied to her about knowing Solomon Mandel.

In charitable moments, she thinks it's because he and the Jew were partners in some conspiracy or other that led to Mandel's murder – that he died trying to protect Gault's identity. But when she's in a more suspicious mood – which is becoming increasingly frequent – she wonders if it might be the other way round: that Gault was involved in the torture and murder of an innocent old man, and that those two scraps of paper might in fact be bloody fingers of accusation. Whatever the truth, she is sure now that Gault invited her to his house for a reason other than the protection of his investments.

Her musings are interrupted as Parson Moody walks in from the dusk, his face troubled. Surely he hasn't come to hear the gossip about Kit Marlowe, unless it's to gloat about the inevitable downfall of sinners.

'Mistress Merton,' he says, like a man bringing news of a massacre. 'It's on the march again. There's been a house closed up on Tar Ally. The parish has put wardens on either end. I am in need of a jug of knock-down before I administer another funeral. I truly think God is testing my resolve.'

Tar Alley. Bianca knows it well – a narrow cut running south from the riverbank where the horses delivering to the grain mills in Bermondsey get led to water. No more than half a dozen tenements, mostly the homes of Dutch refugees from the wars in the Low Countries.

And just two streets away from her shop on Dice Lane.

34

Nicholas opens the shutters and looks out at the full moon rising above the distant Atlas Mountains, their peaks frosted with a ghostly rime and crowned with a mantle of stars. He wonders if this is the picture Adolfo Sykes saw on the last night of his life. He thinks he might go up onto the roof terrace and spend an hour watching the city settle itself for sleep – if he didn't have a more pressing action to perform.

'Careful, *Sayidi*,' Hadir says as Nicholas leans out over the window ledge. 'The Bimaristan will be of no use if you fall from such a height and break your head.'

It takes only a few moments for Nicholas to find the join in the wooden frieze. By touch alone, he slips his hand into the gap from which he'd seen the swift emerge only minutes before.

The space behind is larger than the opening, a cavity where the old masonry has crumbled away with the passing years. Almost immediately he feels something man-made and cylindrical amidst the dried leaves, dirt and bird mess. His instinct is to snatch it out for the hard-won prize he knows it to be. But out of deference to the memory of Adolfo Sykes, he takes his time, treating it more like a holy relic.

By the light of grandmother Tiziri's oil lamp, he lays the object on the plain wooden table to the left of the window. It is a narrow parcel wrapped in what he presumes was once fine English wool, before it was secreted away in a swift's nest. It is tied with spun yarn. Nicholas picks at the knot until it loosens. Then he unrolls the cloth to unmask the contents. He takes his time, because when one man dies to protect a secret it is unworthy of another to reveal it with the flourish of a cheap Bankside street-trick.

Lying on the table in a splash of moonlight is a roll of parchment, three or four sheets thick. The pages curl defensively inwards at the edges, as if protecting to the last what is written on them. For a moment Nicholas is afraid to touch them.

Drawing breath, he tentatively spreads the sheets out on the table, nodding to Hadir to bring the lamp even closer.

The first thing Nicholas notices is that one sheet is different from the others. It is covered in hand-drawn characters set inside boxes, each one linked by a vertical or horizontal line. It is similar to the family lineage he'd seen laid out on the document he'd taken from apprentice Hortop's gabardine coat aboard the *Righteous*.

Peering closer, he sees that's exactly what it is – a family tree.

Studying the document, Nicholas becomes acquainted with Sir Walter Vachel, born in the Year of Our Redeemer 1576, lord of the manor of Melton in Suffolk. It is a simple task for him then to trace Sir Walter's lineage back several generations, following the lines and boxes from the bottom of the page to the top, until he meets one Guillaume de Vachel, Earl of Barentin in Normandy. On the way, he discovers that Sir Walter's ancestors share one outstanding attribute: they have all fought – indeed, frequently died – in every historical battle of renown from the Holy Land to the Low Countries.

A Thomas Vachel was knighted in the field at Agincourt by the fifth Henry. Sir Norris Vachel expired in glory at Falkirk, battling the Scots alongside the first Edward. Yet another Vachel fought with Lord Stanley's men at Bosworth Field and gained himself an estate valued at six hundred pounds from Henry Tudor.

And at the foot of the page, next to the box containing the scion of this redoubtable lineage, Sir Walter himself, is a line identical to the one Nicholas had seen written on Hortop's document:

PROVEN BY DUE AUTHORITY OF THE ROUGE CROIX
PURSUIVANT, COLLEGE OF HERALDS

All in all, it is a pedigree of which any Englishman could be rightly proud, thinks Nicholas, were it not for the fact that it is very likely a complete fabrication.

Nicholas knows this because the manor of Melton, of which the young Sir Walter is apparently lord, is barely an hour's walk from his own home, his father's farm at Barnthorpe. And Yeoman Shelby, being a mildly prosperous farmer, is on nodding terms with all the local nobility. Their family names, from the Howards down, can be seen on effigies and tombs in churches for miles around. Nicholas has grown up with them, heard those names invoked in all manner of situations, good and bad, for as long as he can remember. But never in his life has he heard of a Sir Walter Vachel, or any of his supposedly distinguished ancestors.

The other three sheets are enciphered, a meaningless procession of five-letter groups.

'What does my friend say, *Sayidi*?' Hadir asks.

'I don't know – *yet*. First I must decipher what he has written.'

Hadir looks at him, uncomprehending.

'The words have been changed to make them unreadable,' Nicholas explains. 'I have to change them back again.'

'This is infidel *magic*,' breathes Hadir, an expression of fearful astonishment on his face.

Nicholas tries not to laugh. He reminds himself that not everyone is acquainted with the artful contrivances of a Cecil. 'No, it's not magic,' he says. 'It is just a clever trick to hide what you write, so that your enemies cannot read it. I'd show you how, if the matter wasn't so pressing.'

In the centre of the table is a wooden writing box inlaid with a sinuous mother-of-pearl arabesque that gleams in the lamplight. Nicholas is almost reluctant to touch it, knowing that it once belonged to Adolfo Sykes.

Lifting the lid, he sees a collection of quills, a nib-knife, an inkwell and a pounce-powder pot. As he lifts them out, he cannot help but wonder if the last time they were used was to write these very pages.

'I will need paper, Hadir.'

'I know Sayidi Sy-kess keep parchment with his tally books. I fetch.'

While Nicholas waits for Hadir to return, he gathers the pages to him and tries to recall Sykes's transposition code, the one that Robert Cecil had made him commit to memory before he left.

When Hadir brings the paper, Nicholas takes it from him, ordering him to set down the lamp by the writing box to augment the wash of moonlight. He writes the alphabet in a column on the first blank sheet. Using each letter as a peg, he begins to hang the cipher alongside. To his relief, he soon has all but a handful of matching letters, certainly enough to begin deciphering with confidence. All the while, Hadir watches him in silent bewilderment.

Writing down the first group of letters and their transposed equivalents, Nicholas begins to frown. 'Something's wrong,' he mutters.

The letters spell out nothing but gibberish. He tries again, thinking he's made a mistake. He gets the same infuriating result. The code remains impenetrable. The leaden weight of defeat makes Nicholas slump forward over the table.

'What is the matter, *Sayidi*?' Hadir asks. 'Does the magic fail?'

'Yes, it fails, Hadir. The key I was given by Robert Cecil does not unlock the words written by Master Sykes. And I cannot understand why.'

But Hadir can offer him no comfort, other than a sad expression that's half-pity and half-mystification.

✠

The word in Bianca Merton's imagination needs no deciphering. It is as clear as day, written in letters a yard high: Coward.

No matter how rational the course of action she has decided upon, she cannot rid herself of a sense of shame. No one but a coward would flee because the pestilence has arrived just two lanes distant. But remembering the close shave that followed her visit to Constable Willders's house, she thinks that only a fool would stay.

As she makes her way back to her shop on Dice Lane, Ned Monkton walking protectively at her side in the moonlight, Bianca unburdens herself. It feels strange, she thinks. It should be Nicholas in whom she's confiding.

'What will my customers think of me, Ned? Will they lose heart? Will they say I've abandoned them?'

'There's none would think it, Mistress,' Ned says, in a tender voice that ill-befits his intimidating size. 'All they have to do is walk a little further; the Jackdaw's not ten minutes from Dice Lane.' He smiles. 'Besides, Rose and I would be glad to have you home.'

She places one hand against his arm in gratitude.

In silence they pass Solomon Mandel's old house. Someone else is living there now. On Bankside, a murder is little cause to pass over any half-decent place to lay your head. The landlord moved in a family of French Huguenots the moment the last bloodstains had been scrubbed away.

'I still see him, Ned,' Bianca says, 'telling poor Farzad he hasn't put enough black cumin in that *kubaneh* bread he likes.' It's an image she prefers to the one she'd encountered when she and Nicholas inspected the ruin of Mandel's chamber.

'Hanging's too good for the rogues who did that,' Ned growls as they leave the little house to the shadows. 'Or for those who said he deserved it, because he wasn't a true Christian.'

'Some people have a tendency to dip their tongues in a pot of foolishness before they speak, Ned. Most don't mean it.'

'Aye, Mistress. But that's no excuse for talking ill of a goodly old man.'

When Ned has delivered her safely to the door of her shop she leans up to kiss the wild auburn bank of his bearded cheek, bids him farewell and goes inside. Alone, and in the semi-darkness, she makes a slow lap of the interior, deep in thought. She rubs her fingertips on the sprigs of herbs and bunches of dried leaves, inhales the competing scents of sweet briar, quince and rosemary. She walks amongst the clusters of wound-wort and lovage that hang from the ceiling, as though she is taking a contemplative stroll through a moonlit arbour.

And after a while she comes to a conclusion. Tomorrow she will pack all this away and take it back to the relative safety of the Jackdaw. If she stays here and the plague overtakes her, she reasons, she won't be able to help anyone. Standing in the path of a huge, merciless wild beast that has tasted blood and craves more is not courage. It is blind stupidity.

✠

There is a measure of desperation in the way Nicholas handles the documents Adolfo Sykes has tried so hard to keep hidden. The paper magnifies the trembling of his fingertips, as though a playful breeze is blowing through the open window. The groups of letters blur tantalizingly in the lamplight.

'I can't read them,' he mutters to himself. 'I can't.'

His only hope is that one of Robert Cecil's clever secretaries, skilled in the arts of the cipher, will be able to do so. But that will have to wait until he brings these impenetrable pages back to England.

He is about to return the sheets to their woollen wrapping when he notices something he hasn't seen before. On one of them, written so faintly in the bottom left-hand corner that it is all but invisible in the meagre light, is a single word in clear English.

Matthew.

Nicholas stares at it, willing some meaning into the name. He finds none.

'Is there an English merchant here in Marrakech who goes by the name of Matthew?' he asks Hadir.

If there is, Hadir does not know of him. And Hadir knows every merchant in the city.

Searching for the tiniest glimmer of light escaping the otherwise impervious curtain of Adolfo Sykes's secrecy, Nicholas returns to the window. He stares down into the courtyard. Inevitably his eyes alight on the tiny grey smudge of the stone talisman on the far wall, and the downward-pointing finger that had brought him so tantalizingly close to the agent's last written words. If it's guided me this far, he thinks, can it not guide me all the way?

A talisman on a garden wall in Marrakech. Another one beside a door in Southwark. Two hands, somehow entwined.

And then it hits him: Adolfo Sykes wasn't writing to Robert Cecil. And he wasn't using Cecil's code. He was writing to someone else, because he feared that his dispatches to Lord Burghley's son could be intercepted. He was writing to a friend who shared his faith in the power of a talisman that had ultimately failed them both. He was writing to Solomon Mandel.

From there it is but a small jump in his imagination to Mandel's ruined chamber. He sees himself retracing his steps around the murder bed while Bianca looks on in moist-eyed horror at the devastation. And he sees the one item in that room that has been left untouched: a Bible, open at a page from the Book of Matthew, the parable of Jesus feeding the multitude with just five loaves and two fishes.

Farzad, bring me some more of your fine kubaneh bread, he can hear Mandel saying as he sits taking his solitary breakfast in the Jackdaw.

Five loaves. And two fishes.

The revelation strikes home with the force of one of Ned Monkton's playful punches. Turning away from the window, Nicholas hurls himself back into the chair, leaving Hadir to stare at him as though he fears his master has just been possessed by a particularly energetic demon.

'Matthew,' he announces, holding up the sheet of paper for Hadir to see where Sykes, with the lightest of hands, has written the name. 'It's to tell Master Sykes's friend in London which code he's using. And the key to that code comprises the numbers five and two.'

Nicholas begins to write. Counting five letters into the word *kubaneh*, he sees the next character is an *e* – also the fifth letter of the alphabet. It is all the proof he needs to know he's on the right path. He rings the same letter on the alphabetical column he wrote earlier, when he'd been trying to remember the cipher that Robert Cecil's agent had employed in his dispatches.

Now he faces a choice: two fishes. Two up or two down? He picks the latter. He counts two and then rings the next in the sequence, *h*. Using that as an anchor point, he begins to write a second alphabet in the empty space to the left of the first, *a* against *h*, and so on down the column. Long before he's finished he knows the curtain has been drawn aside, simply by glancing every now and then from the new column to the first encoded page.

Should I make Hadir complicit in this? Nicholas wonders. What else am I to do? He already knows more than is safe for him. Without his help, God alone knows what dangers I'm likely to blunder into in this alien city. And so he lets Hadir watch while he recovers the last written words of Adolfo Sykes. By the time he has completed his task, there is nothing but darkness beyond the open window.

> To my dear and trusty friend, Solomon Mandel, I send you a gentile's greetings, you old rogue. How is it on Bankside? Raining, I don't doubt. Are you still acquainted with the Moor lad, the one who makes kubaneh for your breakfast?
>
> I have contrived another sight of the false pedigree, and can reassure you that the copy I sent you in my last dispatch is accurate in all important respects. I still do not know why these fellows have them, but perhaps the Falconer requires his hawks to be well bred. All I know is that Connell is most certainly the traitor I suspected him to be. He is a devil, stripped by Lucifer of all that was good in him – and I doubt even that was very much.
>
> Connell is paid for his treachery in gold and slaves. He gets first choice in the market. God help the poor souls who become his property. Yesterday I witnessed him houghing a poor fellow who had attempted to escape: two quick slices of his knife and the desperate man was hamstrung. Connell spat upon him, called him dog and sent him crawling away to find his forage as best he might, or starve. What use will he be to anyone, this slave who cannot stand?
>
> When the devil had gone, I bandaged the fellow's wounds, borrowed the cart of my friend Ibn Daoud and took him to the Bimaristan al-Mansur to have his grievous injuries treated. It

shames me that the Moors will treat him better than the supposed
Christian who owned him.

Once I had handed the poor fellow to the physicians, I tarried
a while. I hoped I might discover the secret place where they hide
the oranges, for I am sure now this is the location. The crates are
marked with the symbol ꝛ, two sickles. When you receive this
letter, go to Lyon Quay and watch for cargo marked in the same
manner being taken aboard a Company ship. We will know then
that the source of the oranges is as I suspected.

I do not yet know when they will strike. In the autumn there
is to be a great gathering of Moor chieftains at the sultan's new
palace. It seems likely that this will be when they intend their
perfidy. Urge the Pigmy to alert his watchers in Lisbon and Cadiz
for signs the Spanish are preparing galleys and mustering soldiers.
God willing, we will draw this sting before its venom can flow.

That is all for the present, my old friend. Tonight is 'Ushar. The
moon will be bright. I intend to go once more to the Bimaristan.
God willing, I will discover where they are hiding the oranges.

Say your heathen prayers for me, Hebrew. They will comfort
me if the night is cold. I am, in all faith and honour, your loving
friend: *AS*

Twice Nicholas reads the letter aloud, so that Hadir can grasp
the finer points. In the meagre light, the Moor's face takes on a
harshness Nicholas has not seen before.

'Why did my friend die for oranges, Sayidi Nich-less? If he
wanted them, he could pick them from the trees.'

'They're not oranges, Hadir. They're new English matchlock
muskets. Our queen sends them to your sultan for the defence
of his realm. In return, Sultan al-Mansur sends her his best saltpetre to make black powder to charge our fleet's cannon against
the Spanish. They may not share the same faith, but they share
the same enemy.'

Nicholas has the heart of it now, this conspiracy that has two heads: one in Morocco and one in England. The weapons the Privy Council is sending to Sultan al-Mansur are not reaching him – at least not more than enough to convince him all is well. The bulk gets diverted to his enemy, the 'Falconer'.

'The crates come aboard at Lyon Quay in London,' Nicholas continues. 'They bear a double-sickle wool-mark. If there are papist spies watching, they'll believe the crates contain nothing more dangerous than bolts of English cloth. When the cargo comes ashore at Safi, Connell marks the loading bill in front of Muly Hassan, the customs clerk. He told me it was to identify the sultan's tithe. It wasn't – it was to show which crates contained the matchlocks. Muly Hassan must be part of the conspiracy.'

'Who is this Pigmy my friend Sy-kess speaks of?'

'It's the nickname the queen has given to the man who sent me, Sir Robert Cecil. Master Sykes is telling Cecil to keep his watchers in Lisbon and Cadiz alert for signs that an invasion fleet is being prepared.'

'Are the Portugals and the Spanish infidels coming to make war against us again?' Hadir asks, a splinter of fear in his voice.

'That is what they plan,' Nicholas says. 'This "Falconer", whoever he may be, intends to overthrow Sultan al-Mansur and open your city gates to a Spanish army. And to do it, he's arming his own janissaries with stolen English matchlock muskets.'

'My friend Sy-kess speaks of the Falconer wanting his hawks well bred. What does this mean?'

'I think he wants his janissaries to be men of better quality than poor village boys from the Balkans. He wants men of good blood about him. When he overthrows your sultan and returns Morocco as a gift to Spain, he wants it wrapped in a cloak of nobility. A squalid coup doesn't fit his sense of importance.'

'But you said this family line was false,' Hadir says, picking up the pedigree.

'It is. The College of Heralds in London is responsible for compiling and authenticating the pedigrees of English gentlemen and nobles. One of their heralds – the Rouge Croix Pursuivant – is constructing false identities to make these lads appear to be of noble descent. I wonder how much the Falconer is paying for them: in coin *and* slaves?'

'If they kill my friend Sy-kess for this, then you also are in very great danger, Sayidi Nich-less,' Hadir whispers.

Nicholas gets up and leans out over the windowsill. He lets the night air cool the sweat on his brow. He thinks of how easily Cathal Connell could have contrived his death aboard the *Righteous*, and how al-Annuri's men could have killed him in the storeroom, but chose not to.

'I think they want me alive,' he says to the night, as much as to Hadir. 'If I fail to return, Robert Cecil's suspicions will only strengthen. No, they'd rather I found nothing here, believed the story about Sykes's accident and went home to tell Cecil all is well between Morocco and England. I'm safe for as long as they believe I've not seen Sykes's letter.' He turns back into the chamber. In the light from the lamp, Hadir has only half a face. 'Tell me, do you know of anyone in Marrakech who styles himself "The Falconer"?'

'He will be a rich man, Sayidi Nich-less. Rich men have their hawks as surely as poor men have their cares.'

'Or a clever one – a very clever French Catholic, perhaps.'

'Professor Day-Lyal?'

'The French and Spanish are my queen's enemies, Hadir. They could be making common cause. And there are Jesuits here, too. De Lisle told me they come to arrange ransoms for Catholic slaves. But I know they also send agents into England to plot

333

against us. When we catch them, we execute them. Robert Cecil considers them more dangerous than the pestilence.'

With a bravado that makes Nicholas smile, Hadir announces, 'We shall go to the sultan together and tell him. I shall translate for you. His Majesty will give Sayidi Nich-less more gold than he can count, and Hadir shall be appointed his vizier. We shall be rich men! Very rich – inshā Allāh.'

I'll settle for alive, thinks Nicholas. He hears again the soft voice of the kufiya telling him to go home before it's too late; sees in his mind the butchered flesh of the slave Marcu; the severed heads in the city square. And he hears Reynard Gault as he hands Cathal Connell the package that contained Hortop's false pedigree. *These are the young gentlemen's... Keep them safe. A goodly profit depends upon them...*

'I believe the apprentice boys aboard the *Righteous* were new recruits for the Falconer's janissaries,' Nicholas tells the wash of moonlight on the table, as though by not addressing Hadir directly he may somehow protect him. 'Whether they know it yet is another matter. Follow them, and they'll lead us to the Falconer.'

35

It has taken Bianca most of the day to contrive her escape from the advancing pestilence. Moving the contents of her shop on Dice Lane back to the Jackdaw has not been easy, not with the endless stream of customers demanding her preventatives. Sometimes she has wanted to scream at them: I can't save you! Don't place this weight of guilt upon my shoulders.

She wonders why they still come. If what she was giving them had the efficacy they believed, the plague would not be spreading. Parson Moody would be relaxing in the bawdy-house at the Falcon stairs, not conducting funerals. But they have such trust in their eyes. She cannot turn her back.

Ned, Timothy and Farzad have been ministering angels. She's lost count of the boxes, jars, sacks, pots and bottles they've carried without complaint. If she'd hired day-labourers, the route between the shop and the Jackdaw would be strewn with trampled bunches of herbs, shattered pots and yellow brimstone. They've even carried her jars of live leeches, though Timothy had to do it at arm's length.

The boys depart with their last load as the sun begins to set over the Lambeth marshes. Bianca turns the key in the lock, and her back upon the shop. It's not a defeat, she tells herself, just a sensible precaution. *I will return.*

'Not at Evensong then, Mistress Merton?'

The voice shocks her out of her thoughts. Approaching her is Reynard Gault, his stride confident, arrogant almost. He's wearing a brown velvet doublet and knee-boots of soft leather. The goose feather in his foxskin hat looks freshly plucked. And – much to her amusement, as she remembers the painting – he's wearing a sword at his belt.

'If you didn't dress the gallant so much, you wouldn't need *that*,' she says with a superior smile as she glances at the finely-wrought guard protruding from the engraved leather scabbard. 'On Bankside the cut-purses tend to leave the ordinary folk alone. But my, they do *love* a peacock. And they're fast enough to cut away your coin without you even noticing, so thirty inches of fine Italian steel really is rather wasted.'

Gault gives a little nod of acquiescence. 'You may mock me, Mistress, but I am the one with the fine house on Giltspur Street and gold angels in his purse, while *you* pursue a precarious living amongst rogues, vagabonds and *actors*.'

'Yes, well, we're all living a little precariously now, aren't we? I presume that's why you're here – to collect the preventatives. I'd rather imagined you were going to send one of your bright young boys. I suppose I should be honoured.'

'I came here myself because I wanted the chance to speak privily, Mistress Merton.'

'Oh, do you have *spies* then, in your fine new house?' She looks into his eyes for a telltale flicker of suspicion, an indication that he has secrets he wants to hide, lies he wants to present as truths. She sees nothing but an impenetrable rampart of self-confidence.

'My lads are loyal, and so is my household,' he says. 'Why would I fear to be overheard?'

'I'm jesting.'

'Ah, Bankside wit. I hear it leads to quarrels.' He taps the guard of his sword with a doeskin-gloved hand.

336

'The preventatives are at the Jackdaw. I'm moving back there because there's pestilence on Tar Alley. We can walk along the riverbank if you wish. Will that be privy enough for you?'

The lanterns are being lit in the houses on the bridge, the masts and yards of the ships moored on the river turning slowly into a winter's forest of leafless branches. An evening breeze is blowing off the water.

'We should not be enemies, you and I,' Gault says as they walk.

'I did not suppose we were.'

'We have more in common that you may think,' he says, raising an enigmatic eyebrow.

Like the fact that we both know you were acquainted with Solomon Mandel, even though you denied it.

Bianca lets the voice in her head fade before she answers. 'Is that so, Master Gault? I cannot imagine what that might be.'

'What would you say if I told you that I, too, was a child of the one true faith – a Catholic?'

She doesn't reply immediately. He wouldn't be the first man in this city to claim such a thing, only to betray the subsequently shared confession. There are cells in the Bridewell and the Compter, the Clink and even the Tower playing host at this very moment to those who have been foolish enough to fall for such a trick.

'Does the Grocers' Guild or the Barbary Company know?'

A guilty little *huh* from deep within his chest. 'Would I hold my position if they did?'

'Then what is to stop me denouncing *you*?'

His boyish grin contains a jagged reef of malice just beneath the surface. 'I'd find myself a purchasable magistrate and tell him a Bankside tavern-mistress had threatened to make a false accusation against me, if I didn't pay her twenty pounds. Then we'd see if you're still the one witch nobody dares hang.'

'I can see you've given this confession some thought, Master Gault. Why then are you making so free with your conscience?'

'Because we are allies, are we not?'

'Allies? I'm an apothecary. You're a customer. I'd hardly call that an alliance.'

'But we share a common goal: the re-establishment of God's true Church in England.'

Bianca turns her head away, refusing to acknowledge his words. She looks out over the river and the darkening shoreline to the north. 'Let me make it clear: I have no desire to overthrow the queen, or her religion. I survive here by keeping my faith to myself. Please, may we speak of safer things – like the pestilence, for instance.'

When she looks at Gault again, his face wears the hurt expression of an innocent little boy slapped for a sibling's transgression. 'You misunderstand me, Mistress Merton. I did not confess because I wish to embroil you in sedition. I did it because I want you to trust me.'

'Why, in the name of all the saints, should I trust you? The Grocers' Company has done nothing but stand in my way since I came here. Your friends would rather I went back to Padua and stopped interfering in men's business. And not so very long ago, you were threatening to shut me down for a charlatan. Now, all of a sudden, you're desperate for my trust. I wonder why? What do I have that you desire so much?'

He wrings his gloved hands like a penitent renouncing his sins. 'I admit it. Robert Cecil led me to believe I would find you a deceiver, a dealer in fraud and fakery. Instead, I found a comely young woman who – were she a man – might even give us merchant venturers a run for our money. As to what I want of you, that is easily answered: the Catholic cause in England could make good use of your talents.'

338

Is this contrition real, or a pretence? Either way, Bianca wonders how proficient Gault really is with the sword. Might it not be possible to take it from him and stab him in his patronizing arse?

'I've already told you,' she says firmly. 'There is no alliance we could make that would be of the slightest use to you, Master Gault. Whatever *talents* you think I possess, I have no interest in sedition. I keep my faith to myself. And if you thought somehow to flatter me, you haven't. Now, let us speak of less contentious matters.'

And yet his words are still buzzing in her mind as they approach the Jackdaw.

Why has he confessed such a dangerous secret to her? she wonders – if not to persuade her to reveal whether Nicholas has confided to her the real reason Robert Cecil sent him to Morocco. Why is Gault so determined to know? And why has he lied to her about knowing Solomon Mandel?

There is only one way to find out, she thinks. Earlier, Gault had spoken of alliances. Perhaps it's time to do a little forging.

✠

In the dawn light, the window is a pale square against the dark wall of his chamber. Nicholas calculates that he can't have slept much beyond three hours.

He puts on his shirt and trunk-hose and goes down into the garden to sit under the old pomegranate tree. There he ponders Robert Cecil's simplistic instructions on what to do if he should discover the alliance between England and Morocco broken: *we are all relying upon your ingenuity to mend it.*

It would be easier, he thinks, to perform a successful laryngotomy, or say the right thing to Bianca three times in a row.

The young Berber girl, Lalla, who does his infidel washing, comes to him with a plate of dates. Her gift is all the more touching for the knowledge that she herself is forbidden to take food until sunset. She stands at a discreet distance, watching in utter fascination while he eats, her face serious, her eyes growing wider by the moment. He smiles at her. When she smiles back, he thinks her expression might beat the sun for brilliance.

'Hadir?' he says, exaggerating the movements of his mouth.

Lalla points in the direction of the Koutoubia mosque, to indicate that Hadir is at his devotions. Then, her courage exhausted, she runs back into the house and the safety of grandmother Tiziri.

When Hadir returns, he has news. By some animal ability to sense the currents of the city, he has learned that Captain Connell has arrived with the rest of the cargo.

'Are the apprentices with him?'

'Captain Con-nell and four Christians – this is what my friend, the guard at the Bab Doukkala, tells me.'

'Where are they now? Do you know?'

'Resting in the garden where you and I met Minister al-Annuri. They will not stay long. Con-nell has lodgings in the Aduana.'

Nicholas opens his mouth to instruct Hadir to go there and see where Connell takes the apprentices, but a sudden hammering on the street door silences him. He imagines the white-robed, imperious al-Annuri has come to complete the job the kufiya left unfinished. Hadir looks at him, unable to hide the fear in his eyes. He is clearly thinking the same thing.

Moments later, grandmother Tiziri ushers Sumayl al-Seddik into the garden. He rolls as he walks, like a plumped bejewelled cushion blown on a stiff breeze. He seems in a mighty good humour. The tall, balding de Lisle trails him, observing Nicholas in mild surprise, as if he was making his morning rounds and hadn't expected his patient to survive the night. A small coterie of al-Seddik's attendants make up the rearguard.

'We have been summoned,' the minister says happily, making it sound as though he's received a divine invitation. 'His Majesty the *sharif* has granted you an audience.'

'Today?'

'Within the hour.' A little wince of qualification. 'Though His Majesty's hours are not necessarily the same as a common man's.' He casts a disapproving eye over Nicholas's plain attire. 'Do you perchance have finer apparel than this?'

You sound like Robert Cecil, Nicholas thinks. Next you'll be telling me I look like a Thames waterman. 'I fear this is all I have, sir.'

In a minister's world, apparently, such shortcomings are swiftly remedied. One of his attendants produces a robe of spun silk and an embroidered jerkin that are clearly not al-Seddik's because – by pure coincidence – they fit Nicholas perfectly, almost as though they'd been prepared for the eventuality. As he puts them on, Hadir watches with a proud smile on his face.

'I've never had an audience with a sultan,' Nicholas says, as the attendant fastens a wide tasselled belt with a gold clasp around his waist. 'I was once called before the Censors of the College of Physicians, but they only *think* they're royalty. What is the protocol?'

'It is very simple,' al-Seddik tells him. 'We will approach His Majesty on our knees. When he calls me forward, I will rise and kiss him on the cheek.'

'Do *I* kiss him?'

'Of course not,' the minister says in horror. 'You are an infidel. Imagine if I, a Moor, had sought such a familiarity with your queen when I was in London.'

'You should have taken the chance,' Nicholas replies with a mischievous grin. 'They say she's a dreadful flirt. The Earl of Leicester died before he plucked up the courage. At the

341

moment, in the Jackdaw, all the serious money is on the Earl of Essex.'

Al-Seddik looks at him blankly. 'I will ask you for the letter. You will hand it to me. I shall then break the seal and translate its contents to His Majesty. In return, he may give you a gift. Or he may pay you no attention at all. Whatever his reaction, we shall retire on our knees. After that, I will have a couple of my fellows ensure that you return here safely. I wouldn't want you wandering lost in the lanes, dressed in such tempting garb.'

'I'll get the letter,' Nicholas says, beckoning Hadir to follow him. When they are out of al-Seddik's hearing he says, 'Go at once to where Connell and the apprentices are. Keep watch. Find out where he takes them.'

'But I must accompany Sayidi Nich-less to the palace,' Hadir protests, sounding like a small boy who's been told he can't stay in the same room as the adults. 'I have to – I am your secretary.'

'You will be doing me – and your sultan – a far better service by discovering where those apprentices go. They may lead us to the Falconer.'

Reluctantly Hadir accepts. 'Be careful of Minister al-Seddik,' he warns.

'Why? If we can trust anyone, we can trust him. He is Lord Burghley's friend. I'll tell him about Sykes's letter when de Lisle has gone.'

'I mean, don't trust him not to steal the *sharif*'s reward from me. He is already a rich man. Hadir needs the gold more than he does.'

Nicholas laughs. 'I promise I won't let him cheat you. Just remember to stay out of Connell's sight.'

'He will not see me,' Hadir promises with a grave frown. 'I shall be like the magic letter Sayidi Sy-kess writes to your friends in England. I shall become invisible.'

✠

'It is called, in English, the Palace of Wonders,' says al-Seddik proudly as he leads Nicholas through the immense ornate archway.

The el-Badi Palace seems to Nicholas well named – a secret world with its own horizons of high red walls flanked with shady, pillared pavilions. He gazes out over a vast area of manicured gardens set with date palms, olive and citrus trees. Pathways reflect the dazzling sunlight from uncountable numbers of small glazed tiles, lapis blue, emerald green and blood red, all strung together in geometric patterns, as if the artisans who crafted them had somehow found a way to weave solid stone on a loom. Fountains fill the air with their melodic song. Down the centre runs a broad pool as wide as a river, where birds with long, curving bills wade.

'They are ibis,' al-Seddik tells him. 'It is fitting that His Majesty should look out upon creatures who once graced the palaces of the pharaohs.'

Nicholas searches for a sign of the man on whom this magnificence is lavished, paid for – as Hadir has told him – by Portuguese gold and built by Portuguese slaves. But there is no sign of anyone remotely grand enough.

They are led to one of the tented pavilions, to sink down upon silken cushions and await His Majesty's pleasure. De Lisle is still with them. Nicholas finds himself casting glances at the Frenchman, as if trying to penetrate that aloof exterior to see the conspiracy boiling within. After a while he stops, fearing the Frenchman will grow suspicious of his interest.

And so they wait.

And wait.

His Majesty's hours are not necessarily the same as a common man's...

✠

It is mid-afternoon, shortly after the *al-'asr* prayers, before they are called.

Sultan Ahmad Abu al-Abbas al-Mansur is holding court on the broad top step of a flight of six leading to the arched doorway of a squat gatehouse at the far end of the palace gardens. Shaded by parasols held aloft by bodyguards, he sits on a small stool, staring down the length of the central pool like a Moorish King Canute. He is dressed simply in a linen robe, Nicholas notices with surprise, a plain white turban framing a tightly curled grey beard and prominent cheekbones. Were it not for the grandeur that surrounds him, he could be a village grandfather taking a break from his gardening.

Behind him, in the shadow of the arched doorway, stands Minister al-Annuri, a taciturn spectre in white, his hooded eyes watching Nicholas come forward like a falcon that's just spotted a hare break cover. Yes, thinks Nicholas, I could see you carving flesh off a living body, and smiling while you do it.

The brief ceremony plays out just as al-Seddik foretold. He and Nicholas prostrate themselves at the foot of the steps. When the minister is called forward, Nicholas catches the words *England* and *Elizabeth* in the brief speech he makes.

The letter is duly read. Sultan al-Mansur makes a brief reply, though whether to thank the queen for her declaration of friendship or to comment on the weather, Nicholas cannot tell, because it's delivered without the slightest hint of approval. It is only when, after a brief pause, al-Mansur removes a huge gold ring set with precious stones from his finger and hands it to Nicholas, via al-Seddik, that it becomes clear the queen's greetings have been welcomed.

With the ring clutched tightly in his right hand, Nicholas shuffles backwards on his knees behind al-Seddik's broad, silken rump. Once they have retreated a suitable distance, the minster stands up and start walking slowly backwards. Nicholas follows suit.

And then, from behind the sultan's stool, a man emerges, a basket wedged under one arm. As Nicholas watches, he descends the far right edge of the steps and proceeds to cast sand over the path, moving forward as Nicholas retreats, as though he were sowing a field.

'What's he doing?' Nicholas whispers to al-Seddik out of the corner of his mouth.

There is a slight hint of embarrassment in al-Seddik's reply. 'He's cleansing the pathway between you and His Majesty. Remember, Dr Shelby, in this city you are the infidel.'

It is a poor way, Nicholas thinks, to reward a man who has the power to save your throne. But given the weight of the ring he's clutching, he thinks he'll be able to live with the insult.

Al-Seddik's men escort Nicholas through the lanes towards the Street of the Weavers. Unable to contrive a moment alone with the Moor, Nicholas has consoled himself with an offer to join the minister for the iftar feast at sunset, followed the next morning by a ride out to al-Seddik's kasbah in the mountains for a day's hawking. As De Lisle is to remain in Marrakech, in case the sultan has need to call for him, it promises an opportunity for Nicholas to reveal what he has discovered.

Crossing the open ground where, on his arrival, Nicholas had seen the pitiful clusters of humanity corralled like beasts at market, he notes the space is empty now, save for a few Berbers encamped there with their sheep. He recalls a few words from Adolfo Sykes's letter: *Connell is paid for his treachery in gold and slaves... God help the poor souls who become his property...*

Certain now that poor Hortop was alive when he went into the sea, Nicholas can find little mercy in his heart for a creature such as Cathal Connell. When the plot is foiled, he should count himself lucky to escape with a swift beheading.

Nicholas wonders how many young men have come here on Connell's ships, believing they were embarking upon a lucrative mercantile life? Did any refuse to pay the blood-tax – to sell their souls and become janissaries in someone else's war? He remembers what he told de Lisle in the hammam, when he'd seen the butchered slave Marcu: *Few of us have no limit to the courage in our hearts.*

Nicholas tries to gauge the extent of the conspiracy. He imagines an unbroken line connecting Cathal Connell to Muhammed al-Annuri and Arnoult de Lisle, via Reynard Gault and his fake pedigrees, all the way to the Escorial in Madrid and the throne of Philip of Spain. He sees a new nobility replacing the old in Marrakech – a Catholic Christian government made up of young men with purchased dignity.

By the time he dismisses al-Seddik's two taciturn guides at the entrance to the Street of the Weavers, Nicholas is already imagining himself on the first night home. He has returned to Bankside from Cecil House, crowned with laurels, the garlanded victor of a desperate battle. He is breathing in the rosewater scent of Bianca's hair as he unlaces the points of her carnelian bodice, burying his mouth in the warm arc of her shoulder. Seizing his second chance at life, the bliss he'd thought a capricious god had chosen to deny him.

He pushes on the ornately carved door and steps into the house of Adolfo Sykes.

The first bloodstain lies on the mud-brick wall, beside the doorway that opens onto the courtyard. A handprint – the fingers splayed in agony. Nicholas has to fight every fibre of his body to force himself on into the garden.

346

It is bathed in warm evening sunlight. But the heavenly scent of citrus has gone. And he cannot hear the beating wings of the swifts darting around the upper gallery. All he can smell is the stench of spilt blood and bowels emptied after death. All he can hear is the contented murmuring of the feasting flies. All he can see is Hadir's flayed corpse strung beneath the branches of the old pomegranate tree, like a newly washed coat drying. And huddled around Hadir's bare feet – like petitioners before His Majesty al-Mansur – are the bodies of grandmother Tiziri the Methuselah-woman, Gwata the boy who fetches the water and his sister Lalla who does the washing.

And then the Devil speaks to him from behind his shoulder. Not with a sulphurous pungency, but with a soft Irish lilt.

'I know what these audiences with the daft old heathen are like,' Connell tells him cheerily as Nicholas stares at the carnage. 'They drag on so long you could swear you're going to die before it's over. Well, today you were right.'

36

Ned Monkton glowers at the tabletop in concentration.

'Think hard,' Bianca urges. 'A casual comment. An aside. Something that might have sounded inconsequential at the time. *Anything.*'

It is the evening of the day after the move from Dice Lane. Ned is sitting with Bianca and Rose in a booth in a quiet corner of the Jackdaw, while Timothy plays 'Lady, Weep No More' on his lute to a party of sentimental Kentish drovers. Farzad is tending his cooking pot.

'There is nothing else to remember,' Ned says plaintively. 'Master Nick said the journey was diplomatic, that's all. He told me Robert Cecil would shut you down if he didn't go. He gave me the letter for Lord Lumley, and then he made me swear to keep my gullet shut. He'll be livid when he learns I broke my oath.'

'It will be our secret, Ned.'

Rose asks, 'So why is this Gault fellow so eager to know if Master Nick told you a different story?'

Perplexed, Bianca puts her head in her hands. 'Because, I suppose – like me – he doesn't believe Cecil sent Nicholas to the Barbary shore to learn how the Moors make medicine. Whatever the real reason, I think it has something to do with Solomon Mandel's murder. Mandel was in the service of the Moroccan envoy who came to London some few years ago. He was a translator. To my face, Gault denied knowing him. But he was there in his official capacity as Rouge Croix Pursuivant herald. So he must have met Mandel. He's hiding something, I know it.'

'Perhaps he just plain forgot,' says Rose.

'No, Gault's too sharp a knife to be that easily blunted. Besides, it was the event of the season.'

Ned rises from his bench, his huge form filling the space between the table and the wall of the booth. 'I'll go to Giltspur Street and wring the truth out of the overdressed Jack-a-dandy.'

'Don't be so silly,' Bianca tells him. 'The young men he keeps about him go armed. Besides, it was hard enough keeping Farzad out of the Clink. I don't want to have to worry about you ending up there, too.'

'This is Bankside,' Rose points out. 'Why not lure him into a cross-biting? I'll play the bait and lead him on. Then Ned can burst into our chamber just as Gault's about to drop his hose. If he doesn't spill what you want, we can threaten to haul him before the judge for attempting to seduce a married woman.'

'That's very sweet of you to offer, Rose, dear, but he's not a green-pate fresh in from the countryside. And have you thought how Ned might feel about that?'

'I could tolerate it, if it were done to help Mistress Bianca,' Ned says nobly. 'As long as no clothing other than his own was taken off. An' no pawing. I couldn't 'ave you pawed, Wife.'

Bianca slaps a hand on the table. 'No, I'm not having any of it. It won't work. I don't want Rose's reputation impugned. And I don't want the Jackdaw known for cross-biting. This is about the only tavern in Southwark where new customers can feel safe.'

'Just trying to help,' says Rose with a shrug. 'It goes on all the time in the Good Husband.'

Bianca calls an end to the conversation. 'If I can't come up with something soon, I'll just have to wait until Nicholas returns. Then perhaps he'll tell me what Gault was really up to, and he can have Cecil take a closer look at Master Reynard-peacock-feather-Gault.'

'I wonder where he is now,' says Rose distractedly.

'On his way back to Giltspur Street, I expect.'

'No, I meant Master Nicholas. I wonder if he'll come back to us dressed like a Moor prince? He'd look ever so bonny.'

'Rose, dear, he's a Suffolk yeoman's son. It's all we can do to get him to wear a bright ribbon in the points of that old canvas doublet of his. I don't think you'll be seeing Nicholas dressed up like Master Kit's Tamburlaine this side of Judgement Day.'

'Kit Marlow.' Rose gives a wistful little laugh. 'Mercy, how I remember the look in Master Nicholas's eyes when first you called that saucy fellow Kit. I thought to myself: Hello, that's green jealousy, that is. Our Master Nicholas is afeared Mistress Bianca is smitten with Christopher Marlowe, or my name's not Rose Fludd. 'Course, it's not Fludd now, it's Monkton. But it's a shame he's dead – Marlowe, I mean, not Ned, or Master Nicholas...'

But Bianca isn't listening to Rose's prattle. She's too busy trying to quell the competing voices that have suddenly begun to shout in her head.

Because Rose had just made her realize there is a way to lure Reynard Gault into giving up his secrets. Forget an alliance, she thinks. It's time for Christopher Marlowe to pay for all the tribulations he put her and Nicholas through, by coming to her aid.

Even if he has to make his restitution from beyond the grave.

✠

For Nicholas, the storeroom of Adolfo Sykes's house has become a death-cell. All that is missing is a priest to give him holy absolution.

He has waited all night and much of the following day for the moment when the door is unlocked and they come for him. There has been not a moment's ease. The chamber is as hot and stifling as the hammam, but without the comforts. If he sits against the wall, the rough masonry presses into his sweating back; if he lies on the floor, it's like trying to sleep on a bed of nails. To distract his mind, he's spent much of the time attempting to recite the Hippocratic *Aphorisms* in Latin and then in English. Even so, the expectation has become almost unbearable, an ever-present current of panic. Whenever he catches the sound of movement, every time he hears voices raised, his stomach turns to icy meltwater and he has to fight against a breaking wave of terror.

Not that he's a coward. He hadn't flinched from stepping off the Mutton Lane water-stairs, to finally drown for ever Eleanor's reproachful voice whispering in his head, *Why could you not save me?* During the fighting in the Low Countries there had been times when he'd thought death's eyes were fixed on him, and him alone. And when Dr Arcampora's two murderous rogues had been about to kill him in that warehouse in Petty Wales – before Bianca has saved him – he'd resigned himself to destruction, though admittedly he'd been too roughly used to have much comprehension of what was happening.

No, it's not a lack of courage that threatens to unman him, it's the helplessness. It's his inability to seize Cathal Connell by his sparse hair and smash that salt-scoured face against Adolfo Sykes's stone talisman until the memory of Hortop, of Hadir, of grandmother Tiziri, little Gwata and his sister Lalla is expunged from his mind.

By counting the calls to prayer, he reckons it is early afternoon on the day following the ambush. His captors have given him no food and only a little water since yesterday. Perhaps they mean to starve him to death.

Before they brought him to the storeroom, he had spent several hours in the courtyard hunched beneath Adolfo Sykes's stone talisman, fettered by an ankle-chain. Connell had greedily weighed in his palm the ring Sultan al-Mansur had given Nicholas, then left him with the bodies for company.

Even with his eyes shut, Nicholas had been unable to block out the image of Hadir hanging from the old pomegranate tree, or grandmother Tiziri and the two children lying at his feet. In the heat, it hadn't taken long before the first faint stink of putrefaction began to replace the scent of citrus. And he couldn't shut his ears to the monotone mourning of the gathering flies.

After the *al-'isha* prayers, when the moon bathed the garden in a pale corpse-light, they had unchained him and moved him here, to the storeroom. Thankful to be turning his back on the garden, he'd wondered if they were going to dispose of the bodies before a new sun spread the stench of what they had done from one end of the Street of the Weavers to the other. He prays now that they have done so, because if they take him back there, he's not sure his sanity will bear it.

During the night, sleeping only briefly, he entertained wild notions of escape. Somehow he would reach the Badi Palace and shout al-Seddik's name to the guards until they saw sense and fetched the minister. But there is no way out of the storeroom, let alone out of the house. Even if he managed to reach the roof terrace, it is a thirty-foot drop to the hard dirt surface of the street.

He wonders if Connell might let him have Adolfo Sykes's writing box, so that he can pen a last letter to Bianca. He doubts it. If there had ever been compassion flowing in that man's veins, it long ago turned to bile. So instead he composes the letter in his mind: *I am a farmer's son. I cannot make words like Kit Marlowe, or Philip Sidney. I do not have the graces for it. I cannot make a pretty phrase or write a gallant's verse...*

Shamed by the clumsiness of the words, he strikes an imaginary line through them and starts again: *I had not imagined I should never see you again. The thought of it grieves me past all description. Though I am not of your faith, and confession is not permitted me by the new religion, I would there was a priest here – not to shrive me, but to hear me admit before God the fault of my dereliction: I should not have left you.*

More mental crossing out, followed by further attempts at composition, all of which displease him.

Eventually Nicholas gives up. He covers his face with his hands and simply whispers I *love you*, multiple times, tears welling in the rims of his eyes.

When he hears the sound of the key turning in the lock, it is all he can do to stop himself screaming with a mix of fear and impotent rage.

Connell is the first man through the door. He's dressed in the Moor fashion, in a cloth *djellaba*. It makes him look like a risen corpse in a winding sheet. Behind him come three young Europeans. Though they are not the apprentices from the *Righteous*, he guesses they have each paid the *devshirme* – the blood-tax.

'God give you good morrow, Dr Shelby,' Connell says with a cold smile. 'Because after that, you'll get fuck-all else from Him.'

One of the janissaries places a dish with a few scraps of bread on it beside Nicholas, who tries to eat it without betraying his hunger.

'If I fail to return to England, Connell, Robert Cecil's suspicions will only grow,' he says, swallowing the last of the stale breadcrumbs. 'He'll send word to Sultan al-Mansur. Your conspiracy with the Falconer will fail. You already know how little mercy conspirators get shown here.'

'You're right, of course,' Connell says amiably. 'But we've got plenty of time. When I return to London, I'll be telling them how well you're doing here – being an envoy and all. I'll say you've found yourself a nice little Moor concubine. In fact you can tell them yourself, in your letter.'

'What do you mean, *my letter?*'

'The one you're going to write to Robert Cecil, saying there's naught amiss here – using the cipher that meddling bastard Sykes employed.' He raises his brow in admiration. 'That was clever of you, finding those papers. We thought they might already have reached England.'

'And if I refuse?'

'Don't be a clod-pate, Shelby. Do you think I wouldn't bring down hellfire and chastisement on the whole world, if it could gain me what I want? How long do you think that pretty maid of yours on Bankside would stand what we did to the Jew?'

'So it *was* you who killed Solomon Mandel?'

Connell's mouth gapes in a cold laugh, like a snake swallowing a mouse. 'Not me personally. I was too busy enjoying the wedding feast. But I have friends in England, fellows who help me out every now and then, when little chores need doing.'

'Bianca knows nothing about this. There's no need to harm her,' Nicholas says, his fear doubling.

'Who's speaking of need? I'm talking of entertainment.'

Nicholas is halfway to his feet, his hands lunging at Connell's throat, before one the janissaries fells him with a kick to the stomach. He rolls over, clutching the pain in, as though it's precious to him.

When he's recovered his breath, Nicholas says miserably, 'Why did you kill them all, out there in the garden. They were innocent. Two of them were children, for Jesu's sake!'

'They were untidy, that's what they were. And you know how much I like an orderly ship.' He turns to one of the janissaries. 'Where have you put the bodies? We don't want them stinking the street out. It'll attract attention.'

'They're in the infidel's chamber, Master,' the janissary says. Nicholas recognizes the voice. It's the voice of the *kufiya,* al-Annuri's man, the one who warned him in this very storeroom to go home before it was too late. He nods in Nicholas's direction. 'What about this *berraniyin?*'

Connell squats down beside Nicholas. 'To be plain, I'm not too sure what to do with *you*, Dr Shelby. I could put out the word you slew them all in a drunken rage. How do you fancy being flayed and hung from the city walls? That would answer any difficult questions from Robert Cecil, wouldn't it?'

Nicholas stares back at him with undisguised loathing.

'There again, you're a valuable commodity. A slave who's a qualified physician would be worth a deal of money in the market.' He puts his face very close to Nicholas's. When he grins, it's like the flesh sliding off a rotting skull. 'But I wouldn't plan on siring any heirs, though. There are some masters around here who prefer their house-slaves gelded. Keeps the harem safer, or so I understand.'

He taps Nicholas on the shoulder in a gesture of friendly commiseration and makes to leave. By the door, he looks back at his prisoner, a sad smile on his face. 'What a shame, eh, Dr Shelby? All that promise – and now some other fellow gets to take care of Mistress Merton.'

✠

They come for him again shortly after the *al-maghrib* prayers, though this time Connell is not with them.

They put irons around his ankles and manacles on his wrists. The leg-irons are linked by half a yard of chain, so that he can move his feet independently. To the manacles they attach a second, longer length of chain. The *kufiya* tugs on the free end and Nicholas shuffles out of the storeroom like an old blind man finding his way to the jakes in the dark.

The garden is once again bathed in moonlight. From somewhere in the direction of the Badi Palace a dog howls a plaintive lament. The night is warm and the scent of death still lingers. Nicholas keeps his eyes closed. He knows, from what the *kufiya* said earlier, that the bodies have been removed, but whether or not Connell lets him live, Nicholas has no wish ever to look upon this place again.

They lead him out of the Street of the Weavers and into the darkened city. In London, a man being led about on a chain might raise an eyebrow or two, unless the one doing the leading was a bailiff or a man-at-arms. Here, no one gives Nicholas a second look. Clearly, to the few people he passes he is already a slave.

He thinks of the other transitions in his life: from boy to man; from virgin to lover; from husband to widower; from almost extinguished to a second chance, through the unexpected intervention of Bianca Merton. And he comes to the conclusion that the journey between being a *me* and being an *it* should be better marked. It is a death. And the dead should be mourned.

The *kufiya* is an impatient young man. When his prisoner stumbles, he curses in a language Nicholas thinks might be Slavic. He remembers what de Lisle had told him: *young men from the Christian coastal villages around the Mediterranean... a simple choice: renounce their Christian faith... serve the Moors as warriors – or die...*

To help assuage the *kufiya*'s anger, whenever he berates Nicholas's clumsiness, one of the other janissaries takes a vicious kick at the object of his displeasure. By the time they reach the Bimaristan al-Mansur, Nicholas has learned not to stumble.

Connell is waiting for them in the darkness. Nicholas is not taken in through the entrance he remembers from his last visit; instead, he's hustled towards a narrow doorway in the faceless mud-brick wall some fifty yards beyond. Like a drowning man gasping for air, he throws back his head to catch a last glimpse of the world he is leaving. The sky seems made of black parchment.

It has a brittleness to it, as though the warm desert night has somehow dried it out and if he were to flick it with a finger, it would tear.

He remembers the night Dr Arcampora's men delivered him, bound and bloodied, to a warehouse on Petty Wales. Then, Bianca had found the guile and the courage to save him. She had had to make herself complicit in murder to do so, but she hadn't hesitated. But tonight she is a continent away. Tonight there is no one to save him but himself. And he has no strength left in him to try.

✠

The inside of the Bimaristan al-Mansur is cool and shadowed. From within intricately patterned casings, lamps throw scatterings of golden light against the gleaming white vaults through which Nicholas passes, pale antechambers of some imagined Elysium, whose inhabitants slumber on low divans while nurses in long Moorish gowns move amongst them, moistening lips with water sponged from clay bowls. The air smells of cedar and frankincense, not the fetid odour of sickness and poverty he remembers from St Thomas's on Bankside. He hears the occasional cough and groan of patients in pain or unable to find sleep, but the loudest noise is the sound of his own ankle-chain clanking on the marble floor.

Connell picks up a lamp and beckons the little group to follow him. Nicholas is drawn on into the Bimaristan like a man going to the scaffold. The nurses show little interest in him. He recalls what Sumayl al-Seddik said: *Man; woman; sultan or pilgrim; even slaves are treated here...* Only one nurse looks up from her work. The *kufiya* says something in Arabic and makes a mime of delirium. The nurse nods.

He's told her I'm a poor, deranged madman, Nicholas thinks. They're going to put me in their equivalent of Bedlam.

But they do not. Instead, they bring him to a small chamber with six slender pillars holding up an arched ceiling. It is darker than the others, with only eight beds, four of them occupied. At the far end is a low door.

The *kufiya* gives a short command and the janissary who'd made so free with his kicks walks forward and places a heavy iron key in the lock. As he turns it, a movement behind one of the pillars catches Nicholas's eye. Two women are standing there. They appear to be attending to a patient on a nearby divan – a male patient whose throat is wrapped in cloth bandages. Even in the meagre light from the single oil lamp, Nicholas can see the thin section of reed poking out of the bindings: it's the patient who'd undergone the laryngotomy. And one of the women is Surgeon Wadoud.

Nicholas takes his chance. He turns towards her, yanking the chain out of the *kufiya*'s hands. 'For mercy's sake, help me!' he shouts, his voice echoing into the dark corners of the little chamber. 'These men intend me great harm! I want to speak to Minister al-Seddik. Do you understand? Find al-Seddik. *Please*, help me!'

He has only enough time to register the blank, uncomprehending look on Surgeon Wadoud's face, before the *kufiya*'s fist smashes into his cheek, sending him sprawling onto the marble floor.

As he's dragged to his feet, Nicholas hears the two women speaking. Though he cannot understand the words, their tone is clear: Surgeon Wadoud is troubled more by the disturbance to her patient than by what might be happening to the manacled infidel who has behaved so uncivilly in her presence.

Through the ringing in his ears, he hears Connell snarl to Surgeon Wadoud, 'What are *you* gawping at, ya miserable heathen bitch. Get back to your nursing. This is men's work we're about here.'

Laughing, the *kufiya* translates. Nicholas's last image of Surgeon Wadoud is of the young woman dipping her head in shame and tugging at her companion's robe, in an effort to drag her away.

Beyond the door is an open space that stinks of urine and fermenting fruit. The night feels cold against the bruised flesh of his cheek, even though the air has lost little of the day's heat. The dancing light of Connell's lamp leads them to a low, squat building that Nicholas fears might be a mortuary chamber for the hospital. He can smell the same faint stench of putrefaction here that troubled him so much in the garden of Adolfo Sykes's house.

To his relief, when they unlock the door, Nicholas catches fractured glimpses not of corpses, but of a small ziggurat of crates stacked against the far wall. As the lamplight briefly slices across them, he sees the double-sickle wool-mark painted on one of the crates.

'Don't get your hopes up, Dr Shelby,' says Connell from the doorway as the *kufiya* pushes him inside. 'If you're considering ripping out your fingernails in an effort to get at one of those matchlock muskets, you're wasting your time. We keep the powder elsewhere. We wouldn't want someone getting careless and blowing up the sultan's prized hospital, would we now? Think of all the innocent people who might get hurt.'

And with that, Nicholas is left alone in the darkness – the only person in the Bimaristan al-Mansur without even the faintest hope of recovery.

37

A herdsman drives his cows up Giltspur Street to pasture on Smithfield in the early June sunshine. Bianca steps cautiously in their wake towards Gault's fine new house, one hand gripping the hemp sack slung over her left shoulder, the other battling to stop the hem of her kirtle dragging in the cow dung. As she rams the knocker against the heavy oak door, she hears the bell at St Sepulchre ringing the ninth hour. Like the ominous tolling of a funeral bell, it sends a shiver through her body.

A servant girl shows her into the main hall. When she hears Gault's footsteps, Bianca embarks on the gambit she's been rehearsing all the way from Bankside.

First, flatter his vanity...

She affects a study of his portrait hanging over the hearth, feigning an approximation of a nun adoring a picture of a saint.

'Have you come to tell me you've seen reason, Mistress Merton?' she hears him say to her back.

She turns and lowers the sack to the floor. 'Oh, Master Gault! I didn't hear your approach. Forgive me, I was admiring the brushwork. I've brought some more preventatives. If you can smell cow dung, it's not them – it's the cow turds in the lane.'

Gault makes a bow to her that is only a little less elaborate than the saffron silk doublet with black lace trimmings he wears. He smiles. 'I smell only the perfume of roses. Is it Italian?'

'I make it myself, from oil, rosewater and mace,' she says, pleased that the care she's taken to make the best of herself has not been wasted.

She's wearing her sea-green gown and the carnelian bodice she knows flatters the darkness of her hair. If you're dealing with a canny merchant like Gault, she told herself as Rose helped her prepare, it's wise to ensure the box contains your best wares.

She unties the sack and peers in. 'It's all here: pomanders of rose leaves, tragacanth gum and camphor to hang about the neck... powder of tormentil, clove and lemon to mix in a posset... Also a tincture of bezoar and sorrel. Mix that in water or small beer every morning.'

'I applaud your efforts, Mistress. Would that *all* apothecaries in this city were as diligent.'

Then make him trust you...

'I can recommend each of these personally,' she says confidently. It's a tenuous claim, but her plan hinges on Gault's determination to believe in his own infallibility. 'At least, they worked for *me*.'

He remains silent for a moment, observing her as though her very existence is a vindication of his own certainties.

'So it was true – you *did* cure yourself of the pestilence.'

She lets that go with a knowing smile; no point in overdoing it.

'I should never have let Robert Cecil sow seeds of doubt in my mind,' he says.

'How are your young apprentices this morning? All healthy, I trust.'

'Come and see them for yourself. Having a comely young woman observing their efforts should put an edge to their *riversas*, their *imbroccatas* and their *stoccatas*.'

He leads her to out into the courtyard, where the same lads she had seen on her last visit are practising their swordplay. They are

361

stripped down to hose and garters, their young limbs gleaming with exertion.

'They look very fierce,' she says admiringly. 'But I thought they were destined to become merchants. Are they expecting their customers to put up a fight?'

'Commerce is a martial game, Mistress. Why else would we speak of contracts being won?' He smiles at his own wit. 'Now, tell me the true reason you've returned.'

A little foolish fluttering, to make him think he already has the better of you...

She clasps her hands to her cheeks. 'You've seen through my silly womanly wiles, Master Gault. I should have expected nothing less.'

And he should be yours for the taking...

'When last I saw you, you were uncommonly free with your confidences,' she continues. 'You confessed to me you were a Catholic. You suggested we should be allies.'

'I thought it wise to be open with each other.'

'And I thought you were trying to lure me into giving away things I would prefer to keep to myself.'

'Clearly, I failed.'

'Not *necessarily*.' It is said with just enough flirtation to entice.

'I'm intrigued, Mistress Merton. Please, continue.'

'I believe you wanted to know what confidences might have passed between me, Nicholas Shelby and Sir Robert Cecil.' A bright smile of fake mystification. 'I cannot *possibly* imagine why a *Catholic* would want to know what was in the mind of a minister of the Protestant queen of England. Perhaps you could enlighten me.'

She can see by the almost imperceptible way his jaw tilts that she has him.

'I'm listening, Mistress Merton. You may speak freely here. You're amongst friends.'

Now that he's hooked, all you have to do is pull him in...

'You know that I have a somewhat colourful reputation on Bankside.'

'It has not escaped my attention, Mistress. "The one witch nobody dares hang" was how Connell described you.'

'And you know I was taken to Cecil House to be questioned by Sir Robert on charges of recusancy, and that I returned to Bankside in his very own gilded barge.'

'I seem to recall you told me the story in this very house, only a few days ago.'

'Have you perhaps asked yourself *why* Sir Robert Cecil was stricken by an outbreak of such uncharacteristic mercy, when he could have had me hanged on both charges?'

'The question had crossed my mind. What exactly *does* Robert Cecil get, in return for not indicting you for heresy?'

'Oh, that's easy to answer,' Bianca says, contriving her most enticing smile. 'He gets information – on my fellow Catholics. You see, I am Robert Cecil's spy.'

For a moment Gault says nothing. The only sound Bianca can hear is the rasping of steel as the swordsmen lunge and parry. But there's now a hardness in his eyes that wasn't there before. It hints at a well of violence hidden beneath the gallant's polish. She wonders if he's mulling over the practicality of a tragic accident: a spectator run through whilst watching swordplay.

Then he turns sharply towards the fencers. 'Away with you!' he shouts. 'I can't hear myself think.'

The boys obediently move further down the garden. Gault moves closer to her. Uncomfortably closer.

'I've told you before: if you're planning to denounce me to Robert Cecil unless I pay through the nose, you've picked the wrong victim for a Southwark gulling, Mistress. I shall say you came here seeking to blackmail me. My lads here will confirm it. Who do you think the magistrate is going to believe: a distinguished city merchant or a mere tavern-wench from Bankside?' A triumphant sneer to put Bianca in her place. 'Then we'll see how clever you are at avoiding the hangman's rope.'

Bianca lets the echo of his bluster fade. Then she says, as softly as a lover's whisper, 'Have you *quite* finished, Master Gault?'

'Finished? There's one of us who's *finished*, Mistress Merton. And it's not *me*.'

In a voice that contains just a hint of disappointment, she says, 'Well, in that case I'll be on my way. God give you good morrow. You may keep the preventatives.' She makes a feint of leaving – then appears to remember something she'd almost forgotten. 'Purely as a matter of interest, Master Gault, in the world of commerce what would you pay to know what was in the mind of a competitor?'

Gault scowls. 'Why? What new dissembling is this?'

'I merely wondered – being no more than a mere tavern-wench from Bankside. What would such knowledge be worth?'

'It would be invaluable.'

She purses her lips. 'And if that competitor was – shall we say – Sir Robert Cecil?'

'What are you implying?'

Bianca tosses her head, as though it's such an irritation to have to explain simple things to a clod-pate.

'I would have thought that was obvious – to a clever merchant venturer like you. Have you never put one of your own people into a competitor's enterprise to learn his secrets? Maybe you're not quite as clever as your portrait suggests.'

'Are you telling me you're spying *on* Robert Cecil, not *for* him?'

'At *last*,' she says with a theatrical exhalation. 'I thought we were never going to get there.'

'And who exactly is the recipient of this intelligence?' he asks, a sliver of doubt still lodged in his resolve.

'Cardinal Santo Fiorzi, in Rome,' she says effortlessly, remembering the grizzled face of the man she and her cousin Bruno had served in Padua; the man who bears the ultimate responsibility for the images that still trouble her when she wakes – the image of two bodies falling through the night into the racing waters below London Bridge. 'It was he who sent me into England, to worm my way into the Pigmy's confidence. Surely you don't think I run a Southwark tavern because I *enjoy* the company of heretic drunks?'

Gault seems like a man caught in a hurricane. His mouth opens, but no sound comes out.

And having pulled in your fish, all that remains is to dispatch him with a blow to the back of his gleaming scaly head...

'You've heard about Christopher Marlowe, I take it?'

He stares at her. 'Of course. I can't say I'm surprised. Stabbed, wasn't he?'

'And you know what they're saying about him: that the Privy Council paid him to spy on Catholics, to worm his way into their trust and then betray them.'

He nods.

Bianca thinks, if I were skilled in swordplay, this is how it would feel to deliver the killing thrust.

'Well, it was I who lured Kit Marlowe to his death.'

His jaw sags, spoiling the pleasing symmetry of his face. 'You?'

'He was once a frequent visitor to my tavern. If you were thorough when you asked about me on Bankside, you might have heard the rumour we were lovers.'

Is that a look of intrigue, or envy, she sees in his eyes?

'Well, it's true,' she continues. 'When we lay together, I could not draw a confession from him. He would not admit he was Robert Cecil's informer. And I really *did* try.' She makes a languorous tilt of her head. 'In the end I had to wait until Cecil let it slip that the Privy Council had paid the cheating rogue for his treachery. All I had to do then was pass the information on to some people I know, who believe our faith must be defended by all means possible, and its enemies punished. I would have waited – until we both had grey hair, if it had proved necessary. I'm a very patient woman, you see.'

'That is quite some tale, Mistress,' he says. 'I can think of no woman in London who could match it.'

'Given what we confessed to each other at our last meeting, you should be grateful.' She sighs with mock sadness. 'Poor Kit. Now he has no one to spy upon but Satan.'

Gault is staring at her with undisguised admiration, and not a little unvarnished desire.

'Why have you told me this, Mistress Merton? What is it you want from me in return?'

The smile she gives him contains a galleon's worth of Indies sugar.

'You're the clever merchant, Master Gault. I'll leave you to decide the value of the merchandise. Don't leave it too long – I'm only patient when it comes to revenge.'

✠

Bianca heads down Giltspur Street towards the river, oblivious to passers-by. She wears a wide, triumphant grin that not even the sour stench of cow dung can shift.

Lured, hooked, dispatched and ready for the pot, she tells herself. The gulling of Reynard Gault is very nearly complete. All she has to wait for now is the summons.

What will it be, she wonders, when the confession comes? What conspiracy will he reveal to her, now that he thinks he's found the perfect partner in crime?

As she approaches the Water Gate at Blackfriars she sees a vacant wherry waiting for a customer. She smiles with satisfaction.

Sometimes, it seems, there are days when everything is determined to go your way.

Making herself comfortable on the stern-seat, she thinks: how easy it is to make a vain man – especially one who believes he has power over you – jump to your tune, like poor old Sackerson the bear. The sweeter the promised honey, the livelier his dance.

38

Nicholas has reached the limit of endurance. He will write whatever Connell wants him to write. He will tell Robert Cecil any lie; betray any oath he's ever made; sell his soul to the Devil – do anything demanded of him, if only he's allowed to leave this oven of a torture chamber where every breath feels like hot syrup in the lungs.

There is a grille set into the ceiling, barely a foot square. If he clambers onto the top crates and lies out on his back – a trial in itself, given that he still wears the ankle-irons and manacles – he can breathe fresher air. But he cannot do it for long. Lying beneath the iron lattice is like putting his face too close to a fire.

If he wastes energy shouting for help, the *kufiya* visits him. He brings with him another janissary who speaks in the same Irish lilt as Cathal Connell. They encourage Nicholas to silence by taking turns to lay about him with a cane.

The Irish boy has the face of an angry child, seared by too many hurts delivered too early in life. His companion retains the interrogator's superiority Nicholas recalls from the storeroom in Adolfo Sykes's house: *Take my advice: go home at the earliest opportunity. You would not be the first man who has come here only to disappear into the slave market...*

Nicholas judges it must be around noon when again he hears the sound of the key turning in the lock, though by now his sense of timekeeping is no better than Sultan al-Mansur's. The fear that Connell has come for him turns the sweat on his skin into beads of ice.

But Connell has not come. His visitors are the two lads, though this time instead of beating him, they bring him fruit and water. The water is tepid, but the fruit is good.

'Make the best of this,' the kufiya tells him. 'Captain Connell gave it to us, to keep you alive. Be grateful; only infidels may eat between sunrise and sunset. For the faithful, now is the holy month of fasting.'

'Then you'd best tell Connell to bring me pen, ink and paper as well, because if he leaves me here much longer, he'll not get his letter,' Nicholas says, wiping the sweat from his eyes with the filthy sleeve of his shirt.

'Why do you complain?' asks the kufiya. 'In the bagnios – where they keep the public slaves – they cram them in like fish in a barrel. They would kill their own kin to have a chamber to themselves.'

But then, to Nicholas's surprise, they show him a little mercy. They lead him outside to relieve himself, playfully shaking the length of chain as though they were Bankside street entertainers and he the performing monkey. By the corner of the little building, the Irish lad pays out the chain so that Nicholas can pull his hose down around his knees. He doesn't care about the lack of privacy – serving in the Low Countries soon knocked the bashfulness out of him.

Though it takes his eyes a while to adjust to the blinding sunlight, Nicholas gets his first opportunity to see his surroundings in daylight.

His place of torment is a hermit's cell of mud-brick, set in the centre of a walled enclosure some thirty paces a side. The only exit is the single door they led him through last night. He wonders if this is where the Bimaristan confines those who suffer the worst trials of insanity. He thinks he might soon be listed amongst them, if he has to spend many more hours in that oppressive chamber.

'Don't go, stay a while. Tell me who you are,' Nicholas pleads in desperation, when they prepare to return him to the oven of his captivity. 'I'm not trying to trick you. Just tell me who you are – we're all *berraniyin* here, aren't we?'

The lad with the Irish accent laughs. 'Outsiders? Not any more. When our master is sultan, I shall be a duke in his court.' He adopts a stance of affected nobility, hands on hips, head thrown arrogantly back. 'Why, I'm already the son of an English knight, Sir Thomas Winterbourne. A great man, by all accounts. I have the paper to prove it.' He makes a little dancing mime of dispensing alms to grovelling peasants.

'Proved by the Rouge Croix Pursuivant, no doubt,' says Nicholas, hoping to pique his curiosity.

The lad stops his play-acting. He comes closer, peering at Nicholas as though he were an exhibit in a cabinet of curiosities. 'Captain Connell was right, you *do* know more than you're lettin' on. Did my old master tell you that?'

'That depends on which master you're speaking of: Connell, or Reynard Gault. I'm guessing that you came here on a Barbary company ship, and that Gault gave you a false lineage.'

A sudden flicker of uncertainty in the lad's eyes. 'What do you know of Master Gault?'

'More to the question, what do *you* know of Sir Thomas Winterbourne? Save for the fact that he probably doesn't exist. Or any of his supposed ancestors.'

'It doesn't fuckin' matter if he exists or not,' the lad snaps. 'I'm his son. I have the writing to prove it. That makes me of noble blood. And that means I shall be a duke when we throw down the sultan and—'

The *kufiya* gives the lad a savage push that almost topples him. 'Stop blathering, you stupid *llafazan*. Can't you see what he's doing?'

The Irish boy drops Nicholas's chain and rounds on his companion, using his chest as a ram. 'What did you call me, y'heathen?'

The *kufiya* stands his ground. 'I called you *llafazan*. In my language it means a rattle-trap, a blathermouth. And I'm not a heathen, I'm from Albania.'

The Irish boy fires a gobbet of spit at the other lad's feet. 'Where the fuck is *that*?' he demands to know, giving his companion another shove. 'You can be fuckin' Duke of Albania, for all I care, but only if you've got a pedigree from the College of Heralds to prove it. If not, you'll have to play the churl to those of us who have. What's the word for *servant* in Albania?'

The two janissaries stare each other down, their tempers raw through having spent so many tedious hours guarding the door into the Bimaristan.

Nicholas takes his chance. Moving as fast as his enervated limbs will allow, he seizes the lead-chain in both hands. He swings the loop towards the Albanian's head, with the wild idea of getting it around his throat and choking him until the Irish boy gives up his keys.

Like most acts of desperation, it's been given almost no thought. And it has about the same chances of success. The chain lands ineffectually across the back of the *kufiya*'s neck. Before Nicholas can try again, both lads are upon him, flailing fists pounding at his body. Tripped by his ankle-chains, he goes down hard, the grit rasping the side of his face as he lands.

The first boot takes him just above his right hip. The pain makes his mouth gape, swallowing dirt from the floor of the compound. The next blow lands slantwise below his shoulderblade.

The third is a jab to his right buttock, bringing bile into the back of his throat and rolling him onto his side, so that he's staring at a pair of horizontal boots, and in the hazy background a wall and a door lying on their sides. After that, counting gives way to trying not to vomit.

The Irish lad's voice reaches Nicholas the way the muffled roaring of a wave reaches the man it drowns.

'Don't kill him, Brother. The master will want to hear what he has to say. He's a contrary little bugger, but the knife will make him talkative. It always does.'

Lying curled up in the dirt, Nicholas stares at the tilted world through blooms of sweat that pool in the corners of his eyes and run across his scoured nose and cheek.

And as he does so, he sees the door in the compound wall open. Three figures emerge, floating towards him like spectres in a dream. The boots of his two assailants move away and he hears the Albanian mutter something that sounds very much like a prayer for mercy. From the Irish lad comes a muffled 'Holy Mary, Mother of God!'

Forcing his eyes to focus, Nicholas recognizes the lean, balding figure of Arnoult de Lisle, and beside him Surgeon Wadoud.

But it is the third figure that sears into his vision even more than the stinging grit and sweat. Standing over him, garbed in white, his eyes observing Nicholas with the detached appraisal of a falcon, is Muhammed al-Annuri.

39

Bianca has spent the day returning the Jackdaw's cellar into her apothecary's chamber. Ned and Timothy have done the heavy lifting, passing the bags and boxes down through the open hatchway that gives access from the yard, while Rose has assisted with the bundles of plants and herbs.

Her mind has not been wholly on the job. *What was I thinking of?* she's asked herself a hundred times if she's asked it once. *What temporary insanity made me do it? I went into the lion's den, and for some reason that only my mother could explain – if she were alive, and it's a good thing she's not, because she'd be having apoplexy – thrust my head into the lion's mouth.* Who else but a woman bereft of all reason would make a confession like that to a man of Gault's character and believe it could end well?

She is convinced now that there is a connection between Solomon Mandel's murder and Gault's conviction that Nicholas revealed to her a second reason why Cecil sent him to the Barbary shore. But if there is a second reason – and it led to the Jew's death – that simply compounds her anxiety, because it cannot possibly be a *good* one. If she needs proof of that, Bianca thinks, she has only to recall what Gault said to her that time they walked together along the river: *The Catholic cause in England could make good use of your talents.* That was an invitation to sedition if ever she'd heard one.

Why hadn't Nicholas been open with her? Was it to protect her? If so, it has served only to make things worse. She stamps her foot, raising a little cloud of spilt yellow brimstone. 'Why couldn't you have just told me?'

'What's that, Mistress?' says Rose.

Appalled that her thoughts have taken on a life outside her head, Bianca says, 'Nothing, Rose. I was just thinking.'

The faint sound of St Saviour's bell ringing for Evensong reaches her through the open trapdoor. She sets down her burden of yellow gilliflower that she uses to treat ulcers, laying it beside the bags of brimstone Ned has assembled.

'That's the last of the brimstone,' says Ned, peering down through the opening at the two women below. 'There's still a small chest in your chamber left to bring.'

Bianca remembers the box in which she keeps her father's books, the ones she brought from Padua, and his silver Petrine cross. Bringing them back to the Jackdaw would seem now like an admission of failure. Better, she thinks, to leave them on Dice Lane, as a call to her to return when the pestilence has been defeated.

'Leave it there, Ned,' she calls up. 'You've worked hard enough today.'

Ned sits on the edge of the trapdoor, eases himself down on his arms and – with surprising agility for such a big man – drops easily to the cellar floor. He scoops up his new bride by her waist and sits her down on top of the row of sacks, the better to admire her.

'Husband, 'ave a care!' Rose squeals. 'I don't want brimstone all over my behind. It'll leave a yellow patch on my arse.'

Ned's bushy red beard splits into a grin. 'You don't need no brimstone to set your fundamentals aflame, Goodwife Monkton!'

'This is not a bawdy-house, you two,' Bianca says, rolling her eyes. 'If it were, I'd have Parson Moody serving in the taproom.'

Ned jabs one big thumb in the direction of the cellar stairs. 'I've just heard Alderman Spivey say there's a rumour the queen has ordered the ban on gatherings to include Bartholomew Fair. That's not been cancelled this side of the Flood. Oh, an' the city Companies are to stop all parades and feasts.' He shakes his great head despondently. 'I'll tell you this, Mistress, when Master Nick comes home, he'll find London a sorry place.'

'Look on the bright side,' says Bianca. '*We're* still open. And we can put on a revel here to beat the best of them.'

Rose gives her an alarming wink. 'When 'e does come home, will you be needin' that kissing knot again? Or do you think you'll be able to manage on your owns?'

Bianca glares at her, until the laughter breaks through and she chivvies Ned and Rose up the cellar stairs. 'That's enough idle nonsense for one day, thank you,' she says. 'I think a jug of knock-down is in order, to get the dust out of our throats.'

But as she follows them up to the taproom, Bianca wonders how long she must wait for Reynard Gault to make contact with her again. The satisfaction she'd felt when she left his house on Giltspur Street has vanished. Now she almost dreads the summons. Because whatever he might reveal to her next – whatever it is he's involved in – her own confession to him about being a Catholic spy, fantasy though it may be, is more than adequate to get her hanged.

40

The blows have left Nicholas the sole occupant of a world in which the only sound is a high-pitched whistling in his ears; the only taste, the iron seasoning of his own blood; the only landscape, a vista of pain that has no horizon.

He stares up from the dirt, dazzled by the glare of the sun. Then, as his eyes focus, he makes out al-Annuri's white-robed body looming over him, a curved, bejewelled dagger at his belt. The hooded eyes regard him with satisfied amusement, as though he's prey that it has taken some skill to bring down.

Then the whistling inside his head gives way to muffled voices penetrating from reality: de Lisle speaking Arabic; al-Annuri issuing what sounds like a fusillade of orders; the sound of running feet, sandal-leather slapping against the dirt. Strong arms lift him effortlessly to his feet as though he were weightless – soldiers, he thinks, given the metallic whisper of chainmail against leather. Upright once more, he sways like a creature hooked and dragged from one world to another, unsure if he can breathe its air or stand upright on its surface.

After a few moments, during which they give him water to drink, his senses begin to right themselves, though it is only when he looks around and sees the kufiya and the Irish lad roped together on their knees – under the watchful eyes of two large bearded men in striped linen tunics and mail hoods, loaded crossbows in their hands – that he realizes this isn't the start of some new torture, but a rescue.

✠

'His Excellency says you are most fortunate,' de Lisle tells Nicholas once they've led him back into the Bimaristan, to the little iwan where he had pleaded for Surgeon Wadoud's help the previous night. 'If Surgeon Wadoud had gone to al-Seddik and not to me when you called for help, you would be well on your way to becoming a dead man.'

Looking around, Nicholas sees the ward has been cleared of patients, even the man recovering from the laryngotomy. Through the open door leading to the rest of the hospital he can see more armed men. How they can wear mail in this climate – even in the relative cool of the Bimaristan – is beyond him. But he's glad they're there.

Under Surgeon Wadoud's guidance, an assistant washes his grazes with honey and water, plucking little pieces of grit from his cheek with the point of a small but very sharp knife. Bruised and debilitated, he sits passively on a divan while de Lisle reveals the measure of his good fortune.

'Apparently, Surgeon Wadoud does not like al-Seddik very much,' de Lisle continues. 'She says he treats the hospital as his own personal fiefdom. Everyone here is terrified of him, except her, of course. She knew you were the English envoy, so she thought it proper that the sultan's personal physician should hear of what she had witnessed, not a man who makes a habit of treating the hospital's best surgeon more as a washer of sick bodies than as a healer of them.'

'Are you telling me al-Seddik is behind this? Is he the Falconer?'

De Lisle looks puzzled. 'I do not know what you mean. But yes, Minister al-Seddik has been plotting to overthrow His Majesty.

377

He has confessed.' A look of distaste, and he adds, 'After the confession, I was summoned to keep him alive. They were harsh in their questioning.'

'I believe I owe you an apology, Professor de Lisle,' Nicholas says. 'When I saw you with Fra Cyprien at the hammam, I jumped to the conclusion that if there was any threat to the sultan, it was from a French physician and a Jesuit priest. I was hasty. I should have been less inclined towards misjudgement.'

De Lisle's laugh contains just a hint of reproach. 'A subject of the English heretic Elizabeth jumps to an easy conclusion about a Frenchman! Who would ever have anticipated such a thing.'

'Yes, well, as I said, I'm sorry.'

'I suppose I must be grateful to you,' de Lisle says, relenting. 'Had His Majesty fallen, I suspect that his physician's life would not long have outspanned his own.' He nods towards Surgeon Wadoud. 'But if gratitude is due, the rightful recipient stands there.'

Nicholas thinks so, too. He thinks it in shovelfuls. Climbing stiffly off the divan, he approaches the surgeon and makes a polite bow. The stab of pain from his right buttock as he bends his knee brings a sharp intake of breath, but he still manages a heartfelt 'You have my enduring gratitude, Surgeon Wadoud.' Then, with a glance at de Lisle for his help, he goes on, 'Were it not for your intervention, I would have no hope of returning to the woman I love. I owe you my life. Whatever happiness God sees fit to bestow upon me now, I pray He bestows it upon you twice over.' Another glance at de Lisle. 'Will you say that? Tell her my precise words.'

When the Frenchman has finished translating, Surgeon Wadoud's previously impassive brown eyes become the locus for one of the most beautiful smiles he's ever seen. She makes a brief reply. De Lisle translates.

'Surgeon Wadoud says you have the hands of a good man. And a good surgeon, too. She says: return home and tell them what you saw here in the Bimaristan al-Mansur. Tell them we are not all heathens.'

✠

Muhammed al-Annuri's house is a palatial spread of airy rooms set around a garden five times the size of the one on the Street of the Weavers. Nicholas is installed in a pleasant chamber over-looking a fountain flanked by purple bougainvillea. A servant brings him a clean gown of Berber cloth, dyed the colour of a hot summer sky. Nicholas is ravenously hungry. He makes a motion of putting food in his mouth. The servant looks horrified. Then Nicholas remembers it is the holy month of Ramadan. There will be no sustenance taken from dawn until sunset – in this house-hold, or so it seems, not even for an infidel. He decides a few hours of hunger is a fate preferable to the one that has probably already befallen the two lads who came to him in the compound. He understands now: when the kufiya and the others had interro-gated him at Adolfo Sykes's house, they had not been al-Annuri's men, as they'd claimed, but al-Seddik's. He had sent them to Nicholas to find out how much, if anything, he had learned of the Falconer's conspiracy.

De Lisle and al-Annuri come to him a few minutes later. The minister regards Nicholas with dark, astute eyes. Yet there is a hint of amusement in them, as though he's been pleasantly disa-bused of a poor opinion. He delivers a fast burst of Arabic for de Lisle to translate.

'In order to save time, His Excellency wishes you to confess that you are an English spy. Denial will not serve you well.'

A reprieve then, not an escape, thinks Nicholas as a fresh wave of fear courses through his body.

'I'm not a spy, I'm just a physician. I was sent here to study physic,' he says, knowing as he speaks how lame his denial sounds.

'A physician who happens to be able to decipher coded dispatches,' says de Lisle, even managing to capture some of al-Annuri's scepticism. 'Please don't waste His Excellency's time denying it, Dr Shelby. In your chamber at Sykes's house, His Excellency's men found a paper with certain letters written upon it. He believes it was used to unlock Sykes's code. When he arrested al-Seddik at his dwelling late last night, he recovered Sykes's full dispatch, with a copy of it made in plain English. He presumes that copy was deciphered by you. I read it myself. There were some errors, it is true, though far less than if al-Seddik had been responsible. In English, his hand is not as accomplished as his tongue; though before much longer he will have little need of either.' A twinge of distaste puckers the Frenchman's cheek. 'What His Excellency would very much like to know is how you discovered the original, when the people of the traitor al-Seddik could not.'

Denial is pointless, Nicholas realizes. He looks frankly at al-Annuri as he answers. 'It was luck, really. And the fact that both Sykes and his friend in London put their faith in the same talisman. Otherwise I might never have worked out where Sykes had hidden his letter. How did His Excellency know al-Seddik was plotting against the sultan, before he took possession of Sykes's last dispatch?'

'His Excellency has been suspicious of al-Seddik for a long time. But until now he had no evidence,' the Frenchman says. 'He, too, fought at the battle against the Portuguese and Spanish when His Majesty al-Mansur became sultan, and he has never trusted al-Seddik's protestations of loyalty. Your actions have proved him right.'

Nicholas recalls with anguish Hadir's words on the ride from Safi: *Then al-Seddik comes on his knees to al-Mansur and begs forgiveness. His Majesty shows mercy, and now al-Seddik loves him like a brother...*

He looks directly at al-Annuri and says, 'Then His Excellency is a wise man. In England, Lord Burghley – our queen's most trusted advisor – believed al-Seddik to be a friend. He even wrote a letter of fond remembrance. I handed it to al-Seddik myself.'

'His Excellency regrets he was unable to protect you from such harsh handling, but once al-Seddik had chased away his watchers, it became more difficult. There are only so many times a man can walk down a street and observe a house before his presence is noticed. Otherwise we might have saved the lives of your household.'

The awful image of the scene in the garden on the Street of the Weavers tears into Nicholas's mind. 'If you have al-Seddik, I hope you have that murdering bastard Connell, too. Treat him as harshly as you care to – it will be no more than he deserves.'

De Lisle delivers his message. The reply is not what Nicholas cares to hear.

'Connell was returning to al-Seddik's mansion when he saw His Excellency's men arrive—'

'He escaped?'

'He cannot long evade capture.'

'What about al-Seddik's janissaries? What will happen to them?'

'Sultan al-Mansur's men fell upon them this morning, at al-Seddik's kasbah at Tahannout, in the mountains. Whether they took them all – well, the answer to that will have to wait upon some hard questioning.'

'There are Englishmen amongst them, apprentices that Gault and Connell brought here,' Nicholas says. 'They must be freed; sent home.'

A quick stream of Arabic from al-Annuri. De Lisle translates.

'His Excellency regrets that cannot be. They chose to become mercenaries in a rebellious cause. They will have to face the consequences of their actions.'

'They were given little choice,' Nicholas protests. He thinks of Hortop, the Kentish shepherd's son. 'They're just ordinary lads from poor families. They were promised riches, a new life of plenty, an escape. They didn't know what they were buying. To send them home would show my queen that her ally in the fight against Spain is a merciful man.'

'His Excellency will consider it,' says de Lisle when al-Annuri has digested what Nicholas has told him. 'But he would like to hear from you how Minister Cecil learned of al-Seddik's treachery.'

'He didn't. He simply became concerned when Adolfo Sykes stopped sending his dispatches. So he sent me here to find out what had happened to him. If that's spying – given that it was Sir Robert's only desire to protect both our realms – then yes, I'm a spy.'

Al-Annuri listens to de Lisle's rendition of Nicholas's words with a thoughtful frown. When he replies, Nicholas thinks he hears the name Solomon Mandel.

'His Excellency wishes to know if you have word of his man in London,' says de Lisle. 'A Jew named Solomon Mandel.'

Nicholas raises his eyes to the ceiling, letting out his breath in a long, sad flow. 'So *you're* the Turk. Solomon Mandel was *your* man.'

This time al-Annuri has no need of a translator to understand the meaning of Nicholas's words. The hawk's gaze softens, even as the eyes dart from Nicholas to de Lisle and back again. The neatly trimmed black beard tightens against the jaw with self-recrimination.

'He was murdered,' Nicholas says brutally. 'The conspirators in England thought that Sykes's last dispatch had been sent to him, not to Robert Cecil. I'm sorry. Truly sorry.'

'You knew him?' asks al-Annuri.

'I *found* him.'

Al-Annuri goes to the open window and stares out at the fountain, a contemplative frown on his angular face. He whispers something in the direction of the bougainvillea. To Nicholas, it sounds as though he's making a pledge to a dead man. When he turns back into the room, the faint gleam of amusement in the Moor's eyes has gone, replaced by a frightening intensity. His voice is as sharp as the jewelled dagger he carries. De Lisle catches the measure of it as he translates.

'I know from my friend Solomon that I can trust Captain Yaxley of the *Marion*. He is still at Safi. You will return to England aboard his ship, Dr Shelby. And when you get there, you will do me a small service, in return for saving your life.'

'Of course. Anything.'

'You will find whoever killed my friend Solomon Mandel and erase their presence from this world. You will poison their wells and slaughter the livestock that feeds them. You will burn the sky above them. You will bring pestilence and death upon them, even unto the seventh generation. You will erase their names so that Allāh will forget he ever made them. Will you do that for me?'

Nicholas meet's the Moor's gaze without flinching. 'Yes,' he says, thinking of Solomon Mandel, of Hadir and his dreams of success, of grandmother Tiziri, of Gwata and his wide-eyed sister Lalla, who ran away when he smiled at her. 'I will do it. No matter what it takes, I will deliver them justice. *Inshā Allāh.*'

41

S afi is a town that has fallen to an enemy it never knew it had, caught up in a war it had no idea was being waged. Everyone they pass prostrates themselves before Minister al-Annuri and offers what Nicholas takes to be heartfelt protestations of loyalty to Sultan al-Mansur.

The detachment of Moorish cavalry under al-Annuri's command has made the journey from Marrakech in record time. For Nicholas, the ride – on a rangy Andalusian mare – has been tiring but exhilarating.

In the *Kechla*, the old Portuguese citadel on the hill above the harbour, the governor grovels on his expensively tiled floor and swears by Allāh that he never knew what was going on down in the port. He has never met the infidel Connell. He has never taken so much as a single Christian ducat to look the other way. As proof of his innocence, he produces the customs official Nicholas met when the *Righteous* docked, Muly Hassan. Brought into the daylight from some stinking pit, Hassan is bound as though he possesses a Herculean ability to tear off all but the stoutest chains. From the crimson mess on his face, Nicholas wonders for a moment if he's been gorging himself on the barberry preserve he recalls Connell giving him. But the blank stare in the man's eyes, and the tooth still embedded in his lower lip, suggest otherwise.

Down on the quayside, Nicholas scours the Kasar el Bahr fort and the surrounding warehouses for news of Connell. De Lisle acts as his translator, four of al-Annuri's men as bodyguards.

No one they question admits to having seen so much as a glimpse of the Irishman.

Nicholas climbs the stone steps to the ramparts. He walks along the line of eight massive royale cannon to get a better look at the waterfront. All three English ships – the *Righteous*, the *Marion* and the *Luke of Bristol* – are still moored to the breakwater. Now fully laden, all that prevents their departure is a detachment of the sultan's marines, scowling men in striped tunics worn over mail coats, crossbows drawn, who have come aboard at Minister al-Annuri's command for just that purpose.

But one vessel *is* missing from the Safi anchorage, Nicholas notices. On the strip of beach where – on his previous arrival – he had seen the Moor corsair laid up, now there is nothing but furrowed sand. He wonders if Connell has made an escape aboard her. His fears are confirmed when he climbs over the side of the *Marion*.

✠

Captain Yaxley is a compact, wiry little Devon sea-terrier with a yap for a voice and ocean-grey eyes. The sword he wears is almost too long for his legs. He exudes an air of quiet competence.

'The town has been in uproar since noon yesterday, Dr Shelby,' he says, casting a doubtful eye over Nicholas's blue Berber gown. 'What in the name of Jesu is going on? I can't get any sense at all out of these heathens.'

'A conspiracy, Captain Yaxley. A plot to overthrow Sultan al-Mansur and hand Morocco to the Dons. Connell was part of it. Have you seen him?'

'Aye, he arrived yesterday. Wouldn't speak to a soul, except Stawley, his sailing master.'

385

Nicholas recalls the rough-hewn character who'd stood at his side while the sandglass marked the changing of the watch. 'Where are they now?'

'Only the Almighty knows that, Dr Shelby. Or perhaps the Devil. Connell might be a fine seaman, but I've always held there was a whiff of Lucifer about that man.'

'And you haven't seen him since yesterday?'

'When I asked him what was afoot, he cursed me for a savage and took Stawley away with him. Our people have been asking me what's happening ever since. They're all afeared the Moors will take us ashore and make prisoners of us.'

'How long has that Moor corsair been gone?'

Yaxley casts a glance through the *Marion*'s cordage towards the beach. 'The oarsmen came down to her yesterday in chains, from the Safi slave *bagnio*, just before sunset, along with about a score of janissaries. They're off to do some slaving up the coast towards Lisbon, I shouldn't wonder. They'll have an easy job of it, too – there's precious little wind. With oarsmen who know what they're doing, a corsair galley will outrun a Christian sail easily in this weather.' He lets out a grunt of appreciation. 'It must be a goodly prize they're after; I haven't seen them get a galley that big off the beach so fast in all the years I've been sailing to the Barbary shore.'

Nicholas gives a tight smile of understanding. Connell has taken the speediest means of escape.

'Captain Yaxley, you may know I was sent aboard the *Righteous* by Sir Robert Cecil. I was carrying messages of goodwill from the queen to Sultan al-Mansur.'

'Aye, I'd heard the like.'

'Then hear this also: Sultan al-Mansur is a valued ally of England. The queen's Privy Council must know of what has happened here. In their name, I ask for your assistance to return to England as swiftly as possible.'

Yaxley does not hesitate. 'That's all the excuse I need, Dr Shelby. None of my people fancy getting caught up in a quarrel between the Moors. There's enough English sailors languishing in captivity across Barbary as it is.'

'How soon can you be ready to sail?'

'The cargo's already loaded. The tide's in our favour. But with these slack breezes, we'll have to warp the *Marion* out to sea. We can be away from the quayside inside an hour, but it could be several more before we're far enough out to catch a proper wind.'

'Then look to your task, Captain Yaxley,' Nicholas says. 'In the meantime I'll tell Minister al-Annuri to get his marines off your ship. The sooner we're away, the sooner your men will be downing English ale and spending the Cecils' reward.'

Three children are driving a herd of goats across the track from the *Kechla* down to the waterfront. When they see the imposing figure of Muhammed al-Annuri escorting Nicholas and de Lisle back towards the quay after a final meeting in the governor's mansion, their happy chatter ceases and they fall silent, driving the beasts quickly out of the way. Nicholas thinks how easily he too had fallen into the trap of misjudging the taciturn minister.

When they reach the quay, al-Annuri snaps his fingers. A minion who's been trailing them at a respectful distance hurries up with a leather pouch trimmed with gold thread and pearls. The minion hands it to Nicholas, while al-Annuri makes an account of it in Arabic to de Lisle.

'This contains the letter His Excellency has written to your Minister Cecil,' de Lisle explains. 'It is in Italian, in which His Excellency is proficient. He trusts Sir Robert will be able to find someone to translate it.'

'If it was in the picture-writing of Rameses the Great, Robert Cecil could probably find someone to tell him what it says,' Nicholas replies knowingly.

De Lisle seems uncertain if he's joking. 'Also, the pouch contains the gift the sultan gave you at the Badi Palace – the ring. It was recovered from al-Seddik's house. His Excellency says it was given to you as a measure of the sultan's friendship, and must therefore remain with you. Finally, there are the ducats you left in your chamber at Adolfo Sykes's house. I understand Connell's men would not return to the place where they had taken the bodies of the old woman and the two children. They thought it unlucky. One of them protested – before he died – that he was a warrior, not a common looter.'

'Is that what's happened to al-Seddik's janissaries – all dead? Even the new apprentices from the *Righteous*?'

De Lisle looks troubled. 'His Excellency has not seen fit to tell me. But conspiracy is a dangerous sport here, Dr Shelby. Even more so than in England or France. If you cross them, the Moors have little truck with mercy. Play the game of treason with them, and it's wise to make sure you win.'

✠

Yaxley was right. It takes hours to warp the *Marion* out of Safi harbour. Under a brilliant blue sky and a breeze that barely ruffles the hair, two of her boats row ahead, paying out a cable with the small kedge anchor attached. When the cable is extended, the anchor is dropped to the bottom of the bay. Then the ship's crew toils on the capstan to haul her up to the anchor. The process is repeated, cable-length by cable-length, so often that Nicholas loses count. Eventually the boats' crews are dropping the kedge into ten fathoms of water and the *Kechla* has faded to a pale smudge against the scrub and olive trees. Even the ramparts of the Kasar el Bahr on the waterfront lose their outline, becoming little more than a thin line of sandstone dancing in the heat above the surf.

And then the wind stiffens a little. The long pennants hanging limply from the mastheads begin to dance, and the sea lifts in long, slow heaves beneath the Marion's keel. Captain Yaxley gives the order to make sail. As the crew race into the rigging above his head, Nicholas feels once again the self-conscious embarrassment of the inept thrown amongst the skilful. He allows himself the excuse of his healing bruises to sit quietly by the stern rail.

He has had time during the long haul out of the harbour to take the measure of the Marion. She is smaller than the Righteous, sleeker, with a low, gracefully sweeping prow and a high, raked sterncastle. She carries four cannon a side. He couldn't be in a better ship, he thinks. All she needs now is a good southerly wind to fill her sails.

He is still counting his good fortune when he hears cries from aloft, attracting Yaxley's attention.

Looking up, Nicholas sees several hands perched high in the rigging, pointing in the direction of the headland that Cathal Connell had told him was the Rass Lafaa, the Head of the Snake. He turns in the direction indicated by the outstretched arms.

Low against the glittering wave tops, a dark shape is moving across their path, faster than this breeze should be able to carry a ship. Then Nicholas sees the silver, rhythmic glint of foam marking the sweep of a bank of oars as they strike the water in unison.

'It's the Moor corsair,' Yaxley says, confirming Nicholas's fears. 'I think he means to come down upon us.' He looks at Nicholas, his grey eyes searching for an answer.

'It's Connell,' Nicholas admits, sensing a lifting of the hairs on the back of his neck that has nothing to do with the breeze.

389

'It's me he's after. He has friends in England who will go to the scaffold if I live to reach home. We can fight him off, though, can we not?'

Yaxley gives him a troubled look. 'With a better wind, aye. But at present we've precious little way on us. We can't manoeuvre. He'll be able to keep out of range of the culverins, then cross our stern. All he has to do then is rake us with his bow-chaser cannon until we're a hulk and half of us dead. When he's ready, he'll close and board us.'

'Surely we have some defence against that?'

'Only the rabinet,' Yaxley says, indicating a light cannon set upon a swivel-iron near the stern. 'A charge of hail-shot from that will clear them off. But they're not fools. They won't risk boarding until that's battered down. It doesn't have the range of their bow-chaser.'

'Can we not fly a signal, tell the Kasar el Bahr that we're in danger?'

'We can barely see it from here, Dr Shelby. Besides, we're all but out of range of their ordnance. The Moors are good gunners, but no one can carry a shot further than the God Lord means it to fly.'

'How long do we have, Captain Yaxley?'

'Less than an hour, I'd imagine. She was out of the water for careening – that's why she was on the beach. Her hull will be clean of weeds and barnacles, so she'll cleave the water all the faster. So you'd best get down on your knees, Dr Shelby, and beg the Almighty to fill His lungs and start blowin'.'

No sooner are the words out of Yaxley's mouth than the pennants fluttering from the mastheads fall limply, like accusing fingers pointing down towards the deck. The newly set canvas hangs sullenly from the yards, fractiously banging against the masts until eventually all movement ceases.

The Almighty, it seems, has other things to do today than blow.

✠

Sometimes the corsair is visible from Nicholas's vantage point beside Yaxley, sometimes not. The slight swell, or the glare of the sun on the water, can erase it for minutes at a time. On one occasion it vanishes long enough for Nicholas to hope a sudden catastrophe has swallowed it up. But always it returns, a little larger, a little clearer. By the sandglass next to the compass box, Nicholas can see that half an hour has passed since the first shout from the rigging. The corsair is now some five cable lengths off the *Marion*'s beam, just out of effective range of her armament, manoeuvring to come up from astern – a wolf stalking an exhausted, limping hind.

And still there is no wind. The *Marion* has barely shortened the distance to the Rass Lafaa.

Yaxley orders the sternmost culverin to try its luck with a ranging shot. The concussion feels like a blow against Nicholas's chest. In the still air, the choking smoke drifts slowly towards the bow, filling Nicholas's throat with the acrid, devil-stink of burnt black-powder. The splash of the landing shot rises out of the sea neatly abeam the corsair, but fifty yards or more from the swaying rank of oars.

'The bastard's canny,' Yaxley says. 'He knows we haven't enough way on us to turn the culverins on him, once he's clear of our quarter. If we're not careful, we're goin' to get well and truly bit in the arse, Dr Shelby.'

Yaxley orders the helm put hard over, trying to swing the *Marion* and keep her beam-on to the corsair. But in the calm air and sluggish sea, she merely takes up a crabwise drift.

Now Nicholas can see his enemy clearly. Her oars sweep with a disciplined rhythm, powered by manacled slaves who know that to falter is to invite the lash, or worse. She is a weapon powered not by the sinew of a bowstring or the flame of igniting powder, but by human effort. He sees the janissaries, clad in mail jerkins and helmets, waiting to hurl their grapples against the *Marion*'s stern. And he sees Cathal Connell in her prow, his salt-scoured face grinning like the Devil's dancing monkey.

'Cast me adrift, Captain Yaxley,' Nicholas says. 'It's me they want.'

Yaxley's face seems unnaturally calm, given the circumstances. He seems not to have heard what Nicholas has said. Instead, he draws his sword and waves it aloft. 'Load the rabinet!' he shouts. 'Hail-shot – *two* canisters! All hands muster on the sterncastle to deny boarders!'

It dawns on Nicholas that when a man has watched a wave the size of a small mountain break over his vessel and has lived to emerge on the other side, a battle is not lost until God says it is.

The rabinet's crew load the barrel of the swivel-gun with wadding, powder-bag and two cloth balls containing the hail-shot. Nicholas has seen its effect in the Low Countries: a spraying blast of musket balls that can sweep away men as a thunderstorm can flatten a field of Suffolk wheat. But now, looking at the corsair as she closes, he can see the gun crew crouching by the bow-chaser cannon in her prow. Its heavy shot will soon smash the stern of the *Marion*, destroying the rabinet before it can be effective.

'Captain Yaxley, lower one of your skiffs,' Nicholas shouts, at last accepting the hand misfortune has dealt him, knowing the card he's turned is the one with the skeletal horseman on it. 'It's me he wants. If you set me adrift, Connell will have his prize. If you don't, he'll slaughter every last one of us. I've seen what he can do.'

Yaxley seems torn. His eyes dart from Nicholas to the approaching galley and back again. He seems to be gauging whether his conscience can stomach the knowledge of what will happen to Nicholas if he agrees. With a frown of regret, he calls to the main-deck, 'Lower away the skiff!'

A murmur of approval from one or two of the crew puts the seal upon Nicholas's growing sense of abandonment. He has never felt so alone in his life, not even after Eleanor's death. To be set adrift, certain to fall into Connell's hands, brings fear enough. But to lose all hope of seeing Bianca again – just when it seemed he was free – threatens to turn him from a man into a distraught, howling child. It takes all his will to stay on his feet.

'God Himself knows I wish there was another way, Dr Shelby,' Yaxley says, staring at the deck planks, no longer able to look Nicholas in the eye. 'But I must think of my men.'

'It's the right thing to do, Captain Yaxley. There is no fault to be laid at *your* door.'

'Do you know how to use a wheel-lock pistol, Dr Shelby?' Yaxley asks, drawing one from his belt and offering it to Nicholas.

As a lad, Nicholas had often gone wildfowling with his father's old matchlock in the marshes around Barnthorpe. And in Holland he learned how to use a modern wheel-lock from the Protestant mercenaries he'd served with. He nods.

'Then take this. All you have to do is cock the dog-head. Don't get it wet climbing into the skiff.'

Nicholas understands immediately the implication behind Yaxley's offer. It has nothing whatsoever to do with killing Connell, but everything to do with saving Nicholas from whatever Connell has in store for him.

Taking the pistol, Nicholas imagines the walk from the sterncastle, down the ladder to the main-deck and to the skiff, already being unlashed from its place aft of the mainmast. He does this because he knows that when he embarks upon the short journey for real, his legs will resist. He will have to force himself to move. Seeing the action in his mind might overcome the overwhelming desire to stay rooted to the spot.

He imagines Bianca waiting for him on the main-deck, her hand outstretched, her amber eyes smiling, the faint breeze ruffling those heavy, dark waves of hair. He sees her clearly. Almost as though she's here, on the *Marion*. Maybe Ned and the other Banksiders were right – perhaps she really *can* turn herself into a creature of the air and travel over land and sea to be with him when he has most need of her. He smiles. It will be easier, he thinks, to face what is to come with her beside him. He closes his eyes, the better to see her image.

From somewhere far beyond the lonely centre of his thoughts, he senses – rather than hears – a distant clap of thunder, sharp and brief. He opens his eyes. A moment later he hears the rushing sound of wind like the passage of powerful wings through the air. A tall waterspout bursts out of the ocean barely twenty yards in front of the oncoming corsair galley, hanging like a cloud, before slowly decaying back into the water.

They've opened fire upon us, Nicholas thinks. It's begun.

But he's faced bombardment by cannon in the Low Countries. At this range, the corsair's bow-chaser could not have missed. The shot would have smashed into the narrow, high stern of the *Marion* almost below where he's standing, sending wicked splinters of timber ripping in all directions. The noise of the cannon's discharge should have been a hundred times louder.

Was it a misfire? he wonders. Did the powder only partially ignite, hurling the heavy iron ball barely a quarter of the required distance?

Nicholas is still pondering these questions when two more dull explosions reach his ears, followed moments later by more rushing wings, and two more waterspouts rising from the surface of the sea – one astern of the galley, the other on her seaward beam.

It takes him a moment to realize what's happened: the guns of the Kasar el Bahr have opened fire on the corsair.

But how has the shot reached this far? he wonders, stupefied. The fort on the quayside is all but out of range. Yaxley had told him so when the corsair was first sighted.

And then Robert Cecil decides to have the last word. For what he thinks must be the very first time, Nicholas is actually glad to hear his conversation with Cecil in his head. *We send Sultan al-Mansur new matchlock muskets... In payment he sends us saltpetre... so that we can out-charge Spanish cannon...*

Yaxley grins like a man making the greatest wager of his life. 'Looks like you have friends ashore, Dr Shelby. You'd best pray they have their eye in, or we'll be tinder, too.'

Nicholas cannot stop one short bark of laughter escaping his mouth. He has an image of the taciturn al-Annuri, warned by a lookout somewhere on the Rass Lafaa, stalking the ramparts of the Kasar el Bahr in his gown of white silk, berating the gunners to improve their aim. For he is now certain that these three balls were but ranging shots, to get the gunners properly sighted. And it is fine-quality Moroccan saltpetre that has carried them this far.

The master of the corsair has realized it, too. Astern of the *Marion*, the galley tries to turn away seawards, to get out of range. The bellowing of the officers reaches Nicholas clearly across a hundred yards of ocean.

But her oarsmen have given their all, in the dash to close on their victim. Muscles that have laboured for the past three-quarters of an hour have no more strength to give. The power that a moment before had made the corsair a predator is now spent. She tries desperately to turn away from what all aboard both vessels know is coming.

There are eight cannon on the ramparts of the Kasar el Bahr, Nicholas recalls. Eight royale cannon – the largest calibre of ordnance. It would take a pair of oxen to move one gun and its carriage. It would take a strong man to lift the forty-two pounds of a single solid iron shot. When the salvo hits, the result will be devastation and death. And at this distance, the *Marion* is in almost as much danger as the corsair.

Praying that the Moor gunners know their business, Nicholas listens out for the eight detonations, but the sound of the barrage reaches him as one ripple of distant thunder.

For a moment nothing happens. All Nicholas can hear is the creaking of the *Marion*'s cordage and the slapping of the calm sea against the hull.

And then they come.

They arrive with the sound of a gale that has sprung up from nowhere, a gale that lasts only as long as it takes for the ear to register its passing.

Three of the shots arrive wide – three pillars of green sea-water rising from the surface of the ocean – one of them close enough to the *Marion* to send a spray of saltwater drifting across her stern.

A fourth lands short, perhaps twenty yards to landward of the galley. But Nicholas sees the blur of the ball as it skips off the water to land squarely amongst the rank of oars, splintering them like twigs, before ploughing on into the hull.

The rest land like rocks hurled against a pane of glass.

One moment the corsair galley is a sleek, almost sensuous animal of the sea, and the next she is torn in two, her entrails spilling out in a cloud of sea mist and debris, oars, planks, rigging – and people. Within two minutes the separate parts of her hull are barely visible above the surface, the single mast with its lateen sail still furled looking like a broken cross on an untended grave.

The oarsmen drown first, in neat ranks, chained to their benches. The janissaries, standing on the raised central deck, don't live much longer. Weighed down by their mail coats, they too succumb, the stronger struggling only a little longer than the weaker.

Eventually there is only one survivor – a salt-scoured European swimming towards the *Marion* with long, determined strokes.

To Nicholas's surprise, the crew shout encouragement, willing him on. A moment ago Connell was an enemy. Now he is simply another mariner in danger of drowning – a man to be pitied, to be rescued. Down on the main-deck they are throwing ropes over the side for him to cling to. Seeing their efforts, Connell strikes out even more vigorously.

From his vantage point, Nicholas can see him clearly, perhaps thirty feet out from where he stands on the sterncastle, moving through the water at an angle towards the *Marion*'s side.

There is no conscious thought behind what Nicholas does next – only an animal desire to make an accounting for Solomon Mandel, as he had sworn to, and for Hadir and the others. Noticing the rabinet gunner has left his place to assist with the rescue, Nicholas walks purposefully towards the swivel-gun mounted on the bulwark. It is still primed with powder and loaded with hail-shot, in anticipation of a boarding. Nicholas takes the smouldering match-cord from its stowage. He seizes the round iron button at the inward end of the barrel and aims it over the side of the *Marion*. Squinting down the length of the rabinet, he tracks Connell as he swims. The gun swings effortlessly on its greased swivel. At this distance, Nicholas knows he cannot miss. In an instant there will be nothing in the water except a few pieces of bloody meat for the gulls to feast upon, and tendrils of blood spreading on the current.

As he touches the burning match-cord to the powder vent, Nicholas feels not the slightest remorse.

42

Gault sends her word in the shape of a bright-eyed young lad named Owen, though he waits ten days before he does it.

Owen walks into the Jackdaw early in the morning of a sunny Friday in late June. He is alone, which is unusual in itself. Young men from across the river tend to visit Bankside in pairs at the very least, if only to bolster their bravado with the painted doxies who whistle at them from the doorways of the stews. But Owen – a handsome, well-made lad with fair hair and eyes the colour of lapis – makes it all the way to the taproom with his chastity and his purse intact.

'My master bids me send word he has a tilt-boat moored at the Mutton Lane stairs, Mistress. He wishes to speak to you – privily,' he says, in a gentle Irish lilt.

A boat on the river; Bianca has to stop herself smiling in triumph. Gault must have something remarkable to disclose – something he won't even risk his servants on Giltspur Street overhearing. She wishes Nicholas was here to see how well she's played Master oh-so-handsome Reynard Gault, member of the Grocers' Guild, leading light of the Barbary Company and Rouge Croix Pursuivant of the College of Heralds. He'd be so proud of her!

Owen accompanies her to the water-stairs. Standing beside a comely maid more than a decade his senior, he's taken on what appears to be a permanent case of sunburn about the cheeks. Bianca tries her best to put him at his ease.

'I recognize you, Owen,' she says pleasantly. 'I saw you at your swordplay. I thought you looked the perfect gallant. Very fierce.'

Owen grins sheepishly. 'The master says that only men of courage and skill can expect reward in this world, Mistress. He says that where we're going, a sword and a strong heart are all that's needed to make you a prince. I shall enjoy being a prince. I know I shall.'

Bianca looks at him out of the corner of her eye. 'And where exactly is it that you're going, Master Owen?'

'Wherever Captain Connell takes us, Mistress. Like Drake, Hawkins and Raleigh, we's all going to shake the heathen world by its ears. We're going to bring back more than they ever did from the *Madre de Deus*.'

'How very enterprising. You're fortunate to have a master who desires so much good for his apprentices that he wishes to make them princes of foreign lands.'

'More than princes, Mistress – we'll be kings!'

'How well do you know Captain Connell?' Bianca asks doubtfully, remembering Farzad's dreadful story.

'Captain Connell is a great man. A fine venturer. He and Master Gault grew up together, in Leinster...'

For a moment he falters. He seems to be wondering how much he dares reveal. Bianca suspects he hasn't been in female company for a while. 'Pray continue, Owen,' she says encouragingly.

'The master says you're of the true faith, so I suppose he won't mind me saying.'

'I'm sure he would not.' She touches his arm to reassure him, causing Owen to all but jump out of his skin.

'It was like this, you see,' he begins, turning an even fierier red. 'When they were but boys, they were on a ship together with their parents and their moveables, coming from Wexford to Rome. They were steadfast in the true religion – marked out to be priests when they grew up. The barque was wrecked near Rathmoylan Cove. Everyone got ashore, though they were half-drowned. They thought God had delivered them, but they fell into the hands of Protestant heretics who damned them as papists and put everyone to the sword – save for the two lads.'

The story has the ring of truth, Bianca thinks. She has heard tales of how survivors of the great Armada were butchered on the shores of Ireland, even as they offered up prayers for having escaped the deep.

'They were sold to an English plantation man and his wife – rich but barren – who'd been handed a stolen estate in Leinster by that heretic whore, Elizabeth,' Owen continues. 'They made the boys their own; brought them up in the heretic faith, so they did. But imposed heresy won't stick to men with honest souls. When they died, as the oldest, Master Reynard inherited the property. Captain Connell went sailing to Araby.'

'That is a sad tale indeed, Owen,' Bianca says, remembering the Irish landscape in the painting in Gault's house. She does not like him any the more for hearing it, but she understands him a little better. Connell, too – though she can barely bring herself to admit it.

Gault is waiting for her aboard the small tilt-boat at the Mutton Lane stairs. It has a canvas awning stretched over a wooden frame, like a little tent, to provide privacy. She prays that today will be the one day when Bankside's prurient eyes are looking elsewhere – a young woman taking a trip on the river in an enclosed tilt-boat usually means only one thing.

At the oars are Owen's companions from the house on Giltspur Street. Whatever secret Gault intends to reveal to her, he's guarding it carefully.

'You cannot imagine how much the owner of this thing charged me for just a morning,' Gault says as she climbs in under the awning. 'When I said I wanted my own oarsmen, the price tripled. I think he feared I might not return it.'

'I really cannot see you as a waterman, Master Gault. You're dressed far too smartly.'

'Occasions of great import should not be treated casually,' he says as he helps her to a spread of cushions in the stern, making the boat roll alarmingly.

She notices he's brought a bottle of fine Rhenish and two silver cups. 'Mercy, but this is *very* privy,' she says as they move away from the jetty. 'Are you afraid the walls of your nice new house on Giltspur Street have been built with their own set of ears?'

Gault gives her a tight little smile. 'These lads are bound to me by a sworn oath. I know where each one came from – my estates in Leinster. However, London servants are not always so trustworthy.' He pours the wine and raises his cup. 'A formal toast: to the destruction of heretics and the return of the one true faith.'

It is not a desire uppermost in Bianca's heart, but she goes along with it to encourage him. 'Destruction in any particular manner, Master Gault? Or just generally?'

A brief, indulgent laugh. 'I've been pondering on what you said to me – regarding the demise of that dog Marlowe.'

'You've been pondering, it seems, for ten days. I thought what I had said was clear enough.'

'Oh, unequivocally. But a wise man does not enter into a contract unless he has first made himself fully acquainted with the merchandise on offer.'

'I thought you and Captain Connell had already done that.'

'After what you told me, I thought it best to make a more thorough investigation.'

'And are you satisfied?'

He considers his answer as he sips his wine. 'A number of persons my boys spoke to did indeed swear they'd heard the rumours about you and Marlowe. But they were from the lower sort of woman.'

For the first time since arriving on Bankside, Bianca gives a silent prayer of thanks for the existence of Jenny Solver's loose tongue. She adopts an expression of outraged propriety. 'Perhaps that is because I am not in the habit of inviting a notary into my bedchamber in order to have a signed affidavit when I take a man there.'

To her joy, Gault blushes almost as badly as the lad Owen, at her directness.

'In all other regards, I could not disprove your story, Mistress Merton. There is no doubt in my mind that you would be of great benefit to our enterprise.'

Bianca leans a little closer towards him, as if inviting further intimacy. Inside the awning the air is thick and sultry, ripe for revelation.

'Is this *enterprise* anything to do with the Barbary shore, and your title of Rouge Croix Pursuivant, by any chance?'

If she'd thrown the wine in his face he couldn't be more taken aback.

'How do you know that?'

'Enquiry is not solely a masculine preserve, Master Gault. If it were, we should *all* be ignorant.'

'And what exactly is it you think you've discovered?'

'That the name Solomon Mandel is known to you, even though you told me it was not.' She takes a sip of wine. 'That he died in possession of a document upon which was written your title, the one you hold from the College of Heralds.' Another sip of wine, like the tap of a foot keeping a slow, funereal rhythm. 'That the reason you were so eager to find out from me why Dr

Shelby went to Morocco for Robert Cecil is because you fear Cecil has wind of this *enterprise* of yours.' Another sip. Another foot-fall. 'That you have knowingly engaged a monster in your service, in the form of Cathal Connell.' She fixes him with her amber eyes. 'Given that we have both made confession to each other, let me invite one more. Did you order Connell to murder poor Solomon Mandel?'

Gault regards her impassively for a while, as though he still can't quite believe she could be his match. Then he says, 'No, I did not order him to do such a thing.' He refills her glass, as though he wishes to make her complicit in what he has to tell her. 'But I do know who killed the Jew.'

'Then tell me: who was it?'

Looking into his eyes, Bianca has the chilling feeling Reynard Gault might have brought her to the middle of the river not for privacy, but for a very different reason.

In an unnervingly languid voice, he answers, 'It was me.'

✠

'Mistress Merton... Mistress Merton... Is the river discomforting you?'

Gault's voice breaks through the stuffy air within the awning of the tilt-boat.

'It is nothing,' she says, fearing he's seen the distress in her eyes. 'I found the undulation of the water a little unpleasant. I'm not a sailor, like your brave Captain Connell. I'm fine.'

A sceptical lift of one carefully plucked brow. 'Are you shocked?'

'Of course I'm shocked.'

'That is not quite the response I would have expected from a woman who claims to have brought about the slaying of Christopher Marlowe. Do you wish to amend your story in any particular?'

Bianca fights to compose herself. If he sees weakness in her now, her carefully constructed fiction might well collapse like the froth on a jug of knock-down.

'I'm shocked because I'm not a butcher, Master Gault. I did not know Solomon Mandel was an enemy to this enterprise of yours. To me, he was simply a sweet old man who liked to take his breakfast at my tavern. Why did he have to die?'

'He was a danger to our plans.'

'You couldn't have done it on your own. I saw the aftermath.'

'My boys helped me.'

'You've made killers out of your apprentices? What manner of new world is that for them to inhabit?'

'They are soldiers, Mistress; soldiers in the war against the heretics. Sometimes it is necessary for soldiers to harden their hearts.'

'How could you have done *that* to him – the flaying? He was a helpless old man.'

'He sought to keep from me something I wished to know. Cathal Connell learned the technique from the Moors. It's very effective in loosening tongues.'

'And did it loosen his?'

'No. To speak the truth, that surprised me. I had not anticipated his courage. Or his frailty. Or perhaps it wasn't courage. Perhaps he was just a stubborn old man.'

Yes, he was stubborn, thinks Bianca. And kind. And probably lonely. But most of all, he did not deserve such a dreadful end at your hands.

Gault makes a play of sucking the taste out of his mouthful of Rhenish, betraying a rougher self behind the gallant's façade.

'Let me be direct with you, Mistress Merton,' he says. 'I have considered what you told me about your work for the cardinal: becoming one of Robert Cecil's informers so that you could better serve the one true faith. I confess I had not thought to find such mettle in a woman. And yes, I believe my enterprise could have no better ally than someone like you. *But...*'

He turns the silver wine cup slowly before his eyes, inspecting its finely engraved surface, enjoying the pleasure of owning such an expensive piece of silverware.

'But what? Please do not tell me you doubt a woman is up to the task.'

'Oh no. I have no doubt on that score. It's just that I have always found it wise in merchant venturing to demand proof of trust. Words are all well and good, but nothing can better monies that are put down on account.'

'What is it you want of me, Master Gault?' Bianca asks, feeling an uncomfortable sensation in her stomach that has nothing to do with the river. 'What *proof* will satisfy you?'

He places his hand on her knee, slowly moving it up her thigh so that her kirtle lifts over her shins. His fingers halt just short of her groin, pressing against her flesh.

Oh Jesu, she thinks; for all the display and bravado, you're nothing better than a fumbler in a Southwark stew, the type who thinks he's made the doxy's day simply by turning up. She rotates her heel against the hull of the tilt-boat, the better to position the tip of her shoe for a deft strike between his splayed legs.

'I think I know what you're going to say to me, Master Gault.'

'I heard *that*, too – that you have the second sight.'

'I can also swim.'

Silence for a moment, save for the slap of the river against the hull.

'But can you *poison*?'

Of course she can poison. In Padua, Bianca learned the skill from her mother, who often claimed that before she'd turned from mixing draughts of hemlock to making curatives, it had been a family trade – all the way back to the woman who mixed the draught that Agrippina used to poison Claudius. Bianca can hear her mother now, telling her that if you want to poison your employer because he beats you, or your lover because they've tired of you – for the inheritance, the revenge or just the pure bloody joy of getting the last word – go to the Caporettis of Padua. But don't ever lick your fingers on the way home.

'Of course I can mix poisons,' she says. 'I'm an apothecary. Your guild licensed me, remember?'

'In that case, Mistress Merton, welcome to our enterprise – just as soon as I learn that Robert Cecil is dead.'

43

For eight days the *Marion* has ridden the waves like a grey-hound in pursuit of a coney. Assessing the log, Captain Yaxley expresses a cautious confidence that she can make the voyage from Safi to London faster than any Barbary Company vessel yet.

Forced into close companionship, Nicholas has begun to admire the little sea-terrier from Devon. He commands his ship with a quiet assurance and a care for his crew that makes Nicholas suspect there is no storm they would not follow him through. It is a world apart from Connell's dour tyranny.

On the morning of the ninth day Yaxley calls Nicholas to the larboard rail of the sterncastle and points to a faint smudge on the horizon.

'Falmouth, Dr Shelby. Not long now until we sight good Christian land.'

'Are you suggesting Cornwall is a pagan place, Captain Yaxley?' Nicholas asks, playing along.

'Have you never *been* to Cornwall, Dr Shelby?'

Yaxley's laugh of self-appreciation dies in his throat as the rattle of flapping canvas reaches the deck. The pennants streaming from the mastheads, formerly pointing the way home, begin to droop. Seeing Yaxley look up, Nicholas asks, 'What's amiss?'

'The wind, it's backing. We should be thankful to have had the best of it.'

By the time they encounter the Brixham fishing fleet beneath a cloudscape of gulls, Yaxley's speedy little command is beating long diagonal tacks on either side of the wind in order to fill her sails. Taking a meal of stockfish and biscuit in the cramped confines of Yaxley's cabin, Nicholas's frustration is hard to disguise.

'If it keeps up like this, how much longer before landfall?'

'That depends.'

'On what?'

'On God. He's the one who sends the weather.' Yaxley cracks a wedge of rusk and dips it into his glass of arak to soften. 'If the wind is out of the east from now on, then maybe another four days to London. Five, if it strengthens.'

'And if it gets truly bad?'

'We may have to seek shelter in the Solent or at Chesil Cove.'

'At the present rate, how long till a landfall at Dover?'

'A little under three.' Yaxley smiles at Nicholas's persistence. 'I'm guessing this is only your second voyage, Dr Shelby.'

'My fourth, actually. The first was to the Low Countries, then back again. Not nearly so far. I was seasick most of the time. But the *Marion* seems to have cured me.'

'Then I can forgive the impatience, Dr Shelby.'

'It is a fault in me, I know.'

'It's something you have to learn to put aside. Impatience in a mariner is a greater failing than seasickness.'

Chastened, Nicholas takes a bite of cold stockfish, wishing Yaxley hadn't had to order the ship's oven doused, when the sea began to get up. 'You're right, of course. But you know why I'm in such haste.'

Yaxley studies him carefully. 'I *think* I do. Privy Council business; the queen's business, even.' A knowing look comes into his eyes. 'But you said the plot against old al-Mansur was put down

409

before we left Safi. So maybe there's another reason you're in such a pelt. Would it be a maid, perhaps?'

Feeling like a child caught out in a lie, Nicholas senses the heat flow into his cheeks. 'Am I that plain to see through, Captain Yaxley?' he asks.

'Transparent, Dr Shelby – as a fairy's wing.'

The *Marion* pitches violently as a wave crashes into her bow. Nicholas hears the sound of the sea rushing down her sides, feels the little vessel shake herself free. 'I suppose you can't face danger with your fellow man, or spend a life in such close proximity to him, without learning to see what's in his thoughts. It was the same in the Low Countries, when I was a physician with Sir Joshua Wylde's company, fighting against the Spanish.'

'Who is she, Dr Shelby? Describe her to me.'

Nicholas looks like a man asked to explain the countless spheres of heaven in a single sentence. He shakes his head in defeat. 'I do not have that rogue Marlowe's faculty with words, Captain Yaxley. All I can tell you is that if, tonight, the moon and all the stars above were snuffed out, where she is there would still be light.'

For a moment Nicholas thinks Yaxley is going to laugh at him. But he just drops his gaze, his body moving in time to the swaying of the little ship as though her deck is the only ground he's ever known.

'I knew one like that,' he says contemplatively. 'But I hesitated. And so I was lost to the sea.'

'Is that why this barque is named the *Marion*?' Nicholas asks in a flash of inspiration.

Yaxley nods. Then he lifts his eyes again and fixes Nicholas with an uncompromising stare. 'Does this light of yours know the fellow coming home to her has taken another man's life without a second thought?'

'You mean Connell?'

'Aye. I saw the look on your face, just after you discharged the rabinet.'

'I'm not a murderer, if that's what you mean. At least, I don't think so. You didn't see what he did to my friends in Marrakech.'

'Oh, I'm not judging you, Dr Shelby. I've heard tales of Cathal Connell's time in the Arabian seas that would make such a quick end seem like a mercy. But I presume you swore an oath to heal. And they do say that a man who kills once will find it easier the next time. So I think you should ask yourself: does this light of yours deserve a life wed to a fellow who has strayed off the path of mercy?'

It is a brutal question, but Nicholas does not blame Yaxley for asking it. He considers it in silence, remembering the promise he made to Muhammed al-Annuri: *You will bring pestilence and death upon them, even unto the seventh generation. You will erase their names so that Allāh will forget he ever made them...*

He recalls, too, that night on London Bridge, when Dr Arcampora's men had been preparing to hurl him to his death in the black waters of the Thames. And he hears again the voice of the woman who saved him, sees her now, sees her standing before him in her physic garden beside the river on the day he told her he was leaving for Morocco: *let us face the truth, Nicholas: we are both murderers now...*

Gault has given Bianca a week to devise a plan to poison Robert Cecil. To keep her mind on the task, he assigns another of his apprentices as her shadow, a sour-looking boy named Calum. Whenever he visits the Jackdaw, he sits alone in one of the booths, reading a cheap copy of Hoby's translation of *The Book of the Courtier.* Whether he's learning anything from it is questionable, because it takes all Ned's diplomacy – a substance as rare as powdered unicorn horn – to keep Calum from starting brawls with the watermen, whom he seems to consider himself above.

'Who *is* he?' asks Rose on the fourth day. 'Why is he here?'

'He's one of Master Gault's apprentices,' Bianca explains.

'Well, I don't much care for him. He behaves as if he owns the place. This morning I found him poking his nose about down in the cellar, amongst your apothecary stuff. Said it reminded him of a sorcerer's den.'

Bianca fights back the sudden anger. It's one thing, she thinks, to accept there's a spy in the household, quite another when he makes such a contemptuous display of it.

'Perhaps he wanted to see where I make the preventatives,' she says lamely. 'Indulge him a little longer, for my sake.'

When Rose seeks further explanation, Bianca – uncharacteristically – loses her temper. After that, Calum is not mentioned in her presence again.

Bianca has barely slept since her meeting with Gault on the river. The dread that haunts her mind has become mountainous. Whatever Gault is plotting, she understands now that Nicholas has been sent to Morocco to thwart it somehow. Which means he is in great danger. And if what Gault told her about Solomon Mandel was true, none of them are safe. She has begun to curse herself for taking such an insane risk. What *was* she thinking, when she embarked on unmasking a man she now knows – by his own admission – to be a heartless killer?

At night, when she does finally manage an hour or two of sleep, she dreams of Nicholas being flayed alive like Solomon Mandel. Then she wakes in a drenching sweat, her mouth dry and her fingers clawing at the sheets.

By day, the yearning to have him back with her plays havoc with her reason. Whenever the image of him enters her mind, her thoughts whirl around like leaves in a gale. The customers who come to the Jackdaw – now that her shop on Dice Lane is closed – have to repeat what they say to her, because she appears as distracted as a madwoman. Jenny Solver has even put it about that Bianca is besotted with a rich and handsome merchant from across the river.

On the seventh day, as arranged, she goes to see Gault at Smithfield. Calum tags along beside her, his copy of The Courtier tucked into his leather jerkin. He still seems to have missed its finer points on humility, giving way for no one he encounters, glaring about ferociously as though he owns the city and everyone in it. She imagines teacher Gault must be proud.

The green expanse of Smithfield is unnaturally empty – the ban on entertainments and gatherings has seen to that. There are no lovers making sweet-talk beneath the trees, no pedlars, sharpers or jugglers to be seen anywhere. Even the birds have stopped flying. The cattle she'd followed on her earlier visit to Gault's house on Giltspur Street graze placidly in the sunshine, a single cowherd asleep against the trunk of a beech tree.

Calum leads her towards the half-ruined priory of St Bartholomew. By a section of monastery wall she sees Gault and the other apprentices standing together beside a row of hawks perched on their blocks.

'Well, that explains the paucity of songbirds,' Bianca says. 'I wonder how they know when there are predators about, even when they can't see them.'

'What's that you say?' grunts the surly Calum.

'The hawks,' she says. 'I can see he's training you all very thoroughly. I can see that you're all going to be the model of fine gentlemen.'

413

'Oh, this isn't part of our education, Mistress,' Calum tells her. 'This is our ease. We all learned how to hawk back in Ireland. Master Gault has the finest mews in County Leinster. Everyone there knows that. They call him the Falconer.'

44

In the end it is Nicholas's impatience to be with Bianca, rather than the inclement gale, that determines the *Marion*'s landfall – and the fact that the constable of Dover Castle is Lord Cobham, Robert Cecil's father-in-law. If anyone can promise a fast horse for the ride to London, it will be him.

Just shy of three days after his conversation with Yaxley the little vessel is safely moored beneath Dover's towering ramparts. Before Nicholas climbs down into the waiting skiff to be rowed ashore beneath voluminous white farthingales of summer cloud, Yaxley shakes his hand.

'When you see Sir Robert Cecil, be sure to tell him I had no part in whatever that rogue Connell was about.'

'That, Captain Yaxley, is the very least I can do to discharge my debt to you.'

Yaxley gives him a parcel wrapped in sailcloth. 'Here, take this,' he says.

By the heft of it, Nicholas knows it's the wheel-lock pistol Yaxley had offered him in Safi bay.

'I believe you know why I gave you this before, Dr Shelby. Keep it, as a memento of a fortunate deliverance. You're a man who seems to have the Devil's luck. But even the Devil can have his back turned every now and then, and I wouldn't want anything to stop you reaching that light you spoke of – the one that's waiting for you on Bankside.'

'It's impossible. It cannot be done.' Bianca struggles not to sound as though she's pleading. 'You have set me a trial I cannot pass.'

For privacy, she and Gault have walked a little way from the priory wall. Even though Smithfield is all but empty and there is no one close enough to overhear, speaking openly of poisoning a queen's privy councillor does not come comfortably to her. Her senses seem blade-sharp. She can hear the jangle of the bells on the hawks' leather jesses, and a sudden murmuring of the wind in the grass.

'I thought you were more adroit than that, Mistress Merton,' he says, eyeing her critically. 'Have I misjudged you?'

'Ignoring the fact that he's in Windsor – with the queen, and no one from London is allowed there, and certainly not my sort – how am I to gain access to Cecil's food or his wine? I'm his informer, not his cook.'

Gault looks at her like a schoolmaster who's spotted a glaring error in a pupil's work. 'But you *are* a comely young woman...'

'How is *that* supposed to help – even if it were true?' she asks. 'And I can tell you, Master Gault, if you've ever seen me with an English cold and snot running down my chin, you'd revise your understanding of *comely*.'

'He's a stunted crook-back. An abomination to beauty. *And* a Lutheran. Surely it can't be beyond your imagination. Or your wiles.'

She wonders if she punched Gault, in that otherwise oh-so-pleasing face, she could outrun his apprentices, reach the river and a wherry before they caught up with her.

'Cecil's devoted to his wife,' she says, as an alternative. 'He dragged Nicholas – Dr Shelby – out of bed in the middle of the night to have him treat their child. Robert Cecil is probably the one man in London I couldn't drag to Bankside, even if I promised to dress up as Salome and dance for him in the middle of Whitehall.'

'You'll find a way,' Gault says chillingly.

And to her horror – because she realizes that she's almost as vulnerable here as she was on his tilt-boat on the river – he grabs her wrist. He squeezes it like a lover who's begun to exhibit an unwelcome fondness for insistence. 'Don't disappoint me, Mistress Merton,' he whispers. 'We have made the act of confession to one another. And a confession cannot be taken back. Not without consequences.'

✠

Lord Cobham turns out not to be in residence, but at his home some fifty miles away near Gravesend. After announcing his arrival at the porter's lodge, Nicholas is led to the new battery of cannon at the southern end of the ramparts, where the High Sheriff, a bluff man in his late forties named Sondes, is making one of his periodic inspections. He has troubling news.

'London?' he says doubtfully, when Nicholas tells him he's carrying an urgent dispatch for Cecil House. 'Have you not heard that the city is rife with plague?'

Nicholas feels his legs lose their strength, and not because of his days at sea.

'How rife?'

'Her Grace, the queen, has removed to Windsor,' Sondes tells him, as though Elizabeth were the city's only occupant. 'The Inns of Court and Parliament are shut up, and all the feasts and fairs cancelled. They say the mourning bells have hardly stopped tolling.'

For a moment Nicholas stares at him open-mouthed, consumed by the awful thought that the pestilence might have spread to Southwark. Sondes mistakes his expression for a surfeit of zeal.

'Do not distress yourself, sirrah, you may still deliver this important dispatch of yours to Sir Robert Cecil. I am told Her Grace took many of her Privy Council with her. Sir Robert is most likely amongst them.'

Nicholas doesn't hesitate. He has no intention of riding to Windsor. Robert Cecil can wait another couple of days for his news. After all he has gone through, and with Captain Yaxley's words ringing in his ears – *I hesitated... And so I was lost to the sea* – he desires nothing more than to take Bianca in his arms and confess to being the mightiest fool in Christendom for having set even one foot aboard the *Righteous*. What comes afterwards is not his to determine.

'I will have need of a horse, Master Sondes,' he says. 'A fast one with strong legs. Better still, find me one with wings.'

Distillations, syrups, purges, balms and potions; in her revived apothecary's cellar at the Jackdaw, Bianca has spent the day making a dozen or more of each. It has taken all her concentration not to put tansy instead of walnut leaves in the salve that she makes for dog bites, or hyssop in the headache cure instead of houseleek. More than one customer has enquired if she is feeling a little unwell. 'You appear a mite distracted, Mistress Merton,' Jenny Solver observed barely an hour ago when she'd come in search of some horehound for a wasp sting. 'Are you ailing again?'

Distracted? Ailing? Try *desperate*, she'd wanted to shriek at the woman. Desperate beyond measure. For the first time in her life she feels like a condemned prisoner without the slightest hope of commutation. And she can put her imminent demise down to her own impulsiveness. If only she hadn't tried to get the better of Reynard Gault.

She knows there is no possibility she can do what he has

demanded of her. Even in the unlikely event she could contrive to poison Sir Robert Cecil, every Catholic in the city would be rounded up within the day. The Privy Council torturers would have no rest.

On more than one occasion her thoughts have turned instead to poisoning Gault himself, doing away with the cause of her misery. But his apprentices know her. They've witnessed her visits to Giltspur Street; they know what remedies she brings. They'd have the justices on her inside the hour.

And to cap it all, she has started to weep without warning. It is only a matter of time before Rose or Ned catches her with her eyes brimming.

She stabs her pestle into the mortar as though she means to kill it.

Nicholas, where in the name of Christ's holy wounds are you?

The town is named Faversham. It is a busy little place on the Swale, with an anchorage for shallow-draught vessels, oyster beds and a gunpowder mill. It has cobbles where most places of its size have nothing but ruts, and taverns, too. Nicholas stops at one to rest his horse, and to quench his thirst and take a hurried meal. The landlord regards the *djellaba* he is still wearing, now dust-stained, with consternation.

'You're not some papist priest, are you, come here to corrupt the queen's religion?' he asks, his eyes wide with suspicion. 'Or has a company of players come to town?'

'I've come from Morocco,' Nicholas explains wearily. 'I'm on important Privy Council business.'

'Oh, aye,' the landlord says, as though his custom comprises nothing else but passing couriers in exotic garb. 'You're going to London, then?'

'That is my intention. I hear there's plague there.'

'So there is, an' it's cut our trade in half. Never seen the London road so empty.'

'Do you know if Southwark is spared?' Nicholas asks.

'I have a cousin who's a drover. He took a flock up last Thursday. He told me it's not as bad as in the city, but not healthy enough for him to want to stay more than a night.'

'Do you by chance know which tavern he stayed at?'

The man shakes his head.

'Is he here, your cousin? May I speak to him?'

'Only if you want to wait a day or two, Master. He's away at Canterbury.'

Nicholas finishes the rest of his meal in despondent silence.

Once clear of the town, and with the London road ahead of him, he pauses only to load and prime Yaxley's wheel-lock pistol. There are many more miles still to go, and some of them are across Black Heath. He has not come this far, he tells himself, to fall prey to cut-purses now.

✠

In the garden of his fine new house on Giltspur Street, Reynard Gault listens without interrupting as the lad Calum delivers his daily account of life at the Jackdaw tavern on Bankside. There is envy in his voice, but also a weary disappointment.

'She's had no contact with the Cecils that I could see, Master. Nor could I identify anyone who might have come to her from Cecil House.'

'And you've overheard nothing?'

'They keep their words short whenever they see me around. If she's lying to you, Master, I've no proof of it.'

Gault considers this for a while, studying his fine kidskin gloves. Then he says, 'If we thought to search the place – or if she proved false – how might we gain entry unobserved?'

420

'I can't see how you could, Master. There's always someone there. And it's Bankside, remember. They keep the windows and the street door locked at night – against house-divers. Not that anyone would dare, of course. Not with *her*.'

'It's a tavern, young O'Neil, not a fortress. There must be a way.'

The lad Calum ponders this awhile. Then his face brightens, like a fox that's come across an unguarded coop. 'There *is* the cellar.'

Gault looks up. 'Go on.'

'You wouldn't credit what she keeps down there: enough brimstone to keep hell warm for a week, an' more potions than you'd need to cure or poison half the city. There's a trapdoor in the ceiling, to the yard. The yard wall isn't *that* high. Not if you're fit. Not if you don't mind being cursed.'

45

A day and a half after leaving Dover, Nicholas Shelby rides up Long Southwark towards the southern gatehouse of London Bridge, his sweating mount gleaming in the July sunshine as though it were carved from solid marble. Passing the Tabard Inn, he hears the St Saviour's bell ring out the second hour of the afternoon. When its chimes have died away, he is struck by the uncustomary quiet. Bankside should be teeming with people. But today the twenty-sixth ward of the city – the liberty of Bridge Ward Without – appears almost deserted. A stark contrast, he thinks, to the last time a visitor from the Barbary shore came this way. Then, crowds of Banksiders had turned out to gawp, wide-eyed, at the splendour of the Moor delegation and to marvel at the finery of the Lord Mayor and the merchants of the Barbary Company, who'd come south across the bridge to welcome it. Today none of the few people he passes even notice the dust-stained, weary rider in a blue-cloth *djellaba*, Yaxley's wheel-lock pistol tucked into the belt, who has appeared so suddenly amongst them – even though Nicholas thinks he must look like a supporting character in a performance of Master Marlowe's *Tamburlaine*.

He is filled with a sudden sense of foreboding. He thinks of the promise he made to Muhammed al-Annuri, to bring Gault to a reckoning. Connell is dead, but the second head of the snake still lives. Gault is just as responsible for the deaths of Adolfo

Sykes, Solomon Mandel, Hadir, grandmother Tiziri, Gwata and his sister Lalla – even young Hortop – as Connell ever was. But to discharge that promise he must take another life, a course utterly at odds with another oath he has sworn: the oath to heal.

What am I becoming? he wonders, remembering the total absence of remorse he'd felt when he killed the defenceless Connell.

Thinking now of *Tamburlaine*, he recalls a line from the play, a line that chills him to the core: *I mean to be a terror to the world…*

Bianca hears Rose scream, even in the depths of the cellar where she's at work at her temporary apothecary's table. It slices into her thoughts about Gault and the fatal dilemma he's set her, like an axe through a sapling. She's halfway up the stairs to the tap-room – her head full of dreadful images – before she realizes the scream has given way to a tide of joyful but tearful jabbering. Then Buffle begins to bark rapturously.

He is standing in the street doorway, dressed in some strange garb that might once have been blue, save for the fact that it appears to have been trampled in the dust. His beard is unkempt, his face burned a rich honeyed brown. He looks like the prince of a band of brigands.

But he's back. Her prayers have been answered.

She says nothing. She gives him no greeting. The need to take him in her arms makes the very thought of speech pointless. She hurls herself at him, as though she must pin him to the spot, lest a hurricano – magicked by some malevolent sorcerer – sweeps him away from her again. They cling together, swaying gently to the rhythm of their own relief.

Ned looks on, grinning like a loon. Timothy rushes to find his lute, determined to play the minstrel. Rose makes that strange noise – a cross between a foraging hog and a goose with indigestion – that comes over her whenever she gets over-emotional. Even Farzad comes out from the kitchen to see what the fuss is about, adding an extra chime to Nicholas's happiness.

Bianca has imagined this moment every day since Ned first told her that Nicholas had not left her of his own free will. She has sensed his arms around her body, heard his voice, felt his closeness. At night when she hugs herself to sleep, it has been his fingers she has felt against her flesh. She has rehearsed endlessly what she would say to him on his return. And now he is here. She looks into his eyes, her mouth close to his.

'You smell like a horse,' she says.

His voice is husky. It could be passion. It could be the dust of the Dover road. 'Take that up with Michael Sondes,' he replies.

'Who in the name of all Christendom is Michael Sondes?'

'The High Sheriff of Kent. It's his horse.'

✠

They sit together in a taproom booth. Bianca is leaning against Nicholas as closely as she did on the day of Ned and Rose's wedding feast, when Timothy came to tell her Farzad was missing. If he turns up now, swearing on his mother's life that the queen has reached a rapprochement with the Pope, the pestilence has admitted defeat, and Cardinal Fiorzi has died and left her one hundred thousand ducats in his will, she has no intention of moving.

She has provided a jug of knock-down for Nicholas's thirst and a cushion for his saddle-sores. The trimming of his beard will have to wait for later. He is home. He is fed and watered. The rest is understood.

The expression on his face breaks her heart. It is the look of a man who had been led to the scaffold, had the noose placed over his neck and then – just when he had abandoned all hope – heard the shout that heralds a reprieve. He seems unable to decide whether he should shout for joy or weep.

'Tell me, Nicholas,' she urges softly. 'Why did you *really* go to the Barbary shore? No more lies. I need to know the truth.'

And so he gives it to her – at least a version of the truth, from which the butchery has been expunged. He sees no reason why he should inflict *that* upon her.

'I already know all about Connell,' she says when he's finished. 'Farzad told me. He ran away because I brought that monster into the Jackdaw.'

He gives her a questioning look. 'How did Farzad know what manner of man Connell was?'

'Farzad was taken as a slave, remember? It was Connell who took him.'

'Well, he need fear Connell no longer. Connell is dead. And his master, Reynard Gault, cannot long evade justice. He will be next. I have sworn an oath upon it.'

'I worked out for myself that Gault was the Rouge Croix Pursuivant,' she says proudly.

'How did you do that?' he asks, his eyes widening in admiration.

'He lied to me about knowing Solomon Mandel. I knew he was hiding *something*, so I persuaded Parson Moody to let me see the parish records for when the Moor envoy arrived in London. And there Gault was. It was he who killed Mandel.'

A look of concern clouds Nicholas's face. 'How do you know?'

'He confessed.'

'To *you*?' His concern turns to horror. 'Have you the *slightest* understanding of how dangerous Gault is?'

'Are we arguing? You've only been back an hour.'

'What in the name of Jesu have you contrived to get yourself into?'

'It's complicated,' Bianca says, avoiding his gaze. 'But I had to make a promise – to get Gault to admit it. It's all something of a pottage really. I was trying to find out from him why Robert Cecil had really sent you to Morocco; he was trying to find out from me, because he thought you might have mentioned it...'

Nicholas takes her in his arms and pulls her head into the slope of his neck. 'It's alright, Gault's days are numbered.' He runs his fingers through the thick, dark waves of her hair. 'I'll finish this drink and then we'll take a wherry down to Cecil House. The sooner this is over, the better. What exactly was it that you promised him?'

The reply is muffled by her closeness. He can feel the moistness of her mouth as it moves against his skin. He pushes her away – but only so that his hungry eyes may have a better feast.

'What did you say?'

Bianca bites her lip, bracing herself for his reaction. 'I said, "I had to promise him I would find a way to poison Robert Cecil."'

For a moment Nicholas just stares at her. Then he buries his face in his hands and mutters, '*Oh, by Christ's holy wounds...*'

'It's quite alright,' Bianca says brightly, taking his hands tightly in hers, 'I'm not actually going to *do* it.'

'Oh, some good news!'

'Now that you're back, you can get Robert Cecil to have Gault arrested. But he's not at Cecil House – he's at Windsor, with the queen. It's the pestilence, you see. It's been awful.'

'I'll ride there first thing tomorrow,' Nicholas says, easing the saddle-stiffness in his limbs and buttocks. 'Right now, I'm heartily weary of anything with four legs. Horses, camels...' He glances at Buffle, wagging her tail happily at the mouth of the booth. 'Except for her, of course. In the meanwhile, how would it suit you to be a Suffolk yeoman's daughter-in-law?'

Bianca – who has had proposals from the sons of Paduan gentlemen, couched in poetry as sticky as syrup – tries not to laugh, in case he takes it the wrong way. She gently draws his hands to her lips and kisses them.

And in the adjacent booth the apprentice Calum quietly sets down his jug of ale, tucks the copy of The Courtier into his jerkin and slips silently and unobserved out of the Jackdaw.

46

Nicholas hears the watch calling midnight in the lane, followed immediately by a ribald comment he can't quite catch. Then laughter. The word, it seems, has surged through Bankside like a storm tide through the Deptford marshes: Dr Shelby and Mistress Merton are betrothed.

'We can't have a privy wedding,' Bianca says sleepily as she traces the shape of his far shoulder with her fingers. 'Bankside won't let us. Besides, they could all do with some cheer. It's become rather melancholy around here while you've been away – what with the pestilence.'

'Why would we want a privy wedding?' he says, tugging loose a strand of thread from the coverlet that has somehow got entangled in her hair. 'I want all London to know about it.'

'You're not afeared of marrying a sorceress?'

'Don't tell me you've been putting a love-charm under my pillow all this time, and I never knew it.'

'No, but I warn you: I shall weave magical chains, to stop you going *anywhere* that Robert Cecil commands.'

'Can you delay the weaving until after I get back from Windsor – for Solomon Mandel's sake?'

She raises a cautionary eyebrow. 'After that, no more obeying a summons from the Pigmy – other than to attend the queen's bedside when she's ill. Promise?'

'I promise.'

Nicholas rolls the length of thread between his fingers until it become a little ball. He leans over her.

'What's that?' she asks, as the weight of him pushes her into the yielding comfort of the bed.

'It's a kissing knot,' he replies, letting it fall gently between her breasts. 'Isn't that how all this started?'

✠

It is a witch's night, tendrils of cloud beating across the face of the moon. The river is pitch-black like the inside of a sealed tomb. A single lantern, masked for concealment, glows in the prow of the tilt-boat as it approaches the Mutton Lane stairs.

The boy Owen is ashore first. Hauling on the boat's painter, he pulls her against the jetty and makes the rope fast to a wooden pile festooned with sinking river weed. Calum and two other apprentices are next, showing a practised agility even in the darkness. Reynard Gault is last. He pulls his half-cloak about his shoulders and, with one hand on the hilt of his sword, orders Calum to lead the way into the lanes of Bankside.

✠

The sound of the call to prayer from the Koutoubia mosque brings Nicholas out of a deep and contented sleep. For a moment his senses are confounded. Then the hot thrill of memory infuses his body. Sleepily, he looks around. In the corner of the chamber a candle gutters in its sconce. Beyond the lozenges of glass in the single window the moonlight paints the houses across the lane with a lacquer of ghostly grey.

Then he realizes Bianca is not beside him.

The coverlet on her side of the bed is thrown back, revealing not the amber smoothness of her sleeping body, but a crumpled sheet. And then, to his bewilderment, the high-pitched cry follows him into full wakefulness. It takes him a moment to realize that, somewhere in the Jackdaw, Buffle the dog is howling.

He waits to hear the sound of the street door being unlocked as Bianca lets her out into the lane. It does not come. Curious, Nicholas climbs out of her bed, pulls on his woollen trunk-hose and goes out onto the landing.

He is halfway down the stairs before he smells it: a sulphurous stench that sticks in the nostrils and makes his eyes stream. Then he catches the throat-rasping taste of smoke. By the time he reaches the taproom floor, he can see wraiths of it drifting in the weak moonlight. He turns into the passage that leads to the parlour, the kitchen and the door to the cellar that Bianca has reclaimed for her apothecary store. The stench of brimstone is stronger here. And then he sees a figure ahead of him – a slender figure in a night-shift, leaning against the cellar door as though for support. He hears a woman coughing: deep, lung-tearing rasps.

'Bianca!' he calls, starting towards her.

She turns as though to wave him back, her face contorted by the fumes.

'The cellar... burning...'

Another breath of the sulphurous air cuts her off. Even as Nicholas reaches out to pull her away, he sees her body fold as she chokes. And as she rises again – one hand at her throat, the other still grasping the door-latch – she stumbles forward, dragging the door open behind her.

Nicholas feels a cool draught flow over him. The black doorway to the cellar suddenly turns a brilliant yellow. He hears a deep *whooomph* issue from its depths as the bundles of dried plants ignite, followed swiftly by the oils and the liquors, the pastes made of fat, the desiccated skins, all the flammable materials of the apothecary's art. The night becomes as black as hell, as a dense cloud of smoke bursts up the stairway, bringing with it a heat that chokes his cry of alarm almost before it's left his throat.

He moves without thinking, an animalistic reaction that rebels against the body's thirst for life and overwhelms it. He ducks down into breathable air and lunges forward into the passage. Before he's even conscious of movement, he's stumbling backwards, away from the heat, dragging Bianca after him even as she sinks to the floor.

He pulls her into the taproom as though he were dragging a carpet, shouting between racking coughs, 'Fire!... fire!... hurry – we are undone...'

By the time Rose, Ned, Timothy and Farzad join him, the passageway is ablaze, the flames ravishing the Jackdaw's ancient timbers in a fiery consummation. The air in the taproom is caustic in the throat. Buffle barks in high, agitated yelps in a corner, until Timothy lifts her up and calms her.

Nicholas kneels beside Bianca's body. Cradling her against his chest, he runs his fingers through her hair. A short while ago it had smelled of rosewater. Now it has the sharp tang of burnt straw. Her eyes are open and she seems to comprehend the danger, gripping his wrist tightly as though she fears he's going to leave her again.

'Someone fetch the keys, or we'll all burn here,' Nicholas shouts.

Timothy, whose task it is to lock the street door at night against house-divers, hands Buffle to Farzad and sprints up the taproom stairs to the attic. He returns with a ring of heavy iron keys. In the glare of the spreading flames, he quickly identifies the correct one and advances on the door. He's about to slot the bit into the lock when he suddenly ducks to one side and peers out of the window. He turns back, confusion on his face.

431

'There's people in the lane.'

'Of course there's people in the lane,' growls Ned impatiently. 'The tavern's afire, if you hadn't noticed. Let's hope they've come to help, not gawp.'

'Not just people,' says Timothy, oblivious to the harshness in Nicholas's voice. 'That Gault fellow's there. They 'ave swords. Why 'ave they got swords? You can't fight a fire with a sword. What do they want?'

Nicholas knows exactly what they want. He's seen the bloody proof in a pretty courtyard garden in Morocco.

Bianca, too, understands what Gault's presence means. Tears stream down her face, lacing her skin with a delta of soot. Her grip on Nicholas's wrist tightens. To his alarm, he notices little specks of soot in the spittle around her lips.

'Forgive me, Nick... My curiosity... Kit Marlowe was right: you can't make a bargain with the Devil and expect to come off best.'

He hugs her to his breast.

'Perhaps not,' he whispers into her ear. 'But this, my love, is Bankside. If you can't gull the Devil here, where *can* you gull him?'

He calls to Rose and Ned to take his place. Gently prizing Bianca's fingers from his wrist, he stands up and looks back at the passage leading to the parlour. The far end, by the cellar door, is a wall of roaring fire, smoke rolling along the ceiling of the passage and spilling out into the taproom. He judges that even if he can get into the parlour, he'll have only moments before the fire cuts off his escape. But there is no other way. The choice Gault has given him is stark: die by the sword, or burn like a heretic.

Unless...

The heat almost stops him before he reaches the parlour door. He feels as though he's pushing into the teeth of a gale greater than anything he's experienced aboard the *Righteous* or the *Marion*. Every step he takes is a trial of strength against its

432

scorching breath. But at last he makes it, finding a measure of relief as he slips into the chamber.

The wheel-lock pistol Yaxley gave him as a means of escape from Cathal Connell's vengeance is lying with the dusty-blue *djellaba*, where he'd discarded them before bathing away the aches and dirt of the ride from Dover. Its powder horn lies nearby, beside the pouch al-Annuri had given him at Safi. Nicholas scoops them up and fights his way back through the furnace of the passageway.

In the taproom the air is close to unbreathable. Ned is all for making a charge against the figures waiting in the lane, though he has nothing to set against steel but his bare fists and a courage the equal of his size.

'I'll not make Rose a widow,' Nicholas tells him brusquely. 'It's me they want. And it's me who has to bring an end to all this.'

The wheel-lock is already loaded with powder and ball; he made sure of that before leaving Dover Castle, lest he encountered cut-purses on the road. Thankful now for the skills he learned in the Low Countries, it takes him no more than a moment to make a half-turn on the pistol's wheel with the little iron winding tool, engaging the spring. He checks that the wedge of pyrite is firmly clamped in the dog-head, slides back the priming pan cover and pours in a measure of black powder. He closes the pan lid and swings the dog-mechanism down onto the wheel, praying to God that Yaxley kept the weapon clean of dirt and sea-salt. A misfire now will leave him standing impotently before Gault like the greatest fool on earth.

'Open the door, Timothy,' he commands. 'Ned, stand behind me. Timothy, Farzad – the moment I give the word, help Rose carry Mistress Bianca outside.'

Nicholas knows the night air will rush in and fan the flames. But there is no alternative. Death is waiting – inside or out.

'*Now!*' he cries.

As Timothy swings open the door, Nicholas steps out into the alley. He raises his arm like a man denouncing a traitor, aiming the pistol at Gault's chest. One squeeze on the trigger and the wheel will spin against the pyrite in the dog-head, igniting the powder in the priming pan. At this range he cannot miss.

'*Throw aside the swords!* Throw them, or I swear by Jesu I will shoot you for the deceiver you are.'

Lit by the flames inside the Jackdaw, Gault's striking face has turned into that of a gargoyle, his eyes fixed on the unerring muzzle of the wheel-lock barely four yards from his breast.

'You won't give fire, Shelby,' he says smoothly. 'You're a physician, not a killer. You haven't got the courage.'

'That's probably what Cathal Connell thought. But a charge of hail-shot disabused him of *that* notion. I fired it myself. There was nothing left of him afterwards – nothing the fishes couldn't swallow whole.'

Gault's eyes snap from the pistol to Nicholas's face. 'You're lying.'

'Ask Yaxley of the *Marion*. He can't be more than a day or so away. It was his rabinet I fired.'

Still Gault hesitates. 'I'll let the others live. You have my word upon it.'

'A blood-tax? Is that what you want? Well, Gault, I'm sorry to disappoint, but I don't feel like paying it.'

Nicholas raises the pistol a little, aiming at Gault's face.

'I've forgotten how many wounds made by a pistol ball I treated in the Low Countries,' he says. 'I'm a good surgeon, but not one in ten lived. It's a vile way to die. You'd best hope it's a clean shot through the heart. Oh, and you're going to have to do without the *Viaticum*, which for a man of your faith is an even crueller injury, and a lot longer in the healing. But that's no concern to me, of course. We heretics don't believe in Purgatory.'

A glance to either side at his apprentices and Gault capitulates.

'Lay down your blades,' he orders.

Needing no prompting, Ned moves forward and picks up the weapons.

'Get everyone out of the Jackdaw, Timothy!' Nicholas shouts, without taking his eyes off Gault. He can hear windows opening, voices calling out from the other buildings in the lane. Someone is yelling for the watch, another calling out for water to be fetched from the river.

'You won't dare shoot me now, Shelby,' Gault says, with an easy smile on his face. 'Witnesses. You'll hang.'

'You don't know Banksiders that well, do you? They suffer terribly from poor eyes. It's a well-known condition. I'm forever prescribing balms.'

The edges of Gault's mouth lift in a cold smile. 'It's a temporary reprieve, Shelby. Face it – the road to Windsor can be a dangerous one: cut-purses... accidents... You'll never reach Robert Cecil. I'll make sure of that.'

Nicholas glances at the apprentices. 'What has your master promised you: that you'll be princes when you get to the Barbary shore? That you'll have your own slaves, gold and jewels? That all you have to do is lie about who your parents were, pretend to be noble gentlemen? Well, it's a fraud. I've seen what happens. They sell you into a slavery you can't begin to imagine. It's called the blood-tax. And Gault and Connell took a very profitable cut of it. But it's over. There's nothing there for you now but death.'

The boy Owen turns his face towards Gault. 'Does he speak true, Master?'

'Of course not,' snaps Gault.

Nicholas moves the barrel of the wheel-lock in a small circle, as though marking out the size of the hole he intends to blast in Gault's face. To Owen, he says, 'Has he handed you all a nice, smart

435

family lineage yet – proved by the Rouge Croix Pursuivant?' Then, to Gault, 'How much did Sumayl al-Seddik pay you for each of your boys? How much gold? How many slaves? What price can you get on the Exchange these days for a human life, Master *Grocer*?'

The heat is now almost unbearable. Nicholas feels as though his back is on fire. Clouds of sparks drift in the darkness like fireflies. The apprentices exchange glances. A change has come over them, dispelling their earlier bravado, fatally damaging their trust in Gault.

'The watch... the watch is here...'

The voice is harsh – a woman's voice calling from nearby.

And then one of the Jackdaw's windows explodes, showering glass and lead-beading out into the lane. As Nicholas turns his head, distracted, Gault bolts. He flees down the alley in the direction of the Mutton Lane stairs.

Deprived of his authority, his apprentices seem unable to act. They stand there like sheep without a drover, four young men robbed of a future they now realize was nothing but a fantasy.

Nicholas swings the pistol, sighting down the barrel in the direction of Gault's fleeing back. His finger tightens on the trigger. Gault is still easily within range. One more squeeze and his bargain with al-Annuri is done. *You will bring pestilence and death upon them, even unto the seventh generation. You will erase their names so that Allāh will forget he ever made them...*

For a while he just stands there, breathing in the night air, air that is hotter now than any night in Marrakech, though it has no right to be – given that the moon is yellowed not by a desert mist, but by the drifting smoke from the death of the Jackdaw. He remembers how Eleanor made gentle jokes about his determination to heal, how she'd been horrified when he told her he was going to the Low Countries to treat those who'd been hurt in the fight against the forces of Catholic Spain. And he remembers what Bianca said to him in her physic garden, before he left for the Barbary shore: *let us face the truth... we are both murderers now.*

What am I, he asks himself silently: the physician... or the disease?

And very slowly – though whether in victory or defeat, he does not yet know – Nicholas lowers the pistol.

It takes some time for Ned's voice to penetrate. At first the words are not words at all, merely noises. They are indecipherable, like Adolfo Sykes's last dispatch, waiting for the moment the magic makes them whole again.

Bianca...

The fire...

Hurry...

Dying.

✠

Ned and Rose have laid her down at a safe distance from the funeral pyre of all her hopes and aspirations, as much to shield her eyes from the Jackdaw's destruction as her body from the flames. Timothy and Farzad stand a little aside. Both are weeping, Farzad's tears dampening the top of Buffle's head as he clutches the dog protectively to his breast.

Their mistress's amber eyes have closed. Her chest heaves in desperate spasms as she fights for breath.

Kneeling beside her, Nicholas sees in the light from the fire the black soot around her nostrils and her lips. He gently inserts a finger between her lips and slides it around her mouth. When he withdraws it, the wetness on his skin is slicked with more soot.

He's seen the phenomenon before, in Holland: men who had escaped a burning town, apparently unharmed, dying a short time later as the damage caused by inhaling the fire's breath spread, constricting the windpipe. He knows that if he doesn't act immediately, it will be too late to save her.

And then, from the darker parts of his memory, the old fear comes back to haunt him. His physic had failed to save Eleanor and the child she was carrying. His inability to protect them had been the priming powder that set off the detonation that almost destroyed him. He knows he cannot go back there again – not just because of what it did to him, but because this time there will be no Bianca Merton to bring him back from the Purgatory he told Gault he doesn't believe in, but which he's tasted and knows to be only too real.

He lays his fingers on Bianca's throat. For an instant he thinks she has placed her own fingers upon his, because he senses another's hand about his own. But her arms are lying motionless by her sides. He smiles as he recalls Surgeon Wadoud's impassive brown eyes. *You have the hands of a good man. And a good surgeon, too... tell them what you saw here in the Bimaristan al-Mansur. Tell them we are not all heathens...*

Nicholas searches for the pulse in Bianca's neck.

A risk of severing the carotid arteries, leading to death...

When he feels the beat of her life against his fingertips, Nicholas's fingers linger, fixing the line of the arteries in his mind.

'Ned, I need a knife. A sharp one,' he calls out.

'One of them lads had a poniard as well as a sword,' Ned replies. 'Hang on while I fetch it.'

There is also the danger that the wound becomes foul...

Nicholas calls after him, 'There's a piece of window frame there – to your right – still burning. Put the tip of the poniard into the flames. Count to twenty, then bring it to me.'

The trick is in keeping it clean...

'Timothy, there's good water in the well at the crossroads. Fetch me a little.'

'Water's no use now, Master Nick,' Timothy protests, staring at the flames.

'It's not for the fire! Now, hurry!'

As Timothy sprints towards the well, Nicholas takes Rose gently by the sleeve.

'I want you to run to Mother Fissel at the chandler's on Black Bull Alley. She keeps bees. Tell her we need honey. And clean linen. Tell her it's for Mistress Bianca. If she plays her usual game, don't quibble. I'll pay whatever she demands.'

Rose hurries away at a velocity unseen till now.

'Farzad, give Buffle to Ned,' Nicholas commands.

For a moment he seems reluctant to obey.

'It's important, Farzad. Give Ned the bloody dog!'

'I'm to look after the *dog*?' queries Ned. 'Is that the only task I'm to be trusted with?'

'I want you to hold the dog tightly, Ned, because when I do what is required, your instinct will be to stop me. So I need you to have your hands full. I'll be no use to her if you try to stop me.'

He turns back to Farzad. 'Go to the Pike Garden. Fetch me half a dozen of the strongest reeds, each about the length of a finger.'

'Yes, Master Nicholas,' says Farzad, grinning with the pleasure of responsibility.

'And Farzad...'

'Yes, Master?'

'This time, don't take it into your head to go missing.'

47

The ashlar walls of Nonsuch Palace gleam like bleached bone in the August sunshine. Built by the late King Henry for Jane Seymour, it has for many years been home to John and Elizabeth Lumley. Though Lord Lumley has returned it to the queen in lieu of his many debts to the Crown, Her Grace has granted him enduring tenancy until both he and his long-suffering wife have moved on to more heavenly accommodation.

When not at Bianca's bedside – an excusable intimacy, given that he is her physician – Nicholas is often to be found in Baron Lumley's vast library: the equal, it is said, of those at Oxford or Cambridge. He has spent many hours there, battling the Latin translations of Avicenna and Albucasis, though in his mind they will now for ever be Ibn Sina and al-Zahrawi. He wonders if one day he might read the words of Surgeon Wadoud, though he hasn't yet managed to construct a satisfactory Latinized version of her name. But he has sent a letter to her – via Captain Yaxley – thanking her for the gift she so unknowingly gave him.

He has considered describing to the College of Physicians the procedure he employed to save Bianca Merton's life, but has decided against it. They would most likely denounce him as a butcher.

Thinking of that night – as he does often – he recalls the anguished faces of his friends as he placed the tip of the knife against Bianca's arched throat. Yet not even Ned Monkton had sought to intervene, as he'd feared. They had trusted him to do the right thing. And in so doing, they had given him the strength to trust himself.

Dawn had broken behind the smouldering ruin of the Jackdaw before he'd been even halfway sure that death had been – if not cheated – at least delayed. By then half of Bankside had gathered to gaze in wonder at the destruction, more than a few shedding tears for the Jackdaw and the remarkable woman who had owned it.

Ned had carried her to the vicarage at St Saviour's, where Parson Moody had made a bed available. And there Nicholas had stayed for two whole days, taking it upon himself to clean Bianca's wound with water and honey as Surgeon Wadoud had instructed. To ease the pain of the burns to her throat, and to heal the damage the smoke had done, he'd made her take regular draughts of a distillation of marshmallow root, sage and cinnamon, prepared by an apothecary he trusted on Bucklersbury Lane near Cheapside. Robert Cecil, he'd decided, could wait a day or two. With Connell dead – Sumayl al-Seddik, too, for all he knew – and Gault exposed, the conspiracy was decapitated.

Only when he was sure Bianca was out of immediate danger did Nicholas take a wherry to Cecil House. There he entrusted his dispatch to the same black-gowned secretary who had shown him to Robert Cecil's study the night he'd been so rudely summoned from his bed at Mistress Muzzle's lodgings.

'If he has need to speak to me, you'll find me at St Saviour's,' he'd said. 'If he summons me to Windsor, I shall have need of an armed escort.'

Returning to Bankside, he had spent the next six days at Bianca's bedside. If Parson Moody ever thought his presence in her chamber exceeded his duties as her physician, he never raised so much as an eyebrow in criticism, possibly because of his own propensity for visiting a certain house near the Falcon stairs.

Ned, Rose, Timothy, Farzad – even Buffle – had been closeted with Mistress Muzzle, who, should she ever grow tired of simpering over Ned, could console herself with a goodly handful of Robert Cecil's ducats.

Nicholas had not returned to the Jackdaw until a week after the fire. What he beheld had broken his heart. A tavern that had stood for centuries was now nothing but a mound of blackened debris, bookended by the scorched remains of the gable-end walls. The buildings on either side had largely been spared, thanks to a human chain of Banksiders who had laboured for a whole day bringing water from the river.

Nicholas had wondered what effect the sight would have upon Bianca's recovery. Almost all that she owned – everything she had striven for since arriving from Padua – was gone. The only light in the darkness of her loss was the discovery of the travelling chest containing her father's books and his Petrine cross, which she'd left in her shop on Dice Lane.

But it was the pestilence that finally made him decide to leave London. Towards the end of July plague deaths were approaching a thousand a week. The queen had ordered her Privy Council to send a stiff note to the Lord Mayor, expressing her concern. Hearing of it from Parson Moody, who had himself heard it from an eminent Bankside alderman – though he was a little coy in saying precisely *where* – Nicholas had decided to take it as a sign that luck should only be pushed so far.

And so he had hired horses for himself and Ned, and a cart for Bianca, Rose, Timothy and Farzad to ride in. The two lads had taken turns on the reins, while Buffle barked at every new and exciting sight and smell on the journey to Nonsuch.

Three days after John Lumley took them in, Robert Cecil arrived.

He did not come alone. With him were a score of gentlemen in gorgeous plumage – all of whom, Nicholas assumed, could authenticate their noble lineages without the least help from the Rouge Croix Pursuivant – and a woman of about sixty, whose high, cerise-white brow sat below a crown of tight ginger curls that, in Nicholas's humble opinion, were probably not her own.

✠

'Are you sure you are a physician, sirrah? You do not have an academic look to you.'

'I studied at Cambridge, Highness, under Professor Lorkin,' says Nicholas, rising from where he has knelt in the neatly cropped grass of Nonsuch's fine Italian garden.

The knot of gentlemen surrounding the queen are regarding him with a mix of curiosity and whimsy. But they all share that head-back, looking-down-the-nose expression of superiority he can recall from his days as a *pensionarius minor* at Cambridge.

All, that is, except Robert Cecil.

'Master Shelby has done the realm a goodly service, Your Grace,' Lord Burghley's son is saying. 'He is newly returned from the Barbary shore, where he had an audience with His Majesty the King of the Moors.'

'How interesting,' Elizabeth observes with a slight twist of her narrow, determined jaw. 'Tell me, Dr Shelby, was he *very* savage?'

'Not in the slightest, Highness. I found him to be a very imposing gentleman. He desired me to assure you of the strength of the amity between our two realms.'

'The lasting and *secure* amity,' Cecil says, adding the part of the rehearsed reply that Nicholas has forgotten to include.

'I shall send for you, sirrah, so that you may tell me more fully how the Moors practise their physic,' the queen says, extending one gloved hand for him to kiss.

Nicholas puts his lips reverently to the pearl-encrusted doeskin, then steps aside as Elizabeth and her hive of gentlemen sweep majestically off between the topiary and the Roman columns, towards the banqueting hall set on a gentle hill to the west of the palace.

'Don't get your hopes up,' says Robert Cecil, who has stayed behind. 'She makes invitations like that to every young man whose appearance pleases her. She may never call for you.'

Is that a hint of resentment Nicholas thinks he hears in the crook-backed Cecil's voice? 'Have you found Gault yet?' he asks.

'He's in Leinster. I've had words with my people in Bristol for letting him slip aboard a vessel undetected. But he's of no concern now. The conspiracy ended the moment Minister al-Annuri took al-Seddik into irons.' Cecil purses his lips in surprise. 'My father, Lord Burghley, has been in an ill temper ever since I gave him your news. He is not accustomed to making a misjudgement. Still, I suppose these Moors do not hold constancy in the same regard as Englishmen.'

'Speaking of which, Sir Robert, there are still Englishmen enslaved in Barbary. We should be attempting to arrange ransom.'

'I shall ask the bishops to seek donations from their parishioners.'

'Can the Exchequer not provide?'

Robert Cecil laughs. 'Heavens, no! That would only encourage every Moor corsair to prey upon English ships. England is made out of God's good earth, Nicholas – not out of silver.'

✠

The little private chapel smells of the beeswax the Nonsuch servants use to polish the panelling and the pews. The sunlight streams through the mullioned windows, cutting bright swathes through the shadows and glinting on the dust motes. Unusually for a chapel compliant with the strictures of the new religion, there is also a hint of incense on the warm air. It was here,

Nicholas remembers, that he stumbled upon John Lumley and his wife at their Romish prayers, giving him the evidence Cecil would need to destroy his old adversary. Nicholas had chosen not to reveal that evidence. It is a decision he has never once regretted in the intervening two years, least of all now – because Lumley has offered the chapel for tomorrow's ceremony. It will be a Protestant service. Lumley's generosity does not extend to endangering the life of his private Catholic priest – if he has one, which of course he vehemently denies.

Tomorrow, inshā Allāh, I will wed Bianca Merton, Nicholas reminds himself as he feels the sunlight on his cheek. *Ned, Timothy and Farzad will be my groomsmen. Rose and Elise Cullen – sister of the once-nameless Ralph – will be Bianca's bridesmaids. I did the right thing at last. I became the healer, not the disease.*

He hears the door open softly at his back.

'Are you *sure* you want to go through with this?' he hears Bianca say, her voice now tinged with a permanent huskiness. 'There is no dowry I can bring. It's all burned to the ground. All gone. Everything.'

He turns to face her. She is wearing one of Lady Lumley's cream brocade gowns, a starched linen ruff obscuring her throat. Her beauty steals the breath from his lungs.

'Let me see,' he says, pointing to the ruff.

'I don't like to. It's a blemish. I have enough of those already.'

'I'm your physician. I need to see.'

Coyly, she reaches behind her neck and undoes the band-strings holding the ruff in place.

'Perfect,' he says, observing the red wheal about the length of a small fingernail at the dead-centre of her throat, exactly where Surgeon Wadoud would wish it to be. He blushes. 'When I say "perfect", I mean the incision, not... well, the throat is perfect too – that's a given...'

'I'm serious, Nicholas. I'll understand if a physician on the brink of a royal appointment chooses not to wed the penniless former owner of a Bankside tavern. I really will.'

'Robert Cecil has petitioned the queen for recompense. A tavern can be rebuilt. An empty apothecary's shop can be restocked.'

Her face falls. 'Come now – you know what they're like. They make such easy promises. It could be years before I see a single shilling. I can't pay my lease on Dice Lane. I can't restock. I have nothing.'

'And still you look like a countess.'

'In a *borrowed* gown.'

He smiles. 'It doesn't matter.'

She rolls her eyes at the chapel's panelled ceiling. 'Oh, *mercy*, don't give me the line about love being all. I don't want to force you to rely upon Robert Cecil's stipend, and I can't live on charity.'

'No, it *really* doesn't matter,' he says.

Reaching into his doublet, he pulls out a cloth pouch. It is the powder purse Captain Yaxley gave him, along with the wheel-lock pistol. Nicholas opens the drawstring and extracts an object about the size of a large walnut, covered in a thin layer of black powder. Holding it up to the sunlight, he blows on it, releasing a fine grey cloud. Immediately sparks of reflected sunlight fill the little chapel.

Bianca can find no words. She draws in a slow whisper of breath in astonishment.

'It's... it's... *beautiful*. It's...'

'It's worth a dozen new Jackdaws, at the very least – that's what it *is*.'

And he holds out the ring Sultan al-Mansur had given him, just before having the footsteps of the unclean infidel erased from his royal sight.

446

Historical Note

The plague of 1593 reached its climax in late summer. By autumn it was in retreat, though it returned briefly the following spring. On Boxing Day of that year the Rose theatre on Bankside reopened for business.

At the time Nicholas Shelby entered the Bimaristan al-Mansur, the glory days of Islamic medieval medicine were fading. Yet without the writings of Muslim physicians and the translation into Arabic of Galenic and Hippocratic texts, the progress of medicine in the West would have been incalculably harmed.

The tracheotomy procedure performed by Nicholas and by Surgeon Wadoud was understood by physicians in ancient Egypt. The first successful attempt known to have been performed in Europe was carried out in Italy around the 1540s, by Antonio Brassavola. It was repeated fewer than thirty times in the next three centuries. The operation might well have saved George Washington, who died in 1799 – of bacterial epiglottis – surrounded by three surgeons, one of whom knew of the procedure but did not have the courage to attempt it.

The Catholic friar Pierre Dan, who made ransom missions to Barbary, claimed that around one million Christian slaves were taken by the Moors in the century after 1530. Cervantes, the author of Don Quixote, was a slave in Algiers for five years. The English – who continued to rely on diplomacy and church collections to free those taken – were as troubled by Moor corsairs as any other European nation with a coastline. In August 1625 sixty men, women and children were taken in a raid on Mount's

Bay in Cornwall. Twenty years later, 240 people were kidnapped in another attack on the Cornish coast. But by that time the enslavement of what would eventually become tens of millions of Africans by Europeans had far outstripped the Moorish trade.

Arnoult de Lisle gave up his position as physician to Sultan al-Mansur in 1598, to become Professor of Arabic at the Collège de France. He returned to Morocco in 1606, as ambassador from the court of Henri IV.

Dr Lopez, physician to Elizabeth I, did not long outlive this story. In October 1593 he was arrested, accused of spying for Spain and – worse still – planning to poison his royal patient. Almost seventy by now, and innocent of both charges, he was hanged, drawn and quartered the following summer.

The Barbary Company's charter lapsed in 1597, by which time it had been absorbed into London's other livery companies. The Aduana district in Marrakech – close to present-day el-Fna Square – was closed fifteen years later.

In 1600 the first formally appointed Moroccan ambassador to the court of Elizabeth I arrived in London. His full name was Abd el-Ouahed ben Massaoud ben Mohammed Anoun. For ease, throughout *The Saracen's Mark* I have taken the liberty of using the more familiar, and shorter, version: Muhammed al-Annuri. His extraordinary and enigmatic portrait hangs today at the Shakespeare Institute in Stratford-upon-Avon. It has been suggested that he was the inspiration for Othello.

Author's Note

When the good people at Corvus asked me to continue Nicholas and Bianca's adventure, it seemed the ideal time to write a little about the debt Western medicine and science owe to the world of historical Islam. And then I discovered the extraordinary alliance between England and Morocco that began in the latter part of the sixteenth century. I have to admit that my very next thought was: Oh, good – research in Marrakech! What a chore.

I would like to thank Paul Foulsham for the opportunity to unwind at the Kasbah Angour in the foothills of the Atlas Mountains. If tranquillity can be bottled, you will find a crate of it there.

Adolfo Sykes's house is an amalgam of a number of historical houses and riads that I visited, including the beautiful Dar Cherifa.

Acknowledgement is due to many, but in particular to Dominic Green for his book *The Double Life of Doctor Lopez*, which is a warning never to let yourself become an outsider, and which I mined for the character of Solomon Mandel just as much as for Lopez himself; Comer Plummer for his *Roads to Ruin*; and Jerry Brotton for *This Orient Isle*, a fascinating look at Elizabethan England's contact with the Islamic world. Also of immense assistance were Ahmed Ragab's fascinating *The Medieval Islamic Hospital*; Hakim Chishti's *The Traditional Healer's Handbook*; and of course Miranda Kaufmann's *Black Tudors*. For further reading on the subject of the particular form of slavery contained in this book, I unhesitatingly recommend Robert C. Davis's *Christian Slaves, Muslim Masters* and Giles Milton's *White Gold*.

As always, gratitude is due to my agent, Jane Judd, for her guidance and patience; to Poppy Mostyn-Owen and the crew at Corvus for their belief in what I do; and to Mandy Greenfield for plastering over my many mistakes and grammatical errors.

And finally, my heartfelt thanks to my wife Jane, who redefines stoicism and patience when her husband is locked away in the sixteenth century.